THE ROAD FROM GAP CREEK

Also by ROBERT MORGAN

FICTION

The Blue Valleys
The Mountains Won't Remember Us
The Hinterlands
The Truest Pleasure
Gap Creek
The Balm of Gilead Tree: New and Selected Stories
This Rock
Brave Enemies

NONFICTION

Good Measure
Boone: A Biography
Lions of the West: Heroes and Villains of the Westward Expansion

POETRY

Zirconia Poems
Red Owl
Land Diving
Trunk & Thicket
Groundwork
Bronze Age
At the Edge of the Orchard Country
Sigodlin
Green River: New and Selected Poems
Wild Peavines
Topsoil Road
The Strange Attractor: New and Selected Poems
October Crossing
Terroir

The Road from Gap Creek

A Novel

ROBERT MORGAN

A Shannon Ravenel Book

ALGONQUIN BOOKS OF CHAPEL HILL   2013

ℝ

A Shannon Ravenel Book

Published by
ALGONQUIN BOOKS OF CHAPEL HILL
Post Office Box 2225
Chapel Hill, North Carolina 27515-2225

a division of
WORKMAN PUBLISHING
225 Varick Street
New York, New York 10014

© 2013 by Robert Morgan.
All rights reserved.
Printed in the United States of America.
Published simultaneously in Canada by Thomas Allen & Son Limited.
Design by Anne Winslow.

LIBRARY OF CONGRESS CATALOGING-IN-PUBLICATION DATA
Morgan, Robert, [date]
    The road from Gap Creek : a novel / Robert Morgan.—First edition.
        pages cm
    "A Shannon Ravenel Book."
    ISBN 978-1-61620-161-6
    1. Married women—Fiction.   2. Mountain life—Fiction.   3. Young women—
Fiction.   4. Appalachian Region, Southern—Fiction.   I. Title.
PS3563.O87147R63 2013
813'.54—dc23   2013008906

10 9 8 7 6 5 4 3 2 1
First Edition

For my granddaughter Coralie

THE ROAD FROM GAP CREEK

One

The thing about Mama was she'd never tell you how she felt. When she was feeling bad she'd just go on with her work, washing dishes or peeling taters, or mopping the floor, and I'd know she was feeling pretty low, but she wouldn't say nothing. Work was what she done, what she'd done her whole life since she was a little girl up on Mount Olivet, and she'd keep on scrubbing the dishes and cups with a rag in soapy water and rinse them in cold water and dry them with a linen towel.

It would make Papa mad that Mama wouldn't say nothing when her feelings was hurt or she had the blues. It was a difference between them that went all the way back to the beginning of their marriage, back to the days on Gap Creek. Papa would argue and say she'd spent too much money on flower seeds or a shrub for the yard. He never could see wasting money on beautifying flowers, while Mama was crazy about flowers and liked nothing better than a rose of Sharon bush blooming in the yard and attracting bees and hummingbirds, or colorful geraniums in pots along the edge of the porch. She once said that it was a sign that God loved us that he put such colors in the world as you seen in the red of geraniums or the pink of dahlias or the dark purple of ironweeds along the road.

"Julie, you're going to break us up," Papa would say if she paid a peddler a dollar for some bulbs to hide in the ground. Mama wouldn't say nothing back. She'd just go on with whatever she was doing or maybe start something harder, like washing the chicken piles off the porch or sweeping the backyard. I never saw nobody take more pride in keeping the porch clean than Mama did. Chickens would get up on the porch looking for something to peck and leave their piles like big melted coins on the boards. If the piles got baked in the sun, they'd be hard to get off, set hard as cement or glue in the cracks of the wood. So almost every day Mama would heat a bucket of water on the kitchen stove till it was near boiling. Holding the bucket with a towel or the tail of her apron she'd splash tongues of smoking water on the planks that made them steam like they was burning. And then with the broom she'd scour the chicken piles off, flirting the dirty water into the yard. She'd splash and sweep until the porch was clean as the kitchen table drying in the sun.

About once a week Mama done the same thing to the yard, splashing and sweeping, running away the chickens, sweeping again, sometimes sprinkling white sand she got from Kimble Branch, till the yard looked smooth as a piece of white twill cloth that had been washed and ironed.

That day when the black car stopped in front of the house and the two men in uniforms got out, my heart sunk right to the soles of my feet. It was November of 1943 and you didn't see many cars then because of the gas rationing, even on the big road, and on our little gravel road you could go half a day and not see a vehicle pass except for the school bus. That car could not mean any good as it stopped there on Mama's swept yard beside the boxwoods.

Those two men walked across the ground she'd swept so careful and I wished I could close my eyes and make them go away. We'd read in the paper about two men coming to deliver bad news from the war. It made me cold in the belly to see them, and then it made me mad. I wanted to fling open the kitchen door and tell them to go away. They had no business coming on us all of a sudden like this. I wanted to tell them to get back in their black car and drive back to town or some army base or Washington, D.C., or wherever they'd come from.

They knocked on the kitchen door and when I opened it the taller one said, "Is Mr. Hank Richards here?"

"No he ain't," I said. The truth was Papa was out cutting firewood on the Squirrel Hill with my brother Velmer.

"Is Mrs. Richards here?" the second man said. He took off his army cap and put it under his arm.

"No . . . I'll see," I said, trying to think of some way to keep Mama from having to see them. But the other man took off his cap and looked past me. I turned and seen Mama standing right behind me, in the light from the door.

"Ma'am, I'm awfully sorry to be the one to bring you this news," he said, and handed Mama a tan envelope. Mama held the envelope a minute without opening it, then handed it to me. As I ripped open the paper and looked at the telegram I told myself this was a mistake. We'd read in the paper about men reported killed who later turned up wounded in a hospital or lost from their unit.

The telegram was words printed on paper ribbons pasted to the page. "Dear Mr. & Mrs. Richards, it is with profound regret I report your son Troy Richards, Serial no. 34119284, lost in the crash of a B-17 heavy bomber on Nov. 10, 1943, near the village of Eye in East Anglia. Stop. A grateful nation mourns the loss of your son whose sacrifice for his country will never be forgotten."

I read the words glued to the page to Mama and she just stared at the door like she didn't see nothing.

"Ma'am, if there's anything we can do for you, just let us know," the tall man said. But Mama had already turned away from him. I thought she was going back to the fire in the living room, but she didn't. Instead she walked to the far side of the kitchen and set down in the chair by the bread safe. The two men said more things. They talked real gentle, like they was truly sad, and asked again if there was anything they could do. I reckon it was what they done every day, going around and delivering those telegrams and telling people how sorry they was. Finally they said a letter would be coming in the mail, along with a box of Troy's personal effects. And then they put on their caps and walked slow back to the car and drove away.

"Mama, you go back to the fire. You'll get cold setting in here," I said. But she didn't answer. She just set in that chair by the bread safe looking down at her hands clasped on her apron. I still held the telegram and didn't know where to throw it down on the floor or fold it back up in the envelope it come in.

"Go tell Hank," Mama said.

"I don't want to leave you," I said. Mama's face looked gray, the way somebody with a bad heart looks.

"I can make you some coffee," I said.

"You go on," Mama said. "I'll be fine." She waved me away.

I put on a jacket and tied a scarf around my hair. Clutching the envelope I stepped out into the chilly breeze. Chickens scratched around the edges of the yard. The cotton mill whistle sounded three miles away. It was the end of the first shift. I wished Muir was there so I could tell him. He couldn't tell me what to do, but just knowing that he knowed would help. That's what a husband was for. When something bad happened he was supposed to be there, not off building army barracks at Holly Ridge or Wilmington or preaching at a church down there. It would be comforting to just let him know. Papa had come home for a long weekend and Velmer had come from Columbia, South Carolina, but Muir had stayed in Holly Ridge to preach at a little church near there.

To get to the Squirrel Hill I had to cross the road and then the cornfield.

The corn had been gathered and the stalks leaned this way and that. We'd cut the tops and pulled the fodder back in August, and the stalks was mostly bare and broke. The field looked bad as I felt. I stepped around briars, going real slow. Every second I delayed give Papa a little more time of peacefulness. I wished I could just turn around and go back to the house.

It took me a minute to find Papa and Velmer in the woods. The Squirrel Hill was hit by lightning more than any place I ever heard of. Some said there was iron in the ground under the hill and that's why lightning always come down there. Every time there was a big thunderstorm a bolt hit an oak tree and split it down the middle, flinging splinters and limbs all over the woods. There was dead wood all around the hill to cut up. It was also a place the squirrels loved because of the acorns and hickory nuts, which was how it got its name.

Papa and Velmer was using the crosscut saw. It took a man at either end to pull the saw back and forth. They was cutting up a big limb that had been blasted off that summer by lightning. Papa seen me coming and he must have thought I brought bad news because he turned away like he hadn't even seen me. My breath was short from walking.

"Two men come to the house and brought this," I said, and held out the envelope. Papa looked at the telegram and sighed and put down his end of the saw. Fishing his reading glasses out of his shirt pocket he slid them on and read the words pasted to the page, then let the telegram drop to the leaves.

"Poor boy," was all he said.

"What is it?" Velmer said. I picked up the paper and handed it to him. Velmer read it and shook his head. I was going to say Papa should go back to the house, but he'd already started. His head was down and he stumbled against a bush, and that was how I knowed he was crying. It was the only time in my whole life I'd ever seen him cry. He never cried when his mama died that I could remember. And he never cried when his oldest boy nearly died of typhoid. I followed him as he lurched between the trees and fallen limbs toward the house.

Now when we got to the house, Papa walked straight to Mama where she set by the bread safe. He put his hand on her shoulder, but she didn't even look up at him. I'd seen her do that before. She couldn't stand to be comforted or show affection in front of anybody. He'd touch her, try to put his arm around her, and she'd just pay him no heed. I thought she was too shy to show her feelings when another person was looking. Maybe she thought her and Papa was too old to act intimate. But when she just set there paying no attention to Papa reaching out to her at that awful moment, I seen it was something else. She'd give her life to working for other people and caring for other people. She'd put up with Papa's whims and rages, and all it had led to was this. She'd lived on grits and molasses when they was young down on Gap Creek. She'd give everything to raise her children, and she had lost her favorite child. She didn't want to show no emotion anymore.

"Julie . . ." Papa said as he squeezed her shoulder, but his voice broke and when he seen she wasn't going to answer he turned away and shuffled into the living room and set down by the fire.

"Mama, let me make you some coffee," I said.

"Too late in the day for coffee," Mama said. "I'd never sleep tonight if I had coffee now."

"You could drink just a little; that wouldn't hurt you."

Mama set there and I wondered if she was going to stay in the chair all evening. It bothered me the way she wouldn't say nothing. Ever since I was a little girl it made me afraid when Mama was unhappy or disapproving. I guess that's the way girls feel about their mamas, much more than boys do. A girl has to be close to her mama, and the bottom falls out of the world when your mama is mad at you. Nothing can go right if your mama is angry. Even though I was a married woman, it still seemed everything depended on how Mama felt. There was a big cold empty place in my chest as I watched Mama just set there like she wasn't noticing anything.

And then she looked up like she'd come back to life. "It's time to fix supper," she said. "Look how late it is."

"I'll fix supper," I said. "You just need to rest."

Mama ignored me and stood up, looking around the kitchen like she couldn't decide what to do first.

"You go on into the living room and rest by the fireplace," I said.

"Are you giving the orders here?" Mama said. A pain shot through me. Mama hadn't spoke to me in that tone of voice for a long time.

"I just thought you should rest," I said.

Mama wiped her hands on her apron like she was drying them, though her hands like her eyes was perfectly dry. "This is my kitchen," she said in a short voice like she almost never used.

"I just want to help," I said, and felt my eyes getting wet.

"Then you go down to the basement and get some beans and beets and a pan of sweet taters," Mama said, like she was all business now and time was running out.

I got the saucepan for the taters and stepped out into the gray air. By mid-November it was already getting dark around five. The door to the cellar was at the front of the house. You had to stoop under the front porch to reach the cellar door. When Locke Peace had made the house a long time ago that's the way he'd fixed the basement. There was always cobwebs over the door and I brushed them aside. As I stepped into the dark cellar I remembered what I'd forgot, the flashlight. There was just enough light so I could see the shelves of can stuff. Since I knowed where the beans and beets was, I got the jars and set them at the door. But the tater bin was at the back of the basement and I had to feel my way there, trying not to stumble over any box or keg left on the floor.

When I was a little girl and had to go down there to get something,

I always imagined snakes was watching me from the walls and shelves, big snakes with gleaming eyes. There was a smell in the cellar, the smell of old dirt and mold, of wrinkled or rotten taters, of dust and mildew, which I thought of as a snake smell. I shivered in the cold, sniffing the scent, and reached into the bin of sweet taters. Something scurried away, and I jumped back and listened. All I could hear was pots banging in the kitchen above. My breath was short.

And then I remembered what had happened that afternoon and felt silly to be afraid of snakes or mice. Besides, it was almost wintertime and snakes was asleep deep in the ground.

"Troy is dead," I said, not sure who I was speaking to. It just come out. "Troy is dead." I said it to the dark in the back of the bin, to the smell of old dirt and mildew, to the dust. Troy had come down there as many times as I had, to bring jars still warm from the canner or to get spuds for baking. He'd never come again for a can of peaches at grave level. "Troy is dead," I said again, and grabbed enough sweet taters to fill the pan.

When I got back to the kitchen Mama already had water boiling for rice. She'd made a cob fire in the cookstove and the kitchen was warming up. "You wash the taters and put them in the oven and I'll go milk," she said.

"No, you can fix supper and I'll go milk," I said.

Mama give me this hard look and I seen it was no time to argue with her. Papa still set by the fire, and Velmer had gone out to bring the horse from the pasture. There was nothing to do but humor Mama and try to help her. I run some water in the sink and started to scrub the taters with a brush. Mama poured rice into the saucepan of steaming water.

The kitchen door opened and there was Aunt Daisy holding a bowl covered with a dishcloth. Mama had lit the lamp on the table and the light reflected off of Daisy's glasses. She was married to Papa's brother Russ, and they lived just on the other side of the Squirrel Hill.

"Julie, I'm so sorry," Daisy said. She handed me the bowl and I set it down on the table. "It's just some soup beans," she said. The bowl was warm and I could smell the sweet beans in their broth.

"Thank you," I said.

"I just heard the news from Velmer, and I'm so sorry," Daisy said.

"Won't you set down," I said. I glanced at Mama and at the milk bucket on the shelf. It was past time for milking.

"I'll go get the cow in," I said, and grabbed the milk bucket and flashlight. I still had on my scarf and jacket.

"Troy was an awful sweet boy," Daisy said, and set down at the table. "I always said he was the best this family has seen."

I slipped out into the twilight with the bucket. Velmer had gone to the pasture for the horse, but the cow was still at the milk gap, waiting for me. I put the rope around her horns and led her along the road to the barn. The cow was named Alice and she was a Jersey and the best milker we ever had. She had a tendency to get mastitis after she freshened and was nursing a calf. But otherwise she was a perfect cow. Jersey milk is richer in cream than any other kind of cow's milk.

Once I got Alice to her stall I mixed crushing and dairy feed and cottonseed meal in her feed box. The smell of molasses in the dairy feed was so strong it seemed to light up the dim stall. I got a bucket of water for Alice too. Careful to avoid any fresh manure, I got the milking stool and set the bucket down under her bag.

Alice was nervous because she was used to Mama milking her and because I was late bringing her from the pasture. At first she didn't let down her milk easy, but as she begun to eat from the box, and I leaned my head against the side of her belly and talked to her, she relaxed. A milk cow likes to hear her name said, and I said it again and again. And I told her Troy was dead and wouldn't be coming to the barn ever again. I told her she was the best cow and give the best milk we ever had, sweet golden milk with an inch of cream on top of every quart. The secret of milking is you don't squeeze the teat you pull down. I talked to her and she give down her milk so fast it shot into the bucket with every pull and foamed and filled the air with the scent of sweet warm milk.

"That's a good cow," I said.

"Who're you talking to?" somebody said in the barn hallway. It was Velmer.

"Where have you been?" I said.

"I had to see a man about a dog." It was what Velmer liked to say when he'd been out in the woods to do his business.

"Well, you'd better water the horse," I said.

"Thanks for reminding me," Velmer said.

TWO WEEKS BEFORE I'd had a dream about Troy. Maybe not really a dream, more like a vision. It was a still night at the end of October and the crickets was loud, a weekend when Muir was home from Holly Ridge and we was staying in the Powell house down by the river bottoms. I was about ready to go to bed and had turned off the lamp and Muir was already asleep.

It was the kind of night when there was just enough light to see by, though the moon hadn't come up yet. I was thinking about the war and all the bad news we'd heard about the Air Corps in England where Troy was stationed, how many planes we lost every day, though men sometimes got fished out of the Channel or North Sea before they froze to death.

Troy had joined up in the summer of '41 when he was working at Fort Bragg with Papa and Velmer and Muir, building barracks. It was mighty hot there in August and he watched the soldiers training, the paratroopers climbing ropes, crawling through mud, while sergeants yelled at them, jumping off platforms and towers. Everybody knowed the war was coming. The war had been going on for two years overseas. Because he'd been in the Civilian Conservation Corps and studied welding and learned to

use dynamite when they was blasting rocks on the Blue Ridge Parkway—
they called him a powder man—maybe they offered him a special deal
when he went to talk to the recruiter of the Army Air Corps. Anyway, the
next thing we heard was we got this card in the mail addressed to Mama
saying her son Troy had volunteered for the Air Corps and was training at
the base in Georgia. Though she didn't say nothing, I could tell it made
Mama sick to get that little yellow card. She put it on the mantelpiece
above the fireplace where it was still gathering dust.

After Troy was sent to England in 1942 we just got these little letters
that had been photographed with half the words blacked out. When I
seen Troy's girlfriend, Sharon, she'd say there was nothing in Troy's letters, and rather than get such empty messages about nothing but weather
and mud, she'd sooner get no letters at all. That showed how she didn't
think about nobody but herself. She didn't worry about all Troy was going through day after day. All we knowed was what they said in the papers
about airplanes catching fire or getting shot down. But we'd get a card
saying Troy had been promoted to sergeant with four stripes. And then
one saying he had been raised to a master sergeant.

Troy sent me money to get Sharon a Christmas present. He sent ten
dollars to buy her something nice, cause he had no way of giving her something from way overseas. I went to the best store in Asheville, riding on the
bus with all the soldiers, standing room only, and I bought the prettiest
comb and brush and mirror set you ever saw. It was amber and brown and
gold, the finest vanity set you could get. Because of the war, stores didn't
have as much stuff as they used to, so I was lucky to find it. Would you
believe Sharon didn't even like it? She said if Troy wanted to get her a
present he should get it hisself. Just sending money and letting somebody
else buy it wasn't the same. I was ashamed for her, to think that she didn't
care what he was going through in those dark days over there. She was just
thinking about herself.

In his letters that summer of '43 Troy told us he'd been moved to a new unit and a new job. But he couldn't tell us a thing about it, not even where he was exactly. He just said it rained all the time and the place was an ocean of mud. He was going to be promoted again, but he didn't say what there was above a master sergeant with six stripes. Troy was smart and worked hard and I guess they was going to make him an officer.

THAT NIGHT TWO weeks before as I set by the window before going to bed, looking across the branch toward Chinquapin Hill, which is in the pasture to the west of the Squirrel Hill and makes a kind of bluff above the bottom land, I could see the trees clear against the sky. The moon wasn't up yet, but you could see there was light back there, like the light of a distant town or the light of a fairground. Stars seemed stuck in the limbs of trees like tiny Christmas lights. Maybe it was dew sparkling on the trees and in the pasture, beyond the springhouse and smokehouse and the old molasses furnace above the branch.

Suddenly I didn't see none of that. It was like a light had gone out, and instead of the window, I saw Troy and he was almost close enough to touch. He was setting with his head down and he looked worried. I was so surprised I didn't think to say nothing. He just looked down at something and he seemed terrible sad. And he looked older. His hair was still light red and curly like it had always been. Whatever he was thinking about, it was bad and a weight seemed to be crushing down on his shoulders.

Troy, I wanted to say, but my tongue was set like it was froze, the way your throat and voice are in a dream. I couldn't reach out to him, and I couldn't say nothing, not even his name.

And then he looked at me. It was like he seen me there, so close to him. He turned and it was like he was going to say something, though his expression was awful sad. I thought he was going to tell me where he was and what he was doing. He just wore these drab work clothes, like a mechanic would, not a uniform. He looked like he'd been working a long time without sleep.

But suddenly there was this roar, as if a thousand shotguns had gone off at once. And a whoosh of flame that covered everything fast as lightning. It was a many-colored flame with purple and green but mostly white that flooded out, unfurling like a big cloth, and burned up everything. And then it was all gone. I wanted to see what happened. I wanted to reach out and save Troy, but there was nothing but the window and Chinquapin Hill and the sound of crickets. And I heard the roar of Johnson Shoals over on the creek.

WHEN I TOLD Muir the next morning about what I'd seen he didn't hardly seem to listen. Muir was a preacher who sometimes spoke at different churches, though he wasn't a pastor yet. He didn't like people to talk about superstitions. He said superstition showed a lack of faith. He was making coffee when I told him what I'd seen.

"You must've had a bad dream," he said.

"How could I have dreamed when I was awake before it started and awake when it was over. I was looking out the window toward Chinquapin Hill and I was awake as I am now."

"You just dreamed you was awake. Looking out the window and across the branch was part of the dream."

Nobody can make me mad the way Muir can. I guess it's them that you love that can rile you the most. I reckon a difference with somebody you love scares you cause you expect them to be of one mind and one feeling with you.

"How do you know if you didn't see it?" I snapped.

"Ain't saying you're lying," Muir said. "I just think you forgot you was dreaming." He dippered water from the bucket on the counter into the coffeepot before lowering the holder with the coffee in. Ginny, his mama, had never got running water into the Powell house and we had to carry water from the springhouse out near the pasture fence. The spring itself was way around the pasture hill, beyond the molasses furnace, but Muir's grandpa Peace had piped it all the way down to the springhouse. Muir had got electricity run to the house, but had not put in plumbing.

"No one can tell you nothing," I said, and put on water to make grits. The way Muir acted when I told him I'd seen Troy as close as on the other side of the window made me decide not to tell another soul. Everybody was worried about the war and about getting gasoline and tires and sugar because of the rationing. You had to have stamps to buy almost anything, coffee or meat or tea. Mr. Sharp that was the principal of the school give out ration books and he'd signed some for me. You took the ration books with you to the store, and when you bought sugar or coffee you had to give a stamp with your money. The stamps didn't make nothing cheaper.

Now I kept thinking about what I'd seen in the vision or whatever it was. Maybe it *was* a kind of dream. In the Bible it said young men will see visions and old men will dream dreams. Didn't say nothing about girls or women. What bothered me most was how worried Troy looked bent over that way, like he was waiting for something. Couldn't see where he was, but the awful blast and flash of light just seemed to come out of nowhere. And then as I played it over in my mind I remembered there was something else, something I'd forgot. After the flash and just before it all disappeared there was a smell for an instant, a smell like burnt paint or some burnt chemical. It was a terrible smell, like leather had been scorched, and maybe hair, like when a cat gets too close to a hot stove. That smell come back to me and it made me a little sick.

"How come you know everything?" I said to Muir, but he just laughed and shook his head, like he usually does when I get mad, acting like I'm not worth arguing with, just being an emotional woman. I've seen him do it a hundred times, backing out of an argument and shaking his head and chuckling, like he couldn't make sense of what I said anyway. And that always makes me madder still.

WHEN I GOT back to the house Aunt Daisy had left and Mama was warming up the soup beans and the rice was about ready and the sweet taters smelled almost baked. I strained the milk into pitchers and put them into the icebox. Mama placed bowls and spoons on the table while I washed out the straining cloth and the milk bucket. When I put the rice and taters on the table I called for Papa to come.

"Don't feel like eating," he called back.

"You come on," I said. "You've got to eat something."

Papa shuffled in and set down at the head of the table while I poured each a glass of cold milk. Velmer was still outside, but I knowed he'd come in when we set down. Papa said a short blessing and helped hisself to the soup beans but didn't start eating. "I told that boy to stay away from old airplanes," he said.

Mama set with her bowl empty. "Let me give you some rice," I said.

"He never paid no mind to what I said," Papa said.

"Best not to talk about it," I said. "Won't do no good."

Velmer come in through the kitchen door and set down at the table. I passed him the bowl of soup beans. Just then the front door opened and somebody walked into the living room. "Come on into the kitchen," I called. I looked through the door and there was Preacher Rice.

"If you folks are eating, I'll just stay here by the fire," the preacher said.

"Come on in and set down and we'll find you a plate," Papa said.

The preacher stepped into the kitchen but didn't set down. "I just come to say how awful sorry I am," he said, holding his hat in front of him.

"Won't you have a sweet tater?" I said. Last thing I wanted to do was discuss Troy's death with the preacher. And I guess Mama and Papa felt the same way. For when a preacher comes to comfort you it always makes you feel worser. I don't know why that is, but a preacher's kind words make you feel more miserable. Maybe I shouldn't say that, being married to a preacher. But a preacher's words always seem faraway. You know what he's going to say and what he has to say. And somehow the fact that he goes ahead and says them makes you even sadder. For the preacher will say God's ways are mysterious and beyond our understanding. What seems unbearable to humans must be part of a plan. If something bad is an accident it's bad, but if it's part of a plan that's much worse. I've never understood why preachers think that is comforting. They make you feel so hopeless and stupid. For they remind you there's nothing you can do. Your suffering is all part of God's plan. You don't have control over nothing, no matter what you do. It makes you feel weak and sick in your bones, the way a bad fever does.

"The Lord is looking down in his infinite mercy," the preacher said. "But with our limited understanding we can't always understand."

"That's right, Brother Rice," Papa said, and took another spoonful of soup beans. Mama didn't say nothing, and she still hadn't touched her plate. I eat some sweet tater just to be polite.

"The Lord tries us as he tried Job," Preacher Rice said. "Because he loves us he tries us."

Somebody else opened the front door and walked into the living room. I called out that we was in the kitchen. Helen Ballard stepped into the firelight holding a plate, and her husband, Hilliard, was just behind her.

"I have brought a chocolate cake," she said.

"Your chocolate cake is my favorite," I said.

"Come, pull up a chair," Papa said.

"We'll just stay here by the fire," Helen called. "We was awful sorry to hear about Troy."

I got up and took the cake from her and put it on the counter.

Two

I don't know which come first, Troy's love of drawing or the dog we called Old Pat that he loved so much and drawed so many pictures of. By the time he was in high school Troy must have made a hundred pictures of that dog. The German shepherd was give to Troy by the Osborne family from Columbia, South Carolina. Papa built a summer house for them on the lake and both Velmer and Troy helped him in the summer when there wasn't any school. Velmer had already quit school by then, but Troy hadn't even started high school yet. Troy helped Papa out, carrying nails and boards, going for water, mixing cement to make the foundation.

The Osbornes would come up to see how their house on the lake was taking shape and they brought their German shepherd named Prissy. That dog and Troy took a liking for each other and they played together there by the water. Mrs. Osborne said he'd never seen Prissy take to anybody outside the family. German police dogs didn't usually make friends so easy. But there seemed to be a kind of understanding between her and Troy from the first. I wasn't surprised because Troy always had a special way with animals, even chickens and cats for that matter.

Prissy was one of those police dogs that have silver-and-black fur in different places and a little brown on their shoulders and flanks. She must have weighed a hundred pounds at least, maybe a hundred twenty-five. And she was expecting pups. Mrs. Osborne said since Troy liked her so well and got along so well with Prissy and they was so tickled to have the house by the cool lake that when Prissy got her litter of pups she'd give one to Troy. He could come and take his pick.

As it turned out Prissy had her litter just about the time the house by the lake was finished. School had already started and it was fodder-pulling time. I walked with Troy down to the lake to get his puppy. It was a pretty sunny day, but already there was red leaves on the sumacs and yellow leaves on the poplars and a chill note in the breeze.

The Osbornes had Prissy and her pups on the screened-in porch out over the lake. They give us lemonade, which tasted mighty good after the long walk. City people always knowed how to be real nice when they wanted to be. "You pick any one you want," Mrs. Osborne said to Troy. Me and Troy knelt down to look at the squirming and whimpering pups in the big baskets. They must have been five or six weeks old by then.

Now all those young police dogs looked the same to me as they scrambled and nudged each other. Their noses looked wet and their eyes looked wet. But from the first, Troy seemed to light on one special one. It was not the biggest of the litter, but it wasn't the littlest either. He put his hand on it and it rolled over and licked his hand. It was a girl dog.

"That's the one I want," Troy said.

"Then you shall have her," Mrs. Osborne said.

Mrs. Osborne said the puppy could already drink milk out of a saucer and eat things made out of meat and maybe a little meal or bread with grease. Neither Troy nor me told her we planned to feed the dog scraps from the table.

I told Troy I'd help him carry the dog home, but he picked her up in his arms and never would let me hold her. She whimpered and got restless, but he held on to her. We walked past the store, but we didn't have no money so we didn't stop. All the way up the road Troy held on to his dog like he was afraid she'd run away if he put her down.

At the house Troy fixed up a box on the back porch with a tow sack for a bed. Papa wouldn't let us bring any dog in the house. He got a bowl of milk for the pup and he got corn bread dipped in bacon grease. It was still warm weather, but Troy made a door in the box and put a sack on top to keep it warm.

It wasn't many days after Troy got the pup that he quit calling her Patsy and said instead Old Pat. "Come here, Old Pat," he'd say, like she was a grown-up dog and he'd knowed her for years. For such a young dog you wouldn't think he'd call her old. But he did. Old, I guess, meant affection and closeness. He could have called her just Pat, but almost always he said Old Pat. And first thing you know all the rest of us called her Old Pat too. All the time we had the dog she was Old Pat, and she knowed her name too. It was like she wanted to be called that. Wherever she was, if Troy called out "Old Pat," she'd come running.

It wasn't many weeks after he got Old Pat that Troy started drawing pictures of her. He'd take a pencil and a piece of paper, even a sheet cut out of a paper bag, and sketch a likeness. At first he had trouble making the parts all fit together. The nose would be too long or too short, the ears too far back or forward. He used both sides of a sheet of paper, working on the porch or by the fireplace and sometimes at the kitchen table. He tried drawing Old Pat from the side and from the front and somewhere in between. He drawed her running and jumping up. But mostly he drawed her from the side.

I think Troy discovered his talent for art from drawing that dog. He'd made pictures before, in school and in Sunday school. He could draw birds and color them with crayons. He made pretty cardinals and blue jays. He made a picture of Old Nell the horse and a rainbow trout he caught in the Lemmon's Hole on the river. One time he borrowed Papa's carpenter's pencil, the big flat kind, out of the toolbox, and Papa was so mad he smacked his butt. He drawed clouds and an airplane that he'd seen fly over.

But there was something different about the pictures of Old Pat Troy made. You could say it was the love he felt for the dog that made him draw better. Or you could say it was the practice day after day, in picture after picture, that made him better. Or you could say that as he got older he learned more about art. But in the pictures of Old Pat you could see a real likeness, a living likeness, especially after he started coloring the pictures with crayon, with the gray in just the right places and the black and brown blending into tan just the way a German shepherd's coat does.

But the likeness was more than the color. It was in the way he drawed the eyes so you could see the round shape between the lids and the black spot in the middle with light reflected off it. And the lips. Troy studied the dog's lip and drawed it so you could see just where it drooped and where it held firm. He drawed the shine on the nose and the curve of the nostrils. You wouldn't think a boy of twelve or thirteen could do that. And he got the slope of the shoulder just right so you could feel the bones and muscles under the fur when you looked at the drawing.

As Old Pat got bigger we found she had one bad habit. She got excited if she heard a car or truck coming on the road. She didn't pay much attention to a horse or a mule passing. But the *rat-tat-tat* of a car or the groaning of a truck woke her up if she was sound asleep, and she'd run out to the road and leap at the vehicle and run alongside the tires.

"That dog is going to kill herself one day," Papa said.

"No she ain't," Troy said.

"She'll run under a wheel and be crushed."

German police dogs don't bark much, and she never did. But even if she was in the orchard or in the pasture, sure as she heard a car coming, she run and yelped and jumped at the tires. There was something about the sound of a motor that made her act crazy.

"If you don't break her of that, she'll be killed," Velmer said.

When Old Pat run after a car Troy called to her. We all called to her, but it didn't do no good. Luckily there wasn't many cars on the road then. One time I come around the corner of the house by the cherry tree. Troy was setting on the edge of the porch holding Old Pat in his lap and he was talking to her. "What if you was to run after a car and be crushed?" he said. "What if you was to die and I had to dig a hole and bury you?" He didn't know anybody was listening. "Think how I'd feel if you was in heaven and I was still here," he said. He went on talking like that and I backed away and went around by the hemlocks cause I didn't want to embarrass him. I reckon he talked to that dog all the time just like she was another person.

It was fun watching Old Pat grow up day by day and week by week, almost like watching a baby grow, except a dog grows faster, seven times faster they say. And she drunk milk from the saucer like a cat does and eat table scraps and bread soaked in bacon grease. Her legs stretched out and her feet got big and clumsy. "You can tell she'll be a big dog by the size of her feet," Papa said.

Picking up that dog and holding her in your lap and looking into her eyes, you could think she was almost human, except for her willingness to always be happy, to run wherever you went, to come when you called her. She was a smart dog and learned her name and knowed all of us in the family. But it was Troy she liked best. Wherever he went, whether it was down by the branch to check his rabbit gums or in the orchard or up on the mountain to hunt with his .22 rifle, she followed him.

I don't reckon a police dog has a nose like a hound dog. She wasn't that kind of hunting dog. But she could run after mice or rabbits in the field, jumping above the weeds to see them, following them by sight. She could see and hear things better than any dog I ever seen. Along in October after Troy got her, it come a warm spell, unusual for the time of year. Leaves was already turning, and goldenrod was blooming along the road and edges of the fields. But every day it seemed to get warmer.

"This must be Indian summer," Velmer said.

"Indian summer is later," Mama said.

"It's Indian summer when the leaves are red and yellow," I said.

"That's not what Indian summer means," Papa said. "In the old days Indians attacked the settlements before bad weather set in. That's why it's called Indian summer."

Every day it seemed to get hotter and one Saturday it was hot as July. Because of the warm weather the garden had kept bearing. The late tomato vines was still loaded. Mama said it was a good day to pick them and put them on the porch to ripen so she could can them next week.

As soon as I went out into the garden to gather tomatoes with Troy I was already broke out in sweat. Because it was late summer there was bull nettles and saw briers along the rows, and you had to watch out and not prick your fingers as you picked. Old Pat followed us and run around chasing grasshoppers and then a butterfly. "Here, Pat," Troy said, and the dog come over and watched us pick. For a while.

Velmer come out to help us, but instead of picking ripe tomatoes he picked little green ones and throwed them at me. Velmer always did have a mean streak in his teasing. Them green tomatoes was hard and stung when they hit.

"You quit that," I said.

"Ain't doing nothing," Velmer said.

He was too big to be teasing me like that. He'd already dropped out of school and was helping Papa build houses around the lake. But that didn't stop him from teasing me. "I'm helping you pick maders," he said.

He hit me on the butt and he hit me on the legs and on the back of my neck. When Velmer got started teasing you it was hard to stop him. I looked around for something to throw back at him. I didn't want to waste a good ripe tomato.

The next row over from the row of tomatoes was the old summer squash vines. Some of the squash had not been picked and growed warts and necks long and curved as yellow geese. I looked for a squash to pick up and throw at Velmer and seen one that was so rotten you could almost see through it, like it had turned to jelly. I picked it up and throwed it at Velmer. I meant to hit him on the chest or shoulder. But I must have throwed higher than I aimed for that rancid squash hit him in the face and busted into a thousand pieces. Rotten squash sprayed all over the place and seeds and pieces stuck to his cheeks and nose like it had been a cream pie. Velmer was so took aback he stumbled and then spit seeds out of his mouth and wiped his cheeks. "Damn you," he said, and wiped his mouth with the back of his hand.

"You cussed," I said, and laughed fit to die, and Troy laughed too. Seeing Velmer with rotten squash stuck all over his face made you have to laugh. Velmer was so mad he stomped off brushing squash from his hair and ears. Old Pat danced alongside him, excited because we was laughing so.

That morning we picked only half the tomatoes in the terrible heat. We was going to pick the rest after dinner, and Mama was going to help us. But it must have been two o'clock by the time we washed the dinner dishes and went back out to the garden with our baskets. It was so hot you shivered. A dark cloud had rose from the south over Cicero Mountain. Mama pointed to the yellow light around the edges of the cloud and said that meant it was going to hail. I'd heard her say that all my life. A yellow light around a storm cloud meant hail.

We started picking, hoping to get as much done as we could before the storm hit. But the cloud moved higher and we could hear rain on the mountain across the river. The edge of the cloud straight above us was blinding white. Lightning licked out and clawed the side of the Cicero Mountain and thunder split the air. Rain advanced like an army across the river and through the fields and then into the pasture. Old Pat yelped and whimpered and run around us. Thunder always scares a dog.

"Here, Pat," Troy said, and tried to calm her.

"Let's pick all we can," Mama said.

I tore tomatoes off the vines. Didn't matter if I broke stems and branches since it was the end of the season anyway. The first drops hit my face cold as nickels and quarters. The drops was so heavy they stung my skin.

"Let's carry the baskets to the porch," Mama said as thunder crashed down right on top of us. I picked up a basket and started toward the house. But we'd waited until it was too late. The cold drops hit my face and shoulders like they was shot from a gun, and then I felt something tap the back of my head. White pellets fell all around me, hitting the tomato vines, first the size of aspirin tablets and then big as marbles and mothballs. Old Pat run around yelping and growling, as white hailstones hit her on the nose and back and bounced on the ground.

Troy throwed down his basket of tomatoes and picked up the dog and started running. I followed, carrying my basket and his, but hail hit my back like a hundred whip lashes. "Lord a mercy," Mama said.

The ground was already white and it looked like a ton of mothballs and ice-coated grapes and plums was falling. Hailstones bounced and rolled and banged my head like rocks throwed from the top of a barn. When we got to the hemlock trees Mama said to leave the baskets there under the trees and make a run for the porch. I put my arm over my face as I run. Hail whizzed and whistled and I thought that might be the way a soldier felt with bullets flying all around. It felt like the sky and the whole world had collapsed and was falling on top of me.

Hailstones piled on the steps made it hard to step on them. I slipped and hit my knee and had to hold on to the rail. Hail jumped and bounced on the porch and ricocheted off the wall. Troy held Old Pat and the dog yelped and squirmed, so scared she couldn't be still.

"We'll have to go in," Mama said. Mama didn't say nothing when Troy brought Old Pat inside.

In the house you could hear the hail banging on the tin roof and hitting the walls and windows. A blast of thunder shook the house and rattled the window frames. Old Pat kept on whimpering. That was the first time I seen what a sensitive dog she was. She was as high strung in her nerves as a cat.

We set down and I seen hailstones on the hearth where they'd come down the chimney and was melting in the dark, making pools on the hearth. The whole mess would have to be cleaned up before we could start a fire. "Shhhh," Troy said to Old Pat to get her to quit whimpering.

Next thing I noticed was that the knock of hail on the roof and walls had slowed down and then stopped. I got up and looked out the window and seen it was lighter. It was still raining, but the storm was passing. Even while I was looking the rain stopped, just as fast as it had come.

When we stepped out on the porch I seen that some of the tomatoes we'd laid there in the morning looked like they'd been pecked by chickens. The hail had made chips in their skin. Hail was melting on the porch and in the grass. It felt like the grass was full of marbles when you stepped on it.

Old Pat was so excited she yelped as we walked toward the garden. The baskets of tomatoes under the hemlocks was OK, but Mama gasped when we got to the edge of the garden. The tomato vines was all knocked down and the tomatoes looked beat to pieces. The bean vines was just rags pushed down into the mud.

"At least we got some tomatoes," Mama said.

I NEVER DID understand why men was attracted to me. For I was never much attracted to them. Or I guess I was and I wasn't. It was a kind of surprise when I was about thirteen and just beginning to show breasts and to have hips you could notice that I seen men watching me. It was a little scary to catch men and big boys always looking at my legs. My legs was just beginning to get their shape then. I was a skinny little thing when I was a girl, and the dresses we wore in those days went down to your ankles almost. But I'd see men looking at my ankles and calves. Men always look at a woman's legs first. I reckon they can't help it.

When you're a little girl it don't occur to you how fascinating a woman's butt is to a man. And even if it did, you wouldn't be able to talk about it. But it was shivery to find a man studying your behind, especially when you walked, like they couldn't take their eyes off it. And if you caught them looking, most turned away, like they was ashamed of enjoying the sight of your rear end. But some didn't care at all. They'd look you right in the eye and grin. The bold men was the scariest. They'd stare at you like they could see everything under your dress, like you didn't have no clothes on at all.

There is a way in which men just seem like animals, compared to women. Most of the time all men think about is their bellies. The saying is that the way to a man's heart is through his belly, and I reckon that's true, as far as it goes. Men will set down at the table and eat like hogs, they will. And when nobody ain't looking they'll go out in the garden and eat four ripe tomatoes or half a watermelon that has cooled overnight and still has dew on it.

That was something I learned from Mama. When she had to ask Papa something or explain something that was awkward, she'd wait until he'd finished a good meal and was feeling warm and relaxed, and then she'd ask him. One time I wanted to go on this trip to Asheville to see the movie *Ben-Hur*. Lewis Shipman was taking his big old logging truck, and a bunch of younguns was riding in the back to Asheville to see the movie. There was no talking in movies then, but people still liked to see them.

It costed a dime to go to the movie and I didn't have no dime. I'd have to ask Papa for the dime and that was hard enough. But I had to beg him to let me go to Asheville with all the others and that was the hardest part. I was only thirteen and he wouldn't let me go out with boys. He said a girl my age had no business messing around with boys. If he thought I was going on the trip to be with boys he wouldn't let me go. But there wasn't nothing to do but ask him. It was Friday, the day before Lewis Shipman was taking the kids to Asheville and I had to find out.

Mama said I could go as far as she was concerned, but I had to ask Papa. He was working on a summer cabin down at the lake for cotton-mill folks from Spartanburg. It was the way he made money to pay for our place.

"I can give you a dime, but you'll have to ask him if you can go," Mama said. Mama always had a little money from selling eggs and butter down at the store.

"I'll ask him as soon as he gets home," I said. I was helping Mama shell peas for supper.

"No." Mama said. "Wait."

"I can't wait; they're going tomorrow."

"No. Wait until after supper," Mama said. "When Hank comes home he'll be tired and on edge after working all day and walking home from the lake. After he has eat a good supper he'll feel better and might agree."

That was the first time I seen how smart Mama was at handling Papa. She was so calm and good natured you wouldn't think she was that clever. But she'd lived with Papa a long time and knowed how to persuade him. It was a lesson to me about how to get along with a man. But even more, it was a lesson about women, about what a woman has to do to get along with a man.

Since it was Friday and payday, Mama fixed a good supper of peas and

corn bread, chicken and dumplings. She had a few dried apples from last
fall and made a pie. And when Papa got home she made a pot of fresh
coffee. Nothing makes a meal perfect as apple pie and good strong coffee
at the end. When Papa had eat and went into the living room to read the
paper I followed him and told him Lewis Shipman was taking his truck
to Asheville to the movie.

"Movies ain't good for you," Papa said.

"This is a movie about Jesus," I said. I told him about the novel *Ben-
Hur*. Papa liked to read the Bible and the newspaper and religious tracts.
But he never did read novels that I knowed of.

"Who else is going?" Papa said.

"Just a bunch of kids, Fay Powell, Lorrie Summey, and a few others."

Papa kept studying his paper, but when he looked up I knowed I had
won. When he give in he always acted like he hadn't give in. He never
did want nobody to think he was easy to persuade. He took a square of
tobacco out of his pocket and cut off a corner. "You can't go unless Troy
goes," he said.

"It will cost a dime," I said.

Papa reached into his pocket and took out a shiny fifty-cent piece and
put it in my hand. Then he went back to his newspaper. And I seen that
because I'd waited till after supper I got to go to Asheville and Troy got to
go too, and we had extra money for popcorn and a Co-Cola for each of us.

Three

I reckon a woman knows she's in love when she keeps loving a man she don't want to love. I had every reason not to love Muir Powell. He was a local boy that worked on the farm and done a little house painting and carpentry on the side, and a lot of hunting and trapping in the wintertime. He didn't even have a car and he never did much want to go anywhere. His idea of a date was to walk home with me after prayer meeting on a moonlit night. We'd take the long way round, walking through the pasture by the spring or even down to the river. If it was a little chilly, he'd warm me by putting his coat around my shoulders.

There is nothing like the world at night with the hunter's moon or harvest moon over the mountains. The mountains rise up like big black shadows and the pastures and fields are blue. The river sparkles silver like a road that goes to the edge of forever.

"I never did love anybody but you," Muir said as we looked across the valley toward the Powell place. "All I want is to live here with you."

"Is that why you run off to Canada to trap?" I said. I liked to tease him about the time a few years before when he had a Model T Ford and drove off to Canada to trap in the North Woods. But he got scared by bootleggers somewhere in Ohio and come right back home.

"That's when I was young and didn't know what I wanted."

"You wanted to go to Canada and live like an Indian."

"The dreams of youth seem silly later," Muir said. He could talk proper like a professor when he wanted to. Maybe that's why he thought he could be a preacher.

"But I always dreamed of marrying you, and still do," he said.

There was a place at the top of the pasture hill where you could look across the bottomland toward the Cicero Mountain. We called it the Chinquapin Hill. There'd been an old graveyard just below there and you could see scattered rocks that had been tombstones. Some people said they'd been Indian graves. But others said Indians didn't bury their people under stones. It was the first settlers in the area that was buried there. The place was a little bit scary, but it was also the most beautiful spot on a moonlit night.

Me and Muir walked to the top of the pasture and looked down on the valley. There was no lights to be seen in all the community. He put his arms around me and was just about to kiss me but I pulled away and started walking up the hill away from him. I don't know what come over me all of a sudden, but I couldn't help myself. I just had to get away from him.

"Where are you going?" he said.

"I don't know yet," I said.

"Let me know when you find out," he said, but I didn't answer him.

ONE SIGN THAT you love a man is you get so mad at him and then you get over it. I can't explain it. You argue with a man and get mad and fight with him and hate him, and a few days later, or even a few hours later, it's like it never happened. I don't think anybody understands that. You get angry with some men you don't get over it and you don't forget it. But with Muir I always got over it. Took me a long time to recognize that's part of what love is. He irritated me and done so many things wrong, but in the long run it didn't seem to matter.

I always promised myself I'd never marry a boy from Green River. I wanted a man who could take me places and was going places hisself. I wanted to travel, I wanted fine shoes and clothes. I didn't want to milk cows and pull fodder and go to an outdoor toilet. I wanted a man with a nice car. He didn't have to be rich. I didn't want a rich man necessarily. But he had to have a job and enough money to live on. I told myself I didn't want to marry no farmer where I'd have to work my fingers to the bone and live on soup beans in late winter the way Mama had done.

Now Muir had tried to go with me since I was just a girl. When I was about thirteen or fourteen he'd hang around Velmer and they'd go trapping or hunting. Muir was a year or two older than Velmer and showed him a lot about the woods. And he'd come to the house on Sunday afternoons and set on the porch and talk to Papa. But I knowed he really come to see me. When I turned around he was always looking at me. He was kind of bashful and he'd look away, but then when I glanced that way again he was looking at me.

Muir, from the time he was a boy, liked to dress up on Sundays and for funerals and special occasions. I reckon he spent most of the money he made selling furs and painting houses on clothes. He'd growed up big for his age. By the time I can first remember him he was over six feet tall and still growing. His black hair and fine features made him look awful handsome. He would go over to Asheville on the train and buy a fine suit of herringbone or blue serge. He'd press the suit so it looked perfect on him. There was always a sharp crease in his pants, and his shoes was shined. I never seen anybody that kept their shoes shined the way Muir did unless they was in the army or was a preacher.

He would try to go with me when I was just a girl and since Papa liked him and he was Velmer's friend, Papa never run him off but was always nice to him. But I wasn't nice to him. He was just a neighbor boy and he didn't really have a job except farming, or a car. I wanted somebody different. That's why when he stood on the steps of the church with a flashlight or barn lantern and asked if he could walk me home I kicked him one time. It riled me that he kept asking. It didn't seem like it would be any fun going out with a neighbor boy.

But I did end up going out with Muir even then, because he kept on asking. I was just a little bit of a girl then. Weighed about ninety pounds. Groups of us would walk to Homecomings and singings at neighbor churches, up at Mountain Valley or Mount Olivet, and Crossroads or Double Springs. And I'd walk with Muir and hold his arm. If it was nice weather, we'd sometime go off by ourselves for a while away from the crowd. But mostly we stayed with the group. I even let him kiss me one time at Double Springs, down by the double springs.

When Muir was about twenty-two and I was fifteen, him and his brother, Moody, bought a Model T Ford, owned it half and half. Anybody could have guessed they'd quarrel about who was going to use it and when. They was always fighting about something. You never seen two brothers more different. Muir had always wanted to be a minister. He read his Bible every day. Moody got drunk every weekend down at Chestnut Springs in South Carolina and got in fights there, and he carried liquor up from Gap Creek where there was so many stills. Some people said he had his own still and made liquor with his buddies, Wheeler and Drayton, from up on Mount Olivet. It was one of those times when I was mad at Muir again when Moody stopped the Model T in front of the house and asked me if I wanted to go with him to the homecoming at Cedar Springs the next Sunday. Before I thought, I said yes.

I don't know why I agreed to go with Moody to Cedar Springs. I never did like him much. He was the kind of boy that never said anything and was usually in some kind of trouble. I reckon the fact that he was a

part-time bootlegger must have been a little thrilling, back in those Pro-
hibition days. Bootleggers wore fine clothes and drove sparkling cars with
white-walled tires. I hate to admit it, but I must have done it in part to
spite Muir. For I knowed nothing would make him as mad as for me to go
with Moody and ride in that car they both had bought for two hundred
dollars. Muir had made me mad and I wanted to get back at him.

So that Sunday morning I got up early to help Mama fix dinner before
she left for church. We made a banana pudding and fried a chicken to leave
in the bread safe with the biscuits. Mama said she'd boil the rice when she
got home from church. Then I got dressed and was ready in my lavender
dress with a tight waist when Moody come to the house in the Model T.
Mama was the kind of person that believed that if you went to a homecoming you should take something to add to the picnic.

"You take the banana pudding," she said as I was about to run out to
the car.

"That's for your dinner," I said.

"Not polite to go without taking something," Mama said. "I'll make
another one for us." She wrapped the bowl of pudding in a dishcloth and
I carried it with me.

When I got to the car all Moody said was howdy. He never was much
of a talker, unlike Muir who liked to talk romantic and even poetic. "I have
brought a pudding," I said.

"I have brought something to drink with it," Moody said. He reached
under the seat and held up a quart mason jar of liquid clear as spring water.

"What is that?" I said.

"Just a little peartning juice," Moody said, and laughed. Now I'd vowed
never to go with a boy that was drinking. It never occurred to me Moody
would be drinking in daytime, on a Sunday morning on his way to a
homecoming.

"If you drink, you can just stop this car and I'll get out," I said.

"This ain't ever been opened," Moody said, and turned to me. That's when I seen the swelling under his left eye. He'd been hit there and it was turning dark. I wondered if him and Muir had got in a fight that morning because Moody was driving me to Cedar Springs. The thought excited me and made me ashamed at the same time. I was too young to know any better.

It's a pretty drive up the valley to Cedar Springs. The road winds along the edge of the hills and crosses Cabin Creek, then runs around the edge of the wide bottomlands and crosses Rock Creek below the Briggs Mill. Cedar Springs Church is set on the hillside overlooking the valley and the west end of the Cicero Mountain. The fields along the river are level as a tabletop. The springs that give the place its name are somewhere up the holler behind the church.

We passed people walking up the road in their Sunday clothes on the way to the homecoming. Then, just as we come around the curve at the Beddingfield Place, I seen a tall man walking ahead. He wore a blue serge suit and had black hair and I seen it was Muir. A chill went through me and when we passed him he turned and looked straight at me. It appeared he had a black eye too. It surprised me Muir was going to Cedar Springs, knowing I'd be there with Moody.

"That was Muir," I said.

"Maybe he's hoping they'll ask him to preach," Moody said, and laughed. Everybody knowed that Muir wanted to be a preacher of the Gospel, but when he first tried to preach he done so bad they laughed at him. Even though I was mad at Muir, it made me feel bad when somebody made fun of him for wanting to preach. I didn't want to ever be married to a preacher myself, but it wasn't a bad thing to want to be a preacher. I hated for people to low-rate him.

Once when I was down at the Powell house with Fay and we set down to dinner, Muir said he would ask a blessing. "Muir has to grumble a little over the vittles before he eats," Moody said. It was a witty thing to say, but it made me feel a little sick.

The parking lot at Cedar Springs Church was near full of cars and trucks, wagons and buggies. They'd set up a table of planks on sawhorses under the oak trees. Already women had put tablecloths on the planks and a pot of coffee was boiling over an open fire.

There was a big crowd of friendly people, but nothing seemed to go right after we got out of the car. Moody held my arm and we set down on one of the benches under the trees. He just held my arm like he was afraid to let go and didn't know what to say. We set there and I spoke to lots of people I knowed. Lorrie was there with her new boyfriend, Woodrow, and they come over and talked. Muir arrived and stood by the picnic table staring at me. I guess he was trying to make me nervous, and he succeeded. Moody just set there not saying a word.

After the preacher stood up on a bench and said the blessing, people got plates and moved along the table to fill them. I'd put the banana pudding right in the middle of the table and I wanted to be sure I got some. Fay had come with Lester Jones and I followed them to the table thinking Moody was right behind me. But when I looked around I seen he'd gone back to the car. I knowed he'd gone there to take a drink from that mason jar. When he come back I could smell the liquor on his breath. There was a sweetness to the smell of alcohol, like something rich and mellow from a long time ago.

Since Moody wouldn't hardly say nothing, I talked to Lorrie and Woodrow and Fay and Lester and the others that come around as we eat. Every time I looked and seen Muir he was staring at me. I felt more and more embarrassed to be there with Moody, but there wasn't much I could do about it.

There was ice cream served from big cartons at the end of the table and we went to get cones of that. But while I was getting a cone Moody went back to the car and he must have took a mighty big drink, for when he returned he seemed a little tipsy. I guess he was embarrassed to be with me and so many people around and he didn't know what to say.

After we eat ice cream and people drunk coffee and stood around talking, it was time for the singing to start. Lots of musicians had come, the Raeburn family from Mountain Valley, the blind man from town named Floyd that pulled and pushed an accordion, the Williams Brothers from Brevard. There was a group of singers from up on Mount Olivet that had a banjo and fiddle. I'd heard they played for square dances on Saturday nights, but they also sung sacred music too.

Moody made another trip to the car, and when he come back this time he said he didn't want to stay for no singing. "Let's go drive up to Cedar Mountain," he said. By then he'd had so much corn liquor he slurred his words. He also seemed more talkative.

"It's time for the singing to start," I said.

"Hell with singing," Moody said. "I want to drive to Cedar Mountain and Caesar's Head."

"I want to hear the singing." People had turned to watch us.

"Let's go for a drive," Moody said, and took me by the arm.

"I'm not riding with you," I said, and pulled away.

"Too good to ride with me?"

"You're drunk," I said.

Moody swung his arm like he was sweeping me out of his sight, then turned and lurched toward the Model T. I thought he was going to fall when he turned the crank, but he got it started and drove away. I went on into the church with Fay and Lester Jones. The singing had just started with "When the Roll Is Called up Yonder" when somebody come into the church and whispered to Fay and me that Moody had a wreck. We followed the man outside—I think it was one of the Capps boys—and he said Moody had run the Model T over a steep bank and down into a corn patch by the river.

"Was he hurt?" I said.

"He was throwed from the car and it turned over several times and then landed on its wheels."

"And he's all right?" Fay said.

"He got back in the car and drove it away."

I asked Fay if I could ride back home with her and Lester. I looked around for Muir but didn't see him nowhere.

I WAS BUT eight years old when Muir tried to preach in the church that time. His mama, Ginny, had always took part in church things, and Muir had taught the boys Sunday school class, though he was only fifteen. And Muir was the youngest person in church Preacher Liner would call on to lead in prayer. But when I seen Muir stand up at the pulpit that Sunday I thought he looked awful young to be a preacher.

Before he started to pray he said, "Will Moody Powell please take off his hat in church?" Everybody turned around and there was Moody on the back bench in the meetinghouse wearing this wide-brimmed hat as pretty as you please. You never did see Moody in church. He give a great big grin, then took off the hat and dropped it on the floor.

Muir then led in prayer, but you could tell he was unsure what to say. After the collection was took it was time for him to start the sermon. The congregation was so quiet you could have heard a gnat whine. He stood there looking down at the Bible like he was trying to remember what he planned to say.

"I want to read you a Bible verse," he finally said. He swallowed and tried to speak, and everybody in the church held their breath. Some of the boys in the back of the church snickered. Sweat dripped off Muir's face. He started to read, then stopped. I looked down at my lap. I couldn't bear to watch him.

Muir said he wanted to talk about the Transfiguration. That was a word I'd heard but didn't hardly know what it meant. "This is what can happen when you go up on the mountain," he said. He stepped a little to the side of the pulpit and kicked over the chair he'd set in before. There was more snickers from the boys in the back of the meetinghouse. Muir picked up the chair and set it right and started again. "This is what can happen when we get up close to the Lord," he said, but he stopped again. He looked down at the floor and at the window like he was trying to remember what he was going to say.

"Now let me read to you what Mark says." He flipped through the pages of the Bible in front of him. It sounded like he tore a page or crumpled up the thin paper. It was so hot and tense in the church I couldn't hardly breathe. My chest hurt and the bones in my elbows ached. I felt like it was me up there stumbling for words.

"Listen to this," Muir finally said. His voice was shrill, like he couldn't hardly control it. He read from the Bible like a boy in school that is just learning to read and ain't sure what the words mean.

"There is a blessing for us on the mountaintop if we will just go up there," he said. "We can see the shining face of Jesus, and we can see his raiment white as snow." His voice got a little stronger and I hoped he'd go on and preach like a real preacher. I felt sick inside, afraid that he couldn't go on.

"We can stand with our faces in the wind and feel the spirit moving," he said. I was just a little girl, and Muir was a big boy that was hunting and trapping with Velmer sometimes. And I was friends with his sister Fay. But I felt afraid as if I was the one standing up there trying to think of words to say, trying to find the rhythm of a sermon. The air in that church cut like razors when I breathed.

And then there was a whine in the back of the church. It started out like the whine a dog makes or a wet log as it burns in a hot fire. The whine swelled to a blowing sound, like somebody blowing across the mouth of a bottle, and then blossomed out and flared into the longest and loudest fart you ever heard. And you knowed it was not a regular poot that just happened but somebody trying as hard as they could to make noise. It went on and on and I thought it was never going to stop.

There was giggles and titters throughout the church. People looked around to see who'd done such a thing. The fart was like a comment, a heckling call. When it was over I looked at Muir's face. He'd forgot what he was going to say. He mumbled and stumbled, trying to start all over again. He'd been uncertain before, but the noise of somebody breaking wind louder than a horse and all the people laughing throwed him off completely.

Somebody got up in the back of the church and when I turned around I seen it was his brother Moody. Moody raised the back window with a groan and bang, and then stuck his head outside like he was getting a breath of fresh air. Laughter started in the back rows with the young boys and backsliders there and washed forward.

I was so embarrassed I couldn't look at Muir. I stared down at my hands and at the floor. The air in the room was poisoned and the light was poisoned. There was a terrible weight, like the air had turned to lead. Seconds was so heavy they crushed my breath.

Muir stumbled around a little more, and then Mack the song leader stood up and said we'd sing "Just As I Am." We rose and sung. Mama had the prettiest voice in the church and she sung above all the others, but nobody sung with their heart in the song. They just wanted to get it over with. It wasn't just that Muir had failed to preach most of his sermon. We felt sympathy for him. But the laughter and the giant fart had made a mockery of the whole thing.

When the last hymn was over usually the preacher stood at the door of the church and greeted everybody and shook hands as they went outside. Muir walked down the aisle with his Bible and I expected him to be at the door when we got there. But he wasn't. He'd walked right out of the church and disappeared. I seen Moody and he was walking across the churchyard with a kind of swagger. He almost never come to church and he'd come that day just to embarrass his brother.

I don't know if there was a fight between Moody and Muir after the service. People said they was almost always fighting. I do recall that after that we didn't see much of Muir for a long time. He didn't come around the house for a while. Papa said he seen him way back in the Flat Woods that winter. Muir had sprained his ankle on his trapline and Papa give him a ride in the wagon. Papa was driving a wagonload of tanbark.

Now I wonder how much feeling sorry for somebody has to do with loving them. You might think that pity and sympathy are different from love. But I think they must be close together, especially for a woman. I don't know how to explain it, but I know that to feel really sorry for somebody is almost to love them already. That is different from a crush or a fascination. To really care for somebody is partly to pity them.

I was just a little girl, but always when I looked back on that Sunday and remembered Muir up at the pulpit turning pages of the Bible and trying to recall what he wanted to say, it cut through me somewhere deep in my guts. And when I remembered the awful poot and the laughter it felt like a red-hot knife cut through my chest. I didn't know what it meant then, nor for a long time afterward, but I know now that was love. I didn't understand that for years, and I treated Muir bad from time to time. But I never forgot him. I always compared other boys to him. No other boy I'd ever seen had read as much or thought as much or had such wild dreams. He was always up to something, making plans. He'd talk about things other people had never heard of, in history or in the Bible, or scientific things. Some boys made fun of him because he used big words. I remember I laughed at him sometimes too, but it hurt me to know that other people laughed at him. He read the newspaper every day and he subscribed to magazines and ordered books in the mail. That's how he knowed all these things to talk about. And he had a big dictionary too. When I was visiting

Fay I seen it on the floor of the living room by the chair where he set to read early in the morning before anybody else got up.

The next time I seen Muir was down at U. G.'s store on the highway. Mama and me had carried a basket of eggs and butter to trade for coffee. When you come into the store out of the bright sun you couldn't hardly see nothing, but as my eyes adjusted I realized it was Muir standing behind the counter. I reckon he was shy when he seen me, but he smiled and took the basket and begun to count the eggs. I studied the trout flies and fishing lines, the rifle cartridges and shotgun shells, in the glass case under the counter. I didn't want to look at Muir, remembering the awful Sunday the year before. I studied the candy bars in the other display case and the loaves of bread on the shelves behind.

But Muir didn't seem embarrassed after all. He talked to Mama and counted up how much he owed her. He looked at me and said I got prettier every day. I was nine years old and skinny as a cornstalk. I didn't want to look him in the face.

"Would you like a Co-Cola?" Mama said.

I could only answer in a whisper that I would. And when Muir handed me the foamy bottle with the cap off I turned away to drink it, staring at the paint cans on the shelf.

Four

This is a story I seem to remember like it was yesterday. But the truth is, what I remember is partly what has been told to me by Papa and Mama and Effie and Velmer. It has been told so many times I seem to remember it all, though what I really remember is what has been so often repeated.

The day we moved to Green River, the road from Gap Creek was froze stiff as chalk. I wasn't even five, but I remember that morning was cold. We got up in the dark and Papa built a big fire in the fireplace, burning up the things we didn't need. Velmer was ten then and he helped Papa carry out the stuff we had, including the organ Papa had bought from a peddler for a wagonload of sweet taters. All the stuff we had would fit in that one wagon, or it had to be left behind. Mama made a pot of grits and scrambled a bunch of eggs.

I must have been half asleep as I ate the grits, for I kept thinking that I'd never go to sleep again in this house, which was so close to the creek you could hear the water mumbling when you woke up in the night. Troy was just a baby then and he cried all the time we was eating. I held Troy and tried to keep him quiet.

I thought Velmer and my older sister, Effie, and me was going to ride on the wagon too, but Papa said there wasn't no room. We'd have to walk. Besides, Velmer had to lead the cow by the rope around her horns. It was still dark as midnight when we started out. Papa climbed up on the wagon seat beside Mama, who was holding Troy, and said Giddyup and the wagon started creaking on the gravel of the road. Me and Effie followed the sound of the wagon which we couldn't see at first.

We passed the Poole house where there was a light in the window and smoke leaning from the chimney. You could smell coffee boiling and bacon frying. As we walked on I found I could see the trees on both sides of the road. The sky was just one big shadow and after we passed the Poole house there wasn't no light at all. The road from Gap Creek run right along the creek, but then the road turned away and swung up the steep mountain toward North Carolina, and I was already tired and my side hurt a little like it always did when I walked a long way.

It wasn't too long after we crossed a branch that I could see pretty good in the gray light. The sky was gray and the woods was gray. And I knowed I had to pee. At first it was a vague pressure, a tightness under my belly. I told Mama I had to pee.

"Go to the side of the road," Mama called. I stopped and was looking for a place by the road when Velmer run into me. Maybe I stepped in front of him, or maybe he didn't see me. When he hit me I fell and when I fell and hit the rocks it was like all the strength I had holding back give way and I felt the pee hot on my drawers and on my legs. The pee felt warm and good and it was such a pleasure to let go I just laid there on the cold ground and rocks as Velmer went by and the cow went by. And then I felt the wet in my bloomers get cold at the edges, and the wet on my legs got cold. I pushed myself up.

"You smell like pee," Effie said. "Little baby pee in her pants."

It was harder to walk in my wet drawers, but the pain inside, and the tight soreness, was gone. Papa said we was in North Carolina. I lifted one foot and then another. My bloomers was cold and my legs was cold. Don't seem no different here, I thought. But when I looked around I wasn't so sure. For in the better light the colors seemed a little brighter.

Papa said we would stop at Cousin Johnny's. I noticed that my nose had been running, and I wiped it on my sleeve.

Papa turned the horse into a little rutted road and I seen the house off in a branch holler. It was weathered like the house on Gap Creek and looked like it never had been painted. Smoke from the chimney trailed sideways down the holler. A dog come out from under the porch and barked and a man wearing overalls and no shoes stepped out the door.

"Y'all come on in and warm yourselves," the man said. I figured he must be Cousin Johnny.

It was so dark in the house I couldn't see nothing at first but the fire in the fireplace. And then I seen the cat by the hearth and a girl about my size looking at me. A woman come out of the kitchen wiping her hands on her apron and said we must be froze. Troy started to cry and Mama took him into a back room to change him.

I hadn't knowed how cold I was till I stood in front of the fire and my hands started to hurt at the fingertips as they warmed up. And my toes begun to ache. And I could smell myself. The little girl by the hearth was still looking at me. "You smell bad," she said.

I looked at the fire and felt my face get hot. I didn't look at the girl again because I knowed she was right: I did stink. When Mama come out of the back room with Troy she told Effie to go to the wagon and get some clean clothes for me.

When Effie come back Mama handed Troy to her and took the clean clothes and took me by the hand and led me into the back room. She washed me with warm water and dried me with a towel and slipped on the clean bloomers. My fingers and toes had quit hurting, but they felt itchy and tingly.

"Now you take these out to the wagon," Mama said, and handed me the dirty drawers and stockings.

When I got back in the house everybody had moved to the big table in the kitchen and the whole house smelled like fresh biscuits. Now I was hungry, or I thought I was hungry. I set down and took a biscuit off the big platter and put it on my plate. But where my fingers touched the biscuit it felt greasy.

I got a spoonful of jelly from the jar, hoping sweetness would make the biscuit OK. It was pale orange jelly, June apple jelly. I expected jelly to hold together, quivery but whole. But this jelly fell apart on the spoon, dripping off the spoon, it was so runny. I got a little jelly on the biscuit and put it in my mouth and the jelly tasted slimy, cold and slimy, on the greasy biscuit. I put it back on the table and just set there.

The woman Mama called Feelie looked at me and said maybe I didn't feel good.

"Would you like some coffee?" Mama said. "Maybe you got a chill."

The woman poured a cup from the pot on the stove and brought it to me. The black coffee was so hot it smoked. I was so eager to get the taste of the biscuit out of my mouth I put my lips to the rim of the cup. By just touching the edge of the steaming coffee and sipping a little I could taste the blackness and it didn't burn me. Mixing the coffee with spit I took little sips.

The more coffee I sipped the better I felt. I wasn't used to drinking coffee, except at special times. When we got up from the table the little girl whose name was Lissa handed me a button. It was a button with pearl on one side and blue on the other, the size of a nickel. "You keep it," she said. I put the button in my coat pocket.

Outside the air was brighter than ever, though the sky was still all clouds. And everything, even the distant mountains, had a sharp edge on it.

"How far is it?" Effie said to Papa as he got up on the wagon seat beside Mama and Troy.

"Oh, about fifty miles," Papa said, and laughed.

The road went through a holler between thickets of laurel bushes deeper and deeper and I heard the roar of water. The noise of a waterfall is like a warning. It makes you shudder.

The road come out of the laurels beside a pool, and above the pool a long gray beard of water fell off the lip of rock and tumbled down a slope rough as a washboard. The roar by itself made you think it was something terrible, like the end of the world.

Beyond the falls the road wound on around the hill and plunged down again so steep Papa had to pull on the wagon brake and you could hear the wheel scrubbing on the wood of the brake. My knees got sore from going down the steep hill.

Finally we come to a field and the road run along the edge of the field and dropped into the river. Papa stopped the horse right at the bank. He told Velmer to tie the cow's rope to the back of the wagon. Then he pointed up the river to a foot log and told us to cross there.

Now I'd crossed little foot logs over Gap Creek that bounced and swayed but wasn't too long. But this was a big foot log high up over the river. There was a handrail to hold on to, but I stepped up on the end of the log and stopped. The swirl of water far below made me dizzy.

I watched Effie walk across the swaying log and my knees felt weak. Leaves floated by on the water below. Birch trees and maple trees leaned out over the river. I thought of getting down and crawling across the log. Papa had already drove the wagon across the ford and stopped on the other side.

I closed my eyes and then opened them. I looked across to where the log ended, taking little steps and holding my breath, and holding on to the rail with my fingernails. The water whispered and mumbled below me, but I didn't look down. Taking tiny steps I kept right on going till the log ended and I stepped on sandy dirt.

The foot log scared me so bad my knees wobbled and I had to make myself walk up the steep road from the river. As we come out of the trees I seen the river valley. It stretched between mountains way into the west. There was a house close by the side of the hill and a light broke through the clouds and shined on it. The house had hedges around it and shrubbery and a log barn off to the side.

"That's the Powell house," Papa said, and pointed. The light from the clouds seemed to shine on the place like a spotlight.

The road turned around a bend and I seen a little gray house at the foot of a sharp hill. There was no smoke coming from its chimney. Papa drove the wagon right up into the yard. The windows was dark and leaves had blowed up against the door like nobody had been there in a long time. Papa got down off the wagon and lifted a flowerpot on the porch. There was a key under the pot. Papa helped Mama down from the wagon and then he opened the front door.

The house was so dark it was scary and I shivered when I stepped inside. It felt colder inside than outside and soot had blowed out over the hearth and floor from the fireplace.

There was one old cot in the corner of the front room and a little table in the back room. But otherwise the house was empty and the walls bare. I thought of the warm house on Gap Creek, of the fireplace there and the hot kitchen stove.

Troy started crying and Mama rocked him in her arms.

"Go find some wood and kindling," Papa said to Velmer and me. "I'll bring in the cradle."

When we had got the kindling from under a hemlock tree he sent Velmer to the spring across the field to get two buckets of water.

As soon as Papa had the fire going and Velmer brought the water, Mama give Troy to Effie and started making a pot of grits. I brought her broom from the wagon and she swept all around the hearth and pushed the soot and dust into the fireplace with the ashes.

Papa carried in some old chairs and a bench from the back porch and we set down around the fireplace. The flames made the whole room a mellow orange. Velmer went out to bring a lamp from the wagon and when that was lit and set on the mantel the house looked like a different place.

I reckon the grits was about done when we heard this thud and crack in the ceiling above us. It flew through my mind that the house was haunted. I remembered hearing Locke Peace's wife had died in that house. I shivered and looked at the ceiling and thought I seen dust fall from the boards.

"Who's up there?" Papa called. The footsteps stopped and we waited and listened. Troy whimpered and the fire fluttered, but Mama had quit stirring the pot of grits. My toes felt cold as icicles. There was another step, and then another, going from the living room ceiling to the front room.

Papa took the lamp from the mantel and carried it into the front room and we followed him. We didn't even know where the stairs was, but when Papa held the lamp up in the front room we seen a door that must lead to the attic. Papa held the lamp up high, but he didn't go no closer to the door.

I hoped maybe we'd imagined the steps on the ceiling above, but then they started again. The weight of the steps made nails in boards above us groan and shriek.

"Where is my gun?" Papa said, loud enough so whoever was up there could hear him. But he knowed if it was a ghost a gun wouldn't do no good, for bullets would go right through it and touch nothing. We all stood behind Papa, hoping everwhat it was would stay in the attic, and not start down the stairs.

The steps stopped and we waited. Even Troy was quiet. And then the steps started down the stairs. First one board squeaked and then another, each time lower. Still holding the lamp high, Papa stood back from the door and we all shifted back.

There was not enough light to see the knob on the door turn, but you could hear it work as the bolt was pulled back, and the hinges must have been rusty, for they screamed out and the bottom of the door groaned as it rubbed across the floor. The door opened, but all we could see was a hand and a sleeve, for the stair well was all dark.

"What do you want?" Papa said.

There was no answer, but a man wearing a thick gray coat stepped out into the lamplight. He had a beard and long silver hair like Santa Claus. The coat was ragged and tore in places. He looked almost like a wild thing that had been woke up.

"What're you doing here?" Papa said.

But the man with the long beard and tattered coat didn't answer. He looked at Papa and then at the rest of us one at a time. There was dirt and cobwebs stuck to the wool of his big coat. He looked at us and he didn't smile or frown neither. He seemed like something out of a storybook, a hermit of the hills, a Rip Van Winkle that had woke up after twenty years.

When he walked toward Papa we all stepped back and let him move toward the front door. I thought he smelled like something old, old leather and old wool, or the tarnish on metal.

"We bought this house," Papa said, but the man didn't answer. He opened the door and stepped out into the night and closed the door behind him. Still holding the lamp high, Papa opened the door and followed him out on the porch. "Don't you come back," Papa called. But the man had disappeared into the dark.

"Who in the world was that?" Mama said.

"Just some hobo," Papa said. "I guess we surprised him and he run upstairs. When he seen we was going to stay he had to get out."

We went back to the fire and I didn't feel cold no more.

"Let's go unhitch the horse and milk the cow before we eat," Papa said to Velmer.

IT WAS ABOUT five years after we left Gap Creek when the ty-phoid epidemic come. Before that, after the big war in France was over, the awful Spanish flu swept through and killed people all over the country. They say pregnant women especially took the flu and many died. And them that didn't die was sick a long time and weak for months after that. Mama told me some people was sick with the fever so long their hair all fell out, and because of the high fever some people's minds never did re-cover. When the flu was raging Velmer remembers Papa give each of us a spoonful of whiskey every morning to fight it off, and I reckon it worked because none of us ever did catch it. We stayed at home and didn't go to church when the flu was bad and that might have helped too.

The second year we lived there Papa added to the house: he built a little kitchen in the back with a brick flue for the cookstove, and he added to the back porch a little shed to serve as a smokehouse; he strung a clothes-line for Mama; he built a chicken coop for biddies; then he built a bigger chicken house enclosed in a wire fence; he made a toilet.

But I think the prettiest things about the house was what Mama done, things you can still enjoy right now. She planted hollyhocks by the front of the porch and set out a rose of Sharon bush by the path to the back door and one by the path to the front door. She got rocks and made a path to the steps at the front porch. And she planted thrift on the bank along the road and her and Velmer set boxwoods along the bank every five or six feet. Beside the path to the back door she set a pink rosebush and she rooted periwinkles along the west side of the house under the spruce pine trees.

The prettiest thing Mama done was buy a whole bunch of flowerpots, big terra-cotta things with thick rims, and put geraniums and other flow-ers in them. She set the flowerpots along the edge of the front porch and along the path to the front steps. When those red geraniums was in bloom they seemed to light up the yard and porch. When she bought the pots from a peddler Papa quarreled and said she was wasting money on knickknacks he couldn't afford, but she didn't say nothing. It was not Mama's way to argue. She just went ahead and rooted her flowers in the potting soil and lined them up in the yard and on the porch. I never seen anybody more determined than Mama or less inclined to argue for herself. She just went ahead and done what she wanted to do and let Papa fuss all he would. I reckon that's what she'd learned from living with Papa all them years.

We first heard about the typhoid from somebody up the river. I think they said it was Sam Garnett's wife that got the fever, and then two of her children. That was way up toward the head of the river where the river wasn't no wider than a little creek. I'd only been up that far one time, when Papa took the wagon and we rode up to Long Rock to pick huckleberries.

Now I heard Papa say many times that typhoid fever, whatever caused it, will get in a river valley and start at the top and work its way down the valley. Nobody knowed what really caused it. Something got into the water or air and went from house to house and community to community. Papa said it must be in the water because it started at the head of a valley and moved downstream and couldn't be stopped. People that lived high up on the mountains usually didn't get it.

That should have scared me, but I was too young to be scared. I'd never heard of typhoid before, and when you're young you don't think nothing can harm you, especially something you never heard of. But then we learned about more cases, each one farther down the river valley, coming closer. I'd been told of plagues of locusts in the Bible, and it seemed the typhoid must be something like that, except it was too small to see.

"Some people say you catch it from touching other people or being in the room with somebody that has the fever," Mama said. "But I think you get it out of water. Why else would it go down the river valley the way water flows?"

When we brought buckets of water from the spring across the field

Mama put some in a pot on the stove and boiled it. And when that cooled she told us to only drink from that. Sometimes Papa put a drop of corn liquor in a dipper of water before he drunk it.

In that terrible summer when the typhoid was advancing down the river valley toward us, and we took a tablespoon of whiskey every day again and drunk only boiled water, Effie and Velmer decided to visit their friends down on Gap Creek that they hadn't seen in five years. Effie had got a letter from her friend Brenda Poole inviting her to come back for a visit.

I told Papa I wanted to go, but he said I didn't have no friends on Gap Creek because I was too little when we left there. He said I could help him clear the newground by bringing boiled water to him and holding the other end of the saw. Papa let me hold the far end of the crosscut saw while he cut the timber in the newground. He told me to pull it back after he pulled it to him. I had to pull as hard as I could to bring the saw back to me.

A few days later I was helping Mama sweep the yard when I glanced down the road and seen Effie and Velmer coming back. They looked tired from walking so far in the summer heat. Effie told us Velmer had got so parched on the road he dropped to his knees and drunk from a ditch that run along the road.

"It was a spring branch," Velmer said, and went on into the house.

The next few days Velmer acted sluggish and held back when he was working. Papa said he'd wore hisself out walking down to Gap Creek and back in the hottest part of summer. It was along in the summer when the katydids started chattering at night and the jar flies sung by day, after the dog days had started. Velmer was setting at the table one evening looking red in the face, like he'd been sunburned. He didn't seem interested in eating nothing, which was real unusual. It was one of those nights when all we had was corn bread and milk, cause we'd had a big dinner of roastnears and beans and new taters and fresh sliced tomatoes. Mama said eating a light supper was good for you when you was tired, for it would help you sleep. We crumbled up corn bread in our glasses of milk and eat it with a spoon. Troy was eating corn bread with his own little spoon.

Suddenly there was a bang on the table and Velmer fell over and hit his head on the edge of the table before he rolled over into the floor. Papa jumped up and bent over Velmer. "What's wrong with you?" Papa said. Papa ever did show his concern for them he loved with a rough tone of voice. Velmer started to push hisself up and Papa didn't help him but let him get hisself up. But Velmer was all trembly. Mama put her hand to Velmer's forehead and said he was blazing hot.

We was so scared of the typhoid nobody said a word. I thought maybe if we didn't say it was typhoid, it wouldn't be. But I remembered that Velmer had drunk from that spring branch on the side of the road from Gap Creek. Mama led Velmer to the bedroom and put him to bed. When she come out she told Effie and me we'd have to sleep in the living room. She made us pallets on the floor. Papa said he would go after Locke Peace in the morning.

That night before we went to bed, we washed our feet in cold water from the spring as usual, but nobody said hardly a thing. Papa had us kneel down beside our chairs and he prayed for Velmer not to get typhoid. I'd never heard Papa pray so humble. After we blowed out the lamps and went to bed I couldn't get to sleep but laid there on the floor thinking I could feel the fever coming on.

LOOKING BACK, IT'S interesting that Papa went after Locke Peace the next morning because we was living in the house that had been built by Locke. After his wife died Locke had give his daughter Helen to his sister Florrie and rejoined the army as an army nurse. He'd served before as a nurse in the Spanish American War, and when he rejoined he was sent to California and the Philippines. After he got out of the army for good Locke kept working as a nurse and was called a fever nurse. When a person got typhoid or the terrible flu Locke would come and stay with the family and nurse the patient for weeks or even months if necessary.

I'd never seen Locke Peace before, and when he come back in the buggy with Papa that morning I was surprised. He was smaller than I expected, shorter than Papa. His hair was straight and black and he had dark skin like he might be part Indian. Mama had said he charged a dollar a day and his board for nursing.

Locke Peace carried his little bag into the back bedroom and the rest of us waited outside in the new dining room Papa had built the year before. When he finally come out of the bedroom Locke said to Mama she'd done exactly the right thing. The room must be kept dark and the house kept absolutely quiet. Locke told Papa he'd have to report the fever to county officials and be quarantined. There was a telephone at the store on the highway, but I don't think Papa had ever used it before.

That afternoon a shiny black car drove down the road and stopped in front of the house. We wasn't used to seeing many cars and everybody except Locke went out on the porch to see who it was. As soon as the car stopped you could smell its smoke and hot oil. Two men got out and walked up to the porch. They had sheets of green paper with printing on them and a signature, and they tacked one on the post beside the front porch steps and one on the post beside the back porch steps. They was signs to tell people not to come in because we had typhoid.

The first man asked where the spring was and Papa pointed to the trail along the edge of the field across the road. The men got a leather case from the car and started toward the spring. In a few minutes they come back and put the case in the car, then drove away.

That evening Locke set at the table with us just like he was one of the family. He'd worked all day to clean up the back bedroom and to keep

Velmer clean. Everything around Locke was neat and tidy. He told Mama to wash all the sheets and pillowcases from the sickroom and even to scald the pee pot. He said you had to be careful with the stool of somebody that had typhoid. I figured out that by stool he meant dookie, which sounded awfully funny to me.

Since Locke was sleeping on the other bed in the back bedroom where he could keep an eye on Velmer, and Mama and Papa was sleeping in the front bedroom, where Troy slept on a little cot, Effie and me had the living room all to ourselves at night. It was cooler laying on the floor than laying in bed. After a hot day in the sun it felt good to lay close to the floor and feel the fresh coolness. The smell of ashes in the fireplace was stronger there. Sometimes we could hear mice whispering on their feet in the ceiling above and in the walls.

It was in the second week Locke was staying with us when I woke up and heard Papa and Locke talking in low voices. "Hank, I'm afraid your boy is gone," Locke said.

"I don't think so," Papa said.

They must have gone into the bedroom then for I heard a door close. When the door opened again Locke said, "His temperature is a hundred and six degrees and we've got to do something."

Locke said they would rub Velmer with alcohol.

"While you rub him with alcohol I'll fan him," Mama said. I didn't know she was up because she hadn't said anything till then. I couldn't stay on the pallet any longer. I got up holding my night shift close to me and tiptoed as quiet as I could through the kitchen and the new dining room. The door to the back bedroom was open a crack and I peeped in.

The covers on Velmer's bed was pulled back and he had on nothing but his drawers. His face looked red as a sunburn. Locke rubbed his neck and chest with a cloth. He rubbed his shoulders, arms, and belly like he was washing him. Then he rubbed his legs, first one, and then the other.

The alcohol rubbing must have helped because Velmer was still alive the next morning. The fever had went down as it always did in the morning. But it would rise later in the day and into the night.

TWO DAYS LATER the black car from town drove into the yard and the same two men got out. I seen them coming up the steps and hid behind the door while Mama met them.

"Your spring is contaminated with typhoid," the first man said. "I'm very sorry to have to tell you this. You are forbidden by law to drink from it." He tipped his hat and the two men went back down the steps. Papa met them in the yard and they talked for a little while.

After the two men drove away Papa come into the house and hit the living room wall so hard Locke come out of the sickroom to see what happened. Papa told Locke he had to drill an artesian well in the yard, but he didn't know where he would find the money.

"I think our boy is approaching the crisis," Locke said. "His fever has already started rising, and it's only ten in the morning."

Papa took the wagon to the store and come back with a block of ice wrapped in tow sacks. He put the ice in a tub in the shade of the spruce pine in the backyard, where the breeze would help keep it cool.

That evening Locke didn't come to the table for supper but stayed in the back bedroom with Velmer. When the clock pointed to nine Mama said it was time to blow out the lamp on the mantel and for me and Effie to go to bed. "Time to wind up the cat and throw out the clock," Papa said, as he often did at bedtime. I laid down on the pallet but couldn't sleep. Effie was sound asleep and I finally got up from the pallet and tiptoed to the dining room door. The sickroom door was open a little, and Mama and Locke come out.

"Julie, you must prepare yourself," Locke said in a low voice. "The angel of death hovers over this valley."

I could imagine a giant angel hovering in the air over them. And if it was an angel of death it would have black wings. Tears come to my eyes and I closed my eyes and prayed that Velmer would live through the night. I meant to stay up all night while Velmer reached the crisis, but I must have dropped off to sleep dreaming of the death angel, for the next thing I knowed Mama was waking me and asking what I was doing on the dining room floor. The linoleum was cold on my cheek and there was gray light at the window.

"The fever has broke," Mama said.

It was the best news I could hope for. When I heard Velmer had passed the crisis I was suddenly hungry. I wanted some grits so bad my cheeks ached. When I told Mama I was hungry she said she'd make some grits right then.

WHILE VELMER WAS getting better Mr. McCrary the well dig-ger come. Papa said he lived over near Penrose, everwhere that was, and that he charged a dollar a foot for digging a well. Him and his men come early one morning in August with one little black truck and a big blue truck with a tower laid over the top reaching out beyond the cab. It was the biggest truck I'd ever seen and they backed it right up to the edge of the house.

Me and Troy, who was six then, watched them jack the truck up so it set level and raise the tower on the back so it stood straight up higher than the top of the house. There was a wheel at the top of the tower and a steel rope went over the wheel with a pole at the end. I was so busy watching the pole dig into the dirt and listening to the clang of the machine that echoed off the Cicero Mountain that I didn't see Velmer come to the back door to watch what was happening. But when I turned I seen him there, dressed in overalls and shirt for the first time in weeks. He was pale and thin but couldn't take his eyes off the big truck and the long pole going up and down.

Velmer was so weak he soon had to go set down. He set in the living room eating a piece of cake on a saucer. Because his insides was so thin after the fever, he couldn't eat nothing hard or raw. Locke had said recovering fever patients crave sweet things like cake, so Mama made cakes for him to eat whenever he felt like it. The week the well diggers come Mama made an extra cake that was supposed to be for Sunday dinner. It was a coconut cake, which she set on the table under a glass cake cover. And she killed a chicken and fried it.

With the typhoid over and the well almost dug, Papa was feeling good for the first time in weeks. He was deeper in debt than ever, but he'd got a job helping to build a house down by the lake near the cotton mill. He had one hammer and one saw, but he said that was enough to get started with. As soon as we eat the chicken and rice, Mama opened a can of peaches to go with the cake. The cake had set there for a day looking clean and frosty under the glass.

We all watched Mama press the knife into the giant cake, but almost as soon as she touched the middle of the cake it collapsed. The cake sunk like a thick balloon that busted. I never saw Mama so surprised. Her fine cake had dropped into itself. It didn't make sense that a large cake would be empty inside like it was only a shell.

With the knife Mama lifted a piece off the top of the cake and we could see where the insides had been scooped out by somebody's fingers. She looked around the table and said, "Now who done this?" She looked at Papa and he must have nodded or winked or something because she didn't say no more. But as Mama cut the outside of the cake in pieces and put them on plates we all, except maybe Troy, knowed what had happened. Velmer was so hungry for something extra sweet he'd managed to lift off the top layer of the cake and dig out the heart of it and somehow fit the top layer back on so nobody would notice it. The fact that Velmer was so hungry showed how quick he was recovering from the fever.

When Mr. McCrary finished the well the next week the well diggers fitted an iron pump on the top of the well pipe. By lifting the long arm of the pump you could make the pipe below gurgle and cough and water splash out of the spigot. It was cold water from deep in the ground, and when I tasted it I could tell it had a special flavor from the rock it had passed through far below.

Five

Troy was always good at building things and when Old Pat was about four months old he made her a house that he set on the porch out of the wind, where it would be warmer. It was around Christmastime and he said the house was a Christmas present for his police dog. By then Old Pat come up to his knees and she went everywhere Troy went. When him and me climbed the hill across the pasture looking for Christmas greens she went with us. We pulled up some turkey's paw under the pines on the west side of the hill. And then we broke a few limbs of holly from a tree in an old growed-up pasture. The pine thicket there was full of rabbits and Old Pat started chasing one rabbit and then another.

A young dog, however smart it is, has an instinct to hunt. If a rabbit runs out of hiding, a dog will go after it. That's what it will do as natural as water running downhill. Troy was afraid she'd get lost and called her back, and every time she give up the chase and come back to him. But when we got near the branch with our arms full of holly and turkey's paw, something run out of the brush and Old Pat dashed after it. It didn't run like a rabbit does but kind of bobbed along. I just got a glimpse of it disappearing through some honeysuckle vines and what I seen was a wide white stripe down its back with black fur and a bushy tail.

"My God, it's a polecat," I hollered.

"Come back, Old Pat. Come back here," Troy yelled.

But Old Pat had already gone through the brush, following the skunk, if it was a skunk. Brush had growed up all along the branch there.

"Here, here," Troy called, and slapped his knee like he done to make Old Pat jump up on his britches. And he whistled too, like he did sometimes to call her. I called too, but it didn't seem to do no good. If it was a polecat, I didn't want to get too close. I told Troy we should circle around and see what it was. There was a stirring in the leaves down there.

"Here, Old Pat, here," Troy called again. It was an overcast day and kind of gloomy in the thicket and we couldn't see much at all. The banks along the branch was deep in rotting leaves and there was sink holes all along the stream, some deep as a cellar. Old Pat whimpered and whined, and when we seen her she was standing along the rim of a sinkhole pawing the ground. Whatever she was chasing had jumped down into that sinkhole.

"Come here, Pat," Troy called.

I imagined later that I heard something, a kind of hiss or whiz, a sprinkle of a spray. But I'm not sure I did. But we both smelled it, that awful smell a skunk throws out, like the scent of burnt rubber or the bitterest coffee grounds, except a hundred times stronger. "Oh my God," I said.

And Old Pat pulled back from the rim of the sink hole like she'd been pushed by a terrible wind. And when she run to us the smell on her coat burned my nose. It was a stink so bad you felt it would give you a headache or make you throw up. Old Pat come running toward us and we all hurried back up the hill through the yellow pines and by the holly tree to the open pasture. The stink seemed to follow us, and by the time we got close to the house Mama was already out on the porch. She'd smelled the polecat from inside the kitchen and come out to see where the stench was coming from.

"Did a polecat spray you?" she called.

We told her no, but Old Pat may have got hit.

"Get a tow sack and rub that dog with turpentine," she said. "Do it at the barn and don't get any in her eyes or mouth."

I don't think much of the skunk's spray had actually touched Old Pat's fur, but she still smelled to high heaven, or deep hell. At the barn we rubbed her all over with turpentine and then it was a lot better. But we smelled the burnt-rubber stink on her for weeks, all through Christmas and into the new year.

I RECKON IT was the next spring when Troy was sent by Papa to nail fence wire up on the far side of the pasture where fallen limbs had knocked the wire loose. It was cool in the morning and he wore his coat when he took the bag of steeples and the hammer to work his way around the pasture fence to fasten the barbed wire to the posts again. Papa and Velmer was working on a house down at the lake then and Papa said Troy was big enough to look after the place by hisself. Of course Old Pat went with him.

But that evening when Troy come back for supper the dog wasn't with him. "Where is Old Pat?" I said.

Troy said she'd run off while he was working, chasing a rabbit or maybe a possum through the pine thicket and had never come back.

"Which way did she run?" I said.

"Toward the river."

Troy said he'd better look for his dog and I told him to wait until I'd scattered corn for the chickens and gathered eggs and I'd go with him. It wasn't like Old Pat to run off after a rabbit and not come back. Since she wasn't a nose dog, she'd only run after an animal as long as it was in sight. And then after a few minutes she'd show up again, a little out of breath and tickled with her adventure.

Me and Troy started out toward the river and Mama called after us that supper would be ready in a few minutes. Just then Papa drove into the yard and when we told him we was going to look for Old Pat he said not to bother. "That dog will show up at feeding time."

"A dog can always find its way home," Velmer said.

But we went anyway, walking along the edge of the pasture to the bottomland and along the birch trees by the river. Troy called out for Old Pat from time to time. We seen a muskrat slipping into the water. Wild mustard growed along the edge of the field and soon it would be time to pick it for creasy greens. Coming back, we took the trail over the Squirrel Hill to the barn, but we never seen any sign of Old Pat.

"She'll come back," I said. But there was a chill in the air as we eat supper and I washed the dishes. Troy was so sad he didn't say nothing. I thought he was going to cry. Papa told him dogs always come home after they've been running around. But I know we was thinking that a young dog like Pat could get in all kinds of trouble. She could have been caught in a steel trap some trapper had left or been shot by a hunter or been killed by a pack of wild dogs. She could have been hit by a car or truck since she was foolish about running cars.

After supper Troy kept going out on the porch to see if Old Pat had come back to her house, the house he'd made out of rough pine planks. But the doghouse was empty. I don't reckon he slept much that night, for once I heard him get up and take the flashlight and go out on the porch to look in the doghouse.

Next morning there was gloom all over the house because Troy looked so sad. There was nothing we could say to cheer him up because the dog had not come back during the night. A heavy frost whitened the ground and it was only then that Troy remembered he'd took off his jacket the day before and left it hanging on the fence at the other end of the pasture. He'd got so concerned about Old Pat that he'd forgot about his coat.

There was an old coat of Velmer's in the closet that was about wore out, and Troy put that on to go after his good coat. I went with him to bring the old coat back while he worked on the fence where he had got to the day before. It was so cold our breath turned to smoke as we walked across the frosty pasture. I told Troy that maybe he could get him another dog if Old Pat was lost.

"Don't want another dog," Troy said.

As we come around the hill I seen Troy's coat where he'd folded it across the top strand of barbed wire. It looked a little like a body draped there. Frost made the wool glitter.

"That coat is going to be cold and damp," I said.

As we got closer something stirred in the grass beneath where the coat hung. At first I thought it must be a wild animal, a groundhog or fox. But then it jumped up when it heard us and I seen it was Old Pat. She run and jumped right up on Troy. He hugged her and she yelped.

I looked at the ground under the jacket and there was a bed flattened out in the grass where Old Pat had slept all night, guarding Troy's jacket and waiting for him to return. She'd been doing her duty as a guard dog. It was the first time I seen how she took responsibility for things, which a German shepherd will do.

I NEVER SEEN a dog that loved to swim more than Old Pat. Any time we walked down to the river she liked to jump in to cool off, or chase a duck that was setting on the water. You wouldn't think a dog with such a bristly coat would like the water so much, but she did. Velmer or Troy or me would throw a stick into the river and she'd go paddling after it and bring it to the bank. Nobody ever had to teach her to swim. The first time she seen the river she waded out and started swimming. I reckon she was born that way.

That was trouble for us if we wanted to go fishing. If you took Old Pat with you fishing in the Lemmon's Hole or Bee Gum Hole or over at the Johnson Shoals on Bob's Creek, she'd plunge into the water first thing and scare all the fish away. We liked to fish on a day after it rained and turned the water dishwater cloudy, when the fields was too wet to work in anyway. That was a good time to dig a can of worms out by the barn or below the hog pen. It was exciting to walk down to the river, listening to the roar of the falls on the swollen creek.

But first time we took Pat with us she hopped right into the river and swum around and yelped with delight and we had to wait fifteen or twenty minutes to start fishing to let the trout come out of hiding. "No!" Troy called to his dog when she started back toward the river. "No!" Pat was less than a year old then and she was confused. For she liked attention and approval. Before that, when she jumped into the river, we throwed sticks for her to catch and bring back to the bank. And here Troy was scolding her for even getting into the water.

"Call her back and point to the fishing poles," I said.

"She won't understand," Velmer said. "All she knows is we come to the river."

"Call her back," I said to Troy.

"Here, Pat, here, Old Pat," Troy called and slapped the knees of his britches.

Pat come swimming to the edge and climbed out on the bank. Knowing she'd shake herself and spray water from her fur, we all backed away. When she'd stopped shivering off the water Troy pointed to his fishing pole and said, "Bad dog! Don't go near the water. Bad dog! Stay out of the river."

I don't know if Old Pat understood exactly what he was saying, but you could see she got her feelings hurt. She was used to being praised for going out into the river. And here she was being blamed. Troy pointed again to his fishing pole and said, "Bad dog! Bad dog!"

Old Pat was a sensitive dog. She was so surprised and hurt by Troy's words she slunk off up the bank and whined and laid down under the hazelnut bushes and watched us, panting and whimpering a little. We waited a few more minutes and baited our hooks and throwed them in the water. It was a good day for fishing for Troy soon caught a horny head about eight inches long. I caught a trout a little longer, just long enough to keep. After a while Velmer's pole bent over almost to the water and what he pulled out was so long I thought at first it was a trout, but it was long and round and kind of yellow brown with an ugly snuffle on its face. It was a hog sucker, over a foot long I guess. Velmer took it off the hook and throwed it up into the bushes. "Fisherman's luck, a wet ass and a hungry gut," he said.

But then Troy's pole started whipping down and back and forth at the tip and he pulled out of the muddy water a rainbow trout all silvery and flashing its pink and green. It was at least a foot long and jumped around so lively he had trouble holding it to get the hook out. Velmer broke off a limb with a fork in it and hooked the limb through the trout's gills and stuck the end of the limb in the bank so the trout would stay alive in the water till we started home. There was a big smile on Troy's lips. Catching such a nice trout is a thrill to anybody but especially to a boy twelve years old.

"Where there's one trout there'll be another," Velmer said. "I bet that trout has got a mate at least as big." Troy rebaited his hook and throwed it back out into the Lemmon's Hole. Just then we heard a rustling in the leaves above us and turned to see Old Pat chasing something down the bank. She must have got over her pout for her ears was pricked up. Whatever she was following went this way and that way. I thought at first it must be a mouse, but then I seen a fiery red water dog with black spots race out of the weeds and into the water. Old Pat jumped right into the river after it, but of course she couldn't catch a salamander that must have crawled away into the mud.

"Bad dog!" Troy shouted. "Bad dog!"

Old Pat come back out of the water looking sheepish and ashamed. "Bad dog!" Troy said.

Velmer broke a switch off a birch tree and hit it on his britches leg.

"Won't do no good to whip her," Troy said.

"Got to teach that dog a lesson," Velmer said.

"Don't you whip my dog," Troy said.

Old Pat seen the switch and slunk off up the bank. She was a smart dog and knowed she'd done wrong. I don't think she'd learned the lesson the first time when Troy called her a bad dog. But she'd learned it the second time, because after that she stayed up on the bank, under the hazelnut bushes until we finished fishing. From then on any time she seen a fishing pole at the river she stayed out of the water. You never heard of such a smart dog as Old Pat.

THAT SUMMER WE went swimming every Saturday or Sunday afternoon. If it hadn't rained too much and the river was clear it was the perfect place to go swimming. The river was cold, but in hot weather it felt good, and once you got in after a while you didn't notice the cold when your skin got cold. There was two ways to go into the cold river. You could wade out a little at a time into deeper water and get used to it gradually. Or dive in and take the shock instantly. The boys seemed to prefer to plunge in and the girls to ease in. Effie come with us and Fay and Lorrie too sometimes, and a bunch of boys. I think the boys come partly to see me in my bathing suit. I had a new white bathing suit that I thought was especially pretty.

Because our house was close to the river, everybody left their bathing suits on our clothesline to dry and then they would change in one of our bedrooms. Sometimes the boys would change out behind the barn. Pat soon knowed everybody's bathing suit and I could say to her, "Go get my bathing suit," and she'd run and grab my suit out of its clothespins and bring it to me. But she knowed everybody else's suit also and Fay and Lorrie and all the others enjoyed sending her to get their suits. It become a kind of game, sending Old Pat to get your suit off the line.

One time, when it was just about the hottest day of the summer, we got our suits on and walked down to the Bee Gum Hole because it seemed deeper and colder than the Lemmon's Hole. The Bee Gum Hole is right at the bend of the river where Bob's Creek pours its cold spring-fed water into the river. One of Velmer's buddies brought an inner tube and we had a wonderful time holding on to it and riding down through the Jim Lee Shoals and then coming back to the pool and starting again. I reckon the pool was at least ten feet deep, for you could sink down way over your head, and sometimes you felt a fish brush past you. We was splashing and hollering and having water fights and having a good time when Old Pat swum out to me and started clawing me.

"You get away!" I said. I thought she was trying to drown me. "You go away!" I said, and backed away. But she kept paddling and pushing at me.

"That dog is trying to drown me," I said. I backed into the shallow place near where the creek run into the river, and Pat followed me. "Bad dog," I said. I had red marks where she'd scratched me.

Just then, over the sound of the shoals and everybody's laughter and splashing, there was this terrible crash in the sky and I looked up in time to see the saw-teeth of lightning zap the top of an oak tree high above the river. The top of the tree broke off in steam and dropped right into the Bee Gum Hole where I'd been swimming when Old Pat started pushing me to the bank. If I'd stayed there the tree would have killed me.

We'd been so busy hollering and having fun we hadn't even noticed the thundercloud coming up over the Cicero Mountain. The day was so hot there had to be an electrical storm. Everybody was splashing out of the water and nobody had been hit by the tree. I was trembling I was so shocked. And I didn't pay no attention when Old Pat shook water out of her fur.

"A dog will draw lightning," Velmer said.

Troy pointed up the hill and told Old Pat to run away, to run ahead, and she did. But how did she know lightning was going to strike that tree and that it would fall into the pool? She had some kind of instinct for knowing things I never did understand.

LIKE I SAID before, as she got older Old Pat had quit yelping at cars and running after trucks unless there was something unusual or unusually loud about the car or truck. She was too smart a dog to waste her time that way. Her ears would prick up when she heard a car coming, or she'd stand at the edge of the yard and watch it go by, like she was making sure nothing strange or dangerous come into the yard where Velmer and Mama had set out a row of boxwoods. After all, she was a police dog, bred to look out for things and guard her owners.

But one day, when Old Pat must have been about two years old, a dump truck come up the river road. It made so much noise you could hear it way off, moaning and groaning up the hill. It must have lost its muffler, for it roared and popped in an ugly way. Old Pat run out to the edge of the porch to watch it coming and I stood on the porch to see what was making such a racket. Mama come out of the kitchen too, and Troy, who'd been setting on the living room floor drawing a picture, come out with his pencil still in his hand.

The truck was painted brown and had lettering on the door like it belonged to the county or the state. It must have been loaded with gravel or sand, for it whined along slow with an awful drumming and popping sound. The noise was so loud it made Old Pat nervous and curious. She run out closer to the road, and when the truck passed she stepped out into the road to see it better.

Because we'd been so busy watching the truck none of us seen the car behind the truck. Old Pat wasn't looking back and just as she stepped into the road the car's bumper hit her. The blood froze in my veins and a jolt went through my bones, and I reckon I must have screamed. Mama gasped and Troy run toward the road. The car knocked Old Pat off to the side of the road with a terrible thud and went on.

By the time I got to the edge of the road Old Pat was just laying there like she'd blacked out or was dead. Blood come out of her nose and her eyes was closed. "They kilt her," Troy said, and put his hand on her shoulder.

"No, she ain't dead," I said, for I seen her eyes open. Troy rubbed her back, which was all covered with dirt. Old Pat was breathing and she stirred a little.

"Watch out she don't bite you," Mama said.

"Old Pat won't bite me," Troy said. "She's bad hurt."

"A dog that's hurt will bite whoever touches it," Mama said. "A dog that's hurt ain't at itself."

"We'd better carry her to the porch," I said. It would take two of us to lift Old Pat she had growed so big.

"Best not to move her; she may be all broke up inside," Mama said.

"They kilt her and didn't even stop," Troy said. It had all happened so fast I couldn't even remember what the car looked like except it was black, like the mailman's car. Troy put his arms around Old Pat's neck, but just then she woke up and growled and snapped at him, raking his wrist with her tooth. Troy jumped back in surprise. "Don't you know me?" he said.

"A dog that's hurt only knows it's hurt," Mama said. "She must be hurt bad inside."

I tried to think what we could do for a dog as big as Old Pat that had bones or other things broke inside. I hated to think how much pain she must be in and she couldn't talk and tell you about it.

Troy reached out to caress the top of Old Pat's head, but it must have been terrible sore there for she jerked away growling and snapped at him again. With a yelp she pushed herself away and dragged herself along, getting to her feet.

"Come here, Old Pat, here," Troy said. There was tears in his eyes. He slapped his knees and called her again, but Old Pat walked with a lurch, dragging her left foot. She limped away from us, along the road, and then fought her way through the weeds on the bank by the hawthorn bush and passed between the chicken house and the walnut tree. Troy run after her still holding his drawing pencil, and I followed. Old Pat run into the weeds at the edge of the orchard. By the time I got up on the bank she was already beyond the Winesap and Ben Davis trees.

"See where she goes," I hollered to Troy. When I got to the upper side of the orchard both Old Pat and Troy had disappeared into the pine woods. Briars had growed up thick at the edge of the woods and I had to look for a place to get through without scratching myself. It was cool and dim when I got into the pine trees. Needles fell from the white pines like hairs and piled up on twigs and limbs near the ground. Trees crowded so close you couldn't see far.

"Where are you?" I called, but all I could hear was the breeze sighing in the pines overhead and the drip of needles all around. It seemed like Old Pat and Troy had both disappeared into the shadows.

"Where did you go?" I yelled. I picked my way past a hole where the roots of a big tree had been tore out of the ground when the tree fell in an ice storm. There was a kind of rabbit trail or fox trail and I followed that. The trail led out of the pine trees and into oak trees farther up on the hillside. It was more open there, but still I couldn't see Troy or Old Pat.

And then I seen Troy standing beside a big rock all covered with moss. Tears run down his cheeks.

"Where did she go?" I said.

"Don't know."

We looked around the woods but couldn't find no sign of Old Pat. Troy called out to her again and again, but the only sound was squirrels in the tops of trees and wind stirring the branches. We looked back in the pine woods but didn't see nothing there. After a while we had to give up and go back to the house.

"A HURT ANIMAL will go off and lick its wounds," Mama said. "It wants to be left alone."

"But what if Old Pat needs help?" Troy said.

"I don't reckon there's much help you can give a dog that's all busted up inside," Mama said.

After dinner me and Troy decided we'd try again to look for Old Pat. I got two pieces of corn bread and smeared bacon grease on them and wrapped them up in waxed paper. If anything could help Old Pat, it would be something to eat. I tried to think where a hurt dog would choose to go. She wanted to hide away because she was weak and in pain. She wanted to be at some place where she could feel safe. And she might want to be where there was water. Something hurt or sick would need a drink of water.

"Let's go over to Kimble Branch," I said.

"That's the opposite direction from where she went," Troy said.

"We don't know where she went. She run into the pine woods and she went up the hill. But we don't know where she went from there."

We walked out along the road and then down across the field below the pine woods. Kimble Branch run out through the level woods beyond the field. It was a big branch that went all the way to the river. On the other side of Kimble Branch there was laurel thicket, and a spring come out of the thicket. Between the spring and the branch was thousands of chips of white quartz, milk quartz, where some Indian must have made arrowheads. There was not a perfect arrowhead there, just pieces of broke ones.

When we got to the branch and crossed it we didn't see nothing at first, and then I heard something stir in the leaves and seen a tail. It was Old Pat's tail that moved a little. She laid under a laurel bush not far from the spring, all curled up. The blood on her nose had dried and one of her eyes was bloodshot. She growled a little as we got close. "Go slow," I said. I unwrapped the bread and broke off a piece and handed it to Troy. He reached the bread toward Old Pat's mouth. I thought at first she was going to snap at him, but instead she snapped up the piece of bread.

She must be better if she can eat, I thought. But you could tell it hurt her every time she moved. Troy took off his hat and filled it with water from the spring and brought it to Old Pat. She lapped up the water like she was parched inside. She drunk more water and eat more bread. Troy said he should carry her to the house, but I didn't see how we could tote a dog that big all the way to the house even if she would let us. She needed to lay still and heal up.

"I hate to leave her out here," Troy said.

For the next four days we come back to the place by the spring and brought Old Pat something to eat. Except for the cut on her shoulder that turned into a scab, all the places she was hurt was inside her. There wasn't much we could do for her except bring her something to eat. We come back two or three times a day with scraps of meat and bread. Troy would stay out there for hours with his dog.

It was about a week after Old Pat was hit by the car that we got up one morning and seen her on the porch. The wounds inside her had healed up enough so she could walk. Troy run out and hugged her and she whimpered and yelped.

Six

It wasn't until after Papa started building houses around the lake for summer people that he begun to think about buying a truck. He'd always walked to work, and sometimes he took us to town in the wagon. And sometimes him and Mama would ride in the buggy he'd bought from one of Mama's Johnson cousins. But he wanted and needed a truck to haul things and to go back and forth to work on the other side of the lake.

The new model of Ford, the Model A, come out about that time and Papa saved up enough money for a down payment and went up to the car lot in town and bought one. He didn't tell us he was going to do it. Now he'd never drove a car in his life as far as I know. The salesman showed him how to work the starter and clutch and brake, and told him where to go to get a license, and he just drove away.

First thing we knowed about it was when we heard the rattle of a truck on the road and the *oogah-oogah* of the horn. And Papa drove up into the yard in this shiny black pickup truck. We all gathered round to look at it.

"How much did that thing cost?" Mama said.

"If you have to ask, you can't afford it," Papa said, and laughed.

He told Velmer and Effie and me to climb in the back and him and Mama and Troy got in the front and he took us for a ride up the river. The truck jerked and hiccupped when it started but he got it going. I stood holding the green sideboards with the wind in my face. We drove up the road pulling a train of dust behind us. I hoped people along the road seen us, and knowed that we had a new Model A Ford truck.

Now the truth is that Papa never did learn to drive good. I reckon he was too old when he started, and he never did have lessons. He could get where he wanted to go and that was good enough for him. But he never did learn to use the brakes right. He didn't slow down to go around curves, so when he turned the tires squealed and you felt the truck was going to skid right off the road and swap ends. He just couldn't remember to push in the brake pedal. One time I heard him holler "whoa" when he went around a curve, like he was driving a horse instead of a truck.

It was a good thing Papa bought the truck when he did for the next year the stock market crashed, and after that the banks started failing. And then there wasn't any work to be found. By then Papa had paid off the mortgage and the well digger and the truck. He had two hundred dollars in the bank, but when the bank closed he lost all of it.

It was just when things started looking grim and the banks started failing that Papa said we needed something to cheer us up. There was so much bad news we needed to forget it for a day. He said we'd drive down to Chimney Rock and climb up to the top of the cliff and have a picnic at the park in Hickory Nut Gorge. We kids had never been to Chimney Rock and neither had Mama. We was all thrilled. Mama fixed up a basket with fried chicken and coleslaw and pickles and cookies and a jar of lemonade. We got our hats and sweaters for the ride to Chimney Rock and Effie took her dark glasses for the bright sun hurt her eyes.

But as soon as we climbed into the truck—Troy asked to ride in the back with Velmer, Effie, and me—Papa said no, we couldn't go today. The truck wasn't running right and he had to get it fixed before we could go off on such a trip. I was so surprised I didn't know what to say.

"The truck was running fine yesterday," Velmer said.

"Lord gosh," Effie said.

Mama got out of the cab and took the picnic basket from the bed. "We'll just eat our picnic here," she said. She got almost to the steps when Papa called, "April Fool!" And he started laughing. He laughed so hard he bent over and rested his arm on the fender of the truck.

"You ought to be ashamed," Mama said, and put the basket back in the truck bed.

"You should have seen your faces," Papa said, and wiped his eyes. "Let's go to Chimney Rock."

I DON'T RECKON anybody could see the Depression coming on, unless it was the preachers. Preachers kept saying the world was coming to an end or coming to a terrible punishment for the sins that people had done. It was a terrible time of bootlegging and gangsters and wild parties in the cities, and girls that cut off nearly all their hair and acted like they'd gone crazy, wearing lipstick and rouge and smoking cigarettes in public. But preachers talk that way, don't they? Preachers always see doom and tribulation. That's how they get people to come up to the altar and get saved and join their church and give their money to the collection. They get them scared and then they keep them scared.

But nobody I knowed could tell what was going to happen when we heard the stock market way up north crashed and people jumped out of windows. I thought a stock market was a place where they sold horses and cattle. It sounded like a whole building that had burned and fell down. I was in my last year of high school and everybody seemed to be talking about the Wall Street Panic. Papa said Wall Street wasn't about horses and cattle at all, that stocks was about money invested in business. He said the whole problem was about debt, about people that owed more than they was worth.

But it seemed that everybody had more than they had before. Papa was building summer houses around the lake for rich people from Spartan-burg and Charlotte, and he had paid for the well and Velmer's doctor bills and the new Model A truck. But most people had learned to buy things on credit and all up and down the river valley you seen new cars and trucks and even a few new houses. You seen new farm equipment, and two or three people we knowed had bought tractors. There was talk that electricity was coming out to the country. People would have electric lights the way they did in town and around town.

The first hint I got of what was about to happen was one day I come home from school and Papa's truck was already in the yard. He usually didn't get home from work until five or later. My first thought was that he'd got sick or Mama had got sick and they'd called him to come to the house. And then I seen Papa's toolbox on the porch, and Velmer's tool-box too. Velmer had been working with Papa since he quit school. They usually left their tools in the bed of the truck when they come home in the evening.

Now I knowed Papa didn't like to be asked questions when he was riled, so when I got in the house and seen him sharpening his pocketknife by the fireplace I didn't say nothing at first. I put my books down on the table and went on into the kitchen. Mama was standing at the sink, and I reached into the bread safe for a piece of corn bread.

"Why is Papa home?" I said. Mama turned and looked at me and shook her head. A chill went through me. I figured Papa had got sick or there had been some bad trouble.

"What is wrong?" I said. But Mama turned back to the sink where she was scraping carrots. I'd never seen her act so mysterious. With my mouth full of corn bread I stepped back into the living room. Papa was still rubbing his knife blade on the little stone he kept on the mantel.

"Why is your toolbox on the porch?" I said. I couldn't keep myself from asking it.

"Cause that's where it belongs," Papa said. He kept on whetting his knife on the slender stone and I seen he wasn't going to say nothing else.

"Shell some corn for the chickens," Mama called from the kitchen. Shelling corn for the chickens was something I done every evening, and there was no reason for her to remind me except she wanted to get me out of the house. I crammed the rest of the bread in my mouth and stomped out.

The unshucked corn was piled in the loft of the barn and to get chicken corn I had to climb the ladder in the feed room to the loft. But when I opened the door to the feed room there was Velmer standing by the bins of crushing and dairy feed and cottonseed meal. I didn't know what he was doing in the feed room.

"Why did you and Papa come home?" I said.

I could hear the scribble of mice running along the walls of the barn and stirring shucks at the edge of the pile in the loft above. Velmer looked like he was ashamed of something. I seen he was holding a steel trap, which he was wiping with a tow sack. I guess he was getting ready for the trapping season come winter.

"Why did you all come home?" I said.

"Cause we was fired."

A nerve somewhere inside me shrieked like a sick hornet sting. "What did you do?" I said.

"We didn't do nothing," Velmer said. He wiped his nose with the back of his hand and said Mr. Bishop from Spartanburg that owned the house they was working on today had told them to stop. But Papa had told him the house wasn't even half done.

"Mr. Bishop said his investments in the stock market had been wiped out, and because he couldn't pay his debts, the cotton mill was closing down. The work on the cottage by the lake would have to stop. The house won't be finished."

"There'll be other houses to build," I said.

"But that was not the worst of it," Velmer said. "Old Bishop said he wouldn't be able to pay us what he already owes us. When Papa told him he had to pay the help their wages Bishop laughed at him and said he was declaring bankruptcy and there was no way he could pay. Papa knocked him down right there in front of the half-finished porch. Then he seen what he'd done and helped Bishop up. Bishop didn't say no more; he got in his car and drove away, back to Spartanburg, I guess."

"Can't Papa sue him?"

"What good would it do to sue if Bishop ain't got any money?"

Velmer's story was so strange I felt light headed. Papa had been building houses around the lake for several years. It was the way he made money to pay off the mortgage, to pay the doctor, to pay for the well. He hired his brother Russ and his brother-in-law Elmer to work too. He paid them out of what he got for building the houses. Now he had to pay his help even though he wasn't being paid.

I climbed up into the gloom of the barn loft and shucked ten ears of corn and shelled them in the corn sheller. Mice trickled along the cracks of the barn walls, but I didn't pay them no attention. My mind wasn't on what I was doing. I took the bucket of corn and climbed back down out of the loft. It seemed like the world had changed since I got home from school. We'd been doing better and Papa had paid his debts and I was a senior in high school starring in the school play. And now Papa had no way to make a living.

The light seemed changed when I walked to the chicken house and scattered the corn for the chickens. Everything was the same, but the tilt of the land and the curve of the sky seemed different. The chicken house, the roost poles inside, the smell, was the same, but it was like the world had turned sour and lost its balance. Can't be as bad as that, I said to myself. The world ain't changed. It will always be the same old world. I emptied the bucket and gathered eggs from the nests which was boxes full of pine needles nailed to the walls. When I got to the house I put the eggs in the basket Mama used to carry eggs to the store.

"Careful with them eggs," Mama said. "That's all we got to sell for money." Mama took the bucket and rinsed it. She had to milk the cow before supper.

It was my job to fix supper while she was milking and I poured buttermilk and water and corn meal into a pan and stirred them all together. I thought: Things can't be as bad as they seem. Papa will find another house to build. He always has. I will graduate from high school. The typhoid has gone from the river valley. The sun will come up tomorrow morning.

BUT THE WORLD *had* changed. And nobody guessed at first how much it had changed. The first thing that happened was that all the money disappeared. It was like one day there was plenty of money and then the next day it was all gone. And I never was able to tell where it all went. Had somebody took all the money and hid it? Did the government and the bankers all call the money in? Was it buried somewhere under a government building? Or was all the paper money burned up? I just didn't see how so many thousands of dollars, millions of dollars, could disappear over night. You could see the buildings and cars and things that had been bought. But there wouldn't never be any more bought because there wasn't any more money.

Papa went around looking for work, asking about jobs, but after a few weeks he quit doing that. He said it was just a waste of gasoline. He didn't have money for gasoline. We kept walking to the store to sell our eggs and butter. Lots of people that had been driving started walking again, or riding their horses, because they couldn't afford gas or new tires or everwhat they needed for their cars and trucks.

At home we eat mostly things Mama had canned the summer before. There was old cans of beans and things that had been down in the cellar for years and we eat them. Mama had dried apples hanging in sacks in the attic and we made pies out of them. When the hog meat run out we done without meat except sometimes we had fried chicken for Sunday dinner. We sold our eggs except for the ones we used once in a while to make a cake if the preacher was coming for dinner. Corn bread and milk was all we had for supper most of the time.

Now it hurts for a woman to have to cut back and live without money, and keep wearing the same clothes month after month until the cloth gets frayed and threadbare. A woman worries about what she's going to put on the table the next day, and what she'll wear to church or graduation, or to a funeral. But a man that can't find work and don't have money to buy groceries or put in the collection plate at church or buy gas for his truck is humbled and ashamed. I seen Papa come home after he looked for work and he looked gray. You could see the ton of worry and doubt he carried on his shoulders. It was a blessing that the land had finally been paid for.

A man that don't have a job or no money won't look you in the eye. He looks at the yard or off to the side. A man that can't find work stays away from the house. He can't set on the porch resting as usual. He tries to look busy, cutting weeds around the barn or hog pen, patching up harness, oiling his plows, sharpening his tools. As the conditions got worse Papa took to hunting squirrels in season and fishing for trout in the river. Velmer kept setting traps for muskrats, mink, or fox. Fur still paid a good price and he set traps along the river and up the creeks that run into the river. A muskrat brought a dollar or a dollar and a half, a mink between ten and fifteen dollars. But he didn't catch but one mink in a whole year. Velmer had always liked to trap, and most days he was away from the house, tramping along trails all the way to the head of the river and into the Flat Woods and over to Big Springs in South Carolina.

Papa went about fixing the pasture fence, but he couldn't afford new wire, so he patched up what he had, tightening the steeples on the fence posts, putting in new posts, making a new gate at the milk gap. He didn't even have money for new nails, so he took all the old nails he could find, pulling them out of old boards and posts with a crowbar and straightening them so he could use them again.

I was in the school play in the spring. I learned my part in a few days and had a wonderful time staying after school for rehearsals. One of the boys that had a car would drive me home. And once Mr. Oswald drove me home just in time for supper. It was like jumping between different worlds to spend a day at school, and then rehearse the play, and then go home to shell corn for the chickens and gather eggs in the gloom of the henhouse. Moving between those worlds made me a little confused sometimes. But on the night of the play the audience loved me.

"Did you ever think of being a actress?" Mr. Oswald said.

"How does anybody become an actress?" I said.

"You have to go somewhere and study," Mr. Oswald said. He said I should go to college to study speech and dramatics. He said I could be a teacher while I worked at becoming an actress. I would have to go somewhere there was a theater to act in. But even as he said it I knowed I wouldn't leave home. I didn't have enough money for new shoes for graduation, much less enough money to go to college.

WHEN THINGS FIRST got really bad and Papa couldn't find any work, and nobody could find any work, there was a rumor there was plenty of jobs in Florida. There was jobs building houses on the east coast around Daytona. And there was work picking oranges and grapefruit in central Florida. Papa and Uncle Russ decided they might as well drive down to Florida to find work, for there was nothing at home.

Between them I don't think Papa and Uncle Russ had more than twenty dollars when they started out. Mama packed bread and canned things for them to eat on the trip. It was just after the first of the year. Papa and Uncle Russ took their toolboxes and overalls and work boots.

"If we find work, we'll be back in the spring," Papa said.

With Papa gone me and Velmer did most of the outside work, milking the cow, watering the horse, splitting kindling and firewood. The house seemed mighty quiet. It was about four days after Papa left when somebody banged on the door in the middle of the night. I jumped up and throwed on a housecoat. Velmer and Troy and Effie got up too. When we reached the front room Mama had already lit a lamp. Her hair was down over her shoulders. The loud knocks come again.

"Who's there?" Mama called.

"It's Lum," they called on the other side of the door. Lum owned one of the stores down on the highway. Mama unlocked the door and Lum stepped into the lamplight.

"I got a phone call from Hank," Lum said. Lum told us Papa had a wreck in Florida, but neither him nor Uncle Russ had been hurt. But there was some damage to the truck. Mama had to wire him ten dollars for repairs so he could come home.

"Could you tell if he was hurt?" Mama said.

"He said he wasn't," Lum said.

"Can you wire the money for me?" Mama said. Lum said he would.

Mama went to the drawer at the bottom of the china closet where she kept her egg and butter money. She counted what she had, but it was only six dollars and eighty-three cents. She asked Velmer and Effie and me if we had any money. Just after Christmas Velmer had caught two muskrats and sold their skins for a dollar each. He got his two dollars from the bedroom. I had saved seventy-five cents to buy a hand mirror I'd seen at the store. I give that to Mama. Finally Effie went to the bedroom and come back with a fifty-cent piece she'd been saving.

"There'll be a fee for sending the money," Lum said. Troy handed him a silver dollar, which Papa had give him for Christmas.

"I sure do thank you," Mama said to Lum.

I don't reckon any of us slept much for the rest of the night. And we worried the next day, and the next, waiting for Papa to come back. Had he been hurt bad, in spite of what he told Lum? Was the truck bad damaged? Had we knowed what really happened we'd have been even more worried. For when Papa come back after three days looking wore out and unshaved, he told us an awful story.

Papa and Uncle Russ had got to Florida, but they couldn't find any work. The rumors had not been true. There was no more jobs there than in North Carolina. The roads was teeming with people willing to pick fruit for almost nothing, for a place to sleep and a crust of bread. Papa had started driving farther south, hoping they might find a job around Miami. But near Daytona a farmer in a Model T truck pulled out in front of them. Papa could not avoid slamming into him.

The radiator of the Model T busted and scalded the farmer to death and burned his wife some too. Papa said he'd never forget the screams of the dying farmer.

At that time Florida was having a lot of trouble with hobos and transients and thousands of people looking for work. The police arrested some people and drove the rest out of town. They arrested outside agitators and labor organizers and beat them up. Because the farmer had been killed and Papa was from out of state and had almost no money, the sheriff arrested him and Uncle Russ and said Papa would have to stand trial for manslaughter. An angry crowd gathered outside the jail of Volusia County. Papa said he'd never been in such an ugly situation.

What saved him was the farmer's wife who come forward and swore to the police the wreck had been her husband's fault: he'd drove right out in front of Papa's truck. She said it wouldn't do no good to blame Papa because he couldn't help it.

The sheriff told Papa that if he would leave Florida they'd let him go. But he had to have enough money to fix a tire and pay for gas. And he had to pay a five-dollar fine. That's why Papa had to have the ten dollars wired to him. When Lum sent the money the sheriff held Papa and Uncle Russ until three in the morning after the angry crowd had left, and then he told them to get out of town and out of Florida.

When Papa got back to Green River he had only thirty-seven cents left, but he was mighty relieved to be home. And I was thrilled to see him. The Model A had a bent fender but otherwise looked the same.

About this time we begun to see more hoboes on the road. I reckon it was the worst of the Depression then. The fact there was no job anywhere, and no money anywhere, made men and boys, sometimes women too, wander the roads going this way and that way. You heard about them riding on the boxcars and hiding in boxcars, and walking along the railroad tracks all day and along the main highways. There was hobo camps along the highways and outside the towns. But there was plenty of hoboes walking the little roads out in the country and way back in the mountains too. People didn't know where to go; they went in all directions looking for work, something to eat, a place to sleep.

People passed our house dressed in rags and layers of old coats and any kind of old hat. Some stumbled along with a walking stick or with a bundle over their shoulder. Old Pat watched them from the porch or from the yard. She growled when they called from the edge of the yard asking for a drink of water or a piece of bread. Mama never could turn nobody away that asked for something to eat. She'd bring a dipper of water out to them and a hunk of corn bread, or even a baked sweet tater or Irish tater. In the middle of summer she even had roastnears to give them, and big ripe tomatoes, and later, peaches and apples out of the orchard.

One Sunday when I was home an old man stopped in the yard and hollered out he needed a drink of water. He was all bent over, leaning on a cane, and his overalls was patched and ragged. Old Pat stood in front of him growling. Mama took a dipper out to him and she seen he was so weak and tired he couldn't hardly stand up. She was afraid he might fall down and die right there.

"Thank you kindly," he said after he drunk the water. "Can I just rest a spell? I'm wore out." Mama took him by the arm and led him to the steps, and he set down there. Papa and me come out to see who she was talking to and we seen how weak the old man was.

"Would you like something to eat?" Mama said.

"I thank you kindly," he answered.

We'd already had Sunday dinner and washed the dishes. But there was some leftovers. Mama brought out a biscuit and drumstick and ear of corn on a plate. The old man set on the steps and eat like he'd been starved for a week. When he was near finished Papa asked him where he was going to.

"Going to see my daughter north of Asheville," he said. He said he'd worked at a cotton mill in Pelzer, South Carolina, until it closed, and then he'd lived as long as he could doing janitor's work at a school until he was let go. He'd mowed lawns and cleaned yards. He'd held out as long as he could, but now he had no choice but to go live with his daughter.

"Why are you walking the back roads?" Papa said.

"Big highways are too dangerous," the man said. I don't know if he was afraid of being hit by a car or truck, or being hit over the head by another hobo, or maybe beat up by the police that drove hoboes away from towns. We heard of transients getting run off from any place they stopped.

While the man talked I noticed his shoes. They'd once been fine dress shoes, but they had broke in places and was dirty, tied with rough binder's twine. They was two or three sizes too big for his feet. The cracks in the shoes looked wet, and then I realized it was blood seeping out. The man had walked so far his feet was bleeding. It must have been painful to walk the gravel roads in shoes that was too big and had blistered his feet.

As the man was eating, two other hoboes passed. They didn't stop. One carried a pack on his back and the other led a scruffy-looking dog on a leash. Old Pat growled and trotted out closer to watch them go by.

"Thank you kindly, ma'am," the old man said, and then lurched to his feet.

"You take care," Papa said. We watched him limp out to the road and start north again. I shivered, thinking of his bloody feet in them old shoes, knowing how many miles he still had to go.

But the saddest people I ever saw passing on the road was about a month after that. It was a Sunday morning and we noticed this group of folks coming up the road from the river. It was unusual to see that many people together on the road. But as they got closer I seen it was a family. There was five younguns and a mama and daddy and a grandma. The man carried a big pack on his back that had pots and pans tied to it. And the woman pushed a kind of cart loaded with dishes and blankets and things. The grandma carried a baby, and the four other kids, all ragged and dirty, walked along behind, each carrying something, a lamp, a bucket, a candlestick. It was the sorriest bunch of people you ever saw. They looked wore out and poor as whippoorwills. Old Pat stood on the bank watching them, but she didn't even growl.

I was afraid they'd come to the house, but they didn't. But as they passed the June apple tree one of the younguns yelled, "Apples!" and the other kids climbed the bank and started gathering up all the apples they could find. Mama had come out on the porch to watch them. She rubbed her hands on her apron as she often did when worried. But she didn't say a thing about them taking June Apples. That family looked so bad I reckon she was willing to let them take all the apples they could carry. They must have loaded a peck of apples in the cart and another in the bucket before they went on. As Mama watched them grabbing apples I knowed just what she was thinking. As we'd come up the road from Gap Creek years before we must have looked a little like that to folks that seen us. And if we'd had the bad luck to lose our house, we could still end up on the road like these people. It was a thought that give me a shudder.

It was only later that afternoon when I went to gather eggs in the henhouse that I found all the eggs had been took. While that family was gathering June apples in plain sight and we was watching them they must have sent one of the younguns to rob the chicken house. I thought how clever that was: to be seen stealing one thing in the open while taking something of greater value unnoticed. But that family looked so bad I don't reckon Mama begrudged the eggs they'd took. At least they hadn't stole no chickens.

There seemed no end to people on the road in those days. I thought of the word *pilgrim,* but that meant somebody going to a holy place, hoping for a blessing. As far as I could tell, a lot of these people didn't have nowhere to go. They was just looking for something, anything. Or running from something so bad they had to escape. And some probably didn't know what they was looking for.

One Sunday near the end of the year Old Pat come to the house and yelped, then run a little ways and turned, and yelped again. I knowed that meant she wanted me to see something. It was the way she acted when something important had been found. I got my coat and tied a scarf around my head.

From the way Old Pat acted I thought she must have seen something on the road out toward the church. I was near about afraid of what I might find. But as soon as we got beyond the bend in the road she turned down through the sweet tater patch and into the pasture. "Where you going, Old Pat?" I called. But she trotted on ahead of me, turning back to growl and yelp from time to time.

The winter grass in the pasture had been eat down, but the stalks of indigo weeds was scattered all over the pasture. Old Pat led me around the rim of the gully and down toward the branch and then she turned into the mouth of the gully. The gully was so old it had pine trees growing on its floor, and high walls of yellow clay that made it look like a canyon out west. We throwed trash in the upper end, and Velmer and Troy had dug caves in the walls of the gully when they was boys.

Old Pat stepped between the pine trees and yelped. I seen what appeared to be a gray cloth, and when I got closer I seen it was a piece of ragged canvas hung on a rope between two trees. There was a circle of rocks on the ground with ashes and burned sticks, and tin cans around it. And then I seen the shoes sticking out from under the canvas, and the legs in dirty gray pants. Oh my God, I said. For this was some kind of hobo camp in the gully in our pasture. I wanted to run away, but it was too late to run away.

"Who is there?" I said, trying to make my voice sound strong. But there was no answer. I waited a while and then said, "What you doing here?" Still there was no answer.

The silence and stillness of the place give me a sick feeling. I thought the man under the canvas must be asleep. I waited another minute and thought about running back to the house to get Papa. Wind sighed in the trees on the rim of the gully, but there was no wind on the gully floor.

"Are you awake?" I said. But there was no answer. I stepped closer and stooped down to look under the canvas. The man laying there was so poor he was just skin and bones inside his ragged clothes. He laid perfectly still and his hands and face had turned dark as a bruise. His eyes was open, staring at the makeshift tent above. I knowed then he was dead, and I smelled this sickening stink, like when a dead snake is rotting. He was surrounded by a few cans and ragged paper bags. Looked to me like he'd been staying there a while before he died. I seen an ant crawling on his eye, and I jumped up and run back to the house. Papa would have to call the law to take the body away.

Seven

Mama always said that dog days is when you're liable to see mad dogs. She never did explain why; but it's true that every time we did see a mad dog it seemed to be dog days, that time in late July and August when the heat just sets down on top of us and stays, even after it gets dark, and the haze hangs over the mountains, so you can't hardly see Chimney Top up the river or the tip of the Cicero Mountain or Pinnacle. To the west there is the mountains called the Smoky Mountains, but even here in the Blue Ridge Mountains the haze in dog days gets so thick the sun seems to be hiding and it looks like smoke from a big fire covers everything.

In dog days back then the weeds along the road got covered with dust fine as soot. The trees didn't have the fresh green of spring no more. Briars got tougher in the rows of corn, and the ground baked hard. Clods was sharp as bricks. Pools in the branch got a kind of scum on them, a wrinkled brown scum, and springs lost their boldness and got contaminated. In dog days you could get blood poisoning if you walked in dewy grass with a cut on your toe. In dog days copperheads went blind and would strike at anything that come near them. Since they couldn't see, they crawled at night same as in daytime.

When I was fifteen, before the Depression come, we heard talk there was a mad dog been seen over on Bob's Creek, but we didn't pay much attention, for there was always such reports in dog days. I went as usual in the morning to turn the cow out in the pasture after Mama done the milking. Ever since she was a girl Mama had done the milking wherever she lived. Even in the morning you could tell the day was going to be a scorcher. There was no breeze at all and haze hung so thick on the mountains you couldn't hardly see the tops. It would be a good day to go swimming, but some people said you could catch all kinds of fever from the river water in dog days.

I took the rope off the cow's horns and turned her loose and closed the gate to the milk gap. Just as I was hanging the rope on the post of the gate I heard something behind me like a snuffle, or something trying to cough. I turned around to see who it was and there this dog stood at the side of the road coming up from the river, the road over to Bob's Creek and then down to Gap Creek. It wasn't a dog I'd seen before, but I wasn't scared until I seen the slobber hanging from its jaws. There was foam all around its lips, and it stepped forward with a kind of lurch, like it was walking sideways. A jolt of lightning cut through me, because I seen it had to be a mad dog; it must be the mad dog from Bob's Creek that folks had talked about.

Now I knowed that mad dogs couldn't see too good. Their eyes is so burned by the fever everything blurs, and they have to go by sound and smell. I wondered if I stood still maybe the dog might walk on past me. Maybe it would go on its way and never notice I was there. But as it stumbled on the dusty rocks I seen it was coming right toward me.

I wanted to run toward the house. There wasn't a tree close by to climb up in. But if I run maybe it would run too. Dogs like to chase things that are running. There wasn't a rock or stick close by I could use to hit it.

If I climbed over the fence it could come through the strands of barbed wire. Instead of running I started walking backwards as quiet as I could. Couldn't take my eyes off the dog. I'd be a goner if I stumbled and fell; so I took careful steps.

But you can't walk quiet on gravel. Every time you move a pebble grinds, or one rock rings against another. Just when you're trying not to make no noise a stick or piece of trash gets in your way and scrapes on the packed dirt. As I backed up the road the dog got closer. It was some kind of cur dog, I guessed, not as big as Old Pat but not a little dog either. It was sort of mottled with black and tan, but things was stuck in its hair like Spanish needles, and maybe dried blood and dried snot. It was trembling and panting, and once it fell down. But then it got up and trotted in a kind of zigzag, and I seen it could run faster if it wanted to.

Lord, save me, I prayed. Save me from the mad dog, and I'll never cuss or do bad things again. I'll never make fun of Effie cause she's fat and has bad eyes, and I'll never sass Mama or Papa. I'll never slip away to meet a boy again. I held my breath and backed quiet. The corn rows was still and the grasshoppers was busy in the weeds. But the dog kept coming.

I looked over my shoulder and seen I was about halfway to the house. Papa and Velmer had gone off to work and there wasn't nobody home but Mama and Troy. I didn't know exactly where Troy was, but Mama was probably in the kitchen straining the milk and putting the pitchers in the icebox. Papa had bought us an icebox that summer, and every Monday the ice truck from town come and brought a new cake of ice. I hoped a car or truck would come along and scare the dog away, but nothing come.

The house stood at the forks of the road, but the closest thing was the June apple tree before the fork. I seen I was going to have to make a run for it to the June apple tree, for the mad dog was getting closer. I waited until I got a little nearer to make the dash. But I forgot about the rise of the ground in the weeds along the side of the road, and when I turned and jumped to start running my toe tripped on the lip of dirt and I went crashing down in the weeds.

I rolled over and put up my elbow and seen the cur lurching right at me. Its eyes was devil eyes, crazy and glazed over. I'd heard that if you looked into the eyes of a mad dog you could see Satan hisself looking out at you. I pushed myself away in the weeds and briars, but the dog was so close he'd catch me before I could get up and run. I could even smell him, a thick fever smell like rotten pus and unwashed dog. I'd have to push him away, hoping he was too weak to bite. If his teeth couldn't break the skin, he couldn't give you rabies.

Just then something like a big shadow come out of nowhere and jumped on the back of the mad dog, knocking it sideways. I leapt to my feet and seen it was Old Pat. She circled the mad dog, staying out of reach of its mouth, growling and snapping. I don't know where she come from so quick and so quiet. I run as hard as I could to the June apple tree and climbed up to the fork. A lot of the apples, which get ripe in July instead of June, had fell into the weeds and bees buzzed around the cracked ones.

From the forks of the June apple tree I looked out through the limbs as best as I could to see Old Pat growling and circling the mad dog. The mad dog rolled over in the weeds and tried to get back on its feet. But every time it got up Old Pat jumped on its back and knocked it over again. She was only a little over a year old then, but she was big *and* quick. I just hoped she didn't get bit.

When the mad dog got up a second time Old Pat backed away, and the cur dog followed. I seen Old Pat was drawing the dog away from me and away from the house. The sick dog stumbled and fell and got up again and followed her. Old Pat went along the edge of the joe-pye weeds and the mad dog tried to catch up with her.

That was when I started yelling, "Mama!" I called as loud as I could. "There's a mad dog!" I looked back and forth between the porch of the house and Old Pat drawing the mad dog away. There was still nobody in sight. I was so out of breath and scared I couldn't hardly call very loud. "Mama!" I yelled, and my voice broke. The house was just too far from the June apple tree for Mama to hear me. I called again and again. But finally I seen there was nothing for me to do but jump down to the ground and run as fast as I could to the house while Old Pat was leading the mad dog away.

I started running and hollering and Mama must have finally heard me, for by the time I reached the steps she was standing on the porch drying her hands on her apron.

"Where is the mad dog?" she said. I pointed down the road where you could see Old Pat still jumping and circling around the mad cur. Mama looked around the yard and then remembered Papa and Velmer had gone to work.

"Where is Troy?" I said.

"He's gone to work too."

Mama went into the house and come back with Papa's shotgun. I'd never seen her handle a gun before. She broke the gun down and put two shells in the barrels, and she put an extra shell in her apron pocket. "You stay here," she said.

But when Mama went down the steps and into the road I followed her. I couldn't let her go by herself. She walked toward the dogs, holding the gun out in front of her. When she got closer she called to Old Pat and Old Pat run toward her. Mama stepped closer and raised the gun and fired at the mad dog. It fell and was thrashing in the weeds and Mama stepped up and fired the other barrel. When I got closer I seen blood on the weed stalks around the body and a wheeze come out of the dead dog's chest. Mama sent me to the house for the shovel, and we dug a hole right there at the edge of the field and buried the mad dog.

Cß

By the time Old Pat was two years old she was not only the smartest dog I ever saw but also the best behaved. When Troy told her to set she would set, and when he told her to round up the cows at milking time she would run down to the pasture and nudge and worry the cows up to the milk gap. She knowed everybody's name and if Troy said, "Go to Annie," she'd come to me. Like I said before, she even stopped running and barking at cars unless a car was especially loud or there was a dog in the back of a truck.

One of the first peddlers to come around in a station wagon was the man we called the Raleigh Man. It wasn't really a station wagon but more a panel truck with RALEIGH printed on each side. But people called it a station wagon cause it was long and had windows in the back. He appeared about once a month and stopped in the yard, and he liked to talk if Papa was at home. Him and Papa would sometimes talk religion or politics, and once or twice he'd stayed for dinner.

The Raleigh Man sold all kinds of things he carried in the station wagon. Mama had bought brushes from him for cleaning out mason jars, and oil for polishing furniture. She'd bought silver polish and shoe polish and several kinds of soap. He sold lots of tonics and patent medicines also, including a tonic made of herbs called Wampoles that Mama give us when we got a cold. He sold worm medicine and ointments, aspirins and Black Draft laxative. In that station wagon he carried many of the things you'd find in a drugstore in town, including candy and little bags of peanuts.

It was a hot summer day in the year Old Pat was two years old when the Raleigh Man stopped at the house. It was July after the corn was laid by and before there was berries to pick or fodder to pull. Papa was at work down at the lake and so was Velmer. Effie was out in the yard and asked the Raleigh Man if he had anything that would cure chiggers. She'd caught an awful case of chiggers when she went out in the woods looking for moccasin flowers to set in the yard.

"Nothing will cure chiggers once you've got them," he said. "But you can make them go away faster if you put clear nail polish on them."

"Nail polish?" Effie said.

"Nail polish cuts off their air and they slowly die."

I seen that got Effie's attention because she could use the nail polish on her chiggers and also put it on her fingernails and toenails if she wanted to. She had her purse in her apron pocket and took it out and give him thirty-five cents for the bottle of nail polish.

"Have you got something that will bleach a white bathing suit without hurting the cloth?" I said. My bathing suit had got kind of dingy from being used in the river and no amount of washing made it really white again. And I was afraid that if I used Clorox it might rot the fabric or kill the elastic.

"What kind of fabric is it?" the Raleigh Man asked. His spectacles was thick as burning glasses, and when he stood in the sun the lenses throwed bright spots on his cheeks. I wondered that the bright spots didn't burn him.

I told him I wasn't sure exactly what the fabric was. It might have been wool, but it was also stretchy, especially around the legs. "Let me see it," the Raleigh Man said.

Old Pat was setting at the bottom of the steps watching us. I called her and told her to get my bathing suit off the line. Quick as a blink she was off and come back with the bathing suit in her teeth. I took the suit and handed it to him.

"That's a very smart dog," he said. He didn't even look at the bathing suit. "What's her name?"

"Old Pat."

"Po-lice dogs are smart, like Germans," he said. "But I never saw one that smart."

I asked him what I should use to wash the bathing suit. He finally looked at the fabric and said he had just the thing, something called Wool-bright. It come in a box, a kind of powder, and costed fifty cents. I tried to think if it was worth fifty cents to brighten my bathing suit. I had a little money saved in a jar in the bedroom.

"How much would you take for that dog?" the Raleigh Man asked.

"He belongs to my brother Troy," I said. Just then Troy come out on the porch and the Raleigh Man asked him how much he'd take for Old Pat.

"Can't sell my dog," Troy said. He blushed a little, like he always did when he talked to strangers.

"I need a dog to go with me on my rounds," the man said. "I'll give you ten dollars for her."

Troy shook his head, squinting his eyes in the bright sun. Mama come out on the porch and asked the Raleigh Man if he had any saddle soap, like you could use on shoes and boots.

"I certainly do," the salesman said, and got a can out of the station wagon. Mama come down into the yard and asked if he had any Bag Balm. Since her calf was born our cow Alice had had sore teats. The Bag Balm was salve for udder and teats.

"I don't have any with me, but I can bring some on my next round," the Raleigh Man said.

Mama give him a fifty-cent piece for the saddle soap.

"I want to buy that dog," he said, pointing to Old Pat.

"She belongs to my son," Mama said.

The Raleigh Man held out his hand, but Old Pat didn't come forward and sniff it the way most dogs would. She watched the salesman like she could understand what he was saying. "I need a po-lice dog to go with me on my rounds," he said again. He was sweating in the hot sun, and he took out a handkerchief and wiped his forehead and cheeks and the back of his neck.

"I'll give you fifteen dollars for the dog," he said to Troy.

Troy looked at the ground and shook his head. I reckon he was a little embarrassed because the man was so determined. "Ain't for sale," he said.

"Think what you could do with fifteen dollars," the Raleigh man said. "That's two weeks' wages. You could buy three new dogs."

"I reckon we don't want to sell Old Pat," Mama said, and there was a firm note in her voice. The salesman smiled and said he understood. Every boy loved his dog. But this was a special dog, and he had a special need for a dog to travel with him on his rounds the way a blind person needed a dog to guide him.

We all stood in the yard sweating. It was such an odd thing, the way the Raleigh Man was talking. I decided I would get the Woolbright for my bathing suit. I run into the house to get the fifty cents from my jar, and when I come back out the bright sun like to blinded me. The Raleigh Man was still talking to Troy.

"I'll give you twenty-five dollars for your dog," he said. Nobody ever heard of paying that much for a dog, unless it was a show dog.

"Old Pat is like one of the family," Mama said. "Troy couldn't bear to part with her."

"Twenty-five dollars would feed a family for a month," the Raleigh Man said.

And then the Raleigh Man seemed to get mad, like he thought we wasn't being fair to him. "I'm going to have that dog," he said in a low trembly voice. A chill went through me and I wished Papa was there to talk to him. I was sweating myself as I held the fifty cents and my bathing suit.

"Thank you for your offer," Mama said, "but we can't part with our dog." When she said that it was like the Raleigh Man got hold of hisself and seen how he'd been out of line. He forced a kind of smile on his sweaty face. "I understand," he said. He took the fifty cents and handed me the box of Woolbright. Then he closed up the back of the station wagon and drove away. It was a relief to see him go.

That night after we went to bed we heard Old Pat growling like another dog or a coon had come into the yard. But the growling went on, and a kind of yelping. Papa got up and lit a lamp. I got up too and put on my dress, and Troy got up. We followed Papa to the door and out on the porch. "Who is there?" Papa hollered. We heard steps on the road, but nobody answered.

And then we seen Old Pat at the bottom of the steps eating something. When we got close we seen it was ground meat. "Don't eat that," Troy said. But it was too late; she was gobbling up the last of it. And then we heard a car start and drive away in the dark. The first thing that come to mind was that the Raleigh Man had come back to steal Old Pat, but that was hard to believe. But where had the meat come from?

Papa carried the lamp down to the road and looked around, but he couldn't see nothing. When he come back we seen Old Pat had sunk down on her belly. She was groggy, like she was going to sleep.

"Here, Pat," Troy said, and patted her head. But she couldn't be roused. Whoever had give her the meat had put something in it. "It was that Raleigh Man," Troy said. But Papa said he couldn't believe the Raleigh Man would do such a thing. It was probably some thief.

Old Pat passed out and could not be woke up. We had to leave her laying there in the yard. Next morning she was OK, but a little slow. I reckoned we never would know who'd done it, but I had my suspicions.

It was the summer when the Raleigh Man tried to buy Old Pat that was so dry that fodder had to be pulled early. In an ordinary year you pulled the fodder off the cornstalks at the end of August or in September. But that year everything burned up because of the drought. Trees on the mountainside turned brown under the load of dust. Corn started turning yellow in the dog days, and Papa said it was time to cut tops and pull the fodder.

Now cutting tops was something that men done and not women. They took a sharp knife and cut the stalk just above the top ear of corn and gathered the tops in bundles and then in shocks that stood in the field. Papa said it was better to cut the tops when there was still a little sap in the leaves, before they completely dried. When all the tops was cut you'd carry the shocks to the barn in the wagon to make a great stack around a pole that stood high as the barn roof.

And once the tops was cut you pulled off the leaves lower down and tied them in bundles of fodder. The lower leaves had the most sweetness and richness. Fodder was for horses and tops was for cows. A horse ain't got stomachs like a cow has and needs stronger feed, like oats and even some sweet feed, and sweet fodder.

Cause Papa and Velmer was still working at the lake and jobs was so scarce, Mama and me and Troy had to cut the tops and pull the fodder and carry it to the barn. I said I'd never heard of a woman cutting tops before, but Mama said she'd been doing men's work all her life, all the way back to Gap Creek and Mount Olivet before that and that a woman could cut tops as well as any man if she put her mind to it. Instead of pocketknives we'd sharpen butcher knives to cut the stalks.

We went out early in the morning to start, but the field was already hot and dusty. The thing about a dry cornstalk is when you touch it dust and pieces of dried tassel fall down and stick in your hair and clothes and down your neck. A straw hat helps some, but you still get itchy tassel all over you. Worst is the pack-saddle worm that has stingers like thorns all down its back. You touch one and it's like you got a dozen hornet stings. Besides that, you got to look out for briars and yellow jackets, sweat bees, and a snake in the weeds growed up in the rows.

Mama and me cut the tops and tied them loosely in bundles and Troy carried the bundles to stack in shocks. Like any job it ain't so bad once you make up your mind to get into the heart of the work and sweat and just do it. Dreading it's worse than doing it. I wiped the sweat out of my eyes and cut a stalk and moved on to the next one. "I hope nobody sees me doing this," I said.

"When my papa was sick, me and Lou cut tops on the mountain," Mama said.

"What if a boy was to see me cutting tops?" I said.

"If he was the right boy, he'd admire you for doing it. A smart man wants a wife he can depend on."

I wanted to say no right boy would want to see a girl all covered with sweat and dust and dead tassels, but I didn't. There was nothing to do but keep on slicing off the corn tops and tying them together. I didn't have the strength to argue.

It was near the middle of the morning and I was already wore out when Old Pat come out in the field and started whimpering and whining. She yelped and dashed back toward the house, then come back and yelped again.

"What's worrying that dog?" I said.

"Maybe she seen a snake," Mama said.

"Something has excited her," I said.

When Troy come back to get the bundle I was tying he said Old Pat must want us to see something. "Ain't got time to see something," I said. I was still a little mad for having to cut tops in such hot weather. Old Pat run up to me and whined and grabbed the hem of my dress in her teeth and pulled.

"Don't do that," I said. I was wearing an old dress, but I still didn't want to get it tore.

"She wants you to follow her," Troy said. It seemed odd she was whimpering and bothering me instead of him.

"I think she has gone crazy," I said.

"She's scared or worried," Mama said.

"What is wrong with you?" I said to Old Pat. She looked right into my eyes and yelped and backed away. She dashed across the field, then turned to see if I was following her. Then she come back and grabbed my apron in her teeth.

"Quit that," I said.

But I seen as I was going to have to follow her, to see what was bothering her. "This is a pretty come-off," I said, and started across the field carrying the butcher knife. Old Pat run on ahead and Troy followed me. At least I can get a drink of water at the house, I thought. And I'll bring a jar of water from the house for Mama.

I don't know where I was when I first smelled it, but by the time I reached the road there was a scent of smoke in the air. Old Pat run on ahead, and then come back, jumping and yelping. And I seen the smoke raising up above the end of the house, but I couldn't tell if it was coming from inside the house or outside.

"They's a fire!" I yelled back to Troy and Mama.

"Where?" Mama hollered back.

"At the house!" I yelled, and started running. I was tired and covered in dust and my hand was blistered from holding the butcher knife, but I run as hard as I could into the yard, and Old Pat run with me. I run around the house and seen smoke and flames coming out of the back window of the kitchen. The flames was reaching about tall as a man.

The water bucket was on the porch and I grabbed that and run to the back and throwed the water through the window. But a lot of the water hit the wall and didn't reach the fire.

"Pump more water," I said to Troy, and handed him the bucket. It was a good thing the pump was so close to the kitchen. I run to the porch and got another bucket, the one I used to carry water to the chickens. Troy pumped as fast as he could and water heaved out into the bucket. As soon as it was full I throwed the water through the window again.

"You'll have to reach the fire from inside," Mama said when she got to the pump all out of breath.

I took the next bucket and run to the kitchen door. As soon as I opened the door smoke pushed out and I couldn't hardly see. I stooped down low under the smoke and seen fire on the floor by the window. Holding my breath, I run inside and dashed water on the floor. Mama was right behind me with the other bucket and she dumped that on the fire too.

The curtains by the window was burning and Mama pulled the curtains down into the wet mess below the window. But the flames from the curtains had set the ceiling on fire. I tried to think of something I could smother the flames with. A wet tow sack might do it, but I didn't have a tow sack closer than the barn, and besides it was too high to reach. My eyes burned with smoke and I couldn't hardly see or breathe. I grabbed a bucket and run back out to fill it. Troy had found the canner on the back porch, which he was pumping full of water. But the canner was too heavy to pick up. I dipped a bucketful out of the canner and run back into the kitchen. Swinging the bucket up as high as I could I splashed water on the ceiling, but most of the water fell right back in my face. Mama took the bucket from me and throwed the rest of the water on the ceiling.

It took me and Mama several trips to the pump to put out all the smoldering places on the floor and ceiling. The kitchen was full of smoke and there was water on everything. The floor and window sill and ceiling was partly burned. A pile of dishrags and towels by the stove had caught fire too. We opened all the windows and doors in the house to air it out.

Mama was puzzled about how the fire could have got started. She'd left coals in the stove to keep a pot of beans simmering while we worked in the field. It was such hot weather all you needed was a few hot coals to keep a pot warm. But the stove was all closed in and it didn't seem possible a spark had escaped to start the fire. We looked around the wall behind the stove, and that's when I seen the mouse with scorched fur beside the burned-up matchbox.

"A mouse got into the matchbox and gnawed a match," Mama said. "That's what started the fire." It seemed hard to believe but must have been true. One match had set all the matches on fire, which set the rags on fire and then caught the curtains. The whole house could have burned if Old Pat hadn't warned us.

I stepped out to the back porch where Old Pat laid panting in the heat. My eyes watered from the smoke, but I give her a big hug.

Eight

Now the most embarrassed I ever was in my life was when Papa was mad and said I never could go out with boys again. It was way back in 1927 and I was nearly fifteen years old and I wanted to go places where other young people was. I wanted to go to ice-cream socials and to the picture show. But I could only go if Velmer was going. It didn't count that one of my girlfriends like Fay or Lorrie was going.

Lewis Shipman was still taking kids on trips in his truck from time to time. It was something he liked to do. He'd took kids to the Smokies and to Maggie Valley, and I heard he was going to leave early on Saturday to drive all the way to Mount Mitchell, right to the top of the mountain where you could look out on all creation. I'd never been to Mount Mitchell but had heard all my life it was the highest mountain there was east of the Mississippi River.

I wanted to go so bad it just made me sick to think of being left out. All my life I'd been afraid of being left out of things. All the young people I knowed was going. But Velmer was going out in the mountains to look for sang that Saturday. He was always crazy about digging ginseng, for it was worth a lot of money if you could find some. He said early fall was the best time to dig it.

So I determined I'd go to Mount Mitchell no matter what. It was wrong of me to disobey Papa, but it was like I couldn't hardly help myself. I just had to go. I had a little old coat that I knowed would be needed since the wind would be cold in the truck and on top of the mountain. But if Mama seen me wearing the coat she'd know I was going somewhere. So I dropped the old coat out the bedroom window and then pretended like I was going to the outhouse.

To stay out of sight I walked along the edge of the orchard and through the woods, past the old schoolhouse, to the church parking lot where Lewis Shipman's truck was waiting. Everybody was already there, and I climbed up on the bed and tried to get behind the others where nobody could see me. But when I glanced back down the road I seen Papa coming. I wished Lewis would get in the cab and start going. But he was helping girls up into the truck bed and talking about how fine the weather was for a trip. I stomped my foot I was so anxious to go. But kids kept arriving and Papa got closer.

When Papa reached the parking lot he said hello to Lewis and said it was a fine thing to be taking younguns on an outing to Mount Mitchell. Papa handed Lewis a dollar bill he said to help with the gas. And then he said, "Annie, you get down. You've got to help us strip cane." I'd never been so ashamed in my life. Everybody on the truck was looking at me. And them still on the ground was looking at me. Lewis Shipman looked down at the ground like he was embarrassed too.

Papa stood right there at the back of the truck and glared at me and there was nothing I could do but climb down with my cheeks red, trying not to look at anybody in the face. I was being treated like a little girl. I had to walk down the road with Papa, and I seen he didn't want me to go out with *nobody*.

"You don't want me to have any fun," I said.

But Papa didn't answer; he just walked along aside of me like he didn't want to say nothing or couldn't think of nothing. There was a shy side of Papa and I reckon he was a little embarrassed too. For all his bad temper he'd be at a loss for words at times. I was too mad to be shy, except I remembered I'd have to face Mama when I got to the house, and she'd know I'd slipped away from her. My face got hotter still, and it was not just from anger. I hated for Mama to know I'd deceived her.

After Muir bought the Model T with his brother, Moody, I rode with him and Fay to see the circus parade in town. I'd never seen a circus or a circus parade before. That was when we seen the elephant that killed a man. And the next day we went to the fairgrounds to see the elephant hanged. It was the awfullest thing I'd ever seen, and I wished I hadn't gone.

After seeing the elephant die I didn't ever want to go nowhere with Muir again. Just thinking of riding in his Model T made me sick. There was a thousand boys besides Muir in the world, and I would go with one of them after church or to homecoming picnics. I'd find somebody with a good job and a good car and escape from Green River.

Watching the elephant hang must have had some kind of effect on Muir too, for the next thing I heard was that he told people he was going to build a church on top of Meetinghouse Mountain. And he was going to build it out of rock, rocks he got out of the river. It was Velmer who heard the story first, down at the store.

"That's plumb crazy," I said.

"All I know is what I heard," Velmer said.

"You can't even get to the top of the mountain with a wagon," I said. "Much less carry rocks all the way to the top to make anything." It give me a bad feeling to think Muir might not be at hisself and to know that people was laughing at him. They'd laughed at him when he tried to preach, and now they was telling rumors about his big plans to build a church on top of the mountain.

"Who would go to such a church?" I said to Papa a few weeks later, after he seen Muir cutting trees and starting to make a road up the mountain with his horse, Old Fan.

"I reckon he wants to move the church from the foot of the mountain to the top," Papa said.

"Ain't none of his business to move the church," I said. "He ain't the pastor or even a deacon. He don't even own the land."

"His mama, Ginny, owns the land," Papa said. It surprised me that Papa liked the idea of building a church on the mountaintop. I expected him to say how foolish it was of a young boy to build a church all by hisself on top of a ridge. In fact Papa seemed to admire Muir's plan.

"At least Muir wants to do *something*," Papa said. "That's more than you can say for most people around here."

I don't know why the news of Muir planning to build a church made me cringe. After all, I'd washed my hands of Muir. It was none of my business. If his mama would let him try such a fool thing, well, just let him. It hurt me to even think about it, like I was afraid people would be laughing at *me*. I promised myself to stay away from where he was cutting a road up the mountain and making a fool of hisself. I didn't even want to see it.

But as I walked home with other boys and went out driving with other boys, and acted in plays in school, I couldn't help but hear talk of what Muir was doing. People talked about him like he was a lunatic, and that embarrassed me and made me mad. They said he'd cleared a spot right on top of the mountain and made a level place with a pick and shovel. It was a place where you could look out across the whole valley.

I don't know where Muir got any money except from selling muskrat hides and sometimes a mink. Maybe because he done all the work hisself he didn't need much money. Or maybe his mama give him some money.

Everybody knowed Ginny wanted him to be a preacher. I was sure his brother, Moody, didn't give him no money, for everybody said Moody made fun of Muir all the time.

Muir got down in the river and carried out rocks and stacked them on the bank. It took him months in all kinds of weather to gather enough rocks for the building he planned. Papa said Muir had made a drawing with a pencil of the church he wanted to build. The drawing seemed to please and impress Papa.

"Everybody is laughing at Muir," I said.

"What difference does that make?" Papa said. "If we waited for people to approve, we'd never get nothing done."

"That church ain't built yet," Velmer said. "I don't think it'll ever get off the ground."

Next Muir loaded the piles of rock on his wagon and carried them to the top of the mountain. The road was so steep he could only carry a few rocks at a time. He worked day after day and week after week, and people shook their heads and said he was out of his mind, and I wondered if they might be right. I heard that after he got the foundation laid somebody took a sledge hammer and busted it apart. He thought Moody had done it, and they got in a awful fight.

After the Depression come nobody was building houses at the lake no more, and Papa couldn't find work that paid a wage. One day he carried his toolbox to the top of the mountain and offered to help Muir build the joists and sills, the beams and flooring. From the beginning Papa had took a special interest in Muir's church. When people criticized Muir's big plans Papa never argued with them. He just smiled like he didn't care what they said. It didn't matter to him what they said. Since he couldn't find work anyway, he might as well give Muir a hand with the church.

"Nothing ever gets done unless somebody has the idea and the will to do it," Papa said. Papa always said a good builder had to have an "idea," that is, he had to be able to see what a building would look like even before he started making it.

We heard Preacher Liner climbed up the mountain and give Muir a piece of his mind, but Muir didn't pay him no heed.

One Saturday Mama sent me to carry dinner to Papa when he was working on the mountaintop. She put enough biscuits and sausage in the bucket for Muir's dinner too. It surprised me how much both Mama and Papa liked Muir and thought his big plans for a rock church on top of the mountain made sense. I hoped nobody would connect me with such shenanigans.

Muir was embarrassed to see me come with the dinner bucket. I guess I was embarrassed too and tried not to look at him. I was took aback by how much work him and Papa had done. There was big piles of rocks and piles of lumber among the trees at the edge of the clearing. The floor had been made and two-by-fours that would hold the wall stood in place. Papa and Muir was hammering the rafters that would hold the roof up.

I don't know where Muir got the money for the lumber or how he got the trees sawed up for planks. I know Papa didn't have no money to give him. But I could see how Papa and him had become a team. They'd learned to work together, one handing a board up to the other or driving nails at the other end of plank. Papa was cutting the pitch on rafters at a mortar box and handing the long pieces up to Muir on the roof. It embarrassed me to see what friends they'd become. It was like Muir was winning his way into the family in spite of me. I was more determined than ever to not go out with him again.

Everything about Muir riled me, even his looks, his good features and black hair, his height and broad shoulders, his big strong hands. He'd made enough money before the Depression started to buy a fine blue serge suit in Asheville. And he also had an outfit with a tweed jacket, white riding pants, and shiny riding boots that he wore sometimes. He thought it made him look like a movie star, or somebody that owned a yacht.

It bothered me that he liked to talk about all the things he'd read in history books and newspapers. You would have thought he was some kind of professor. I reckon he thought sometimes he was some kind of professor. He was just a Green River boy like everybody else, but he would talk like he'd been off to college.

It made me mad just to think about how he'd tried to go with me since I was a little girl, the way he kept coming back, the way he kept watching me. It made me mad the way he'd become friends with Papa. Papa was a man of good sense, yet he seemed took in by Muir's scheme. And Mama liked Muir too and made lemonade and carried it herself to the top of the mountain to give to Papa and Muir when I wasn't at home. It seemed sneaky of Muir to have become such good friends with my parents. When I went up there I heard him and Papa talking about religion and politics and history and hunting. Papa loved to talk about politics and never got tired of running down Democrats.

I tried to let Muir know every way I could I was going with other boys. I invited a boy named Mike Caldwell from Travelers' Rest down in South Carolina to come to church in his fine new car. I rode out on Sunday afternoons with Mike on double dates with Lorrie and her boyfriend. I always let Fay know what boys I was dating, hoping she would tell Muir. I wanted Muir to know I never fancied myself a preacher's wife. And never would be engaged to somebody that was crazy enough to build a church on the top of a mountain that nobody wanted and he couldn't afford, when he wasn't even an ordained minister yet.

After Preacher Liner told him off Muir didn't come back to church services for a long time. His mama come and his sister come, but he never did show up at Sunday school or preaching. I don't know what he done on Sundays. Maybe he stayed home and polished his riding boots or went for long walks in the woods. Maybe he went to church somewhere else, though I never did hear about that. But I do know that when Papa got another paying job down at the lake, and Muir run out of money for more lumber, and a tree fell on his half-built church in a windstorm, Muir told everybody he was going to go to Canada to be a trapper. I heard he loaded all his guns and traps in the Model T Ford and headed north.

I don't know what all happened to Muir on that trip to Canada. He never would talk about it much. He did say he went up Highway 25 all the way through Tennessee and Virginia to Cumberland Gap and on into Kentucky. And he crossed the big bridge to Cincinnati and drove through the fine farm country of Ohio where they was doing the fall plowing with their big Percheron horses. He said the country beyond that was flat as a tabletop. Finally at a place called Toledo he turned around and come back home.

There was rumors that Muir had been scared by bootleggers or gangsters somewhere in Ohio. They'd flagged him down because they thought he was going to Canada to buy a load of liquor. Whatever they said to him scared him so bad he turned around at Toledo and started back to North Carolina. All I knowed was we didn't see him for a while, and then he was back, looking like he'd lost weight, like he might have been sick.

Some people said that after he got back from Ohio he'd gone straight to the eastern part of North Carolina to trap muskrats on the Tar River. It was a lot warmer there than in Canada. He'd bought a boat to travel on the river and almost got drowned in a flood they had. He lost the boat and all his traps and equipment. I reckon the story must have been true for Muir acted different after he come back. Didn't seem like nothing that he done worked out for him.

One day while he was gone I walked up on the mountain with Fay to see the church he'd abandoned there. The road had partly washed away in a big rain and me and Fay had to jump over logs that had fell across the ruts. There was something spooky about that place on top of the mountain. I shivered as we got close to it.

"Only Jasper would think of building such a foolish thing as this," Fay said when we got to the top of the mountain. Sometimes Fay called Muir "Jasper" after a figure in the funny papers. I reckon it was a joke between them. I agreed with her of course but resented the way she said it. I was surprised that it bothered me when she made fun of her brother. I remembered what Papa had said when people criticized Muir: "At least he tries to do *something.*"

"At least he tried to do something," I said to Fay.

"And everything he does turns into a mess."

After Papa went back to work around the lake Muir had got the roof, or part of the roof, of the church finished. Boards had been nailed to make walls, but the rocks had not been put on the walls. The piles of rocks around the clearing had weeds growing around them. As I looked at them a black snake slipped under one of the heaps. Stacks of boards was turning gray in the weather. Odds and ends of lumber was scattered all around the clearing. A joe-pye weed growed by the steps at the door.

Part of the roof had caved in where the big oak tree fell on it. Through the opening rain had got in and mold and leaves covered part of the floor. It was such a sad mess I shuddered.

"Let's go back down the mountain," I said to Fay.

It wasn't long after Muir come back that we heard Moody had been killed. Some people said he'd been shot way back in the Flat Woods by rival bootleggers. Others said he'd got in a fight when he was drunk at Chestnut Springs down in South Carolina. Moody had been in a lot of fights, and he'd cut people with his knife. Once he'd cut a man's face and neck in South Carolina so bad he'd almost bled to death.

And then we heard that Preacher Liner didn't want them to have Moody's funeral at the church because Moody had never joined, and one time when he was mad Moody had broke every window and every lantern in the church and never paid for it. Papa said Preacher Liner couldn't do that, because Ginny and the rest of the family was members. And the land for the church had been give by Ginny's papa, Mr. Peace.

After Moody died it was like Muir come back alive. He walked around to every house in the valley and told people he was going to have Moody's funeral in the half-finished church on the mountaintop, and he was going to conduct it hisself. It was like Moody's death had let loose a shock and a determination in Muir. I was scared for him, for I remembered what had happened when he tried to preach all them years ago. To make it even worse he asked Mama and me to sing at the funeral. He said we had the prettiest voices he'd ever heard and he'd be grateful if we could sing.

Mama told him we would sing and I had no choice but to agree too. It's hard to say no when somebody wants you to sing at a funeral, and what Preacher Liner had done made us ashamed for Ginny and the Powell family.

"What do you want us to sing?" Mama said to Muir.

"Whatever you want to," Muir said. "Whatever seems right for Moody's service."

Mama and me looked through the hymnbook. We thought of "Shall We Gather at the River" and "Battle Hymn" and "When the Roll Is Called Up Yonder." But Mama said the best thing would be "How Beautiful Heaven Must Be." It was a simple song and it wasn't too sad.

For the service in the unfinished church Muir made benches out of planks, but there wasn't a pulpit or even a table at the front. People kept arriving that afternoon, mostly climbing the mountain on foot, and soon the room was packed. Luckily the weather was good. I guess some people come out of curiosity just to see the church Muir had started. But most come out of respect for Ginny.

When Muir stood up and said me and Mama would sing, I was afraid

I couldn't open my mouth. But I seen I was more scared for Muir than for myself. I hated to think of him having to preach his own brother's funeral. And when Mama and me sung it went better than I expected. We always did sing good together. It was like our voices depended on each other.

I was so worried for Muir my knees trembled after we sung and he stood up. I was afraid something awful was about to happen, that he would be tongue tied or say the wrong thing. Everybody got so quiet you could hear the breeze in the trees outside. I jerked I was so nervous, and felt like I was going to pop out of my skin.

But when Muir started talking I seen how much he'd changed. It was still his voice, but it was like he was a different person too. He didn't seem like the boy I'd always knowed. For one thing, he spoke slow, like he was thinking about what he was going to say next, like he was saying just what he felt. It was the honesty and plainness of his talk that surprised me. I'd never heard a preacher at a funeral talk like that. I think everybody was as surprised as me.

There in that half-finished church on top of the mountain Muir talked about Moody's troubled life and how only God could look into the heart of a person. He talked about how we don't know about the pain others are suffering and how we're all sinners. And he read from scripture the prettiest passages. He read from Revelation about the Alpha and Omega and about a new heaven and a new earth coming down to replace the old one. "The tabernacle is with men . . . former things are passed away." "I am the root and offspring of David . . . I am the bright and morning star . . . The spirit and the bride say come . . . let whosoever will take the water of life freely." It was the best sermon I ever heard, and it was preached by Muir there on the mountaintop.

After Moody's funeral Muir begun to preach at other places too. He preached at Mount Olivet and Mountain Valley. He conducted services at Refuge and way off at Fruitland. He'd always studied the Bible, and he'd always wanted to be a minister. And now in his midtwenties he discovered that he could preach after all. But he never did go back to building the church on top of the mountain. He seemed to lose interest in that once he started preaching.

When Muir tried to go with me again it surprised me that I still didn't want to date him. He'd growed up and he was a preacher, and I had to admit he was a good one. But when he stopped by the house and asked me to ride with him to Berea Church where he was conducting a service I told him no. It surprised me a little that I said no. But I didn't want to be no preacher's wife. That wasn't what I had in mind at all.

All my life I'd seen how preachers' wives had to go to church and set quiet while their husbands preached. They had to smile at everybody and be friendly. But nobody paid much attention to them. They had to dress well but not too well. They had to eat dinner at other people's houses and compliment the cooks. Most had to work to support their husbands cause the churches paid them so little. Most preachers' wives was gray and mousy. That kind of life was not for me.

I was going out with lots of boys. I sometimes went out with Mike Caldwell in his fine car. I was working in the dime store and didn't want to get married anyway, unless I could go away to a different kind of life. I thought about becoming an actress or a model. And everybody said there was going to be another war.

Nine

When Effie come from Flat Rock with her husband, Alvin, the day after we got the telegram the first thing she done was bust out crying as soon as she walked through the door. It was always her way to cry when she was embarrassed or disappointed. But I thought what had happened to Troy was too awful for crying. Crying was what you done when you got your feelings hurt, when a friend was mean to you. I'd cried when Old Pat was killed on the Fourth of July before Troy left to go overseas. But when the worst thing you could think of happens crying is too easy. Maybe I was wrong to feel that way, but I was bothered by Effie's tears, a whole day after we got the news. Mama hadn't cried at all. Alvin stood by the door holding his hat and said nothing.

About the time the war had started Alvin had got a job as caretaker at one of the big houses at Flat Rock. He'd never liked to farm, and he'd never become a carpenter the way Papa did after the well was dug. Alvin moved slow and didn't talk much. But when he did say something it was usually funny. When Bill Durham was running for sheriff Alvin quipped, "Some people say they won't vote for Bill Durham because they don't know him. I won't vote for him because I do." Alvin had worked as a laborer for the Durham construction crew, digging footings and mixing "mud" for the masons.

Caretaking for the rich in Flat Rock seemed to suit Alvin and Effie just fine. Effie did housekeeping and Alvin mowed grass, trimmed shrubbery, and did minor repairs to the house and outbuildings. They had a small house back of the big house, and Alvin drove a 1932 Buick with yellow fog lights and shiny chrome headlights.

Effie stood in the kitchen bawling like a baby, but Mama didn't go to her to hug her. Mama set at the table peeling taters for dinner, and she kept peeling taters. I was mixing up batter for corn bread and didn't put down the spoon or the bowl. For some reason in our family it was awkward to hug each other anyway. Papa stood in the door from the living room looking at Effie and Alvin like he wasn't sure what to say.

"Will Velmer be coming home?" Effie gulped.

"He's already home," I said. "He come home for the weekend."

Just after the war broke out Velmer had studied to be a barber. He said you could make five dollars a day and it was light work, compared to farming or carpentry. He'd never been too strong after the typhoid. But by taking care of hisself he could work like anybody else, avoiding heavy jobs when he could.

Now the saddest thing about Velmer was that after he married Aleen their baby was born with a bad heart. It was what they call a blue baby and that must have damaged its heart. For no matter how much the doctor done for the baby it never got no better. It's name was Ronald and he was as pretty a baby as you ever saw. A long baby too, with red hair. But the bad heart kept him from growing right. They took him to doctors in Asheville and even to Charlotte. But along about six months later he got weaker and weaker. Aleen was just a young girl and she would hold the baby all night, afraid to put him down in the crib. Like she was trying to make his heart keep moving with her own strength.

When baby Ronald finally died it broke my heart to watch her. I never seen a woman go to pieces any worse. She screamed and would not be comforted. She cried herself to sleep. And then she got sullen and wouldn't talk to nobody. She'd go through the motions of work, kind of. I could tell Velmer didn't know what to do. He'd finished the barber training and needed to go off to the army base at Columbia, South Carolina, to cut the hair of soldiers. The draft board told him he was too old to join the army, but he could cut the hair of servicemen.

Aleen had took a course in typing and one in bookkeeping in high school. And when she announced she was going off to Washington, D.C., with her younger sister to work for the government in one of the offices there, it was a kind of relief. For nobody knowed what to do to cheer her up. She wouldn't talk to nobody, and Velmer had to leave to go to Columbia. Her and her sister took the bus to Washington, and she'd only come back home once, and that was last Christmas. Velmer come home about once a month from his job at the army base.

"This is a pretty come-off, if you ask me," Effie said when she finally stopped crying. "A boy volunteers to serve his country and then just gets killed."

"It's a war," Alvin said. He opened the back door and spit tobacco juice into the yard.

"How come he was killed in a plane crash when he was just a mechanic?" Effie said.

"Maybe he'd worked on the plane and was trying it out," Papa said. We'd read in the papers that bombers that flew out to Germany come back, the ones that made it back, all shot up, sometimes with pieces of the wings gone, and had to be fixed during the night so they could fly out again next morning. Sometimes planes lost motors or landing gear and had to crash land.

"What did the telegram say caused the crash?" Effie said.

"It didn't," I said.

Mama had finished peeling the taters and she just set in the corner looking at her lap.

"Was the body recovered?" Effie said. "Sometimes in an airplane crash everybody is burned up. When they ship the body home there's nothing in the casket except a bone or a little bit of uniform."

"That's enough of that kind of talk," I said, and nodded toward Mama.

Effie looked at me over her glasses. She ever did have a quick temper when I disagreed with her. "I'll say what I want to say," she said. "Who are you to tell me what to talk about?"

"Talk like that don't do no good," I said. I took the pan of peeled taters from the table in front of Mama and poured them into the saucepan of heating water.

"Are you the boss who tells everybody what they can say and can't?" Effie said.

"At least I have sense enough to try to help people and not rub their faces in shit," I said. But even as I said it I was sorry I had.

Now the thing about Effie was she'd get mad and say something hateful, but she couldn't argue. As soon as you answered her she'd get her feelings hurt and start to cry. We'd been quarreling since I was a little girl, and I learned to get the best of her by plunging ahead in an argument. She'd snap at you once or twice and then she couldn't think of nothing else to say. Effie's lip begun to tremble and she started to cry again.

"We don't know a thing about Troy's death," I said. "What's the use of imagining terrible things?"

Effie walked toward Alvin and said, "Let's go."

"We just got here," Alvin said. When other people got upset Alvin always acted calm and skeptical.

But I wasn't finished. "Just because something's terrible don't mean you have to talk about it," I said. "Just because something hurts don't mean you have to drag it through the mud." When I got mad, words come pouring out of my mouth, sharp hurtful words. I didn't want to stop. It's a bad habit I have.

"I'm going home," Effie muttered.

"You come here and make Mama upset and then you run away, like always," I said.

Mama stood up and walked into the dining room. I seen I'd gone too far, and I was ashamed of myself. I followed Mama into the dining room where it was cold as ice. She stood by the window looking out into the backyard where it was starting to get dark already.

"You'll freeze here," I said. I hoped Mama would say something. I hoped she'd tell me I'd been mean to Effie. But she didn't. She just looked past the cherry tree toward the orchard on the hillside.

"Come back where it's warm," I said.

"What does it matter?" Mama said.

"It'll matter if you take pneumonia," I said, trying to sound strict, like I was her parent.

"Can't see it would make much difference," Mama said. In the gloom I couldn't hardly see her face as she turned and started back toward the kitchen, and I followed her.

"Will you have a funeral?" Effie was asking Papa. She'd not left after all.

"We'll have to wait and see what the Air Corps says," Papa said. "A funeral may have to wait until the war is over."

THAT EVENING SHARON come from Saluda. Her daddy drove her in his pickup truck from their orchard farm. She brought her suitcase like she meant to stay a few days. She was my friend and I had to be friendly. It was me that introduced her to Troy when we both worked in the dime store. But when I seen her come through the door with her suitcase I remembered I didn't want her there. I thought she'd just upset

Mama. But to tell you the truth I wasn't sure why I disliked her so much at that moment. I thought it was because she was selfish and didn't appreciate the presents Troy had give her and the little letters he sent her from England. Or maybe it was because she'd tried to rope him into marrying him before he left to go across the water. She was no great beauty, but she did have a dark look, like she might be part Indian or something. She was slim and petite with no great figure.

As I said, when Sharon walked through the door with the suitcase it surprised me how much I didn't want her to be there. She had no right to be there since she was not married to Troy. I reckon I was afraid she'd claim rights she didn't have. She dropped the suitcase on the kitchen floor and run to me and hugged me and I hugged her back. It was not a time to be cold or start another quarrel. I felt guilty for quarreling with Effie. Most of the time you can't show how you really feel about people anyway. If we always spoke our minds we wouldn't have no friends at all, and no love, and the human race would die out.

When Sharon finally let go and stepped back she wiped her eyes with the back of her hand and said, "What kind of a god would let Troy be killed?"

"We can't understand these things," Effie said.

"I understand what a good person Troy was," Sharon said. "He didn't deserve to die."

It was only then that she seemed to notice Mama setting at the far end of the table. She run to Mama and bent over and hugged her. I felt she had no right to do that because Mama had not said a word to her and Mama wasn't the hugging kind. Sharon got down on her knees and looked right into Mama's face and said, "I am so sorry, Mrs. Richards. I don't know what to say."

"I'm sorry for you too," Mama said. As bad as Mama felt she was always polite, especially to Sharon. She'd always tried to be more than kind to the woman Troy was supposed to marry.

Then Sharon got up and went into the living room where Papa set by the fire. She bent over and hugged him too. He patted her on the back and said, "Yes, we have lost a great friend." There was tears in Papa's eyes. He'd always liked Sharon better than me and Mama had. She had always kind of flirted with him. But then a man can never see through a woman the way another woman can. When we was growing up Effie would say, "Girls are smarter than boys." I guess I would say girls are smarter than boys about some things. Girls understand people better than boys do.

About machines and things boys are real smart. And they don't get lost as easy as girls do when they're driving and trying to find a place. But girls are willing to ask directions, and boys ain't, and they usually get there sooner than boys. When men like Muir read books they remember everything they've read. Even though he is just a farmer and housepainter and preacher, he has read every book and magazine he can find. The thing about Muir is that he has in his mind all the things he has read and all the things he has thought about. But he never could see through Sharon the way I could. He thought Sharon was pretty in her dark Indian way, and it didn't bother him that she was trying to rope Troy into marriage. He could remember who was president a hundred years ago, but he couldn't see how selfish Sharon Peace was. He thought she was a cousin because Ginny's maiden name was Peace too.

When Sharon come back into the kitchen she said, "Mrs. Richards, I want something to remember Troy by. I don't have a thing except my engagement ring. Could I have some of his arrowheads and some of his paintings?"

I was about to say, "No, they should stay here with his family," but before I could speak Mama said, "Why, of course, honey. I know he'd want you to have them."

"I expect Velmer will want some of the arrowheads," I said. Velmer and Troy had hunted arrowheads together in the bottom fields after the spring plowing. One of Troy's many talents was for finding arrowheads. He could spot them where others had looked and found nothing. His eyes was sharp, but it wasn't just his sharp eyes. He seemed to know where to look. Sometimes I thought the arrowheads found him instead of the other way round.

Back in the Depression there was nothing for boys to do on Sunday afternoons, when there was no singing at church or Homecoming picnic. Sometimes they got together and walked down to the bridge on the highway to watch the cars pass, hoping to see a Packard or Pierce-Arrow. They didn't have no money to spend at the store. Other times they climbed up on the mountain above the church and rolled rocks down into the holler. They had contests to see who could pick up the biggest rock and hold it above his head. While a boy was straining to lift a rock another might pee on his leg for a joke. Sometimes they got in rassling matches or fights.

But after the fields was plowed in early spring Troy and his friends would walk over the turned and harrowed dirt and look for arrow points and pieces of Indian pottery. They found gray flint and black flint, milk quartz and orange quartz points. They found spearheads and tomahawk heads, and pieces of pottery with marks of the basket in which the pot had been molded and fired. Troy would come home with his pockets full of arrowheads. He filled boxes and boxes with them. He sorted out the broke ones from the perfect ones. When he left to go to the war he put his arrowheads in boxes in the attic.

"The arrowheads and paintings are upstairs," Mama said to Sharon. "You go look at them and see which ones you want."

"It's cold in the attic," I said. "You'll need your coat. I'll come with you."

I wanted to keep an eye on Sharon to see what she took. She had no right to take Troy's arrowheads and pictures. But Mama had told her to pick what she wanted. There was no way to stop her.

There was one lightbulb hanging in the attic and the arrowhead boxes was stacked by the chimney. One little cigar box had black "bird" points and another had white quartz arrowheads. Troy liked to explain that different shaped arrowheads belonged to different tribes from different times. Only the most recent arrowheads had been made and used by the Cherokees. There was bigger boxes of broke arrowheads and pieces of pottery. There was only one small pot that had not been broke and Sharon took that and the cigar boxes of black, white, gray, and orange perfect points. There was one tomahawk that didn't have a scratch or a chip on it and she took that. There was a stone that had two holes in it, and Troy had guessed it was used as a button. Sharon took that and two spearheads.

Troy's paintings and drawings leaned against an old bedstead near the chimney. Some had been put in frames, but mostly the canvases had not been framed. Many of the drawings was rolled up like scrolls. The paintings on Masonite was wrapped in brown paper. Sharon held up a water color of an eagle in flight. "Oh, that's so pretty," she said. "He was so gifted." She broke into tears. I touched her on the shoulder.

"It's cold up here," I said. My teeth chattered a little. I hoped that if we went back downstairs to warm up Sharon would forget about the pictures. But she would not be distracted. She wiped her eyes and uncovered another picture and another.

One of the paintings on Masonite looked dark in the dim light of the attic. "What is that?" Sharon said. I knowed it was a picture of moonlight on the river, looking upstream from the bridge, but I didn't say so. It was one of Troy's best paintings. Sharon put it aside and reached for another.

What she uncovered next was a watercolor of Old Pat. The picture made her look like a happy dog. "I want this one," Sharon said, and placed it with the soaring eagle.

"Mama will want to keep some of the pictures," I said, and shivered.

"Oh, I just want a few," Sharon said.

She pushed aside a portrait of Uncle Russ and one of Uncle Zeke that lived in Asheville. Troy had drawed with charcoal a portrait of Abraham Lincoln, like the one on the penny, and she placed that with the eagle and Old Pat. It occurred to me she was looking to see if Troy had painted a picture of her. As far as I knowed he hadn't.

There was a picture of a rainbow trout leaping out of the water, but she didn't take that. Another watercolor showed a barn with a horse cropping grass beside it, and Sharon picked that one. There was a picture of the river valley with the mountains lavender and then blue in the distance where the ridges touched the sky. If you looked close there was an Indian at the bottom of the picture, almost hid by underbrush, but I don't think Sharon seen it. I was relieved when she moved on to the next picture.

In the CCC camp Troy had painted the trucks and tractors they used. One oil painting showed the rock side of a mountain exploding with dynamite. The rocks looked like smoke blowed out of a hole in the mountain. The woods below was colored with fall colors. "I'll take that one too," she said.

Troy had done drawings of hammers and rakes, shovels and picks, drill bits and transits, but Sharon didn't seem interested in those. I think she was disappointed as she looked through drawing after drawing. And then suddenly there was a picture of a naked woman. And it wasn't just a nude woman, but a woman leaning back on a couch or chair with her legs spread and you could see everything. Sharon gasped and then laughed. "Now who is that?" she said. The face looked like her, but I didn't say so.

"Shame on him," she said. "Who in the world did he get to pose like that?"

Sharon added that drawing to the others she was taking, and I had the feeling that was the one she'd been looking for. I decided I'd say nothing about it and helped her carry the boxes of arrowheads downstairs where it was warm.

ↂ

I'D TOOK OFF my coat and was warming by the fire when some-body opened the front door. Into the living room walked Velmer looking cold and pale. I reckon he'd been walking in the woods or maybe along the river. "You must be froze," I said.

I hoped Velmer wouldn't mention Troy until somebody else did. The death of Troy was the great fact hovering over us, too big and too awful to discuss. Because it was so overwhelming it must be sidestepped with small talk and everyday details.

"Mama, would you like some coffee?" I asked when the coffee was done.

"Not just now."

I offered Sharon some coffee, but she said coffee this late in the day would keep her awake all night. I brought coffee for Papa and Velmer.

"You're lucky to still get coffee," Velmer said.

"It's half chicory," I said, "and we can only get a pound a week."

"When will this awful war be over?" Sharon said. "You can't even get clothes anymore."

"I'm afraid the war is just getting started," Velmer said.

"Don't say that," I said.

"Velmer is still clipping hair," Papa said.

"That's my weapon of choice," Velmer said. "A pair of hair clippers and a comb."

"Lucky they didn't draft you," Alvin said.

"Right now they need barbers more than riflemen," Velmer said. "My war is with fast-growing hair."

"At least nobody is shooting at you," Effie said.

"Some of them officers might threaten to shoot you if you cut their hair wrong," Velmer said. I expected him to laugh, but he didn't. Instead he shook his head like he was remembering something he'd just as soon forget.

"You can't cut a head of hair to please them officers," he went on. "No matter what you do they ain't satisfied."

"At least you don't have to crawl through mud or climb ropes," Papa said, and spit tobacco juice into the fire.

"I have to hold my temper when them officers cuss me," Velmer said.

"Since you ain't no soldier, you don't have to take their cussing," Papa said. "Boss man treats you bad, bash him over the head with a shovel if you have to."

"Don't have no shovel in the barber shop," Velmer said, "only a straight razor."

"That ought to scare them," Papa said.

Mama got up from her chair and said it was time to milk before it got dark.

"You stay by the fire and I'll go milk," Velmer said.

"Milking is my job and I'll do it," Mama said, like that was the last word, and she wouldn't hear any more argument. It seemed a shame to let Mama go out in the cold and set in the stinking cow stall to milk when she was so sad. But she meant to do it. And I thought it might be better for her, to go on doing the work she was used to doing. Milking the cow was better than just setting in the corner grieving and saying nothing. Maybe going on with her work was the only thing that would help her.

"I'll shell corn for the chickens and gather eggs," I said.

"When is Muir coming home?" Velmer said.

"I don't know. Maybe whenever he can get a ride from Holly Ridge," I said. I wondered if Muir had got the telegram I sent him from the cotton-mill store. I wanted to get out of the house same as Mama did. I needed some cold fresh air.

I helped Mama feed and water the cow, and while she was milking I climbed up in the barn loft and shelled corn for the chickens. It was a relief to be out among ordinary things, doing ordinary jobs. I tried not to look at Troy's canoe laying by the heap of unshucked corn. After I scattered corn in the chicken yard I gathered eggs and carried them to the house and come back to help Mama carry the milk to the kitchen. After she strained the milk into pitchers I washed the straining cloth, which was just a piece of flour sack, and hung it by the stove to dry.

All the time I was thinking about where everybody would sleep. Effie and Alvin could drive back to their house in Flat Rock. Sharon and me could sleep in the back bedroom, and Velmer could sleep on the couch in the living room. I didn't think he would want to sleep in the same room with me and Sharon. If he didn't like the couch he could make a pallet on the floor. People used to sleep all in the same room in little cabins in the mountains, but that was a long time ago.

After the milk was put in the icebox I helped Mama put on a supper of leftovers but made a new cake of corn bread. While I was at the barn Aunt Daisy had brought a bowl of boiled cabbage. Hot corn bread and milk with all the leftovers of chicken and green beans people had brought earlier would have to do for company.

Since we'd got the telegram it had seemed the strangest time. I knowed it was the saddest time in our lives and I should set down and think about it, and think what it meant, the way Mama was doing. But I didn't. One thing after another kept happening. People come and brought things to eat and stayed to talk. The preacher come and prayed. Effie and Alvin come, and then Sharon come. The most awful thing we'd ever knowed had happened and yet time went on and ordinary things followed one after another.

I felt like I should go out and talk to the chickens, and to the cow, to the road and field, to the walnut tree and the spruce pine tree, to the oaks and hickories on the Squirrel Hill. I should tell them that Troy was dead and never coming back. I should scream it at the church and at the sky and at the side of the mountain. I should holler it down to the bottom of the well. But at the same time I seen that was silly. People had to keep doing what they always done. You couldn't stop time or make the world quit turning. There was no way to make people do different. I'd fix supper and wash dishes and mop the floor and fix my hair as usual. I'd expected it would be different. But things was just what they was. And people was just what they was. Everything just went on as always. And I guessed that far away the war went on as usual too.

We'd just started eating when the kitchen door opened. I looked up to see who it was this time and there was Muir in the doorway. Never had I been one to run and hug nobody, but this time I got up and just held him around the waist and put my head on his shoulder.

"You're just in time; go get a chair," Papa said.

"Yes indeed," Muir said. And I seen how uncertain he was because he hadn't knowed what he would find here. With such terrible news he wasn't sure what to expect.

"Take off your coat," I said. Muir was carrying his toolbox and he set it down by the kitchen stove.

"How is work at Holly Ridge?" Papa said.

"The barracks are about finished," Muir said. "I reckon they'll be painted by soldiers, not outside contractors."

"Soldiers will do a rough job," Papa said.

"Anything done by the government is a rough job," Muir said.

"At least you don't have to cut hair to please officers," Velmer said.

Muir was a bigger man than Velmer and Alvin. He was taller than Papa. Him and Troy was about the same height and build, though I reckon Muir's shoulders was wider. As Muir took off his coat and set down at the table it give me a shiver of pleasure to see how strong he looked in his khaki shirt and overalls. I knowed I was supposed to feel sad and not think of such things, but I couldn't help myself. As Muir set at the table eating corn bread and milk I just wanted to reach out and touch him. But I didn't.

And then while Mama was washing dishes and I was drying them, and everybody else was setting in the living room by the fire and talking, I started to think again about where we would all sleep. Muir and me could walk across the pasture in the dark to our cold house by the river. It had been Ginny's house before she died. But I couldn't leave Mama at this time. I was worried about her and knowed she needed me to stay close by. As much as I wanted to go away with Muir I knowed I couldn't.

One solution would be if Sharon volunteered to sleep on a pallet in the dining room or on the couch in the living room, while Velmer took the other option and Muir and me took the back bedroom. But since Sharon was the guest I couldn't suggest she take the couch or pallet. Surely she'd see that Muir had been away almost three weeks and we needed to be together. You'd think any woman would understand that and sympathize.

After the dishes was done Mama took a chair in the corner of the living room and didn't say nothing. I stood by the fire and said it had been a long day for everybody.

"I'm not sleepy," Sharon said. "I guess I'm too sad to be sleepy."

"I'm plumb wore out," Velmer said.

I knowed Muir had carried his toolbox all the way from the highway. After riding all day from Holly Ridge he must be a little tired.

"I just keep thinking about Troy and wondering what kind of funeral he'd have wanted," Sharon said. "That's one thing we never discussed."

"We can't have a funeral unless the body is brought back," Effie said.

"After an airplane explosion there may not be any body to bring back," Alvin said, and spit tobacco juice into the fire.

"We'll find out about that later," I said.

"There could be a memorial service, even without a body," Sharon said.

Papa looked at Mama and said, "Julie, it's time for bed."

"We've got to light a rag out of here," Alvin said. It was what he always said when he was ready to leave. I never understood what he meant unless the rag was the wick of a lantern.

As Effie and Alvin got up to leave I was still hoping Sharon would volunteer to sleep on the couch. But she was asking Muir how he got back all the way from Holly Ridge. He told her he rode in the back of a lumber truck to Raleigh, and then took a bus from Raleigh. He walked from the store on the highway to the house.

"Well, Sharon, you can sleep in the bedroom," I said. "Velmer can sleep on the couch here, and Muir and me will sleep on a pallet in the dining room."

"Whatever is best for you all," Sharon said.

I got quilts and blankets and pillows and put them on the floor of the dining room, between the table and the china closet. Muir stepped outside to pee while I got undressed and Sharon went into the bedroom. While the house got quiet I slipped under the covers and felt the hard floor under me. You don't appreciate a mattress until you don't have one. Every time Muir was away I worried about us getting together again. As silly as it may sound, I was afraid we'd be strangers when he come back and we got in bed again. I guess people, no matter how long they've lived together, are a little bit strangers. Intimacy seems like something that might disappear and never come back after people have been apart.

And I wondered what was proper given the sadness of the time, the grief we was all suffering. Would it be too unfeeling to love as usual at a time like this? When Muir come back in he brought a flashlight that must have been in his toolbox. He walked quiet to the pallet between the table and china closet and switched the light off to get undressed. His knee knocked the table and I said, "Shhhh."

I was so worried I felt prickly when he got under the quilt. We held each other and I was glad we was laying on the floor and not in a creaky bed. In a house full of people you had to be careful at night not to make too much noise, for everybody could hear and know what you was doing. You had to wait until deep in the night when everybody was asleep. But on the floor you could be very quiet.

Muir reached under my gown and touched me between my legs and shifted his weight, and the floor creaked a little, but just a little. "Shhhh," I said, and we both giggled.

What surprised me, as it always did, was how good it felt for Muir to touch me. For I was worried, and it was the saddest time of my life. I wasn't even sure it was the right thing to do, to be loving when things was serious and awful. But Muir rubbed between my legs and I didn't want him to stop. All I could think of to say was "Shhh," and we giggled again.

Because it was dark and we was on the floor, I kept thinking we was in some kind of basement, or maybe it was a tent. As Muir and me moved slow to make no noise, I thought of different kinds of cloth in a store basement, hundreds of kinds of fabric, red silks and blue watered silks, black velvet, gray flannel and herringbone, taffeta, green and red and yellow plaids, and a blue-and-red tartan, and the white on white of fine blouses. And I kept thinking of the names of cloth, of chambray and denim, seersucker, calico, poplin, oxford cloth and broadcloth, chenille, and whipcord. I don't know why. I seen chiffon and corduroy, and different shades of tan and brown, khaki and silver gray.

And then I thought of the pallet as a magic carpet like they talked about in the stories. Instead of laying on the cold floor in the dining room, me and Muir was flying faraway over the mountain and sunset all the way to dawn. The clouds was all shiny fabrics, sateen and knitted wool. Gabardine and yellow linen, which was my favorite.

Ten

By the time Troy started high school he was already nearly six feet tall. Working in the fields and with Papa and Velmer building houses on the lake had made him strong, and he could move quicker and run faster than anybody I ever seen. As soon as he started freshman year the coach asked him to play basketball. Troy stayed after school to practice with the team and caught a ride home however he could if the coach couldn't drive him.

Troy had never played basketball before, and I don't reckon he'd ever seen a basketball goal. But once he started playing he learned fast. He didn't have no place to practice except the gym at school, but that was too far to go on Saturdays and Sundays when other members that lived closer got together. Troy decided to build his own place where he could practice.

To practice for the team he needed a basketball, a hoop and backboard, and a level place to run and dribble and shoot. There was no place around the house that was right for that. But Troy found a stretch at the lower side of the orchard, the ground between two apple trees, that was almost level. He cut off the weeds and took a shovel and rake and leveled it as smooth as he could to make half a court. Then he dug a hole and put in a pole about ten feet high. For a backboard he got four planks and nailed them together on the pole.

"What are you going to use for a net?" I said.

"Don't need a net," Troy said. "All I need is a hoop."

What he done was take the wooden band off an old bean hamper and wrap wire around it to make it strong, and he nailed that to the backboard at just the right height. It was not strong as a steel hoop, and it drooped a little. But it was something to throw a ball through.

Troy didn't have enough money to buy a basketball, but the coach found an old one that was scratched and had been used for practice, and he let Troy take that home. Playing basketball and having that goal and ball at home started a whole new life for Troy. Velmer had never been any athlete, and Papa hadn't either. We lived too far from town for them to take part in any team sport. But the high school coach had asked Troy to play on the team and give him a locker in the gym in which to keep his uniform and shoes.

Whenever Troy was home and not doing some job for Mama or Papa, he was up there in the orchard practicing with the basketball. He dribbled and shot, dribbled and shot. We could hear the ball slam on the backboard and rattle on the rim. The bouncing ball echoed off the house and the noise excited Old Pat. She whimpered and yelped as Troy bounced the ball, and she tried to run around him and play with the ball. She'd never seen anybody play basketball, and the sound of the ball disturbed her.

Troy would have to stop dribbling and order her to set. And then she'd get excited again and run around him, yelping and snapping at the ball, until he ordered her to go set again. But after about a week Old Pat did get used to seeing Troy play with the ball and toss it through the hoop. She'd run up to the orchard when he took the ball out of the house, and when he started practice she'd run around a while and then calm down. She'd watch him play until a rabbit or mouse or bird got her attention, and then she'd run away, chasing through the weeds.

The ground around the basketball goal got packed down from all the walking and dribbling. Soon it was wore bare and packed down hard as the road, until a rainy spell come and the ground turned muddy. Troy carried gravel from the road and put it there, but the gravel didn't do much good. The pebbles just got packed down in the mud. The basketball got dirty and he had to wash it off after every practice.

In dry weather the ground around the pole turned to dust, and the ball and Troy's sweaty hands and feet got covered with dust. After every practice Troy would wash off at a pan on the back porch. We didn't have no shower bath or bathroom. All we had was water from the pump, unless we heated a kettle on the stove. But he washed often and kept hisself clean and always neat.

Playing basketball made Troy grow up faster. He'd always been serious and well behaved compared to other boys his age. At fifteen he was tall as a man and near strong as a man. But after the coach asked him to join the team you could tell a difference. I reckon being on the team give him a new confidence and a new ambition. Nobody in our family and few in the community had ever played on the team and got to go to games around the county and in town and sometimes even in other counties. Troy acted more growed up and he kept up with his homework and his drawing too. But he done that at night, after it was dark, when he couldn't practice basketball no more.

Even though he was a freshman the coach let Troy play on the team in almost every game. He learned fast how to be a guard or forward, how to pass off, do a jump shot, a hook shot, a layup. I got to see some of the games and I seen how good he could play. He wasn't the best player yet because he was new to the game. Sometimes if I had a date we'd wait until Troy changed and then drive him home. He would smell fresh from the shower and be tired from all the running and jumping.

Papa was proud of Troy for being on the team, but he kept warning him about getting injured. "People that play sports always get hurt," Papa said.

"They do things to theirselves that they never get over. Usually to their knees or hips or ankles."

"I'll be careful," Troy promised.

"Somebody could hit you and break your leg," Papa said. "Being careful won't be enough."

"I've heard that people who play sports die young," Velmer said. "They wear their heart out."

"Everybody lives their allotted time," Mama said.

Troy played in almost every game his sophomore year, and people said that by the next year he would be the star of the team. He'd be the player the school depended on. It got up late in the season and our team had had a good year. It looked like they'd get in the play-offs and maybe play another county. I was at the game with the team from town, and I seen Troy jump high above a guard to shoot. When he come down there was a pop and he crumpled right to the floor. They had to stop the game and help him off the court. From the sound of the pop I thought Troy must have broke his leg. But when the doctor examined him he said no bones had been broke. It was only a bad sprain. Troy would have to walk with crutches and he wouldn't play no more basketball that season.

Troy's foot swelled up and turned dark blue or black. It must have been awful painful, for they give him some pain pills to take. He had to hop around from table to chair in the house and use the crutches if he went outside. You could tell how much it hurt him from the way his lips tightened when he moved. But I think the worst pain was not being able to play basketball, missing those last games leading to the play-offs. For a year and a half Troy had built his life around playing basketball. Everything had changed, everything centered around being on the team. And now all he could do was limp around and watch.

Troy was so used to moving and exercising he couldn't set still even with the sprained ankle. He had to be doing something. On the Sunday evening after he got hurt he took the crutches and walked out on the porch. He took the basketball from the shelf and dribbled it on the porch a few times.

"You're not going to try to play on crutches?" I said.

"I don't know; I just might."

He asked me to hold the ball while he made his way down the steps, working sideways one step at a time to the yard. Then he called to Old Pat and handed me the crutches and took the basketball. Standing on one leg he slapped his knee and motioned for Old Pat to push up beside him. Resting the knee of his hurt leg on her shoulder he held the ball in his left hand and gripped her collar with the right. Then he took a step and she moved forward. I thought he was going to fall, and he did fall, but then got back up and tried it again.

"Here, old girl," he said to Old Pat. She was patient and careful and let him rest the weight of his leg on her shoulder. They started walking again, and he was just barely able to keep his balance. He hopped and held on to Pat's collar and they made it up to the orchard. Standing in front of the basketball goal Troy throwed the ball through the hoop and caught it bouncing back. Resting his knee on Old Pat's shoulder he could just barely keep his balance, but he throwed the ball through the ring again and again. I never seen anything like it.

Old Pat was as patient and careful as if she'd been a guide dog for a blind man. When Troy needed to move to retrieve the ball she would move. She followed the ball as it arced through the air and fell and bounced, and was ready to move in the direction it fell. I watched them for a while. They must have stayed up there an hour, while Troy practiced throwing the ball and getting it back, leaning on his dog. How many dogs would have done that?

The summer before Troy was a senior in high school him and Papa and Velmer worked on a house down on the lake owned by a Mr. Huger.

They didn't actually build the house but just added a porch out over the lake that served as a kind of boathouse where the Hugers could keep their boats under the deck. Mr. Huger took a liking to Troy, as people always did, and at the end of the summer he told Troy he could borrow his canoe and keep it over the winter. He would take the speedboat back to Charleston.

So along in late September Troy paddled the canoe across the lake and up the river. It must have been a mile up the river to our field. At the Jim Lee Shoals he had to pull the canoe over the rocks because the water was too fast to paddle up the chute. And then he left the canoe on the bank at the end of our field cause it was too heavy to carry all by hisself up the road to the barn. Later Velmer and me helped him tote the canoe all the way to the barn and put it under the shed where the wagon stayed. That canoe was heavy and it took all three of us to carry it, Troy at one end and me and Velmer at the other.

"Maybe I could use this this winter for trapping," Velmer said.

"Help yourself," Troy said.

The canoe was one of the prettiest things I'd ever seen. The inside was made of cedar, the curved ribs smooth and fragrant. The boards fit perfect together in the rounded and tapered shape. The two seats was made of white oak or ash wood with a kind of wicker webbing. The ends was sharp in just the right way to cut through the water.

The outside of the canoe was stretched with canvas that was painted green. The canvas had been fixed to the wood so it was perfectly smooth. The canoe seemed like a work of art. Everything about it was firm and streamlined as a fish.

"Just make sure it don't get stole or damaged," Papa said. "You couldn't afford to pay Huger for it."

"Nobody's going to steal it," Troy said. "It's too heavy."

Troy said when he had a free day he'd take me riding in the canoe. "We'll go for a picnic on the river," he said. But that fall he was the captain of the basketball team and had to spend every free minute practicing basketball. And besides that he was drawing pictures for an art show they was having in town. He'd made dozens of pictures of Old Pat, and of the horse Old Nell, and one of an eagle flying. He'd painted a portrait of Uncle Russ, and one of Papa. He wanted to paint my picture too, but I was already working in town at the dime store and come home only on weekends.

There was a girl that lived up the river named Amy Finch. She was a little younger than me but she was a friend. She had a terrible crush on Troy, and he was nice to her but really wasn't interested in her as a girlfriend. She was a big girl, almost six feet tall, not fat, but not willowy either. Like a lot of tall girls she was a little shy and liked to act like a little girl. One Sunday in late October she come home with us from church for Sunday dinner. We was good friends, but I knowed she was mostly keen just to be around where Troy was. Like any girl in love she just wanted to give the boy a chance to fall in love with her. She was wearing a pink dress that had bows and ribbons on the shoulders.

It was just about the prettiest fall day you ever seen. After dinner and after me and Amy washed the dishes and dried them, I said to Troy, "How about taking us for a ride on the river?" I was sure he'd say he had to practice basketball or do homework or draw pictures for the art show, but he didn't. "Do you want to go for a canoe ride?" he said to Amy.

"Oh yes," she said, like she was ten years old, and blushed.

Even though Amy was wearing her pink Sunday dress and was too tall to fit any of my clothes, she helped carry the canoe down to the river anyway. She didn't mind that her white Sunday shoes got in the dust. Old Pat run alongside of us, excited there was an extra person and we was going to the river.

My arms was wore out by the time we got down to the sandbar opposite the Lemmons Hole and set the canoe down. Troy said he'd ride in back and paddle and I could set in the front and paddle and Amy would set in the middle with Old Pat. The dog whimpered she was so thrilled. We got in our places and Troy slid us into the water and jumped into the back. It was a wonderful feeling to be gliding out above the water. It was like being weightless or something. Leaves was floating on the river and more leaves was falling from the river birches and maples.

"Turn it with your paddle," Troy called. But it was almost too late. We come close to hitting the far bank. I'd never paddled a canoe before and it took me a minute to figure out how to push to the left or the right. I pushed to the left and we got turned right and headed down the winding river, toward the Bee Gum Hole. Troy done most of the guiding, I'm afraid. But I slowly learned to turn the paddle a little as I made a stroke to keep the front of the canoe pointed straight.

"I just can't believe it," Amy said and patted her hair. "It's all so pretty."

One of the things that struck me was how different the river looked if you was in the middle of it. Looking up at the trees and the mountains beyond I'm not sure I would have recognized the scene if I didn't already know where I was. By us being out on the river everything looked strange. I'd never seen anything prettier than the clear water with leaves floating and more falling. I guess the fact that it all seemed so strange made it even prettier.

When we bumped against a log Amy screamed and then laughed. The water was perfectly clear, and you could see the rocks on the bottom. I watched a crawfish in the sand behind a rock, and then this big shadow shot by and I caught the flash of a silver rainbow side. A muskrat slid into the river and shot out of sight.

"Let's go down to the shoals," Troy said.

"No," I said, and giggled. "We'll tip over or hit the rocks and be drowneded."

"Got to run the rapids," Troy said, and laughed.

The river slowed for a long quiet stretch under the birch trees. Except for the splash of the paddle and settling of leaves on the water, there was no noise. Leaves fell in the river, and one fell in Amy's hair. She picked it out and held the leaf, looking at the pretty golden color.

I could have set out there on the river for hours, maybe forever. I'd never seen anything as peaceful as that stretch of still water with the leaves rocking down and the blue sky beyond. The world and all its troubles, the Depression and meanness and sickness, seemed too far away to remember. Breadlines and riots and Roosevelt seemed to belong to another world entirely. "Let's just stay out here," I said.

Suddenly there was an explosion on the water head of us. There was splashing and swooshing and all these wings flapping. It was a bunch of ducks taking off from the water. They must have been drifting on the river so still even Troy hadn't seen them, and Old Pat hadn't heard them or smelled them. Their wings seemed to burn and beat the air as they flew up through the trees. Old Pat was as surprised as any of us, and she put her paw on the side of the canoe. The canoe was rounded on the bottom and the least little thing could roll it over. Old Pat put all her weight on that side and jumped into the water. She was so heavy that before I knowed it the canoe tipped and flipped over and we all fell into the river.

The cold was a shock that made me gasp. Water hit my face and went right through my clothes. I held on to the paddle and started to swim. But the river wasn't deep there. It was only up to my waist. And then I heard Amy screaming. I didn't know if she'd ever been swimming or not, but the cold water scared her and she cried like a baby that had been smacked.

"Hold the canoe," Troy called to me. He started wading toward Amy and I grabbed the canoe, threw the paddle in it, and pushed it toward the bank.

"The water ain't deep," Troy said to Amy. He took her by the arm and led her to the shallows. Her dress was pressed against her chest and her hair was ruined. She kept crying and Troy patted her on the back. Old Pat had run after the ducks, but they'd flown away. She come back and stood dripping on the bank, watching us.

"Ain't we a pretty sight," Troy said. He looked Amy in the face and she quit crying and smiled at him. In the sunlight Troy's curly red hair gleamed like fine copper spun into silk. "You won't ever forget this Sunday," Troy said, and laughed.

BEFORE TROY GRADUATED from high school he was give a letter for playing basketball. It was a big pretty letter, fuzzy as sheepskin with a blue backing, but he couldn't afford a jacket to put it on. He laid the letter on the mantel where everybody could see it. He couldn't afford a suit for graduation and had to borrow some slacks for the ceremony. Troy had growed too tall to wear any of Papa's or Velmer's clothes.

The summer of 1933 after Troy graduated things got even worse than they had been. There was not a job to be had in all the county. Rich people had quit building houses on the lake, and Papa and Velmer couldn't find any more work. Papa had lost the two hundred dollars he had in the bank when it closed. There was a new president in Washington, but things got harder rather than better.

Velmer had made a little money trapping muskrats and minks that winter, but once the trapping season was over he had no way to make another cent. Papa sawed down dead chestnut trees and hewed cross ties for the railroad. The chestnuts had all died in the blight of 1924, and the dead trunks stood around everywhere on the mountain. It took Papa all day to make a good cross tie, and when he hauled it to the depot he got seventy-five cents or sometimes only fifty cents. Nobody could explain where the money had all gone. There was plenty of things in the stores to buy but no money to buy them with.

Only one in the family that could find a job was me. I'd put on a little lipstick and my best dress and got a ride to town and found the job as a clerk at the dime store. It paid a dollar fifty a day, or nine dollars for a six-day week. I got a room at a boardinghouse on Church Street and come home on Saturday night if I could get a ride, and returned to town early Monday morning. The boardinghouse cost me five dollars a week, and I give Mama three dollars every weekend. That left me one dollar a week for spending money, so I couldn't save much.

That three dollars a week I give Mama was all she had to buy groceries, except the money she got at the store for butter and eggs. With that money she bought coffee and sugar, salt and flour, the things she couldn't grow. When there was no sugar she used molasses for sweetening, or honey if she had any. I don't reckon Mama had had a new dress for years that wasn't made out of a feed sack. In winter she wore the same old coat she'd always wore.

Troy had graduated and he was a star basketball player, but he couldn't find a job nowhere. He was tall and good looking and popular, but there was no opportunity for him. He worked in the fields, and he caught trout for dinner. He drawed more pictures and took some up town where they sold art supplies, and I think he sold two pictures for a dollar each. When cold weather come he set rabbit gums in the pasture and caught rabbits and possums, which he sometimes sold at the cotton-mill store for a quarter each. There was plenty of mill hands happy to buy a rabbit or possum for their dinner.

But in the worst times us people in the country was lucky because we could raise enough stuff to eat. When the garden was in we eat fresh peas and beans, corn and squash, new taters, okra, lima beans, and peppers. We dried apples and canned peaches and made jelly and preserves. Canned blackberries was good. And after a hog was killed you had ribs and tenderloin, souse meat, sausage and ham, and streaked bacon. You had eggs and chicken for Sunday dinner. All through the winter you had grits and mush and sweet taters, when you didn't have nothing else.

The leanest time was late winter and early spring, after the hog meat run out and the taters was getting dried up and wrinkly in the cellar. In the spring you started craving meat and something fresh. You thought about bacon and ham and roastnears. If you was lucky you had soup beans left or maybe crowder peas.

That's when you went out along the edge of the woods looking for pokeweed sprouts. Pokeweed was tender when it first come up and if you washed it and boiled it and sprinkled vinegar and slices of boiled egg on it, it was mighty good, with a special tang all its own. It was poison if you eat it raw.

Even better was creasy greens, or wild mustard, which you gathered along the lower edge of the field along the river. You boiled them and put vinegar on them and it was like a tonic to tune your system, a taste of the fresh new season and the summer ahead, full of all the minerals from the soil. Papa said it was the minerals, the salts and metals extracted by roots into plants, that made us healthy, give us strong bones and rich blood.

Some of the old-timers used to eat dirt every spring to stimulate and nourish their systems. Well, it wasn't dirt exactly, it was white or gray branch clay, pipe clay Papa called it. Every March Papa would go down to the bank of the branch where the clay was exposed and clean away a place and take about a spoonful of buttery clay. He'd eat that and wash it down with coffee. He said it would thin his blood in spring after the long winter. Him and Mama both would eat a little clay every year, but none of us younguns would.

Effie had got a job as a maid in one of the houses at Flat Rock. I don't think they paid her anything but her board and maybe a dollar a week. She'd come home about once a month if she could find a ride, but she never did have enough money to help Mama and Papa out. She had broke her glasses and it took everything she had to buy new ones.

I don't know when it was that we first heard about the CCC. It was one of the programs President Roosevelt started to help people get back to work. We may have read about it in the paper, or maybe one of Troy's friends told him about it. But one Sunday when I was home Troy showed me this pamphlet describing the program. It sounded a little like you was going into the army. You lived in barracks and did athletics every morning. Boys that joined worked at making roads and bridges, planting trees, filling in gullies, building parks and recreation sites. Some worked in the high mountains building scenic highways. Others worked on the sea coast planting grass on dunes, building boardwalks at parks. Troy said if you went into the CCC they paid you thirty dollars a month, but most of that was sent home to your family and you was left with a few dollars of spending money. It was the best way he could help Papa and Mama.

The pamphlet said there would be classes taught to the boys in the CCC. Skills such as welding, carpentry, and mechanics would be taught, and basic subjects like English and math for those that hadn't graduated from high school. And some camps would offer instruction in bookkeeping, typing, and even accounting. The whole idea was to give the boys a job and help prepare them for the future.

Troy had never lived away from home and I could tell he was excited and nervous about going to the CCC. He'd filled out the application and been accepted and was waiting to be called to town to meet the truck that would take him to the camp somewhere in the mountains north of Brevard. He was told to carry very little because they would provide work clothes at the camp. Sometimes on Saturday night there would be parties and dances where people from town could come, but no fancy clothes would be needed.

"I'm going to miss Old Pat," Troy said. He called the dog to him and stroked her head and the back of her neck.

"Not as much as she'll miss you," I said.

"Wish they'd let me take her to the camp," he said.

It took about three months for Troy to be called to the CCC. So many boys had joined, so many was out of work all over the country, it took a while to get all the camps set up to accommodate them. Clothes had to be made, barracks finished, instructors and foremen trained. The newspaper said army officers that had been retired or let out of the service would be running most of the camps. There would be some drills and inspections just like in the army.

When Troy finally got the letter telling him to report, it was late winter. The first green was showing on the poplars along the branch. At a distance the maples looked like red mist. It was plowing time and that week him and Velmer was going to drag-harrow the fields. Troy was to report in town on Sunday evening with just a bag with a few clothes. He'd got a ride to town with the McCalls whose boy Jake was also going into the CCC.

I was at home that Sunday and helped Mama fix dinner. After we washed the dishes I stood on the porch with Troy and Old Pat, waiting for the McCalls to come. Troy had packed his underwear and toothbrush and shaving stuff, along with a sketch pad and pencils, in a brown paper bag. That was all he was taking. "They'll give me everything else I need," he said.

Old Pat could tell that something was about to happen. Maybe she even sensed that Troy was leaving. She paced back and forth on the porch, and then she run down the steps and back up. "Here, old girl," Troy called. She come to him and Troy patted her on the head and stroked her ears.

When the McCall car stopped in front of the house Old Pat whimpered and yelped at it. Troy give me a hug and patted the dog, and when Mama come out on the porch he give her a hug. And then he took his paper bag and dashed to the car. As they drove away Old Pat stood in the yard and watched the car disappear around the bend. She yelped and whined and then run after the car.

Later she come back and laid down on the porch where Troy had stood, and whined and groaned. I tried to get her to go for a walk down to the river, but she wouldn't go. That night she just laid there on the porch and groaned and whined, like her heart was broke. I never seen a dog grieve so. I guess for Old Pat nothing made sense unless Troy was around. That was all she understood.

In the days after Troy left for the CCC Old Pat would go off into the woods and be gone for hours. Once I found her in the barn loft laying beside the canoe. And sometimes she'd lay in the sun on the steps to the road where Troy had got in the McCalls car, like she expected him to reappear right where he had disappeared.

But Old Pat got closer to me in the months after Troy left. When I was home she'd follow me around and hardly let me out of her sight. I was not Troy, but maybe I was the next best thing. I bought her a new collar at the dime store and sometimes I brought home a can of sardines for her. She liked sardines as much as a cat does.

Eleven

Next Sunday morning Mama said she wouldn't be going to church. That surprised me because Mama always went to church every Sunday for as long as I could remember. She went to church on Gap Creek till just before Troy was born. Only times I could remember that she didn't go to church on Sunday was when she was sick with the flu and when we was quarantined because Velmer had typhoid.

"Mama, don't you want to go to preaching?" I said.

"I'll stay home today."

"Why don't you want to go?"

"Because everybody will come up to me and talk about Troy."

Mama was a quiet person, but when she made up her mind there was no use to argue with her. She'd do what she thought it was right to do. The way she'd decided so certain made me wonder if it was wrong for the rest of us to go to church. Maybe it was not fitting for people grieving to go to service as usual. On the other hand, maybe it was just the thing to do, to show how everything was in the hands of the Lord.

Muir and me got ready to go, and Papa said he was going. Papa was a deacon and he liked to set up front on the right side of the church with the other deacons, in what was called the Amen Corner. A lot of people had expected Muir to become the pastor, but that was another story, and one he didn't like to remember. When they'd been considering a new pastor there had been such an argument over doctrine and Baptist discipline that Muir had give it up and said he didn't expect to ever preach there.

Sharon come back down that weekend, and she'd bought a new suit, maybe expecting to wear it to a funeral. It was gray and tight waisted and looked a little too fancy for a country church. She had new shoes too, and a dark purple hat, with gloves and purse to match. "You look awful pretty," I said when she come out of the bedroom.

"It's good to be respectful of the Lord's house," she said.

And it's good to be noticed, I could have said, but I didn't. It was Sunday, a day to hold your tongue. Now that the bedroom was free I went there to put on my black dress with the lace around the square neck. I'd carried it up from the Powell house, not wanting to wear good clothes as I crossed the pasture and climbed through barbed-wire fences. It was the only black dress I had and I figured this was a good time to wear it. I put a touch of red on my lips.

Muir had always loved to dress up whenever there was an occasion. When we was courting he would sometimes wear his riding boots and tight plaid jacket just to go on picnics or go to Asheville for lunch at Grove Park Inn. But Sundays he liked to wear one of his two suits, a blue serge and a gray herringbone. The gray suit was the one he liked to preach in, when he did have an invitation to preach. I was glad he didn't preach too often, because he never could sleep before he was supposed to preach, and then he'd worry for days after he preached if he'd said the right thing or left out important points. I never mentioned his preaching because it made him sad that he wasn't asked to conduct many services, since the war started.

Velmer did have a suit, but it must have been in Columbia or packed

away with his and Aleen's things. Some of their stuff had been left with
Aleen's family when she went off to work in Washington, D.C. Velmer was
wearing his clean khakis.

The church was so close we walked out the road past the garden and
the woods where Troy had left his cot, past the field where the old schoolhouse had stood. Before we got to the church steps people stopped us to
say how sorry they was to hear about Troy. Florrie Stepp wiped tears from
her eyes and said she always thought Troy was the finest boy the community had produced. She was Muir's aunt, and before we was married
she'd tried to persuade Muir that I was the wrong girl for him. He told
me she said I was lazy and the worst flirt in the whole county. But Muir
hadn't paid no attention, and I never let on to her I knowed what she'd
tried to do.

"Just let me know if there's anything I can do to help," people said. I
know they meant well, but I wondered just what they had in mind that
they could do, if they had anything in mind except just saying the usual
thing. We'd not come in time for Sunday school, and the singing had
just started. I took my seat with the women on the left side at front and
Papa and Muir joined the deacons in the Amen Corner. Velmer never
did pray in church. He always set about halfway back on the right side of
the congregation.

When the collection plate was passed I put in a fifty-cent piece, which
was all I had. It was best to give something. I always felt better when I give
something to the church. After the offertory hymn was over it was the
usual time for the preacher to get up and make announcements. If there
was some special event like an upcoming revival he would mention that.
If people had asked for special prayers he would mention that and give the
names of bereaved families.

"We offer all our sympathy, our prayers, and our help to the Richards
family that has suffered such a tragic loss," the preacher said. "We all loved

Troy and will always remember him. He was among the finest this church and this community has to offer. He served his country in the Civilian Conservation Corps, and he served it again in the Army Air Corps. He gave the ultimate sacrifice for his country and for freedom around the world."

"Preacher," somebody called from the back of the church. Everybody turned to see who'd yelled out. Somebody had stood up near the back of the church. At first I didn't recognize him, and then I seen it was that half-wit Edward Peace. Edward wasn't exactly a half-wit. He could work, and he could read and write his name, but everybody that knowed him knowed he wasn't right in the head. And strangest of all, he wanted to be a preacher.

"I have something to say," Edward said. He swayed back and forth holding on to the bench in front of him. You could tell how surprised the preacher was, and he waited a few seconds before answering. Finally Preacher Rice said, "Tell us, Brother Edward, what it is you have to say."

"The Lord has sent me a vision and told me to be a witness," Edward said. His voice trembled as it always did when he spoke in church. But the shaky voice never stopped him. If a preacher made a mistake and asked him to pray, Edward might pray in that trembly voice for ten or fifteen minutes, or even more.

"What was your vision?" the preacher said.

"It come to me while I was awake and standing out by the barn," Edward said. "The Lord said come with me, and he took me to a place high on Mount Olivet, above the Mareslide, where I could look down on the whole valley. 'Edward,' he said, 'there is one family in the valley that has sinned and gone against my commandments. That is the family of Hank Richards. You must go to them and warn them that my patience is wearing thin. I will send a terrible plague on them, and I'll send you to explain it to them. The death of Troy is my warning to Hank Richards to get out of this church and out of this community before more terrible wrath is visited on his family.' "

"Thank you," the preacher said. "And now we'll all rise to sing."

But Edward wasn't finished. "I come only as the spokesman," he said. "I fear the wrath of God. When the vision was over there I was standing by the barn again."

"We'll sing 'Leaning on the Everlasting Arm,' " the preacher called out. We all stood up and the preacher led in the singing. I couldn't tell if Edward had continued talking or not. If he did, his words was drowned out by the singing.

Since they was boys Edward had fought with Velmer, and he'd picked on Troy. When Troy was little Edward would catch him in the churchyard and hold him up by the heels and shake him. Him and Velmer would fight and roll on the ground and bloody each other's noses again and again. As far as I knowed Edward hated Papa because he thought Papa had opposed him being ordained as a Baptist minister. Papa was a deacon of the church, and the board of deacons had decided that Edward was not mentally fit to be ordained. They'd knowed him all his life and knowed how crazy he could act and what kind of silly things he could imagine. The whole board had voted against ordaining him, but for some reason Edward blamed only Papa.

I was afraid Edward would try to interrupt the preacher when he started his sermon, but he didn't. It would have been a terrible embarrassment if he had. The preacher took his text from Psalm 103. "As for man, his days are as grass. As a flower of the field so he flourisheth. For the wind passeth over it, and it is gone, and the place thereof shall know it no more." As the preacher talked about how we would all die and be forgot, unless we repented and got saved and went to heaven, I kept waiting for Edward's trembly voice to call out from the back of the church. You could tell that Edward's outburst had put a chill on the preacher's sermon because he seemed to preach faster than usual. He said the words you'd expect, but you could see his mind wasn't completely on what he was saying. You could hear it by the way he didn't pause at the right places, and then, after he hesitated, he said some sentences too fast.

When the service was over and the invitational hymn was sung, nobody come forward to the altar to be saved. It was not a day for people to get saved. The mood and the spirit was not there. "Let whosoever will come and take the water of life freely," the preacher said. But not one single soul come forward. While we sung "Just As I Am" the preacher walked down the aisle to the door of the church, and he prayed the final prayer standing at the door. From there he'd be ready to shake hands with everybody as they walked out of the church.

I introduced the preacher to Sharon when we reached the door and he said, "Bless you, sister. The Lord sees us and loves us in the time of our sorrow. He has sent the Comforter to be with us."

"Thank you," Sharon said.

When we got outside and walked down the steps the sunlight was almost blinding. It was not a sunny day, but the light in the clouds was glaring. It seemed almost strange to me to come out of the church and see the trees and feel the wind. I was almost surprised to see the road and the fields, the parked cars and cattle in the pasture, and the gray and blue mountains, and everything going on about its business, like nothing had happened in the church, nothing had been said. There seemed little connection between the words inside the church and what went on outside. But the strangeness was not bad. In fact it was comforting, to see the peacefulness of the shrubbery and parking lot, going on in time as always. It was both good and scary to see that time didn't stop for nothing. We might all be getting older, and a dear one was gone, but life and time went on, no matter about the talk of hell and heaven, sin and getting saved.

I seen Edward standing to the side near the bottom of the steps. I turned my head to Sharon and walked on by like I didn't see him. He'd tried to date me when I was about seventeen, and I'd always been a little afraid of him. We walked on down to the parking lot below the row of junipers and turned to wait for Papa and Velmer. I seen Velmer over by the corner of the church talking to one of the Beddingfield boys that wore an army uniform.

Then I seen Papa at the top of the steps shaking hands with the preacher. Papa was smiling and saying something, probably trying to cheer the preacher up. The preacher was younger than him and Papa was the oldest of the deacons. Then as Papa started walking down the steps Edward pushed through other people toward him. My mouth felt dry as the scales on a snake's belly as I watched him move toward Papa. I wished there was something I could do. Muir was still in the church, probably talking to somebody. Surely the preacher or Velmer or somebody could tell Edward to go away.

"Hank, you've had your warning," Edward said.

"Yes, Edward, we heard," Papa said. He looked Edward in the eyes, then turned and walked toward us. But Edward stepped after him.

"The Lord has made it clear that you have to leave this church and this community," Edward said, loud enough so everybody could hear. Papa stopped and faced Edward. Papa was a little taller, and he looked down on the excited man. "If the Lord had a message for me, don't you think he would have told me hisself?" Papa said.

"I've been burdened with a message and a vision," Edward said.

Just then Muir come out of the church and seen what was happening. He hurried down the steps and put his hand on Edward's shoulder. "Edward, I think you should go on home," he said

"Maybe your message is from the devil," Papa said. "Did you ever think of that?" Papa took a cake of tobacco from his pocket, opened his knife, and cut off a slice and put it in his mouth.

"I know the voice of the Lord when I hear it," Edward said.

"You go on home now," Muir said to Edward.

Papa chewed on the tobacco and turned and walked down the road and me and Sharon joined him. "I know you stopped me from being ordained," Edward called after him. "And you talked to the draft board and told them not to let me join as a chaplain."

I looked back and seen Muir put his hands on Edward's shoulder and guide him toward his pickup truck. People stood in the parking lot watching them. I don't know what Muir said to Edward, but the crazy man finally got in his truck and drove away. Muir hurried to catch up with us.

"The army rejected Edward and he has to blame somebody," Muir said.

"Too bad they didn't take him," Papa said.

I was glad Mama hadn't come to church. It would have killed her to hear Edward's ranting in front of everybody. She'd have been embarrassed and ashamed, even though she knowed as well as anybody that Edward was touched, especially about religion and our family. From all the stories Mama told about the early years of her marriage and the time on Gap Creek, it was clear she was the strong one then. Papa had been excited and lost control when the flood come, when Ma Richards come to visit, and when he lost his job at the cotton mill. Mama was the one who stayed calm and got them through the terrible times.

But over the years Papa had got stronger and calmer. Usually when he was really worried he just laughed about something. From Mama's stories it was obvious he'd growed up a lot since those days. He still had a temper, but when things was really bad he could not be riled. Over time Mama had got wore down. Maybe it was working so hard over the years. Maybe it was having children and raising children. Maybe it was the typhoid, and the quarrels in the church, and the quarrels with Papa over spending money on flowers and such.

But it puzzled me how Papa had become more confident and Mama less certain, like the wind had been knocked out of her. Maybe that's what happened to women. The world wasn't fair to women and always wore them down. It made me shiver to think that. And now Troy's death had put a crushing weight on Mama's mind and spirit. I wondered if it could ever be lifted.

"Somebody needs to knock some sense into Edward," Velmer said.

"Wouldn't do no good," Papa said. "He can't tell sense from nonsense."

"Why do they let him go to church?" Sharon said. I noticed her fine shoes had got dusty on the road.

"You can't stop people from going to church," Muir said, "not that I ever heard of, any more than you can make them go if they don't want to."

WHILE WE WAS gone Mama had been fixing Sunday dinner. I reckon she'd been working all the time we was away. She'd caught two hens and chopped their heads off, placed them in boiling water and then pulled out the feathers, and singed away the pinfeathers with a burning newspaper. She'd gutted them and cut off the feet, sliced them up into drumsicks, thighs, breasts, back and neck, with liver and gizzard. All had been rolled in flour and fried. She'd cooked rice and green beans, opened a can of peaches, and made a coconut cake. I guess she'd been saving the coconut for weeks. And she had a pot of coffee perking on the stove.

As soon as I got home I put an apron over my Sunday dress and started setting the big table in the dining room. It was cold in there, but I figured if we left the door from the kitchen open it would get warmer. With hot food and people setting around the table it would warm up more.

"How was church?" Mama said.

"About as usual," I said. I didn't want her to know about Edward. There was no reason for her to know what he'd said and done. She was sure to hear about it later from somebody, but by then it wouldn't matter as much. But just then Papa walked into the kitchen and said, "That idiot

Edward has made a fool of hisself again." I wished I could stop him, but he went on ahead and told Mama what Edward had said, every word of it. She didn't seem to pay no attention, just went on stirring flour into gravy. She made the best gravy I ever tasted, with juicy crumbs from the frying pan where the chicken was cooked.

"No use to pay attention to a fool," I said. We all set down at the table and Papa said the blessing. Mama stood by her chair like she was waiting to serve us.

"Come on and set down, Mama," I said when the grace was over.

"I'll set down later," she said. She brought a plate of biscuits that had been keeping warm in the oven.

"Edward thinks he's a prophet out of the Old Testament," Muir said, and laughed. "He sees portents and messages everywhere."

"Somebody ought to shut him up," Velmer said. "Somebody ought to cut off his tail right behind the ears." It was an old saying, usually about a dog or cat.

"Let's forget about Edward," I said. "He ain't worth thinking about."

"I'll say amen to that," Sharon said.

"Can I bring somebody more milk or coffee?" Mama said.

"Why don't you set down," Papa said.

Just then I heard a car drive up and stop. Mama stepped back into the kitchen and looked out the window. "Who is it, Mama?" I said.

"It's the Asheville cousins," Mama said.

Oh my God, I thought, and looked around the table. There was hardly room for any more. The Asheville cousins was the children of Papa's older brothers, Zeke and Dave, who had moved to Asheville many years before. They drove down to see us about twice a year. Uncle Dave had spent time in prison for embezzlement, framed, he said, by crooks in the Buncombe County Highway Department who stole funds and made it appear he'd took them. On his deathbed Uncle Dave had swore his innocence.

Papa stood up to greet the cousins. I was relieved to see there was only five of them.

"I was so sorry to hear about Troy," the one called Ancell said.

"It breaks my heart," his wife, Gladys, said, and give Papa a hug, and then Mama.

"My heart goes out to you," said Cousin Helen.

"You all are just in time for dinner," I said.

"We don't want to be no trouble," Clarence said.

"We've got enough chicken here for an army," Papa said.

Muir went into the front room and got two more chairs and Velmer brought two chairs from the living room. I took a chair from the back bedroom. The air in the bedroom smelled like frying chicken. It always surprised me how smells would linger at the back of the house, long after they was gone in the kitchen or rooms where people was talking and breathing. I helped Mama bring extra plates and silverware, and when we all got seated Ancell said, "Hank, how have you been?"

"Same old sixes and sevens," Papa said, and chuckled. It was what he always said, meaning everything was out of whack and nothing fit or matched.

"At least there is jobs," Ancell said, "not like in the Depression. I got on at the chemical plant in Enka."

"What do they make there?" Muir said.

"Oh, some kind of chemical for the army. We're not supposed to talk about it."

"The war has been good for business," Clarence said.

"Shame on you," his wife, Olivia, said and looked around the table.

"I only mean people has jobs," Clarence said. "The store does four times the business now that it did in 1940." Clarence worked in a hardware store on the west side of Asheville. Or maybe it was a feed and seed store; I have forgot which. I know it sold tools, like rakes and shovels, and equipment, like plows and mowing machines.

"As long as there is war, business will be good, for the government is buying everything people can grow or make," Ancell said.

"Buying it all with borrowed money," Muir said.

"What if the Depression comes back after the war?" Velmer said. "I don't see that there's anything to stop it."

"There won't be another Depression," Clarence said. "All the businesses started by the war will continue. There'll be prosperity."

"I just want this war to be over," Gladys said.

"This war ain't even half over," Muir said. "It won't be over till we land an army in Europe and drive the Germans back."

"Not to mention the Japanese all over the Pacific and the Philippines," Clarence said.

"It's a wonder the Japs never landed in California," Ancell said.

"They might yet," Clarence said. "This war is just beginning in the Pacific."

"I hate to think that," Sharon said. "I'm tired of this awful war."

Nobody said anything for a minute, but kept on eating. Then Clarence said, "Do you know exactly where Troy died?"

"It was in a place called East Anglia," Papa said.

"Do you know where that is?"

"The man that come here said it was in a place called Suffolk, near a village named, of all things, Eye," I said.

"Spelled the way you spell 'eye'?" Ancell said.

"I reckon that's the way it's spelled," I said.

"That is in the eastern part of England," Muir said. "As I recall it's northeast of London. The air bases are put there to be as close as possible to France and Germany." Muir always did love geography. He subscribed to the *National Geographic* and would spend hours studying maps.

"Close to the Channel?" Olivia said.

"To the North Sea, to Holland," Muir said.

"Why was Troy on the plane?" Gladys said.

"We don't know that," Papa said.

"Maybe he was testing it out, after it was fixed," Clarence said.

"Could be," Papa said.

"I've seen pictures of the bombers, the Flying Fortresses, coming back from a raid," Clarence said. "They come back with parts of the wings shot off, or a motor gone. Some have to crash land and some have to ditch in the ocean. I heard one come back and landed with most of the nose gone."

"Now they have the Liberator, the B-24," Ancell said. "It's an even bigger plane."

"Not as pretty as the B-17," Muir said.

"I hate to think what a crash would look like, with a plane exploded by bombs," Clarence said.

Mama had not said nothing. She stood behind Papa's chair holding a dishcloth. She'd brought a pitcher of milk from the icebox and refilled everybody's glass. I wished I could turn the conversation to something else. But once men start talking about war it's hard to get them to think of anything else. Their eyes light up and their faces glow when they talk about airplanes and guns and fighting.

"When a bomber crashes they try to save the bombsight," Clarence said. "I've read that's the most valuable thing on the plane."

"When a bomber crashes there's not much left to save," Ancell said. "The bombs go off, and the fuel tanks, and everything burns up. Even dog tags get melted."

Sharon stood up so sudden her chair fell over behind her with a crash. "You all are a bunch of vultures," she said, her voice rising to a high pitch. "You can't get enough of the horrors. You feed on it and wallow in it like a dog does with carrion. I'm sick of it." She turned and run into the back bedroom. Everybody at the table set quiet after she left. Finally Mama said, "Would anybody like some coconut cake?"

AFTER WE'D FINISHED eating Sharon had still not come out of the bedroom. I helped Mama clean the table and put the leftovers in the icebox and bread safe. The kettle on the stove was already hot and Mama washed the dishes while Gladys and me dried them. When I threw the dishwater out into the backyard I seen the sky was darker, like it was going to rain.

"Was Troy and Sharon married?" Gladys said when I come back in.

"Only engaged," I said.

"That's what I thought," Gladys said.

At just that moment Sharon appeared at the door from the dining room. "I'm freezing," she said.

"I bet you are," Mama said. "Here, stand by the stove and get warm."

"Let me pour you some coffee," I said.

"I'll just stand here until I thaw out," Sharon said. "It's icy in that bedroom." She was trying to act cheerful, like her outburst had never occurred. I'd always noticed that people that get mad and tell everybody off soon get over what bothers them.

"Maybe you ought to go set by the fire," I said.

Papa and the cousins and Muir and Velmer was setting around the fireplace in the living room talking about Roosevelt and how he ruined the country and got us into the war.

"Going to war was the only way he could make people forget the mess he'd made," Ancell said.

"He never was able to help the farmers," Papa said.

"He started the CCC," Muir said. "Many people think that was good."

"I think the CCC was just a way of getting thousands of boys ready to go into the army," Clarence said. "I've heard soldiers say that what they learned in the CCC has made life in the army seem easy."

I was stacking plates on the shelf when I heard another car stop outside. Mama stood at the window and said, "Why, it's Lou and Garland." A thrill flashed through me for none of Mama's family had come to see her yet. Most of them didn't have any way of coming. But if there was anybody who could cheer Mama up it was Lou. Since they was girls they'd worked together and laughed together and teased each other.

I stepped out on the back porch and called out to Lou and Garland as they got out of the Model A Ford pickup. "I'm mighty glad to see you," I said.

Aunt Lou come up the steps and said in a low voice, "How's Julie?"

"She has been quiet, like she's just thinking about things."

"That's her way, to brood over a thing," Lou said.

Garland reached the steps and give me a hug. "How's my favorite girl?" he said. I could smell whiskey on his breath. He'd took a dram before he got out of the truck. I reckon he needed a drink before visiting in-laws at such a bad time. Garland made pokeberry wine for his rheumatism, claiming it was the only thing that kept his joints from swelling up. Him and Papa used to drink together, before Papa quit, about the time I was born.

"I almost forgot the pie," Lou said. She hurried back to the truck and returned with a cake box. I could smell the lemony meringue in the cold air.

"I think it's about to snow," Garland said looking up at the sky. "The clouds have what we used to call snow light."

"Come on in before you freeze," I said. Seeing Lou and Garland made me feel better than anything had that day. They was the kind of people that whenever they entered a room people cheered up. I don't know what it was; it was like some kind of feeling they give off.

Lou walked into the kitchen and give Mama a hug. "I come to see if you was behaving yourself," she said. Mama didn't answer, which was unusual since her and Lou liked to make teasing remarks.

"Brought you a pie," Lou said, and put the box down on the table.

Papa heard Lou and Garland come in and he greeted them at the door to the living room. "You never know what the cat'll drag in," he said.

"Got to be nice to in-laws whether you like them or not," Garland said, and punched Papa lightly on the shoulder.

"How are you, Hank?" Lou said, and give Papa a hug.

"You know me, same old sixes and sevens."

As I watched Lou and Garland shaking hands and chatting and laughing with everybody it come to me how important acting was. What Lou and Garland was doing was acting. There was no way they could actually feel so light and cheerful coming to a place of bereavement at such an awful time. But instead of acting mournful and quiet, as would be natural, they knowed how to be lively and full of affection and humor. They hugged people and made teasing comments, like everything was all right and it was a happy get-together. It come to me that most of the smart things people do are a kind of playacting. It would be awful to just act the way we feel. Better to behave for a purpose, with good sense. Use our minds and not just our feelings of the moment. Act the way you need to. It was something I'd thought about before but never seen so clear.

"I think it's going to snow," Lou said. "That's why I told Garland to bring his chains. I told him I wouldn't come a step if he didn't bring the chains."

"It's too early to snow," Gladys said.

"Not that early; it's almost Thanksgiving," Ancell said.

"It'll be hard to have Thanksgiving this year," Sharon said.

"Indeed it will," Garland said, and nodded.

"It's almost deer hunting season," Velmer said. "The problem will be to get ammunition."

"There's people that has hoarded ammunition," Clarence said. "I know somebody at Enka that has bought a hundred boxes before the war started."

"Look, it's raining," Lou said, and pointed to drops running down the window.

"I hope it don't freeze," Garland said.

I stepped to the window and seen the fine drops making dark spots on the edge of the porch and on the steps. I couldn't see the drops fall, only the dark dots appear, and new ones filling in the space between other spots. Soon the boards and steps was wet and the boxwoods by the road shined with drops on their tiny leaves.

"If the roads freeze we may have to stay here," Lou said. "Never thought you'd have so many people to feed," she said to Mama.

"We've got plenty of can stuff and taters in the cellar," Mama said.

"And a hog in the pen that's ready to be killed," Papa said.

"They predict more snow this year than usual," Ancell said.

"I've heard things the government shoots up in the air can make it snow," Helen said.

"What could you shoot up in the air to make it snow?" Clarence said.

"That's just what I heard," Helen said.

"The government is always tampering with something," Ancell said.

"The government is always tampering with people's lives," Sharon said.

"People ought to have patriotism and serve their country the way Troy did," Gladys said.

"There's not much patriotism anymore," Ancell said, "just when we need it."

"Patriotism gets you killed," Sharon said.

"What we need now is some Americanism," Ancell said. "We spend our money and our lives helping other people instead of ourselves. If we had a little Americanism we might do better."

"Look," Garland said, and pointed to the window. "It's snowing."

I didn't see nothing at first when I looked out over the front porch to the road. And then I seen what seemed like flies or little moths flourishing over the shrubbery and in front of the dark hemlocks. It had been raining, but now the flakes was replacing the drops. It must have been getting colder. The rain was turning into snow. As I looked across the road to the field beyond I seen the air was now filled with flitting things, like mayflies hatching above a stream. The sky was falling in flakes that swung and rocked and playfully dodged each other like swarming butterflies. Even as I watched, the road begun to turn white and the hemlocks appeared to be catching thistledown. Flakes big as butterflies fell past the porch, and then the flakes got smaller and was steady.

"How will we ever get back to Asheville?" Ancell said.

"I'm glad I brought my chains," Garland said.

"And I'm glad you thought of it," Lou said, and giggled.

"Would anybody else like some fresh coffee and lemon pie?" Mama said.

Twelve

When Troy come home from the CCC after a year, he had a few weeks of leave before he went back to the camp. He'd signed up for another year of work on the road high in the mountains. Troy never had told us exactly what he done in the CCC until he wrote in a letter near the end of his first year and said that he'd been trained as a powder man. That meant he was in charge of the dynamite. Where they was blasting away rocks to make the road, men drilled holes into the rock. It was Troy's job to place sticks of dynamite in the holes and set caps on them attached to a fuse. The cap was like a big firecracker, and when the fire reached the cap and made it go off, that shook the dynamite and made it explode.

The other way to set off dynamite was through a long electric wire. The cap was then set off by a spark of electricity. You could send the spark either from a battery or from a box that worked like a generator when you pushed down hard on the handle. Handling dynamite was the most dangerous job in the CCC. I'm sure they assigned the work to Troy because he was so calm and careful. If Mama had knowed that's what he was doing she'd have been worried sick. I guess that's why he told us only after he'd almost finished the first year.

Velmer said dynamite would go off if you dropped it or hit it with something. He said lightning or some other electric charge could set it off. He said when you was handling dynamite you had only one chance to make a mistake. There wouldn't be a second chance.

Troy was coming home on Saturday while I was working in the dime store. So I wouldn't get a chance to see how happy Mama and Papa and Old Pat was when he arrived with his duffel bag. Troy said that on Saturday evening he'd take Papa's Model A truck and drive to town to bring me home for the weekend. I was excited all week knowing Troy was coming home, and on Saturday I couldn't hardly wait for work to be over at six. Finally when they locked the doors and dimmed the lights I run to the back room where clerks kept their stuff and got my purse and my bag of clothes. Wilson the manager seen I was in a hurry and said, "Did you clean up your counter?" We was supposed to clean up our work space before we left every day.

"I cleaned it up," I said.

"Let's just have a look," Wilson said. I hurried after him carrying my bag. I'd cleaned my glass display cases and swept the floor behind the counter, but I'd left a stack of paper bags on top of the counter. "Look at that, Annie," he said. "That won't do." I quickly placed the bags on a shelf under the counter.

"If you're in too big a hurry to do the job right, others are waiting to take it," he said.

"Yes, sir," I said.

When I finally got outside I seen Troy parked just down the street and Old Pat was in the back of the truck. I turned in that direction and almost run into somebody. "Why, hey there, Annie," they said.

It was Mike Caldwell, the boy I knowed from South Carolina. I'd only gone out with him a few times and then stopped seeing him. "What a surprise," he said.

"How are you?" I said. I started to edge away, but he took me by the arm.

"I'm so glad to see you," he said. "Why don't we go and get some ice cream?" Mike Caldwell was a nice boy and his family owned a Ford dealership in Traveler's Rest. He always had a new Ford to drive and he was handsome. But as much as I wanted to like him I just never could. I didn't know why.

"Troy is waiting for me," I said. "He's been away in the CCC a whole year." I started backing away.

"We can all go for ice cream," Mike Caldwell said. I could see that he'd drove all the way from Traveler's Rest just to meet me when I got off from work and pretended it was a coincidence. It was like him to do a thing like that. Maybe it was because he was so nice and forgiving that I couldn't like him. I know that sounds awful. I hated to hurt his feelings. He started to follow me toward the truck.

Just then I heard Troy say, "No, Old Pat," and out of the corner of my eye I seen the dog jump out of the truck bed and gallop toward me. Everybody on the street turned to look and Mike Caldwell froze where he was. When Old Pat got to me I took her by the collar and led her back to the truck. Troy got out and opened the door for me to get in. I was happy to see Troy and I was happy Old Pat had saved me from having to say anything else to Mike Caldwell.

HAVING TROY AT home after a year was like a vacation for all of us. It seemed like a new start in life somehow. We walked down to the river and had picnics at the Jim Lee Shoals. Because I had to work in the dime store, I only seen him on weekends so I didn't go on most of his trips. One Sunday we drove to Asheville to visit Papa's cousins there. We went swimming in the lake and drove Mama up to Mount Olivet to see the place where she was born and raised. Often there was one of my friends coming along just to be close to Troy.

I told Troy he was lucky to be alive, working all year with dynamite.

"I may have the easiest job in the CCC," he said, and laughed. He said dynamite was safe as sticks of peppermint candy if you obeyed the rules. "The first rule is never to be in a hurry," he said.

For three months there'd been a class in drawing taught at the CCC camp. The instructor was a professor of art from the University of North Carolina that had been let go because of the Depression. In the class they'd drawed from a model and from nature. Troy said that teacher had taught him a lot about perspective, about depth in pictures, and how to model with shading. To his surprise Troy had a lot of time for drawing in the CCC camp. After work and on weekends when most of the boys just loafed, or played Ping-Pong or poker, or sometimes slipped away to town, he took his pencils and pad, or his box of paints, to the recreation center where there was a kind of library and worked until the lights went out. He painted pictures of the boys in the camp and animals like deer they seen in the woods. But mostly he painted pictures of the mountains, of Pisgah Mountain, and Horsepen Gap, of Looking Glass Mountain. He painted pictures of the Pink Beds, the meadows of phlox in bloom, and the slopes of mountain laurel in bloom. He had painted waterfalls so tall they disappeared in mist at the bottom. He painted a black bear that come into the camp to eat garbage. There was a picture of a dynamite explosion, with dust and rocks flying every which way off the side of a cliff.

Mama had saved most of the money the CCC had sent home, and she give it to Troy to buy new clothes. He only took fifty dollars and he bought presents for everybody and a new set of paints. He took some of his pictures up town to Baker's art supply store and they put them in the window where people could see them.

Because of the pictures in the store window there was even a little piece in the paper about Troy and his paintings. The article said he was serving in the CCC and he was a graduate of the county high school. There was a photograph of him and Old Pat that must have been took by the reporter. Girls that I worked with asked me if I would introduce them to my brother.

It was because of the article in the paper that the woman named Mrs. Ellen Anhalt wrote to Troy while he was at home. The Anhalts had retired from some place up north in New York State and built a house on Cabin Creek. Though the house was made of logs, it was a big fancy house. Before there was electricity in the valley they had their own generator.

The Anhalts didn't have much to do with the local people, though they was friendly enough when you seen them. They went to church in town and had friends in town, but they sometimes bought milk and butter from their neighbors. Mrs. Anhalt's sister had come from up north to live with them. About two or three years ago Mr. Anhalt had died. And about a year after that the sister had died and Ellen Anhalt was left alone in the big log house.

It was the same year Troy went into the CCC that we heard Mrs. Anhalt had had the bodies of her husband and sister dug up to be sent back north to be buried among their kin there. Joe Williams had been one of the men hired to dig up the caskets from the local cemetery on the hill above Cabin Creek. But Mrs. Anhalt herself had not gone back to New York State.

When I come home on Saturday I read the letter Mrs. Anhalt had sent to Troy. It was typed on fine business-size paper.

Dear Troy Richards,

I have seen your pictures in the window of Baker's store and I am impressed by your talent and accomplishment. I am proud to have such an artist from our Green River valley.

The reason I am writing is that I would like to commission you to paint portraits of my late husband, Arnold Anhalt, and my sister, Mertis Edwards. They have both passed away and I would like to have life-size portraits of them. I can provide you with photographs for you to work from.

I am also interested in purchasing some of your landscapes for my parlor. Could you visit me this Sunday and bring some of your paintings also?

Sincerely yours,
Ellen Anhalt

Troy asked me if I'd go with him to the Anhalt house and I said I would. As we drove up the Cabin Creek Road I held his paintings and drawings in my lap. It was late summer and some of the sumacs along the creek and the poplars on the ridge had already started to show their fall colors. Old Pat rode in the back; she liked to put her paws on top of the cab and feel the wind ripple through her fur in warm weather. It was awful pretty, driving up that winding road into the deep valley of Cabin Creek. The big flat face of the rock called the Mareslide gleamed high on the mountain above.

"What if she don't want to pay you nothing?" I said.

"We'll just see what she says."

Troy and me had seen Ellen Anhalt at the store several times, and we'd seen her with her husband and sister earlier, at school events like the Halloween party and the Christmas party. But we didn't know her well, and neither of us had seen her since her husband died. She was said to give Christmas presents to some of the kids on Mount Olivet and in Mountain Valley.

Her house was back off the road up the holler and there was a sign at the entrance that said PEACEFUL VALLEY mounted on an old wagon wheel. The road was neat, with white gravel on the tracks and the brush trimmed on either side. First thing I seen at the house was a bank covered in flowers, including chrysanthemums, and stone steps going up to the porch. The house was made of logs, but it was twice as big as most houses in the community, with dormer windows and what must have been a big attic. And at the side of the house there was a garage with two doors. It would take a lot of money to build and keep a house like that.

When we got out I carried some of the pictures and Troy carried the rest, as Old Pat followed us up the steps. Troy told her to set on the porch until we come out. Before we knocked, Mrs. Anhalt opened the front door. She was wearing brown slacks and a kind of embroidered cowboy shirt.

"Thank you so much for coming," she said, and showed us into the dark living room furnished with leather chairs and couches, and a glass-covered coffee table. The ceiling was high as a church, with the beams exposed and polished. First thing I noticed was all the Indian things on the walls, a feather headdress, a blanket, tomahawks, spears, the head of a buffalo.

"My husband collected Indian artifacts," she said. "He was an ethnologist." She told us to set down and asked if we would like some tea.

"No, thank you, we just now finished dinner," Troy said. Troy had learned it wasn't polite to accept refreshments when people offered them.

"I love art, especially local art and folk art," Mrs. Anhalt said.

"Yes, ma'am," Troy said.

"I didn't mean to imply that your paintings are folk art," she said, and laughed.

"No, ma'am," Troy said.

Mrs. Anhalt took her glasses off the coffee table and said, "Now let's see what you have brought me."

Troy laid the pictures on the couch beside him and handed the first one to her. It was an oil painting, mostly dark blue, of a trail of moonlight on the river, like you would see if you was standing on the bridge looking west. It was painted on Masonite. Mrs. Anhalt turned on a lamp so she could see better.

"Oh, this is wonderful," she said. "I love it." She laid it on the end of the coffee table and Troy handed her the next picture, a water color of a golden eagle soaring against a blue sky. It was one of my favorites of Troy's pictures.

"You do have a gift," she said, studying the picture like there might be a secret hidden in it. "I like this one especially," she said.

The next picture Troy handed her was a painting of Pisgah Mountain seen from the CCC camp. The dark peak shot up into the sky steep as a fodder stack. A touch of ice gleamed near its top like a diamond eye.

"This is heroic," Mrs. Anhalt said. "You have caught the nobility of the mountain, its dignity and authority." I thought that was an odd way to talk about a mountain peak, but there was a kind of truth in what she said.

Next Troy handed her his painting of the Pink Beds, which showed pink phlox covering a meadow and the blue mountains beyond, with the curved face of Looking Glass Mountain reflecting the morning light. It was an awful pretty painting.

"You have caught the magic and the splendor of the mountains," Mrs. Anhalt said. She held the painting in the lamplight like she wanted to eat it. I was thrilled that she liked Troy's pictures so much and I know he was too. Every picture he showed her she *ooh*ed and *aah*ed over, except maybe the picture of the dynamite exploding the side of a mountain. I don't think she liked that one as much.

"It's a shame to tear off the beautiful face of a mountain," she said.

"With a scenic road more people can see the mountains," Troy said.

"That may be," Mrs. Anhalt said. "But it's still a shame to blast away the ancient shape of the ridge."

When she'd looked at all the pictures Mrs. Anhalt stacked them carefully on the coffee table. "We'll come back to them later," she said. "Now I want to show you the photographs of my husband and my sister."

She went to a chest of drawers and took out two pictures in frames and brought them to us. They was the kind of pictures that had been took in black and white and then colored so the eyes was blue and the hair brown, and the sister's cheeks had a little pink on them, and the lips was touched with red.

"Wasn't Arnold a handsome man?" Mrs. Anhalt said. "Of course I may be biased." She laughed.

"He was a handsome man," I said. He looked like somebody that might have been a bank president.

"I met him at the University of Chicago. I was a student in an anthropology class." The picture of Mr. Anhalt must have been took when he was around forty.

"I always said Mertis was the prettiest of us sisters," Mrs. Anhalt said. The woman in the other picture had her hair cut short, like the style had been fifteen years before.

"She's awful pretty," I said.

"It seems impossible she's gone," Mrs. Anhalt said. She put the two pictures side by side on the coffee table and looked at them a long time without saying nothing. I couldn't think of anything else to say myself. Finally Mrs. Anhalt looked up at Troy and said, "What I want is a portrait of each, about twice the size of these photographs, to hang on the wall either side of the fireplace. I want them done in color, as lifelike as you can make them. Do you think you can do that?"

"I haven't done a lot of portraits," Troy said. "I've done one of Uncle Russ and one of the instructor at the CCC camp."

"Of course you can," Mrs. Anhalt said. "You'll have the photographs to go by."

I knowed Troy wanted to paint the portraits. He loved to try new things. But he was slow to answer her. I reckon it was the way she insisted that made him hold back. "I have to go back to the CCC camp next week," he said.

"But you can work there," Mrs. Anhalt said. "Look at all these pictures you've made in the camp." She pointed to the pile of pictures on the end of the coffee table.

"I'll give you ten dollars each for the portraits and five dollars each for three of the paintings. That's thirty-five dollars all together." I almost gasped at the amount of the money.

"I'll do my best," Troy said.

Old Pat had been whimpering and whining on the porch, but we'd ignored her. But when she started yelping and whimpering I couldn't ignore her no longer. I knowed from the sound of her voice she was excited and upset. She was no longer on the front porch but at the side of the house, or the back of the house.

"I'll go see what's the matter," I said.

"You should keep your dog in the truck," Mrs. Anhalt said.

"I'll put her back in the truck," I said. I figured Troy could finish making his deal with Mrs. Anhalt while I went to see about Old Pat.

I had to walk around the house to find Old Pat. She was standing on her hind feet with her paws on the sill of the window at the back of the garage, whimpering and yelping. She was so nervous she dropped down on the ground and then jumped back up on the window ledge.

"What's wrong, old girl?" I said.

I looked through the window, but it was too dark to see anything at first. I thought there might be a dog or other animal in the garage. But as my eyes adjusted I seen lace on a pillow and a head laying on the pillow. It was the face in the photograph of Mr. Arnold Anhalt. I shivered and hollered out because I seen it was a coffin with the top open. And then I noticed a funny smell a little like some chemical from biology class. As my eyes adjusted even more I seen there was another coffin and the woman from the other photograph was laying in it. When Mrs. Anhalt had had the bodies dug up she'd not sent them up north for reburial but brought them to the garage.

The back door of the house opened, and Mrs. Anhalt seen me looking through the window and called out, "You get away from there!" I was too stunned to answer her. Troy come out of the house and asked what was wrong.

"You two can leave right now," Mrs. Anhalt said.

Troy come over and looked through the window and gasped. Pat yelped and whimpered.

"I couldn't bear to live without them," Mrs. Anhalt said. "I couldn't leave them in the cold ground."

I took Old Pat by the collar and backed away. When I got to the corner of the garage I hurried toward the truck, and Troy followed me. But then he run back in the house to get his paintings before we drove away.

That visit with Mrs. Anhalt seemed stranger and stranger in the days afterward. It begun to seem like something that never happened, just something we'd dreamed. I wasn't sure I believed it was real, but Troy had been there, and Old Pat had been there too. And then it was in the paper, how the man who come to work on the generator had seen the bodies in the garage and reported it to the law. There was even a picture of Mrs. Anhalt on the front page, and a reporter had interviewed her.

"I know people will think I'm awful and weird," she told the reporter. "But I'm just an ordinary person, and I love my husband and sister so much I couldn't be without them. It was such a comfort to keep them near me."

The law couldn't decide what to do with Mrs. Anhalt for a while. The paper quoted some people saying she hadn't broke any laws. The sheriff said it was against the law to dig up a body without permission of next of kin. But Mrs. Anhalt *was* next of kin. Finally a judge ruled that it was unlawful to keep a body aboveground unless it was sealed in a vault or mausoleum.

The paper said Mrs. Anhalt had a mausoleum made out of bricks in her backyard there by Cabin Creek. The mausoleum was locked up, but there was a window in its wall where the morning sun could shine on the faces of her husband and sister and she could look at them at any time. People on Green River talked about it and some boys even slipped in at night with flashlights to have a look at the bodies in the caskets. But Mrs. Anhalt had rigged up a light that flashed on when somebody come near that little brick building. When the floodlight blazed on in the dark it nearly scared those boys to death. As far as I know they never did go back.

But the saddest thing about that visit to the Anhalt house was how it seemed to cool Troy's enthusiasm for drawing and painting. He never said so, and I never did either, but after that he never seemed to work at his pictures as hard. You might have thought it would have the opposite effect. You might have thought that after Mrs. Anhalt had showed so much interest in his work and praised his talent he would have been more determined than ever to draw and paint and sell his pictures.

Maybe he got too busy working in the CCC and, after that, in his job at the cotton mill and then building barracks at Fort Bragg. Or maybe he spent his free time with Sharon instead of his sketches and canvases. But whatever it was he didn't devote as much energy to his art anymore. He did keep drawing and painting pictures—he never give it up completely—but it was not the same.

Some might say that as Troy got older he kind of outgrowed his pleasure in art. It didn't give him the satisfaction it had before. But I think it was two things that caused him to make fewer pictures. One was Sharon, who did take up more and more of his free time. She was jealous of any time he didn't spend with her.

The other was that visit to the Anhalt house. There was something about Mrs. Anhalt's *ooh*ing and *aah*ing and choosing some pictures and passing over others, and offering him so much money and then telling us to get away, that soured Troy a little on the picture business. His hopes had been built up high, and then smashed. He felt ashamed, like he was guilty of pride and overreaching. I can't quite explain it, but I could feel it without him telling me. That visit jolted him and made him feel ashamed, about hisself and the pictures, and he started turning away from making more pictures. Maybe it would have happened anyway and Mrs. Anhalt only made it happen sooner. We'll never know for sure. But the fact is his mind was never on his art the way it had been before.

THE FIRST TIME I seen Sharon Peace at the dime store I thought she looked skinny and young and scared. I reckon she'd just graduated from high school three years after I did. She looked so dark skinned you might have thought she was an Indian. The manager brought her over to the candy counter and told me to break her in.

"I'm moving you to cosmetics soon as Sharon can take over here," he said. He'd flirted with me and tried to go with me when I first come to work. But I'd brushed him off the way some of the girls couldn't. I wasn't afraid of him because I knowed he was married and had to do everything on the sly. Once he whispered to me, "How about a date, Miss Annie?" I pointed to the place on the counter where boxes of dates was kept. "Do you want a pound or half a pound?" I said real nice. He never asked me again.

That first day Sharon worked was a Monday and business was slow. I showed Sharon how to open boxes of candy and fill the bins, and how to scoop out and weigh a pound on the balance scales. The little weights was kept under the scales, quarter pound, half a pound, pound. Most people bought either a pound or half a pound.

Sharon said her daddy owned an apple orchard down toward Saluda, beyond the so-called Blue Ridge Divide. They also had some cows and sold a few gallons of milk a day. But the price of milk had gone so far down in the Depression you couldn't make a profit from apples and milk. That was why she'd took the job in the dime store, that and so she could live in town. "I figured I'd see more good-looking boys in town," she said, and giggled.

"This is the place to be seen by good-looking boys," I said.

Maybe because Sharon had come from the country to work in town and was nervous about getting started, I kind of took her under my wing. I told her where I was staying and she asked if she could board there too.

"I don't see why not," I said. "The food's nothing to brag about, but it just costs five dollars a week."

Sharon was grateful for any advice I give her. She was the kind of girl that was eager to please everybody and I warned her about the manager and other married men that would flirt with her. But she learned her job quick enough and I moved over to the cosmetics counter, which was considered a step up from the candy counter. It was thought the prettiest girl in the store would be placed at the cosmetics counter where face cream, bath powder, perfume, nail polish, nail files, eye shade, eyeliner, lotions, conditioners, colognes, and other beauty products, including combs and hairbrushes, was sold.

I soon learned that the cosmetics counter was a much harder job than the candy counter. Almost all the customers of cosmetics was women, and women are much harder to wait on than men. Women will come and look at things for what seems like hours, opening bottles and sniffing. They'll spray samples of perfume on their wrists till they smell up the whole store, then walk away without buying anything. Some old sisters will say cutting things to you, and some will slip a bottle of perfume or nail polish in their coat pocket. I had to learn when to be nice and when to be cool. That was the hardest part. Yankee women and Florida women in the summer would treat you like dirt under their feet. I reckon they seen local store clerks as nothing but servants or trash.

It was a relief to get off from work and walk back to the boardinghouse with Sharon. She looked up to me because I was older and more confident and got the attention of more boys. She felt nervous to be in town where she didn't know many people, and she depended on me to guide her. We eat together and listened to the radio together, and sometimes went to the picture show together at the theater on Main Street that cost a dime. Sometimes we wrote postcards to our folks at home even though we'd see them on the weekends.

It was the third week when Troy was home from the CCC that I invited Sharon to come stay with me. I told her she'd have to help with work because Mama was drying apples for winter and I'd have to peel and slice apples. Sharon said that was fine because she was used to doing that kind of work at home.

Now I knowed Sharon was already struck on Troy because she'd seen him when he come after me on Saturday evening one time. But then all girls was interested in Troy, though he didn't seem especially interested in any of them. When we come out of the store with our bags Troy was waiting there in the truck. He got out and opened the door of the cab, letting Sharon get in first to set beside him. He put our bags in the back of the truck. All the way home he asked her questions and told jokes. I'd never seen him pay that kind of attention to any girl before.

I don't reckon anybody knows what draws a man and a woman together. It must be some kind of sixth sense, something nobody understands. I didn't think of Sharon as especially good looking at all. She was kind of skinny and dark like she'd been out in the sun all summer. She had brown eyes and a kind of round face. Her hands looked a little too big for the size of her arms. I thought I knowed what attracted men, but now I'm not so sure. Sharon was slim and well made, that was all.

But all that weekend Troy opened doors for her and pointed out things to her. He was usually friendly and always polite, but this was different. It surprised me and pleased me to see love take hold of him and Sharon. I guess I was a little jealous too, for he paid less attention to me. You could see the love growing in their eyes when they looked at each other, when they stood close together, when Troy took her hand to help her down the steps or through a fence.

To watch somebody fall in love helps us see the world in a new and better light. Most days are just for work and waiting, getting along from hour to hour. But love puts everything in a new brightness and sets the world at a new angle. People in love may look the same, but if you watch them they seem different too, willing to take risks, see things they hadn't noticed before.

Troy took us walking down along the river. We took off our shoes and waded across below the shoals, and he helped Sharon climb up on the rocks. Sharon couldn't take her eyes off him. I never seen a girl so happy. She held up her dress and the water splashed her lean brown legs. The roar of the shoals sounded like the buzz in the blood of lovers.

"Next time you come I'll bring the canoe down to the river and we'll go for a ride," Troy said.

"I'd love that," Sharon said.

Old Pat come running through the river and jumped up on the rock and shook water on all of us. "Don't do that," Troy said.

"She must be a Methodist, sprinkling us," Sharon said, and laughed.

I'd hoped that Old Pat wouldn't be so friendly to Sharon. She usually only liked members of the family. But Sharon could see how much Troy liked his dog, and she went out of her way to make friends with Old Pat. She petted her and talked baby talk to her. She wiped the flung water off her arms and legs. It annoyed me a little to see how she worked to make Troy like her. But she was my friend too, and my guest, and there was nothing to do but be nice to her. There was a slot where most of the river poured between two rocks. Troy took a run and jumped across from one rock to the other. I'd seen him do it before, but nobody else could do it.

Sharon gasped and clapped her hands when he landed on the other side, like she'd seen a god perform a miracle.

"How do you do that?" she called. Troy took another run and jumped back across the roaring chute.

As we started back up the hill Troy helped her across a boulder and held on to her hand until he seen me looking. But then he put his hand on her back to help her across a log.

That evening at supper Papa said he was going to take a job at Fort Bragg building a barracks for the army. He said Fort Bragg was near Fayetteville, North Carolina. Papa hadn't had a real building job for years. He'd done little jobs for neighbors, sometimes for people in Flat Rock, repairing chicken houses, fixing a leak in a roof. But he'd had no steady work since he built houses on the lake. Him and Mama had lived on the money I give them and the money Troy had sent from the CCC. The only money Velmer had made was from selling muskrat hides and a little ginseng.

"How long will this job last?" Mama said.

"Could last a long time," Papa said. "They're building dozens of barracks."

"How come, when times are so bad?" Sharon said.

"Because they know a war is coming," Velmer said. "Roosevelt is getting ready for war."

"I hope not," Sharon said.

"There'll be work for all of us there," Papa said. "We can all go down and work as long as we want to."

"When will you come home?" Mama said.

"Every weekend," Papa said. "I'll drive my truck down there and back."

The way Papa talked you could see the Depression was coming to an end. There was new work to be had, but it was different from what we expected. It was not jobs at home, but way off somewhere, and the jobs had to do with the army and with the war everybody said was coming. It was good news and bad news at once, the way so many things are.

"That's a long way to go for work," Mama said.

"This work could last for years," Papa said.

Early the next morning Troy drove Sharon and me back to town. He got out of the truck and hugged Sharon before we went into the store with our bags. Old Pat yelped from the back of the truck.

"Thank you for such a nice weekend," Sharon said with a big grin on her face.

"You're welcome," I said, and headed for the cosmetics counter.

Thirteen

I never did have any extra money back then in the 1920s like other younguns did. Papa was paying for the place and paying doctor bills from the typhoid and paying for the new well and pump. Only money I had for months at a time was what I got catching rabbits in a rabbit gum and selling them down at the cotton-mill store. The store sold them to mill workers for their dinner. Me and Troy would carry a rabbit gum out into the field along in November after frost had killed the goldenrod and asters and other weeds. A rabbit gum was just a hollow log of black gum fixed up with a sliding door and a stick trigger. You put a piece of apple in the back and when a rabbit hit the stick trigger inside, the door fell and trapped him. If you skinned and gutted a rabbit, you could usually get a quarter for it.

When big boys started noticing me and I started noticing them, I didn't have no money for fancy clothes or jewelry. And Mama said it was wrong to wear lipstick or paint your face. Effie had some face powder and lipstick and I slipped into the bedroom and tried them. But I seen I didn't need any makeup. Whatever it was about me that attracted boys it didn't have nothing to do with makeup. My skin was soft and smooth and my hair was blond and naturally wavy. And my figure was beginning to fill out in the right way.

But to tell the truth, as I said before, I never did know what it was about me that attracted the boys. Sometimes I think it was the fact that I never did care nothing about them. I liked to flirt with them, but I never was crazy about boys the way other girls was. I remember my friend Grace would come to church just to hear a boy, Raleigh, sing. He was an awfully good singer. And she'd say, "Ain't he pretty; he's just so pretty." And she followed him from church to church wherever he was singing at revival meetings and prayer meetings, homecomings and singing schools. And when she was just fifteen she caught him and married him. They started out with nothing and had to hew cross ties just to make a living, him chopping out one with an axe while she chopped out another. And every weekend she'd go around with him wherever he was singing.

But I was never like that at all. I wouldn't hardly pay attention to the boys that was interested in me. And the more I ignored them the more they seemed determined to go out with me. I can't explain it except to say boys seem to want what is hardest to get. The boys would line up at the door of the church at night after service to ask if they could walk me home. It was the custom at the time to ask a girl if they could walk her home after church. They'd stand on the steps of the church pushing and elbowing each other to see who would be first. I remember Blake there every night, holding a big barn lantern and saying, "Walk you home, Miss Annie?" The one time I let him walk me home he held my arm so tight it got numb, and he couldn't think of nothing to say. Blake never was much of a talker. I reckon I never did walk with him again.

Now the one that bothered me the most was Muir. I'm ashamed to tell it now, but one night when Muir come up to the door of the church holding a lantern and asked if he could walk me home, it made me mad. I don't know why I done it, but before I even thought about it I kicked him in the leg. Everybody seen it, and some people gasped and some giggled. I know it was a terrible thing to do, but I couldn't help myself. It just happened, like that.

The girls all laughed at me, and the boys laughed at Muir. Poor fellow. I couldn't explain why I done it, why he bothered me so. He was silly just like all the other boys, and he was crazy about me. But to this day I have trouble explaining why I kicked him there in front of all the other people on the steps of the church. Except sometimes when I'm honest with myself I think it was because even then I liked him and didn't want to admit it. I was attracted to him and was afraid. The other boys didn't mean nothing to me and had no power over me. I liked their attention, but I was afraid of boys and wouldn't let them reach me inside, where I really felt things. It riled me that I was attracted to Muir, with his odd ways and book reading and bashfulness. It was a weakness I didn't want to have, and it made me mad and I kicked him.

From the time I was young Mama acted like she didn't want me to ever marry. And I didn't want to get married either. I told myself I'd never marry. What was the use of it? And I think Mama had had such a hard time herself, going back to the days on Gap Creek, and all the years since, paying for the place, dealing with typhoid, and Papa's quarreling, that she didn't want to see me tied to a husband.

Thrilling as it was to see how I could attract the attention of men and boys, there was something silly about it too. For it made me feel icky to be in the sights of mean and evil people. One time when I was walking home from school, from the store where the bus let us off, the boys went on ahead of me cause I stopped to talk with my friend Lorrie. Lorrie had a dime for candy and we stood just outside the door of the store eating Milky Way bars and talking about the school play. And next thing I knowed the boys had gone on ahead and it looked like rain. Lorrie went the other way and I hurried on down the highway and up the dirt road that followed the river. I hadn't felt any drops yet, but the sky looked like it was serious.

I'd got above Florrie's house where she had all the beds of thrift on the bank and a kind of rock garden too when this big old truck come snorting and blustering along and stopped. I guess it was a kind of dump truck, painted brown. This man leaned out the window and said, "You better get in because it's about to start raining."

I was so surprised I just stood there, like I didn't have a bit of sense. The truck rattled and smoked out of its tailpipe this awful burnt oil smell.

"You don't want to get wet, girl," the man said, grinning like I was the funniest thing he'd ever seen.

"I can't," I said, trying to think of a good excuse why I couldn't ride with him.

"You sure can," he said, and laughed. He was wearing a dirty yellow cap, the kind they give away in feed stores.

"No I can't," I said.

"I ain't going to let you get wet," he said. "You go ahead and get in."

There was a threat in his voice, like he didn't want me to feel I had a choice. I'd never felt so caught and helpless. I wished Velmer and Troy had not gone on ahead of me. I looked up the road, but they was out of sight. The big dirty truck trembled and idled and give off its bad breath. It seemed to fill up the whole road. I wished a car would come along, or another truck.

"Am I gone have to get out of here and put you in?" the man said. He lit a cigarette with a lighter and blowed smoke out the truck window. I felt the skin tighten over my forehead. I was so embarrassed and confused. I'd always promised myself I'd never let any man get me all flustered. And here I was embarrassed and scared.

"I ain't going to get in that truck," I said, and started walking on the shoulder of the road. But the big truck moved right along with me, its wheels crunching on the gravel.

"I'm going to give you a ride," the man said. "I'm not gone let you get all wet and take pneumony." You could tell from his voice he could be mean toward women. That kind of man just thinks girls are to be teased and pushed around. Good men are a little bit shy around women because they don't understand them, and because they want to impress them and be admired.

"You can't get away from me, little girl," the man said. He wasn't grinning no more. There was something hard and ugly in his voice. I tried to think how I could run away. The truck was between me and the bank along the edge of Florrie's yard. There was a fence on my side of the road, below the road. I could crawl through the fence and run through the pasture toward the river. But if the man jumped out of the truck and run after me there wouldn't be nobody to stop him. If I run on up the road he could follow me, but I might be able to catch up with Velmer and Troy.

Just then I looked down the road toward the highway and seen a Model T coming. I looked up at the man in the truck and said, "I'm just waiting here for my daddy and here he comes now." I pointed down the road to the Model T.

The man must have seen the car in his mirror for he slammed the truck into gear with a great grinding noise and jerked ahead and kept going, leaving a cloud of stinky smoke. The Model T passed me and the first drops of rain fell. I was so shook up I was trembling and out of breath. But I was also relieved and didn't hardly feel the rain.

And then it occurred to me that the truck driver might come back and see me still walking along the road, cause I still couldn't see Velmer and Troy ahead. When the road reached the end of Meetinghouse Mountain at the bend, I jumped down the bank and crossed the little creek and started climbing up the mountain. It was raining hard by now and the water was streaming from every leaf and limb. I had to fight my way up through the laurel thicket into the woods on top of the ridge. I walked along the comb of the mountain with rain hitting my face and then slid down in the leaves and rocks on the steep side above our orchard.

When I got to the house my hair was pasted to my head and my dress stuck to my shoulders and legs and was muddy where I'd slid down on my butt. My shoes squished with every step I took. When I stepped into the kitchen Mama was fixing to start supper. She seen me and gasped, "What happened to you?" I told her I'd walked across the mountain and about the man in the dump truck, and she hollered to Velmer that was setting by the fire drying out, "Don't you never leave her to walk home by herself."

"She wouldn't come on; she just kept talking to Lorrie," Velmer said.

When Papa come home from work and Mama told him about the man in the truck Papa was so mad I thought he was going to take off his belt and whip Velmer even though Velmer was near grown. He told Velmer to never let me out of his sight again while walking on the road. And he told me to stay with the boys always when I was coming home from school. He said I'd come close to real trouble that time and it was a miracle I'd got away.

After that every time I seen a dump truck on the road it scared me. And I stayed close to Velmer and Troy or everwho was walking with me.

I always thought cars was exciting. There's something about an automobile that stirs your heart. Maybe it's the speed or the sleek lines. Seeing a roadster passing a wagon or buggy on the road you feel that power, that soaring into the future. A car makes you feel that the world is moving ahead toward the wonderful, and you are moving ahead with it.

I don't even know why I dated Moody Powell again, after that time at the Homecoming at Cedar Springs, unless it was to get back at Muir. Moody had the Model T that he owned with Muir, and it was Moody that you seen driving it all the time. People said Moody was in the liquor business down on Gap Creek and in Chestnut Springs. I guess he must have been. But when he asked me to go riding with him again I didn't say no.

I reckon I was mad at Muir again. Maybe I was trying to get back at him. Maybe I was just mean. I never did care nothing about Moody Powell at all. But I was mad at Muir for no other reason than I was afraid I liked him. I can see that now. I didn't want to be in the power of no man or boy. So I mostly went out with boys I didn't care nothing about. I went out with Moody because I knowed it made Muir mad, and when him and Moody had a fight it tickled me to hear about the fight. Moody never had nothing to say. He wasn't at all like Muir and he didn't read books. I don't reckon Moody ever read the newspaper.

But what cured me of going out with Moody forever was one Sunday afternoon when we went driving with Lorrie and Woodrow. It was a pretty fall day and we drove all the way up to Brevard with the top of the car down. Moody had a mason jar of corn liquor under the seat and him and Woodrow had took several swigs from it. You know that straightaway on the road up to Brevard across the bottomlands of the French Broad River, where you can see all the Pisgah range spread out ahead? Moody was driving too fast and my scarf was flapping in the wind and we was laughing when this police car come up behind us with its light flashing on top and Moody said, "Ah shit!"

Moody pulled over to the side of the road and the cop come up and stepped on the running board. "Let me see your driver's license," he said.

"Now, officer, I ain't done nothing," Moody said. That was his first mistake because when Moody opened his mouth the officer must have smelled liquor on his breath. If he'd just handed over his license he might have been all right.

Moody reached into the glove compartment and fished out a card and give it to the officer. It must have been Muir's license because the policeman said, "Muir Powell, would you step out of the car." They both kept their driver's licenses in the glove compartment. The rest of us didn't say nothing; we just set there as Moody got out and stood beside the road as other cars passed by.

"Let me see you walk along the white line," the policeman said to Moody. Moody tried to walk straight ahead, but I seen he leaned a little this way and then that way and then stepped off the line. It's hard to walk in a straight line when somebody is watching you. I tried not to look at Moody or the policeman. I looked straight ahead. Lorrie and Woodrow giggled in the backseat. "Lordy, Lordy," Lorrie said. I just hoped nobody we knowed passed by on the Brevard Road and seen us. They'd tell everybody at church.

The policeman told Moody he couldn't drive no more. He was too drunk to drive. He said Woodrow would have to drive the car home. And he wrote Moody a ticket for driving under the influence. So me and Moody got in the backseat and Lorrie and Woodrow got in the front seat. But the funny thing was Woodrow was much drunker than Moody was. Woodrow had set in the backseat with Lorrie and took two drinks from the mason jar for every one Moody took.

I was scared I'd never get home that afternoon. I said to myself that if I did get home safe I'd never go out with Moody again. I'd done it again just to spite Muir, and I felt double silly and stupid and I had learned my lesson.

To avoid the law again Woodrow drove us home the back way, going all the way up the mountain to Cedar Mountain, and then turning onto the dirt road that comes by Blue Ridge Church and all the way down the river by the Abe Jones Flats and the Brack Shipman cabin and then the Cedar Springs community. The road was so rough we bounced and jerked so bad it like to have broke my tailbone.

When Papa heard what had happened he said I wasn't never going out with no Moody Powell again. He said I was never going out with *no* boy again till I was twenty years old. He said he didn't care if I lived to be an old maid, I'd never go out like that again. I thought he was going to whip me he was so mad. Papa almost never did whip me when I was little. It was Mama that switched my legs with a hickory when I sassed her or done something bad.

Now when they come and arrested Muir for driving under the influence because Moody had give the patrolman Muir's drivers' license, Muir had a terrible time. He had to get witnesses to prove he wasn't even driving the car that Sunday afternoon. He'd gone to the baptizing at Mount Olivet. He got witnesses, including the preacher at Mount Olivet, to swear he was with them and he did eventually get off.

But the thing was that after that for more than a year, if that patrolman seen me in a car he'd stop it and ask to see the license of the driver. I don't know if he ever figured out what had happened. I was near about afraid to ride on the highway. But after a while he must have give up or been moved to another part of the state, for after that I didn't see him no more.

WHEN I WAS a senior in high school me and Lorrie left school at lunchtime and went down to the store for a candy bar. Lorrie always had a dime and bought two candy bars, one for each of us. Her daddy had a job as a mail carrier and they had money during the Depression when nobody else did. There was this boy that was the nephew of Mr. Fletcher that run the store and filling station. His name was Glenn and he worked at the jewelry store in town. And for some reason he was always at his uncle's store when we come down at lunchtime. I thought maybe he was on his lunch break from the jewelry store then.

Glenn had a kind of limp. I don't know if he'd had polio or had hurt his leg somehow. But you could see him lurch a little when he walked, like he was struggling to keep in balance. He had a nice car so he must have made good money at the jewelry store. I don't know at what point I noticed he was always looking at me. He'd be talking to his uncle but be looking toward Lorrie and me. And he'd come over and ask how I was and how school was going. He wore one of these tweed cloth caps and he'd take the cap off when he greeted me.

"I bet school ain't hard for a smart girl like you," he said.

"Ain't too hard," I said.

"You're too pretty to work hard," he said.

"I don't work too hard," I said.

"I bet you got lots of boyfriends," he said.

"Ain't got a boyfriend," I said.

"Sure you do." He grinned like he knowed a secret.

"I wouldn't go out with a boy unless he had a college education," I said. I don't know why I said that.

"Whoa now; hold on," he said, and laughed. "I've been to jewelry school; I guess that's a kind of college."

Most every time Lorrie and me went down to the store Glenn was there. It didn't occur to me for a while that he was there to see me. But then one day he told me to come to his car; he had something to show me.

"I ain't going to your car," I said.

"Don't you want to see what I got?"

"I have to go back to school," I said.

"Then you just come here to the door and wait," he said.

I stood at the back door to the store while he went out to his car and come back with something held in his two hands. He smiled like somebody about to tell a big secret, then opened his hands and there was a little velvet-covered box, the kind a ring or piece of jewelry would come in. He handed the box to me, but I couldn't open it.

"Here," he said, and opened the box like a mouth. Inside was white silk and what looked at first like a bracelet. And then I seen it was a watch, the prettiest watch I'd ever laid eyes on.

"Well, put it on," he said.

The watch was stretched around a silk-covered stump. It was white gold and gleamed with little diamonds around the face. The band shined and the tiny face was magnified by the thick crystal. I was almost afraid to touch it. But I took it out of the case and slipped it on my wrist and it was cold on my skin but fit just perfect.

"This ain't for me," I said.

"Ain't for nobody else," Glenn said.

The watch looked like something a princess or movie star might wear.

"I can't take this," I said. I didn't know what to say because it didn't seem possible he was giving it to me.

"Oh yes you can," he said. "I work in the jewelry store and I got it for you."

"For me?" I said.

"Just for you and nobody else."

As we walked back to the school Lorrie kept *ooh*ing and *aah*ing over the watch. She said, "That means he wants to marry you."

"It don't mean no such a thing," I said.

"Else why would he give you such an expensive watch?" she said.

"I don't know," I said. "I guess he likes me."

"I never seen such a fine watch," Lorrie said. I could see how jealous she was. She kept looking at the watch on my arm even after we went back to geometry class.

Now I was afraid to show the watch to Papa because I knowed he'd have questions about it. I didn't know myself what the watch meant or what it was for. I just knowed it was about the prettiest thing I'd even seen. When Mama seen it on my wrist she gasped, "Where did you get that?" I reckon it flashed through her mind it might have been stole.

"Somebody give it to me."

"Who would have give you that?"

There was no way I could lie to Mama. I told her about Glenn that worked in the jewelry store in town.

"That must be a fake," Velmer said. "I bet it ain't real gold."

"Why would he give you such a present?" Mama said.

"I guess he must like me."

"You're too young to get a present like that," Mama said.

When Papa got home Troy told him I'd got a new watch. I'd took it off and laid it on the counter beside the stove while I helped Mama peel taters. I tried not to look at Papa when he come into the kitchen. He picked up the watch and looked at it. I wished I'd kept the watch a secret and not told nobody.

"Who is this boy?" Papa said.

I told him his name was Glenn and he worked in the jewelry store in town. He was the nephew of Mr. Fletcher that run the store beside the school.

"You don't know a thing about him," Papa said.

"He's a nice boy," I said.

"How do you know that? You don't know nothing about him."

I understood Papa was right, but the watch had been give to me and it was my watch. Papa didn't want me to have such a fine thing, finer than anything he could afford. I knowed before he said it what he was going to say.

"You give that watch back to him," Papa said.

"How can I give it back to him?"

"When he comes to the store you hand it back to him."

"Why can't I have something of my own?" I said.

"Don't you sass me," Papa said. "That boy is a stranger and has no business giving you such a present. And for all you know he stole it from the store."

I stood there looking at the wet taters and the knife in my hand. A tear fell into the pan. The watch was the most precious thing I'd ever owned. It broke my heart to think of giving it back. I wondered if I could secretly keep the watch and not let nobody see it. But I seen that was impossible. If you couldn't wear the watch, it wouldn't be no good to own it. And I couldn't just flat-out disobey Papa, however much I wanted to. He wanted to show me again how he was in charge of everything till I was all growed up. I had no choice but to do what he said.

When I took the watch back to the store the next day I hoped Glenn wouldn't be there and I could keep it for another day. But he was there. When I handed the little velvet box to him he said, "No, it's yours."

"Can't keep it," I said.

"Sure you can; it's all yours."

"Papa said I have to give it back." I shoved the box into his hands and walked away. He come running after me and said he didn't want it back.

"I bought it for you," Glenn said.

"I don't want it," I said, not telling the truth.

What Glenn done then shocked me. Tears come into his eyes and he looked at me and sobbed. "I love you," he said. "And I want to marry you." I couldn't think of nothing to say and I started to walk away.

"I know I'm not nothing special," he said, like he was choking.

"I got to go back to school," I said.

That was the first time I seen how a man could make it up in his mind about being in love with a girl that didn't even know about it. A man could plan it all out in his mind without a girl being hardly aware of him. I don't know what he done with that watch. He probably sold it back to the jewelry store. But I do know that love gifts look awful sad and silly when the love is over. Love gifts remind you of how foolish people in love can be and how much that kind of love is an illusion. The gifts, even expensive gifts, seem cheap afterward, and tainted by the ridiculous. It near killed me to have to give that watch back, but I bet it broke Glenn's heart to have to look at that watch later and see how his love had all been made up in his mind.

IN HIGH SCHOOL they started putting on school plays every year, one in the fall and one in the spring before commencement. I'd been in church plays before at Christmastime and found how much I loved to go up on a stage and pretend to be somebody else from a different time and place, in different clothes. I always thought it was odd that I liked to take part in plays and act a part since I was too shy to ever get up in front of an audience, even a small group, and give a speech. Even the thought of having to give a talk made me so nervous my breath got short. If I had to give a report in class I worried about it so much I couldn't sleep at night. Just the thought of having to speak in front of people made my back ache and my stomach churn and my knees weak.

But starting with the Christmas pageant at church I found that if I put on a costume and become somebody else it wasn't hard at all to get up on a stage with people looking at me. In fact I enjoyed it. And I was always able to memorize things. I could memorize anything: poems to recite in class, a passage from the Bible, and the lines of talk in a play.

So when Mr. Oswald that taught English announced he was going to direct a play for the school and asked who would like to take part I volunteered. He said it was going to be a play about a girl that breaks every boy's heart until one day she meets a boy that she falls in love with and he breaks her heart. I went to the school library and got a copy of the book and memorized a whole long scene. When I went to see Mr. Oswald in his office he asked if I would read a few lines. Instead I recited the whole scene, where the girl brags about how much fun it is stealing other girls' boyfriends and then dumping them when they get stuck on her. I made her seem mean and shallow, just like the part was wrote. Mr. Oswald was so surprised he didn't say nothing at first, and then he exclaimed, "By golly, you *are* Priscilla. The part is yours."

Most of the students in high school was from around town, and they looked down on us kids from the country, way out in the river valley. So it give me a special thrill to get the lead part in such a romantic and sad play. I read all through the play and found Priscilla dies at the end with a broke heart after she learns what it means to be truly in love and is sorry for all the people she has hurt. It was an ending that would bring tears to anybody's eyes and teach them how important love is.

I learned all the part and we rehearsed every afternoon, first in the classroom and then on the stage in the auditorium. Since I knowed my part from the first it bothered me it took so long for others to memorize theirs. Mr. Oswald would stand there with a copy of the play and remind them of the lines they'd forgot or correct them when they remembered them wrong. Jason Gooch that played the lead boy's part, the one Priscilla finally fell in love with, kept forgetting his lines in the middle of one of the most important scenes. We'd have to keep stopping and starting over.

Now I'd never been on a stage in front of so many people before, and I admit I felt a little nervous as the big night approached. I knowed nearly the whole school and families and people from the community would come. Papa would drive us to the school in his new Model A truck, with Mama and me in the front and the boys riding in the back. When I got to school and went back stage to put on my dress I could hear the crowd on the other side of the curtain and my hands trembled a little. My costume was a kind of sundress with low shoulders and a short skirt, almost short as shorts. I swallowed and suddenly felt so scared I wanted to tell Mr. Oswald I was sick or just run away into the night.

But other kids in the play started coming in and putting on their costumes and it was too late. I prayed that if I could get through the play without making a complete fool of myself I'd never act again. Some people said the theater was a sin and maybe I was being punished for taking part. Before the curtain went up I was trembling, and it felt like my feet had turned to ice.

But as the curtain lifted and the lights hit my face, it was like a weight was lifted off me. I opened my mouth to say the first lines and stepped forward into my part. Nobody in the audience could see me. All they could see was Priscilla. It was like I stepped through some kind of wall and was in contact with the people out there in the dark. I said my lines with all the feeling and meaning I could give them.

From the first, the audience hung on every word and every move I made. Jason forgot his lines once and Mr. Oswald prompted him from behind the drapery, but it didn't make no difference. The audience laughed at things that was funny and kept quiet most of the time. There wasn't even much coughing.

In the last scene, after I'd died of a broke heart, Jason was supposed to carry me off stage. I told him at every rehearsal to carry me with my head toward the audience, for if I was turned the other way wearing the short skirt the people could see all the way up to my bloomers. Well, we got through the play and the audience liked us and even clapped sometimes after a scene they liked special. So when I died Jason picked me up, but I reckon he was nervous and forgot and held me so my legs was toward the audience and my skirt was pulled up even higher. Even though I was supposed to be dead, I reached out and pushed my skirt down as far as I could. And the audience started laughing and then they roared. Maybe they thought that was in the play, for they started clapping like they would beat their hands to rags and bones. Mr. Oswald was beaming as we come off the stage. Now Mr. Oswald was a very shy man. He'd blush even talking to a class. But I reckon he was so thrilled to have the play over and to have such a big crowd and such applause, he wasn't hardly at hisself. As soon as Jason put me down Mr. Oswald run over and hugged me and kissed me on the cheek. There was tears in his eyes and he said, "You're wonderful, wonderful." But the clapping continued and we had to go out on the stage and take a bow.

After that I had a part in every school play, and I thought of being an actress. I knowed I could be an actress, for I felt more like myself when I was playing a part than I ever did when I was just being me. I never was sure who myself was. But if there was a part that had been wrote, then I knowed how to play that part. And I could learn any lines that anybody wrote.

But to be an actress I had to go off to New York or Hollywood, a long way from home where I didn't know nobody. I'd have to leave home and go there as my nervous self. I didn't know how to play the part of some-body that is going off to study to be an actress. And I didn't have the money to go somewhere like that. The Depression had come, and there was no money for groceries, much less for traveling to some far-off place that would be expensive once you got there. I thought and thought about going away to be an actress, but I never did. The only part I would play would be myself, and that wasn't wrote too good.

One time after I got the job working in the dime store a man seen me and asked if I wanted to be a model. I was working at the candy counter and he come up and said I looked perfect to be a model. I was just a slim little thing then. He said he was a talent scout for some agency in New York and he looked for girls that wanted to be models. He give me his card and said he was giving interviews with people at the Skyland Hotel. Them that was chose for training would be sent to New York. He said I was a natural; I wouldn't need much training.

I looked at the card that evening after work. It would be wonderful to be paid for modeling clothes in a big city like New York, to be photo-graphed wearing fancy rags. But I'd heard stories about men that lured girls by promising them a chance to be a model. When I got back to the boardinghouse where I was staying I looked at the card and thought about it. Even if the man was telling the truth, I couldn't go off and leave Mama and Papa. I couldn't leave Mama to do all the work by herself. The next day I throwed the card away.

THE ONE TIME I was glad Papa was strict and determined where I was concerned with boys was when the Henderson boy got interested in me. He belonged to the family of Hendersons over near the South Carolina line, and I never would have gone out with him in a thousand years in any case. He'd dropped out of school when he was about fourteen and he was knowed to be a heavy drinker. I don't know when he got so interested in me. He was about four or five years older than me. But one time we was having a revival meeting at church. You know, the meeting they have after the corn is laid by and before it's time to pull fodder and cut tops, in the heat of the summer, when it feels good to get out at night after the heat of the day goes away.

His name was Gus and he come up to me on the steps of the church like the other boys done. His face was red and I could smell aftershave and then I realized it was the scent of corn liquor that I smelled. "Miss Annie, I come to walk you home," he said, and kind of bowed.

"No, thank you," I said, and turned away from him. I took Mama's arm and walked down the steps and out of the churchyard, without looking at any of the other boys standing there. I wouldn't be seen dead walking home with the Henderson boy.

But after the revival meeting come the baptizing and that was the summer I got saved and joined the church. I didn't have a special dress for the baptizing and just wore an old gray frock I had. The baptizing was down at the river, at the sandbar across from the Lemmons Hole. The river was just a little cloudy, for it had rained the night before.

Now baptizing is a kind of shock when they plunge you down into the water over your head and then raise you up streaming into the light. Some people scream because of the cold water, but I gasped and called out to Mama and everybody on the bank laughed. But I stumbled to the bank wiping the water out of my eyes, and first thing I seen was Gus Henderson standing on the bank above the others looking at me. It was the kind of stare that was scary, like somebody that ain't at theirself. I shivered with the cold water dripping off me and looked away. Mama handed me a towel and I dried my face and waited at the edge of the water with the others for the singing to be over. But every time I turned I seen Gus still looking at me. I stayed close to Mama when we walked home, and Troy walked with us. It was a relief to change my clothes in the bedroom.

What happened after that was every time Gus got drunk he'd come to the house to try to see me. He didn't have the nerve to come when he was sober. But on the weekends when he'd had a drink or two here he'd come, sometimes pretending like he come to see Velmer or was on his way to the store. But he'd hang around waiting for a chance to ask me to go out with him. There was always something a little thrilling about a drunk man, because he was out of control and you didn't know what he might do. He didn't know hisself. It was the thrill of danger. But really Gus was pitiful, always a little drunk, stumbling around, hoping maybe I'd go out with him.

And then one night he come over and knocked on the front door. He called out and he sounded different. He sounded like he was mad or determined to get an answer. Maybe he thought he was trick-or-treating. Papa went to the front door and told him to go on home. I looked out the window and seen Gus was carrying a big old lantern.

"Mr. Richards, ain't got no call to run me off," he said.

"Don't come around here no more when you're drunk," Papa said.

"Didn't come to see *you*," Gus said. "Come to see Annie."

"Annie don't want to see you," Papa said. "Nobody wants to see you when you're drunk."

Gus took a step like he was coming into the house anyway. Papa shoved him back and Gus staggered, almost falling down the steps. He swung the lantern like he meant to hit Papa with it. Next thing Papa done was grab a rocking chair that set on the porch and push it out in front of him. It was the way a trainer in the circus might push a lion away with a chair.

"Don't you come around here no more," Papa said.

"You ain't got no right to treat me thisaway," Gus said.

But Papa held the chair out and pushed him back a little at a time until Gus was standing on the top step. I thought he was going to fall backward down the steps and drop the lantern. Instead he pitched the lantern onto the porch where it broke and spilled kerosene that flared up. I guess he run away after that, but I didn't pay no attention to him with the flames leaping on the boards of the porch. I run to the kitchen and got the water bucket. Papa took the bucket from me and splashed it on the kerosene and broke glass. There was just barely enough water to put the flames out.

"He's worse than Timmy Gosnell," Mama said. Timmy Gosnell was a drunk man on Gap Creek that used to come and bother Mama and Papa when they first got married.

But after he threw the lantern and set the porch on fire Gus Henderson never did come back to the house. Or if he did he slipped around in the dark and nobody seen him. That was about the time Troy got Old Pat, and if he'd come around then, Old Pat would have let us know.

Fourteen

I never did plan to start going out with Muir again. Sometimes I think it was just a happen. I tried to fall in love with boys one after another. But every time I dated a boy, the longer I went out with him the less I liked him. Sometimes I wondered if I liked boys at all. I wanted to be in love, and I tried to be. I kissed boys and let them hug me. I let them give me presents and drive me to the picture show. But every time I got tired of them. I told myself it was because I wanted to move on. I wanted something more than just settling down to raise babies and keep house and go to church on Sundays. I wanted to make something of myself. I had to go somewhere else and meet other people. But I didn't know how I was going to do that.

Muir lost the Model T, which he co-owned with Moody when Moody died and it was found out he owed a bunch of money to his buddies Wheeler and Drayton. Muir didn't have no money, so he had to sell the car to pay Moody's debts. Without the car he had to walk or hitch a ride to a church where he was going to preach. Sometimes when Effie and Alvin drove him to Tracy Grove or Saluda I'd go along with them. Wherever Muir preached they'd take up a collection and Muir would give Alvin a dollar for driving him. I told myself I was just going along to be sociable.

One night in the fall of 1939 after Muir had preached at Double Springs and we was driving back toward home Muir told Alvin to let us out at the highway and we'd walk up the Green River Road to the house. I wasn't sure I wanted to walk that far, but I didn't say nothing. We got out and Alvin and Effie drove on toward Flat Rock.

It was a night with a full moon and the road run along the sparkling river. There was just the faintest chill in the air that made things seem more alive. Muir put his arm around me and that felt good. He was warm and strong. The mountains rose like shadows up into the moonlit sky. The light on the road made everything almost clear as day. The valley in moonlight seemed not only like another world but also a different time, either long ago, or maybe in the future.

We come to the bend in the river where the road climbed up high above the water. The moon was reflected in the big pool there, and seemed bright as footlights on a stage. Muir had said little, which was unusual for him. I wondered if the preaching had wore him out. We stopped and looked down at the river.

"I won't ever ask you again," he said.

"Ask what?"

"You know what."

I thought at first he meant ask me to go out with him. But then I seen he meant asking me to marry him. Twice he'd asked me before, when I was just fourteen, and then after I graduated from high school.

"I've always loved you since you was a little girl," he said. "And I always will love you. But if you say no now, I'll leave you alone and never bother you again."

I didn't know what to answer. His proposal was not a complete surprise, but I was not expecting it at that time. I thought of all my dreams of going away and doing something with myself. I thought of having my own business or living in some city, of being my own boss.

"I think the Lord meant for us to be together," Muir said.

That seemed unfair to me, to make the proposal a religious thing. How did he know what the Lord wanted? I couldn't see any way the Lord would care one way or another. But on the other hand, I couldn't be sure. Maybe there was something I just didn't understand.

"This is the last time," Muir said. "You are twenty-seven and I'm thirty-four. I won't try again."

As I stood there in his arms I wasn't confused. I could think clear, and the thing I thought about was why I hadn't married none of the other boys that had asked me. I could have married any of them, but I hadn't. I'd got rid of every one of them when they got more serious. I'd done that in each case.

And why had I not gone off to the city and got a job as a model or an actress? Why had I not gone out to Asheville or Charlotte and got a job? Surely I could have done it, if I'd really wanted to. But I hadn't. Something had held me back. The question was: What had held me back? Was I just too scared to go off and trust myself in another place? Was I that timid?

And then I wondered if I'd not gone away because I secretly wanted to marry Muir Powell and refused to admit it. Suddenly I seen that must be the case. I seen that I'd always come back to Muir and that if I didn't marry Muir, I'd never marry anybody else. I would always reject other boys. None of them seemed right to me. If I didn't marry Muir, I'd be an old maid. Maybe the Lord did intend for me to marry him. I'd been in love with Muir all along, but didn't understand what love was. I'd thought love was something way off yonder, something in a storybook, but I seen it was right here. It was what had been already in me all along.

And I seen also how he needed me. Muir couldn't help hisself. He couldn't stay away from me. He couldn't manage his life without me. He'd never been able to handle his money. People had made fun of him for his preaching and for his church on the mountaintop. His own family had made fun of him for reading books and tramping in the woods and never making no money. He needed somebody to look after him and take care of him. He had no head for business at all. I'd thought I wanted to marry a businessman, but I didn't. I was the one who was good at business.

"What do you say, Annie?" he said. "If you say no, you'll never hear from me again."

"Yes," I said almost in a whisper.

"What did you say?"

"Yes," I said, and seen my whole life take firm shape before me. Before, my future had been murky as dishwater; now it come into solid, sharp focus. And I saw how hard it would be, and I didn't care.

He kissed me on the lips and I enjoyed the kiss. But when he pulled away I said, "But let's not tell nobody yet."

"What do you mean not tell anybody?"

"Let's just keep it to ourselves, for a while."

"How is that possible?" Muir said.

"We'll get married and not tell nobody. I'll live at home and you'll live at home as before." I don't know why I said that. Maybe it was because I couldn't bear to tell Mama I was getting married. She didn't want to hear of me getting married. She had had such a hard life and worked so hard she needed me to stay home and help her. She was afraid for me to get married.

I guess I was afraid of marriage too. I never wanted a man to handle me and force his way with me. I never wanted to be under the will of a man. I wasn't going to be the play toy of no man. So even though to my surprise I was willing to marry Muir, I wasn't willing to live with him just yet.

"If you will marry me, that's a start," Muir said. He was surprised I'd agreed and surprised that I wanted it to be a secret. But mostly he was relieved that I'd agreed.

It was just before Thanksgiving when Muir got the license. I told Mama I was staying with Effie and Alvin on Thanksgiving night. It had turned awful cold and Alvin's Buick didn't have a good heater. Me and Muir set in the backseat all bundled up in our overcoats and with a blanket over our laps. There was a new preacher at church named Preacher Rice, and he'd agreed to marry us and keep it a secret for a while. He lived all the way up at Brevard in Transylvania County.

We waited till after supper to go, and Alvin decided to take the little road all the way up Green River to the Blue Ridge Church and Cedar Mountain. It was the roughest road you ever seen. We bounced over rocks and ruts till our behinds was sore, and we laughed and laughed. We woke the preacher up and he performed the ceremony right there in his living room. I was surprised how quick it was over. Mrs. Rice served as witness. Muir give the preacher a five-dollar bill and then it was done. Before I knowed it we was in the car and headed back the same way we'd come.

"You all are welcome to stay the night with us," Effie said.

"Muir is going back home," I said.

Effie turned and looked at me, and I looked at Muir, and he said to Alvin, "Yeah, take me back home."

"Well, I never heard of such a thing," Effie said. She was like Papa. She always said what was on her mind. I thought I could see a grin on Alvin's face in the rearview mirror.

"We want to keep it a secret for a while," I said. "So please don't tell nobody."

"How can you keep it a secret?" Effie said.

"Just for a while," I said. "I want to wait a while to tell Mama."

I never felt more nervous in my life than in the weeks after me and Muir got married but didn't live together and didn't tell nobody. I couldn't bear to tell Mama I was married, and I couldn't bear to leave and go to live in the Powell house. I told myself that I didn't want to upset Mama, and I wanted to find the perfect time to tell her I'd be leaving home. She'd come to depend on me as the years passed, not only on the money I brought home every week from my job and the work I helped her with when I was home. It was more than that. Later in her life she was less sure of herself. She'd always been sure and determined, but as she got older she got scared. Partly it was the talk of war and fear that Velmer and Troy might have to go off to war. As she got older she was afraid she wasn't attractive no more to Papa. I think that was a part of it.

When Mama had to make a decision she wanted my support. Even if it was something as little as choosing the color of curtains or buying a new shrub to set in the yard. It was almost like I'd become the parent. She wanted my approval for ordering Christmas cards, and she wanted me to be there to help when the preacher come to Sunday dinner. I liked it that she needed my help, and maybe I didn't want to give that up.

But the truth was I'd always been afraid of marriage. Even I could see that. I'd never wanted to be in the power of no man. I didn't much want to be bothered by a man running his hands over me and having his way with me. Other girls said it didn't hurt and besides it was fun and some said loving was the most wonderful thing they'd ever done. And I was curious and attracted as any girl is. But I felt a dread also of laying night after night with a man and letting him do whatever he wanted to with me. I couldn't admit it even to myself that I was that timid. But the fact is I was. Nothing in the world scared me as much as the idea of having sex, unless it was the fear of having to make a speech in public.

But as I'd agreed to marry Muir and had gone through the ceremony in front of Preacher Rice, I knowed that according to the law I had to live with my husband. And besides, Effie and Alvin knowed. I was living on borrowed time. While I was working every day, and while I was laying in bed at night, I thought about when I was going to tell Mama. And I thought about *how* I was going to tell Mama. Would I make like it was a joke and didn't matter, like it was just a matter-of-fact small thing? Or would I break down and cry and beg Mama not to be mad and even give me her blessing? Or would I talk firm and businesslike and tell Mama it was my business and not hers? I was old enough to know what I was doing.

As it turned out Muir give me a deadline. He said we had to announce our marriage by Christmas. War had started overseas in September and things was moving in a dark direction. And we had to act like responsible grown-ups. He made me feel a little ashamed and a little silly. So I waited till everybody had gathered at the house to open presents by the fireplace on Christmas. Effie and Alvin was there, and Troy and Sharon was there. Velmer was there. I had got Mama a pretty lavender shawl at the best store in town. When she opened the box and held the shawl up in the light to see the sparkling colors, I said, quick before I lost my nerve, "Me and Muir has got married."

I didn't think Mama heard me because she kept admiring the shawl.

"Me and Muir got married back in November," I said.

"Well, it's about time," Papa said.

"That's wonderful," Troy said, and jumped up and hugged me. Sharon hugged me too and kissed me.

"So that's the Christmas surprise," Sharon said.

Mama folded the shawl and put it back in the box. She laid the box on the floor, stood up, and walked into the kitchen. I run after her and found she'd gone on into the dining room.

"Mama, I had to tell you some time," I said.

She opened the closet where the towels and best dishes was kept and took out several towels and dishes and set them on the table. And then she opened the drawer where the silver was.

"What are you doing?" I said.

"If you start keeping house, you'll need some dishes and silverware and towels," Mama said.

"There is dishes and silverware at the Powell house," I said.

"But you'll need some of your own. A woman needs to start housekeeping with her own stuff."

"We can worry about that later," I said. "It's Christmas. We need to finish opening presents."

"You'll need to take a frying pan," Mama said. "And some of the apples we dried."

It was Mama's way of not talking about my marriage. She was not going to approve or disapprove. Instead she went right to work, doing what was practical, as she always done. When she was hurt or confused or surprised she just kept on working. She worked until she had got a box of things packed and a bunch of my clothes folded in a brown paper bag. She done everything that she could to make it easier for me.

When Muir arrived at the house a little later Papa stood up and shook hands with him, and Troy shook hands with him, and Sharon run and give him a big hug. I waited to see what Mama would say, because she'd avoided talking to me, except about the things I'd need to carry with me to the Powell house. She was never one to say much about how she felt anyway. But after all the handshaking and hugging she stood on the other side of the fireplace from Muir and said, "I hate to see Annie get married and leave us, but if she has to I'd rather it was you than anybody else." That's when Muir stepped over and hugged Mama and she didn't back away from him.

Once I announced that I was married and going to live with Muir at the Powell house it was like things just moved of their own accord. I'd dreaded the moment so long and now that it was here it was like everything fell into place. Sharon helped me pack a few more things and was so excited she was shaking. I knowed she wished that it was her that had been married. I got my overnight case and my three pairs of shoes in a bag.

Effie and Alvin said they'd drive us down to the Powell place. "What a relief," Effie said. "I'm tired of keeping your secret."

To get to the Powell house you had to drive through two pastures, stopping to open and close the gate at every fence. Muir got out each time and opened and closed the gates. It was only as we approached the house that I remembered that Ginny Powell would be there. I don't know why I'd thought only about Mama. We'd have to announce our marriage to Muir's mama, and we would be living in her house. I can't explain why I hadn't thought much about that before. I swallowed with surprise and tried to think what I'd say to my new mother-in-law. Ginny was known as a great talker, opinionated and lively. She'd been a Pentecostal Holiness in the revivals that come through years ago.

Ginny must have seen the car drive into the yard, for she opened the door before we got to the porch.

"Well, this is a surprise," she said.

"Annie and me has got married," Muir said.

"I won't say it's a complete surprise," Ginny said. She hugged me and kissed me on both cheeks. She took the bags from my arms and led me into the parlor where a bright fire was burning in the fireplace and tinsel sparkled on the Christmas tree. The Powell house was bigger than our house and had better furniture too.

"You just make yourselves at home," Ginny said. "I'm so pleased that you and Muir are to start a family. You've got to live here, of course."

Ginny was opposite to Mama in every way. She spoke everwhat was on her mind and she moved quick. She loved to read and she loved to argue about scripture. She was tall and had black hair and black eyes, but now her hair had streaks of gray. "I'm just so happy," she said, and clapped her hands.

There was books and magazines and newspapers on the couch. She moved them to a table so there'd be room to set down in front of the fire.

"I'll reheat the Christmas ham," she said.

"I can help you," I said.

"You just sit down," Ginny said. "I'll fix supper for you two and then I'll go up to Fay's to spend the night."

"You don't need to do that," Muir said.

Fay had got married to Lester two years before and she lived on the road by the church. She already had a little boy named Duane.

"No," Ginny said, "What you two need is to be alone. You don't want to be bothered on your wedding night." She said it in such a determined voice you didn't want to argue with her. Ginny Powell was the kind of woman that knowed her own mind. The words *wedding night* made me shiver. But I'd got this far and there was no turning back. I set down and looked at the fire. I had been to the Powell house many times before, but now that I'd be staying here it appeared like a different place. The fire in the fireplace looked like some kind of gate leading to a road that wound far back into dark mountains.

"Here is some mulled cider," Ginny said, and give me a mug of steaming cider that smelled of cloves and other spices. I sipped the cider and wondered if I should volunteer again to help fix the supper. I didn't know what was the polite thing.

"Do you want me to gather eggs and feed the chickens?" I called to Ginny in the kitchen.

"Already been done," Ginny called back.

"I'll go water the horse," Muir said.

"Already done," Ginny called.

When the supper was ready Ginny said she was going to put on her coat and walk up to Fay's house. "You're not going to eat?" I said.

"No, no, you two need to be on your own this night." She looked at me and rushed over and kissed me on the cheek. "I am so happy for you," she said. "I always thought you two would get together."

Then she was gone and there wasn't nothing for us to do but set down and eat Christmas ham and sweet taters. There was biscuits and canned peas and apple pie. After we eat I heated water in the kettle on the cook-stove and washed the dishes. The Powell kitchen was bigger than ours, and I had to look around to find where things was. Ginny was not neat as Mama, and to tell the truth I seen places that could have used a good scrubbing, especially under the counter, behind the bread safe, and below the table. I figured I'd have my work cut out for me to keep the place clean without offending my mother-in-law.

Muir got a dry towel and wiped the dishes, and he showed me where to put them on the shelf. It come to me that a woman's work is the same whether she's married or unmarried, at one house or in another. But working for your own husband and your own family had a satisfaction, I would have to admit. Later we set by the fireplace and Muir read in the Bible. He had a pile of history books stacked beside the fireplace, and you could see that's what he done when he was in the house. He read either the Bible or one of these history books. They was big thick books that would take a long time to read, books on the Civil War and George Washington and such.

I told myself as bedtime approached that everything would happen as it happened. There was something inevitable about marriage. Once it was set in motion one thing followed another as it had to. I wondered if I really had any choice at all, even when I thought I did.

"Are you sleepy?" Muir said. I said I was, though in fact I didn't feel the least sleepy. He picked up a lamp and I followed him down the hall and into the farthest bedroom. It was cold so far from the fireplace and I shivered so hard it made my shoulder blades sore. When Muir set the lamp on the night stand I seen all the knives and trapper's equipment on the wall and on the floor. There was rifles and shotguns on pegs on the walls, and boots on the floor, and a mackinaw coat hanging on a hanger.

There was a red plaid hat and two large hunting knives, fishing tackle, a pair of binoculars. There was a pair of weblike things, which I guessed was snowshoes. But the floor was neat and the bed was carefully made.

"This was Grandpa Peace's room," Muir said. "Him and me slept here when I was a boy."

"Is this the same bed?"

"No, no. I made this bed myself from chestnut wood." It was a beautiful big bed with high posts and a headboard carved in the shape of a flying eagle.

Muir said he would go out, and he pointed to the pee pot in the corner of the room. When he was gone I started to get undressed and then remembered my nightgown was in the bag Mama had packed. It was in the living room. Instead of taking the lamp I felt my way down the hall and found the bag and brought it to the bedroom. By then I was shivering even more. I wondered why in a house this big they'd not made a fireplace in the far bedroom.

There was an old trunk at the foot of the bed and I took off my clothes and folded them on that. My feet was ice, after I'd put on the gown and used the pee pot; then I pulled the quilts back and got into the big bed. The sheets was so cold they burned my back and shoulders. But the heavy covers settled around my belly and shoulders and I could feel the heat reflected from my body. I wondered if I should blow out the lamp; but if I did that Muir wouldn't have no light when he come back.

This is a night you'll always remember, I said to myself. This is something that happens only once to a woman. I shuddered with the cold in my bones, but the sheets was already warming up. You will never be the same again, I thought. And then I laughed at myself, for I seen that every day we're different from the day before. You're acting silly, I said to myself.

When Muir come in I could smell the cold on his clothes. He took off his shoes and blowed out the lamp, and then I could hear him slide off his pants and shirt. It sounded like he hung them on the bed post. And I thought: That's what bedposts are for. When he got in on the other side of the bed it shook the mattress like an earthquake. Muir was a big man and he was all muscle, which is heavier than fat.

I just laid there for a little bit, and then he put his big hand on my breast. Muir had the biggest hands with the longest fingers I ever seen. His hand was so big it could cover most of both my breasts. At that moment something occurred to me that I hadn't thought of before. I'd been thinking, as I guess most girls do, that a wedding night is when the man does things to you. It's what girls whisper from the time they're just beginning to grow up. But it come to me that a wedding night could also be things a woman done to a man. It could work both ways.

I reached out and put my hand on one of his nipples. It was firm and good to the touch. He seemed to like that and I put my other hand on his other nipple. And then I run my hand through the hair on his chest. There was something about that that relieved me. I can't describe it, except to say it was a surprise. All the time I'd thought it was just a question of what my husband would do to me, and that had scared me. But looked at this way it wasn't as scary.

He run his hands over me and I run my hands over him. You are a woman and not a little girl, I said to myself. Women and men have been doing this since the beginning of creation. It must be what people was meant to do. It must be why they have bodies shaped the way they are. I felt all over Muir's body; he was so big and strong, he felt like a giant in the bed beside me. He seemed to like for me to touch him all over as he was touching me. I could see how excited he was. I thought, this is the way things have to be. It was like we didn't have no choice.

By the time Muir pushed up my gown and got on me it all seemed inevitable. I didn't mind that it hurt a little. In fact you could say I almost welcomed the little pain, for the pain made the pleasure more real. And I thought if this is the worst you have to fear then you have nothing to fear. And something else I seen was that I had a greater effect on him than he had on me. A man gets so excited he just loses control of hisself.

Now the thing was that while we was making love I was thinking how strong and quick Muir was and how close we was, and I knowed I would enjoy it even more in the future when I got used to it. But at the same time I thought how *ordinary* it was. It was not the strange thing I expected. It was like you remembered things from a former time, that you'd knowed it all along. I wondered if deep down you could remember the moment your parents created you or the moment when all your ancestors created the generations before you going back to the beginning.

And I thought it must be the same in the future too. Our grandchildren and great-grandchildren would do the same and seem to remember what we'd done to create them. But all the time I was so relieved I thought of other things too. I thought of bright washing on the line blowing in the wind and grass on the hillside rippling in the wind. I thought of the way wind presses through the gap in the mountain and the stories of pigeons that used to fly through the gaps by the millions. It was silly the way I thought of trout flashing in the river and butterflies bouncing in a breeze. And I thought of birds that circle all in a swarm before landing in a maple tree.

Later, when it was over, Muir must have gone right off to sleep for next thing I heard was him snoring. I laid on his arm and thought about how things just went on the way they would. Didn't seem to have much to do with our intentions. Everybody said the war was coming and if it happened they'd be drafting boys from all over. I wondered if they drafted preachers. Surely preachers wasn't called on to fight. It would not make sense to order preachers to kill.

And I thought about where we would live. Would we continue to live in the Powell house with Ginny, or would Ginny move in with Fay and her husband? But this was Ginny's house. While Ginny was awful nice to me, I knowed she was a headstrong woman and a neglectful housekeeper. At some point we'd argue: I was sure of that. If Muir went off to war, I'd go back to live with Mama and Papa. Mama would need me to help her if Papa continued to work at Fort Bragg and Velmer and Troy was gone too. War would change everything, as the Depression had. I shivered, thinking of the bad things that might happen.

As I laid there I heard a knock on the side of the house close by and then another not far away. And then a tap on the far end. It sounded like somebody was walking around the house hitting the boards. Was it somebody trying to scare us? I'd heard of shivarees where they tried to scare new marrieds with guns and throwing rocks on the roof. Old houses popped when the boards got cold and shrunk. And then something thumped in the attic like a heavy weight had fell. Was it mice or snakes up there? There was rattles and taps all through the house, like it was haunted.

And then something screamed out on the pasture hill. Was it an owl or a wildcat? It sounded so close. And there was a screech, and a dog barked somewhere way off.

Fifteen

Now I know Ginny was a good woman. She may have been a better woman than me from some points of view. But she was a woman used to getting her way. And she was used to thinking she was always right. I don't reckon any woman ever got along perfectly with her mother-in-law, especially if they had to live in the same house. A mother-in-law wants to be the boss in her own house, and a young wife has to find her place and learn to be a wife to her husband.

Ginny read her Bible and religious magazines and talked about religion a lot, but I didn't mind that so much. She could talk religion as much as she wanted to for all I was concerned. It was little things that irked me, like if I started to straighten up the living room she'd say, "Don't you bother with that, Annie, I'll do it later." But of course she wouldn't. She'd let the clutter of newspapers and magazines build up on the floor and leave coats and dirty clothes throwed over chairs and on the couch. She didn't much want me to sweep, but she wouldn't do it herself. If I took up a broom she'd say, "Put that down; you're still on your honeymoon."

Though I was married now, I kept working in the cotton mill. Every morning I walked across the pastures to the church and caught a ride with Joyce Benson to the cotton mill. In the evening after work I always stopped at the house to see Mama before walking back across the pasture to the Powell house. If Mama needed something I could get it the next day at the store.

The first quarrel I had with Ginny come when Muir announced he was going with Papa to work at Fort Bragg. He'd not been able to find work at home and when a church invited him to preach they sometimes paid him nothing at all. And even if they did pay it might be only two or three dollars. I told him I'd keep working at the cotton mill and he could keep preaching. But no local church had invited him to be its pastor. And no man likes for his wife to be making more money than he makes.

With the war coming Muir thought he should do his part. Troy had joined up with the Air Corps, and Papa needed extra hands on the crew. Muir was thirty-six, too old to be drafted. And I don't think he wanted to carry a gun and kill anybody either. The army was building barracks and other buildings as fast as they could get the lumber and concrete and somebody to throw them up. "It's the least I can do," Muir said. "I can help build barracks and I can preach sometimes on weekends."

I think he also wanted to help Papa out too. Papa had encouraged him and helped him build the church on the mountaintop. And Papa had encouraged him over the years when he was courting me. Velmer was going off to barber school. And now, when Papa needed more hands to hammer barracks together, Muir seen that was the way to help him and serve his country at the same time.

But Ginny was not pleased at all when she learned that her son was going away to work at Fort Bragg. She'd always wanted him to be a preacher, and now that he was a preacher she insisted that he be nothing but a preacher. I don't think she wanted him to go work with Papa either. It was too much like he was joining my family and leaving her.

"I'm surprised you'd agree to that," she said to Muir when he told her he was leaving for Fort Bragg.

"I didn't agree to anything," Muir said. "I asked to go."

"And what about your ministry?" Ginny said. "You were called to preach."

"I can still preach on weekends if somebody invites me."

"No one will want a preacher that works faraway building army barracks."

"I think it's my duty," Muir said, "and my business. It's my chance to serve the country."

"What about your duty to the Lord?" Ginny said.

Now I know a wife ought to avoid quarreling with her mother-in-law at all costs. Once two women start fussing with each other there will be no end to it. Mama had told me many stories over the years about her arguments with Ma Richards. And, after all, I was living in Ginny's house. But when she accused Muir of failing the Lord I just couldn't keep quiet no more. I couldn't stand the way she took advantage of him to make him do what *she* wanted.

"He said he'd keep preaching on weekends," I said.

"He has no business being a weekend preacher," Ginny said. "He should be holding revival meetings, even if it's only in a tent or brush arbor. He should be making a name for himself. Besides, no church will want to give him the call to be pastor if he's off building barracks all the way across the state."

"He said he wants to serve his country too," I said. I could feel my blood rising and my tongue getting quicker.

Ginny turned like she was going to speak to Muir and ignore me. But then she turned back to me. "You seem awfully anxious for him to be away all week," she said.

"I think he should do what he thinks is right," I said. "It's not a matter of what I want."

"Muir has always been ready to run off and follow his fancies," Ginny said. "You don't know him as well as I do. He drove all the way to Canada once to get away from home and then come straight back. He nearly drowned trying to trap muskrats in the Tar River at the other end of the state. The last thing he needs is a wife to encourage him in his whims and fancies."

"The last thing he needs is a mama to treat him like a little boy," I said. I'd never been so mad at another woman. I could see how Muir had been burdened all his life by a mama that worked to control him, like he was just a part of *her* ambition and desires.

Muir stepped between us and said, "This is shameful. We must pray about this." He dropped down on his knees, and Ginny looked away and then dropped down on her knees too. I had no choice but to kneel down also. Muir prayed that there would be concord and love in the family and in the household. He prayed that the two women he loved would be friends and love each other. By the time he'd finished Ginny was crying and I had tears in my eyes too. All three of us stood up and hugged each other. Such a thing would never have happened in my family. Ginny was an emotional person, and all her anger was gone.

But I could see it was only a matter of time until we clashed again. She had such a strong will and was used to getting her way. I'd heard stories about all of the troubles she had with her husband, Tom, about the brush arbor meetings, about her going against his wishes. She was a woman who meant well, but she also meant to have everything on her own terms.

So when Muir left to go to Fort Bragg with Papa I moved back to Mama's. I couldn't bear to think of staying in the house with Ginny all week while Muir was away. And besides, I had to walk all the way across the pastures and get my feet wet every morning to catch the ride to the mill when I stayed at the Powell place. It was much easier to walk to the church from Mama's house.

"You don't need to move out," Ginny said when I told her. "You know you're perfectly welcome here."

"I think Mama needs me to help her," I said. "And it's easier to get to the cotton mill in the morning from there."

"You must do what you think best," Ginny said. When Ginny wanted to be cold she could talk like some high-class educated woman, not a mountain farm woman. It was always surprising to see that change come over her. Her family had always had more money than mine. But it was still surprising to see her act like a high-toned lady.

It pleased Mama that I was moving back to the house. While Papa and Velmer was away she had to take care of the horse and cow, the hog and chickens, all by herself. She had to make the garden and can peaches, hoe corn and gather fodder, chop kindling and carry wood for washing. She'd always done those things, since she was a girl on Mount Olivet, but she was getting old. Sometimes I was astonished at how frail she looked. When I got home from the mill every evening I helped her work. We picked blackberries at the edge of the pasture and canned tomatoes. I helped her wash windows.

Every month when she got the allotment from the government that Troy had sent home from the Air Corps she put it in a bowl on the top shelf of the china closet. I don't think she ever spent a dime of Troy's money for herself. The only money she spent was what she got from selling eggs and butter at the store. She kept that money in the drawer at the bottom of the china closet. When she opened or closed the drawer you could hear the coins rattling.

"Troy said to use some of that money for everwhat you need," I said.

"That money is to be saved for Troy," Mama said. "When he comes home from the service he will need to build a house for him and Sharon." There was a spot in the pasture near the big cedar tree where Troy had said he'd like to build a house. He'd showed me the level place where we used to play kick ball in the evenings after supper when we was kids. It was a perfect spot.

"I hope Muir will build a house when the war's over," I said.

"Let's hope it's not on the mountaintop," Mama said, and laughed.

IT WAS LATER in the fall when I begun to think about Ginny and feel a little sorry that I'd left her house and never did go back to see her. She was after all my mother-in-law and a good woman, however high handed she could act at times. She was Muir's mama and had been awful nice to me when I first got married and went to her house. It's true she wanted everything done her way. She wasn't like Mama at all. But then most people want things to go their way.

I kept thinking what I could do to be good to Ginny. I seen her at church and smiled at her, and once or twice I'd gone with Muir to visit her on weekends. But I knowed I needed to show more respect to her. It come to me I should go to visit her myself and I should take something; I'd take her a pie. We'd had a big crop of pumpkins that summer in the field between the orchard and the garden. When frost killed the pumpkin vines it looked like the field was full of orange moons and planets. I cut up one of the big ones and made three pies, and after I got off from work the next evening I took a pie and walked across the pastures to the Powell house.

It was a pretty time of year because the hickories on the hill was dark gold and the black gum trees was turning purple and some of the oaks was bright red. The sun was out but it was cool in the shade. I could smell apples on the breeze coming from the Powell orchard. It was cider-making time and I wondered if I might find Ginny making cider. She always made gallons of sweet cider in the fall.

But when I climbed through the fence and passed the springhouse I didn't see her by the cider mill. The press was standing beside the smokehouse and a basket of apples set on the ground nearby. She must be getting ready to crush the apples. Yellow jackets and bees circled around the basket.

Among neighbors and kinfolks we didn't even knock on the door in those days. We just hollered out to let people know we'd come and opened the door and walked right in. I wanted to seem friendly to Ginny and I called out "Hello" and stepped into the kitchen. But she didn't answer back and I didn't see her either.

"I brought you a pie," I said. After the bright light outside I couldn't hardly see into the living room. I figured she must be down the hall in one of the bedrooms. But just as I stepped into the living room my foot hit something and I stumbled forward and the pie went flying out of my hand. I fell on my knees and elbows, and when I got up and looked in the dim light I seen it was Ginny laying on the floor that I'd tripped over.

"Ginny, what's wrong?" I said. I bent down close and seen her eyes move. She made a gagging sound but didn't say nothing. She stirred one arm a little.

"What is wrong?" I said again. And then I seen the water on the floor. She had dropped something. No, she must have wet herself. She laid there helpless except she could move her eyes. It come to me she must've had a stroke: that was why she couldn't talk.

"I should get you to the couch," I said. Ginny was a tall woman. She was bigger than me and in later years she'd put on a little weight too. I tried to think how I could pick her up and get her on the settee. I tried to put my hands under her arms and lift her. She was so heavy I could just barely get her head off the floor. Even if I could drag her to the couch I couldn't lift her onto it.

There wasn't nothing to do but go somewhere for help. For there was nothing I could do for her. But something should be put under her head and a blanket or a quilt should be spread over her. It was cold down on the floor. I looked around the room and stepped in the mess the pie had made when it hit the floor. I tried to wipe the pie filling off my shoe before running to the bedroom. There was a quilt folded up on the trunk in her bedroom and I grabbed that.

Covering Ginny with the quilt, I told her I had to go get help. I'd run to Fay's house and I'd be back as soon as I could. We would lift her onto the settee. I don't know if she could understand me or not. But her eyes moved and I hoped she understood I was going for help.

I run out of the house and past the springhouse and the molasses furnace. When you're in a hurry distance stretches out ahead of you and the place you want to get to seems to retreat the harder you run. I crossed the pasture, climbed through the fence, and skirted the edge of the big gully. I climbed up through pines and laurel bushes to the field below the old schoolhouse. Limbs hit my face and pine cones rolled under my feet.

Fay and Lester lived in the house on Green River Road just beyond the church. I cut through the line of junipers around the churchyard and went around behind the church, thinking that was the shortest way. But they'd let all kinds of honeysuckle vines and briars grow up there and I scratched my arms and legs fighting a way through.

But when I got to Fay's yard I was relieved to see that Lester's car was there. He must have just got home from work. I run up the steps and opened the kitchen door. But when Fay and Lester come into the kitchen to see who it was I was so out of breath I couldn't hardly talk.

"Ginny," I gasped.

"What about Ginny?"

"In. . . the floor . . ."

"In what floor?" Lester said.

"Her house," I said. "Must've had a stroke."

Fay's face turned white as the sand in an hourglass. "Oh no," she said.

"You'll have to drive us down there," I said to Lester.

"Let's go," Lester said. "I'll get my keys."

Fay had her hands over her mouth. She looked around like she was confused. I handed her the sweater that was on the back of a chair. My chest hurt, but I was beginning to get my breath again.

"No," Fay said. "Somebody has got to go to the store and call an ambulance."

"We need to go see about Ginny," I said.

"I'll drive you down to the house and then I'll go call the ambulance," Lester said.

Fay run into the bedroom and got little Duane who'd started to cry because of all the excitement. He was only about two years old. "Everything will be all right," Fay said to him. After we got in the car it seemed to take forever to reach the Powell house. I got out and opened the gates three times and closed them after Lester drove through. Fay just set in the front seat holding Duane and wiping her eyes with the back of her hand. When we finally reached the house Fay and me got out and Fay put Duane in the back seat. Lester turned around to drive to the store where the telephone was.

Fay wouldn't go into the living room until I went in ahead of her. It was even darker in the house now and I couldn't see a thing as I looked into the living room. As my eyes adjusted a little I gasped, because Ginny didn't seem to be where I'd left her. Was it possible she'd moved or that somebody had moved her?

And then I seen her laying there under the quilt perfectly still. I'd misremembered where she was, maybe because I was so surprised and scared before. I pointed to her on the floor and Fay turned away like somebody had slapped her in the face.

Kneeling down, I said, "Ginny, Fay is here. We're going to put you on the couch." Her eyes was open and I expected them to move, but they didn't.

"Lester has gone to call an ambulance," I said. "We're going to take you to the doctor."

I thought I seen her eyes move and I bent closer. But her eyes was fixed, not looking at nothing. I put my ear next to her chest but couldn't hear no heart beat. I was going to tell Fay to help me move her to the settee but seen there wasn't no use now. Lester could help us when he come back. I didn't know how to tell Fay that her mama was dead.

"What is this mess on the floor?" Fay said.

"That's a pumpkin pie I made. I dropped it when I come in and seen her there."

"I don't think we can lift her," Fay said.

"We don't need to lift her now," I said.

"What do you mean?"

"Fay, Ginny is dead," I said.

"No!" she said and pushed me away. She bent down over the body and then stood up and walked to the cold fireplace and started to cry. The clock on the mantel chimed five o'clock. I felt guilty somehow, like it was my fault, though I couldn't say why. Maybe I should have come to see Ginny before. She'd been all alone down there. And then I remembered I'd have to tell Muir. I'd have to send a telegram to him at Fort Bragg. I hated to do that. Somehow it seemed my fault that his mama had died.

It was getting dark in the living room and I lit a lamp on the table by the couch. "You set down," I said to Fay. "I'll clean up this pie on the floor."

There was nothing to do but scoop up the sticky pie filling with my hands and put it back in the plate. And when I'd got up all the mush I would bring a wet rag from the kitchen and scrub the floor. And I'd take a towel and wipe up the wet spot by Ginny's body. It was what Mama would have done.

AS SHOCKED AS I was by what had happened to Ginny, so unexpected, so awful, I thought having to break the news to Muir was the worst of all. There is no worser news you can give a person than the death of their mother. Even though Muir and his mama had fussed and quarreled a lot, I knowed how much he'd depended on her. He was her favorite. All her ambitions and hopes had been placed on her younger son. I wished I didn't have to be the one to tell him.

And I admit I felt some guilt too. Not that I blamed myself for Ginny's death. I don't reckon anybody could have prevented that. No, what I blamed myself for was ignoring my mother-in-law all those months. After we quarreled and I moved out of the Powell house I'd left her alone. She was a proud woman, and she was determined to have her way, but she was still Muir's mama. I'd failed in my duty. Taking that pie down there after staying away so long seemed like a silly gesture.

Trying to think clear, like Mama would have done, I told Fay and Lester that I would get somebody to drive me to the store at the cotton mill to send a telegram to Muir and then I'd come back and help them lay out the body. I'd never done anything like that before, but as the daughter-in-law it was my job to help prepare Ginny's body for a funeral and burial. There had not been a funeral in my family since Ma Richards passed away when I was still a girl.

Lester said he'd drive me to the store hisself, but I told him he'd better look after Duane and stay with Fay who was on the couch sobbing. I would ask somebody to come and help lift Ginny's body onto her bed. Besides, somebody had to be at the house when the ambulance come, to tell them it was too late, they could just go back to town.

"You will need a cooling board," Lester said.

That was a name I hadn't heard in years. A cooling board was a flat thing made of wood on which a corpse was laid to be washed and kept straight so it would fit into a coffin. "I don't know where we might find one," I said.

"I'll go see what I can find," Lester said. "An old door might do."

I found a lantern on the back porch and lit that to carry across the pasture. Though I was familiar with the trail past the molasses furnace and across the branch and through the grove of pines to Papa's pasture, it all looked different in the glow of the lantern. Shadows swung around bushes as I walked like they was mocking me. Dew sparkled as if a thousand toads was watching me. A whippoorwill called somewhere up on the hill like a ghost lamenting some awful deed.

When I got to the house and told Mama the news she said she'd go right down to the Powell house to see what she could do to help. I don't know why I'd told Lester somebody would drive me to the store, for Papa was away at Fort Bragg and there was nobody else with a car or truck. I guess I was so stunned I just wasn't thinking. I give Mama the barn lantern to carry back to the Powell house and I took the flashlight. There was no choice but to walk to Lum's store on the highway and get Lum to drive me to the cotton-mill company store to send the telegram.

As I walked along the road, following the spot of light from the flashlight, I rehearsed in my mind what I'd say in the telegram. Would it be better to say that Ginny was bad sick and Muir should come home at once? Would it be better to say she'd had a stroke but not say she'd died? Or would it be better to tell the truth at once and say "I'm sorry. Ginny has had a stroke and died. Love, Annie." I kept saying over and over in my mind one short sentence and then another. In the end I seen I had no choice but to tell Muir the truth, however awful it was. If I told him Ginny had merely had a stroke he'd rush back home hoping to see her alive, and he'd find I'd not told him the truth.

Lum was nice enough to not only drive me to the store at the cotton mill to send the telegram, but he drove me all the way back to the Powell house. Lum was Ginny's cousin. He come inside to see what he could do to help.

Lester had found an old door in the shed and washed it off and dried it and laid it over four chairs in the living room. Mama and me helped Lester and Lum lift Ginny's body off the floor and place it on the door. She was almost as long as the door.

"You men go on about your business," Mama said to Lum and Lester. "Annie and me will wash her and put her in clean clothes."

Fay was still crying on the couch where Duane had gone to sleep and Mama suggested to Lester that he take Fay and the boy home. Once again I was astonished at how calm Mama was when things had to be done. When bad things happened she seemed to know just what to do. Her confidence and patience made the rest of us calmer too.

When the others was gone and we was alone in the house with Ginny on the cooling board Mama placed lamps on chairs around the body.

"Help me take off her clothes," Mama said.

I DON'T KNOW what I would have done without Mama's help that night. I'd never laid out a body before, but Mama had done it many times. She'd prepared Ma Richards for burial when she was just a young wife. And she'd helped neighbors with the sad ritual all her life. She started a fire in the cookstove and heated water and we washed Ginny thoroughly and soaked a handkerchief in camphor and laid it on her face. Ginny, who'd always been so spirited she was a little scary, was now growing cold as a lump of clay. All her enthusiasms and will and knowledge had vanished from the earth, or was returning to the earth. Except that a lot of it had been left in Muir.

I went to Ginny's closet and got what I thought was her best blouse and skirt. She'd always wore dark clothes, with fancy white blouses. I guess she thought of herself as a kind of deaconness or even minister. I picked her silkiest and whitest blouse, one with pleats down the front, and a long black skirt like she wore to church. And she had a silver brooch with amethysts that I pinned on the blouse. It was way in the night when we finished and I told Mama to go on home.

"I'm not going anywhere," Mama said. "Somebody has got to stay up with the body to show respect. You never leave a corpse unattended."

I went back to the kitchen and rebuilt the fire in the stove and made a pot of coffee. Mama added wood to the fire in the living room and we set on the couch sipping coffee and keeping our vigil. Mama talked about Ginny and her ways and her life in the house by the river. Mama talked more than I'd ever heard her talk before. She could remember Ginny from when she was young. Mama said that with her black hair and black eyes she'd looked part Indian.

"There was a rumor the Peaces was part Indian," Mama said.

"Then Muir is part Indian," I said.

"No shame in that," Mama said.

Later we both got quiet. I think Mama must have dozed off a little. But I didn't. I set there thinking how quick a life can be over. And wondering where do people go when they die. Do they just vanish? What is the meaning then of all the things they have done and thought, the things they wanted and cared so much about, all their dreams and hopes?

Far into the night with the house still the flames in the fireplace fluttered like they was saying something. I got up and put two more sticks on the blaze. And then I heard this noise. It seemed to come from the orchard or the pine woods above the pasture. It was a rush of chattering or mocking; it was a crazy sound. It come again like somebody afflicted out in the night raving and guffawing in the dark thickets. And then I knowed what it was. It was the kind of bird called a laughing owl. And it was shrieking and laughing at all the folly and foolishness of the whole world. With Ginny laying there cold and still it was reminding me how little any of us mattered, in the big dark silly and confusing scheme of things.

PAPA AND MUIR arrived just at daylight. I was afraid Muir would be awful upset, and he was. When he got out of the truck he hugged me with tears streaming down his face. I'd never seen a man so heartbroke. When he went into the house he took the handkerchief off

Ginny's face and kissed her on the lips. He dropped to his knees beside the body and howled with grief. No man in my family had ever done that, and I seen how different Muir was from the Richards men. I stood beside him and tried to think of something to comfort him.

After a few minutes Mama went to the kitchen and come back with a cup of strong coffee. "Here, you drink this," she said, and held it out to Muir.

Muir turned to her, his eyes veiled in tears, and stopped crying. He couldn't refuse Mama's offer and command. He wiped his eyes and took the cup.

"You'll need some breakfast," I said.

Muir cleared his throat and sucked in through his nose. "No," he said. "I'll make a casket."

Papa come forward and was about to speak. I know he was going to offer to help Muir make a coffin; but then he stopped. I reckon he seen Muir wanted to make the burial box hisself. Papa said he'd drive to the sawmill and get some cedar boards, and he'd stop at Lum's store and get brass handles for the coffin. Muir went with him, and when they got back Muir spent the whole day sawing and sandpapering and nailing together the coffin.

The cedar was the prettiest boards you ever saw, rosy pink and tan. Cedar takes a wonderful shine, and Muir sanded and varnished the wood. He carved Ginny's name with a chisel on the lid of the coffin. It was a pretty piece of work, and Papa stood by and let Muir do it. It was the careful and thoughtful work on the casket that helped Muir more than anything else. I don't know what he'd have done if he hadn't had that work to do.

While Muir was finishing the coffin Papa got his brother Russ and they took their shovels and picks and dug a grave in the Peace cemetery on the hilltop below Buzzard Rock. Some other men come to help them too, and by suppertime the grave was dug. Papa said they'd dug into rock, but it was soft rock, a kind of rotten rock, and they cut through it with mattocks and picks.

THAT NIGHT WHEN we went to bed I wondered what was the best way to comfort Muir. He'd not slept for two nights, and he'd worked all day on Ginny's coffin. Fay and Lester and little Duane come down in the afternoon, and Fay had helped me greet people when they come bringing platters of chicken and cakes and pies and casseroles. Everybody in the church seemed to bring something. Preacher Rice stopped by and most of the deacons. Everybody seemed to have forgot that they'd once voted to drop Ginny and her papa from the church membership. Her sister, Florrie, came by and said I'd done a good job laying out Ginny.

"I done it with Mama's help," I said.

"I'm sure you did," Florrie said. For some reason Florrie never approved of me, and even now she couldn't resist letting me know it.

When it come time for bed and everybody had gone home except Florrie, Florrie said she'd stay up with the body.

"You don't have to do that," Muir said.

"Well, I'm doing it anyway," Florrie said. She was as independent and headstrong as Ginny had been, though she never was as religious and intellectual. After her husband, David, had died she'd remarried twice. When the second husband had died, she married a Mr. Connell down in South Carolina. There was rumors that that husband had kept his hunting dogs in the house, and they would grab her biscuits or whatever she was fixing as soon as she took them out of the oven.

"Either them dogs go or I go," Florrie had said to him.

Mr. Connell walked to the door and opened it and said, "Go."

People told the story and laughed and said somebody seen Florrie come walking up the road from Gap Creek with a basket of dishes under one arm and her favorite laying hen in the other. After that she'd not married again.

When me and Muir left Florrie setting in the living room and finally went to bed I figured Muir would be so tired he'd sink into sleep at once. But he didn't. I guess he was so disturbed by Ginny's death and memories of his quarrels with her that he couldn't sleep. He laid in bed and talked about how Ginny had read the Bible every day and subscribed to the *Moody Monthly*. She could quote the Bible better than any preacher he knew. In the brush arbor meetings a long time ago she'd shouted and danced in the aisles, and spoke in tongues, and even rolled on the floor. She'd had what they called the baptism of fire. She'd quarreled with her husband, Tom, but that hadn't stopped her from attending the revivals and taking part.

As Muir talked and couldn't sleep I held him for what seemed like hours. I could hear Florrie stirring in the living room and kitchen. She must have made herself some coffee for I could smell fresh coffee down the hall. Far in the night I heard the laughing owl in the thicket again. Muir turned over and raised my gown and we made love like we never had before. I reckon it was the power of grief in him that worked so intense and loving. It was like he was possessed with some larger and forgotten power. And I was possessed too, like I was out of myself and in myself at the same time, and it seemed like I had sprouted wings. And it was like we discovered the true lesson from Ginny's death: that we was still alive and that it was our job and our joy to be loving and alive for each other. After that we slept.

NOW I EXPECTED that Muir would want to preach Ginny's funeral, like he'd preached Moody's. He'd done such a fine job after Moody died, and now he was even more used to preaching. And Ginny was his mama, and he was her favorite child. But the next day when I asked him he said, no, Preacher Rice was the pastor and it was the pastor's place to conduct the funeral for a member of the congregation. I reckon he remembered all the trouble with Preacher Liner about Moody's funeral and he wanted things to be peaceful and dignified with Ginny's funeral.

But Preacher Rice was not Preacher Liner, and when the pastor come to the house the next day to discuss the funeral he asked Muir if he'd like to speak at the service for his mother.

"No, you're the pastor," Muir said.

"Could you say a few words about Ginny before I speak?"

That took Muir by surprise and he hesitated for a moment, like he was about to say no, and then he said yes, he would like to say a few words for the memory of Ginny. I could tell how pleased he was.

After the preacher left, Muir took a tablet of note paper and a pencil into the bedroom. I seen he was going to write down some of the things he planned to say. He'd learned to write notes for his sermons, and I guess he wanted to say something good for Ginny's memory. I shuddered just thinking about having to get up in church to say some words at a funeral. And it was twice as scary to think of speaking about your own mama. My knees wouldn't have held me up for such a talk.

Muir must have worked for two hours in the bedroom on his sentences about Ginny's life. When he finally come out he looked tired but relieved. The funeral was to be that afternoon, and after dinner Papa and the other pallbearers put Ginny's coffin in the back of the Model A truck and drove it to the church. I put on my black dress that had the smocking below the collar. Muir put on his blue serge suit and a silver tie, and if I do say so myself he looked like a Philadelphia lawyer. He folded the sheets of notes he'd wrote and put them in his breast pocket. Fay and Lester drove down to the house and give us a ride to the church.

I won't even try to describe the funeral service except to say Muir's speech was awful fine. There was flowers all around the altar that people had brought, and the coffin made of cedar wood and varnished looked better than anything you could have bought. It was a fine fall day with sunlight streaming through the open windows mellow as the scent of ripe apples. The crickets called from the weeds outside, the ting of the meadow mole tolling and tolling the end of summer.

Muir had chose not to say the usual things preachers talk about at funerals. He didn't mention heaven and hell or the many mansions in the sky, the way preachers usually do. Instead he just give a long list of the things that Ginny had loved. It was the simplest funeral speech I'd ever heard, and maybe the best. He said Ginny had loved her house, her rose garden, and the stately junipers around the yard. She'd loved sewing white blouses and making black skirts. She loved giving to the poor and coming to the aid of anyone in need. She'd nursed the sick and comforted the bereaved. She liked to set on the Sunset Rock beyond the pasture and watch the stars come out in the evening. She'd done that since she was a little girl.

Muir said Ginny loved to walk along the river, all the way down to the Jim Lee Shoals, and she loved to climb the hill above the orchard when the gold leaves was blowing off the hickory trees there. She loved to read the Bible every day as well as stories in the *Moody Monthly,* and newspapers, and she liked to talk about all the things going on in the world. When she was younger she'd loved Pentecostal services where she danced and spoke in tongues.

Ginny had loved her husband, Tom, Muir said, however much she'd argued with him, and she had worked hard with him to make their place beautiful and fruitful. Ginny loved her children, and her grandson, Duane. She loved her sister, Florrie, and her brothers Locke and Joe, however much she might disagree with them about some things.

Muir said that Ginny loved words. She loved the feel of words, their textures, their hints and echoes. She loved to look up words in Grandpa Peace's big dictionary. She loved to talk and discuss the Bible and the most difficult problems in theology. She loved to tell stories about the old days, about her pa in the Confederate War. She loved to tell stories about Indians, and ghosts, and snakes and panthers, mad dogs and bears. She loved the church and community and worked to help out wherever she could.

And then Muir described how Ginny had helped him and encouraged him to become a preacher and even to build the church on the mountaintop. He was lucky to have had such a mother. There was not many dry eyes in the church by the time Muir set down.

It was the week after the funeral, after Muir and Papa had gone back to Fort Bragg to work, that I found Muir's notes for his talk at the funeral. He'd left the pages on the chest of drawers by the closet in the bedroom. It had been such a good speech I couldn't resist reading the notes for myself. The ending he'd wrote brought tears to my eyes again.

"Ginny loved the future," Muir had wrote. "She loved to think of the time when the war everybody predicts will be over and the boys will come home and the world will be at peace again. It was like she was already in touch with the future and could see her grandchildren and great-grandchildren and all the generations ahead and the world they would make. She loved to think of the generations who came before us and how they inspire the things we do and think every day. She loved to think that the best in people would always come to the surface. I was certainly the beneficiary of her love. I am indeed fortunate to have known her. I feel the strength of her love and vision even now as we are gathered here, even as we say good-bye to her on the banks of the river of forever."

Sixteen

One of the trickiest things for me after I moved back with Mama in 1938 turned out to be knowing what to do with Old Pat when she was in heat. Before that it had been somebody else's problem. Big as she was and smart as she was, she was still a healthy female. When she was spreeing she wasn't hardly at herself. She whimpered and run around and you could see blood under her tail. I didn't want her to run off and mate with some old hound dog or cur dog and have a litter of mongrels to get rid of. The fact was she was too big to mate with most of the dogs around the valley. Maybe that was why it hadn't happened yet.

After Troy left with Papa and Velmer to work at the barracks at Fort Bragg I had to look after Old Pat when I was at home. But I wasn't at home except on weekends. And then I heard they was hiring at the cotton mill down at the lake. No, I never wanted to work in no cotton mill where it was dusty and lint filled the air and your nose got stopped up with lint, and your hair and clothes got covered so you looked all fuzzy. The cotton mill didn't pay no more than the job at the dime store, but I could live at home and save the five dollars a week I was paying at the boardinghouse.

But the real reason I quit the job at the dime store and took the job at the cotton mill was that Mama needed somebody to stay with her while Papa and Velmer and Troy was away and Effie was now married and living in Flat Rock. She never would say it herself, but I knowed Mama needed help with all the work at home, and somebody should be there at night with all the tramps and hoboes coming through the country. Every weekend she could, Sharon come down when Troy was at home. But from Sunday night through Friday it was just me and Mama to look after the place.

I never was sure about predicting when Old Pat would start spreeing. But I come to recognize the signs when she got a little slower and less interested in people, including me. She'd yip and trot off by herself. I'd call her and she'd come but act like she didn't really want to be with me. I reckon a dog that's in heat can't really help the way she feels and acts.

The surest sign was that other dogs, male dogs, started coming around. The day I'm talking about was one of the warm afternoons in winter when the sun on the south side melts the hoarfrost on the ground and bleaches the old leaves pressed by rain and snow. You feel it's almost spring, though it's just February and there'll be snow to come and maybe blizzards. But because of the warmth and light everything seems open.

When I got home from the cotton mill around three-thirty there was this little dog following Old Pat around, growling and barking. It was bigger than a feist but littler than a terrier. It was just some kind of mutt, but it wouldn't go away. I picked up a stick and threatened it, and it backed away but then come back to Old Pat as soon as I turned around. Its thing was hanging down long as a wiener. I wasn't too worried about that dog, but then I seen two more. One was a beagle and one was a bigger hound, what is called a black and tan. I wasn't much worried about the little dogs, but the bigger one might actually mate with Old Pat.

I wasn't completely ignorant, for I knowed even a big dog like Old Pat could lay on her belly with her tail raised and let a smaller dog mate with her. A bitch in heat just wants to be bred, and she might do whatever is necessary to be bred. I knowed Old Pat couldn't hardly help herself and could push herself down on the ground so a smaller dog could reach her. It made me mad to see these dogs gathering in our yard and growling and snapping at each other.

Mama come out on the porch and I asked her what I was supposed to do. She never did let Old Pat in the house. Mama didn't believe a dog should ever be brought into a house. A dog would bring ticks and fleas inside.

Just then I seen this dog with long shaggy hair come out of the orchard. It was a collie or part collie, with pretty tan and white and gray hair. A taste of sick dread caught in my throat. The collie was not as big as Old Pat, but bigger than the other dogs. The little dogs barked at the collie and Old Pat pricked up her ears. The collie didn't come straight toward us but circled the yard, slipping under the Wolf River apple tree and then around the hemlocks. You never heard such barking and yapping as the little dogs made. When the collie got to the hemlock by the chicken coop Old Pat whimpered and started moving toward it.

"Here Pat, come here," I said in as strong a voice as I could. When she stopped I grabbed her by the collar. I knowed I couldn't really hold Old Pat if she lunged away. But she was used to minding me, and I hoped she wouldn't try to break away. It was a matter of my will against her instincts.

One of the places I could put her was in the cellar where we kept the canned stuff and sweet taters and Irish taters. But the door to the basement didn't close completely and there was no lock on it.

"Put her in the feed room," Mama said. I seen that was the best hope, for the door to the feed room locked from outside. If I could get her in there and latch the door, none of the other dogs could reach her.

"Here we go, old girl," I said to Old Pat. "You're going to have a new home." She was reluctant to go, but as I pulled her collar and talked to her she obeyed me. The other dogs barked and yelped and followed us. The collie snarled and snapped at the others.

"You get away," I said. "You get away from here." I was afraid Old Pat would break loose and I gripped her collar as hard as I could. If the collar broke, or she took a leap away, there was nothing I could do.

As we got closer to the barn I seen what was going to be my biggest trouble. I could lead her into the dark feed room, but how was I going to let go of her and get out and latch the door before Old Pat jumped back out? Mama must have seen that was the danger too, for she followed us out to the barn. "You take her inside and I'll latch the door behind you," she said.

"How will I get out?" I called over my shoulder.

"I'll go back to the house and get her water pan and something to eat," Mama said. "Then while she's eating you can slip out."

It always did surprise me how clear Mama could think when there was an emergency. When other people got excited she stayed cool as silver in a drawer. I'd heard Papa tell of the flood on Gap Creek when they both almost drowned. Papa said Mama never lost her nerve or good sense.

I opened the feed room door with my left hand, but Old Pat hesitated. "Come on, old girl," I said, trying to sound playful. Finally she stepped across the threshold, and Mama latched the door behind us. It was dark in the feed room, but streaks of light come through the cracks like pinstripes on a dark suit. The bins of crushing, shorts, cottonseed meal, oats, dairy feed, and sweet feed filled the air with their aromas. The strongest smell was the molasses in the dairy feed. Some of Velmer's steel traps hung on the wall, among the dusty old harness that was no longer used.

Old Pat whined and whimpered and the dogs outside barked and growled. One scratched on the door, and one pawed the logs at the base of the wall. The hound dog howled. I patted Old Pat on the head and tried to calm her down. I'd never seen her so restless. She yelped and walked under the ladder to the loft above where Troy's canoe was, then come back and pushed against the door.

When Mama returned she said she'd hand the dish of bread and streaked bacon through the space at the top of the door, then while Old Pat was eating she'd open the door and hand me the water dish. She was afraid the water would spill if she handed it over the door. I set the dish of bread and bacon as far as I could from the door and then took the water from Mama and placed it beside the bowl of food. Old Pat looked back at me before I slipped out, but I guess she couldn't resist the bacon.

When I got outside I tried to shoo the dogs away, but no matter what I done they come back. The big collie had found the toolshed beside the barn and clawed at the wall behind the feed room. I chased it out of the toolshed and closed the sliding door.

By then more dogs had showed up. There was a coal black dog that I hadn't seen before and a tall dog with curly hair that must have been an Airedale. I tried to run them off, but it didn't do no good. There was nothing to do but hope Old Pat wouldn't get out of the feed room, and the other dogs couldn't get in. I hurried to the milk gap to get the cow so Mama could milk. The dogs made the cow nervous, so Alice didn't let down her milk at first, but finally Mama got the milking done and put her in her stall.

It was later, just before dark, after I gathered the eggs in the henhouse, when I seen the pack of dogs gathered at the end of the barn yapping and snarling at each other. They kept looking up and it took me a second to see what they was looking at. It was Old Pat standing in the door of the barn loft. I thought at first she was going to jump out and maybe kill herself. But she didn't. It was just too far down and she had too much sense to try it. She stood there in the door whimpering and yelping, and the dogs below snapped at each other and whined and barked.

Later the next day when I got home from the cotton mill the dogs seemed to be gone. I could see the scratch marks they'd made on the door of the feed room. I opened the door but Old Pat wasn't there. I was so afraid she'd got out my chest felt sore. I climbed up to the loft and at first I didn't see nothing in the gloom there. And then a tail moved and I seen her laying on the floor beside Troy's canoe.

WHILE HE WAS working at the army base at Fort Bragg Troy had met a man who bred dogs and trained dogs for the army. I'd never heard of the army keeping dogs before, but Troy said they used them for guard dogs and to sniff out buried explosives and things like that. Troy visited the kennels at Fort Bragg and got to know the man in charge of the dogs. They talked about police dogs, and Troy told the officer about his dog Old Pat back in the mountains. The officer said he wanted to breed Old Pat to one of his finest German shepherds and raise the pups for the army. There was going to be a war soon and he needed all the bright German shepherds he could get. And he needed new blood for his kennel.

When Troy come back home the next weekend, not long after Ginny's death, he said he was taking Old Pat with him to Fort Bragg. It surprised me how much his announcement riled me.

"You can't just take her and give her to the army," I said.

"I'm not giving her to the army."

"She'll be killed when the war comes," I said.

Sharon was visiting that weekend. She patted Old Pat's head and stroked her neck. "She knows you're talking about her," she said.

"She'll just be used to breed more pups," Troy said. "The army needs more really smart dogs."

"How do you know what the army needs?" I said.

"Because I know the officer in charge. He wants to breed the most intelligent dogs he can find. When I told him about Old Pat he said they'd give anything to be able to breed her."

"Is he giving you anything?" I said.

"No, it's my contribution to the country."

Knowing that Old Pat was going to Fort Bragg with Papa and Muir and Troy put a chill on the weekend. We done some of the usual things. We drove up town for ice cream, and went to an all-day singing at Mountain Valley church. But all the time I kept thinking about Old Pat and how dangerous it was that she was going to the army base. We walked down to the river and Troy threw sticks into the water for Old Pat to swim out and bring back.

"How long will she stay with the army?" I said.

"Until she has her pups and they're weaned."

"That will be months and months."

"They'll take good care of her. They know just what to feed her," Troy said.

"Don't you think Troy knows what he's doing?" Sharon said. "After all, it's his dog."

I was so surprised my breath got short. It was the first time Sharon had sided with Troy against me. After all I'd done for her, letting her come down to the house for weekends, being her friend when Troy was away. "I hope you know what you're doing," I said to Troy, ignoring Sharon, and then I didn't say no more.

Late Sunday evening they left for Fort Bragg. Troy tied a rope to Old Pat's collar and tied the other end to the sideboards of the truck bed so whatever happened she could not be throwed out or jump out of the truck. Me and Mama stood in the yard and watched them go. Troy was driving and him and Muir waved to me as they drove out past the barn.

When Papa and Troy and Muir was gone away it seemed mighty lonesome around the house. It's the people that make a place seem like home, not the house and yard and land around it. Now with Old Pat gone too the place seemed even more deserted. The chickens still pecked in the yard and the hog grunted in his pen. The cow and the horse was still in the pasture. But the place seemed awful quiet, like it was empty. I'd moved back home to keep Mama company, but now she was the one who tried to cheer me up.

"They'll be back before long," Mama said as we looked down the road where the truck had gone.

"Not if the war comes," I said. "If a war comes, they'll draft Troy and Velmer and probably keep Old Pat."

"Maybe there won't be a war," Mama said. "Roosevelt said on the radio he didn't want war."

WITH EVERYBODY GONE all week except me and Mama I took to listening to Papa's radio. I'd never paid much attention to the news before, but every evening if there was time I'd listen to the news at six o'clock. I'd switch on the radio in its wooden cabinet and roll the needle in the lighted window to find a station in Greenville that was telling the news. It was terrible news. They spoke about Germans bombing London and other cities in England, about people being blowed up and burned. They told about the German army invading Russia. You never heard such awful stories, about whole cities burning up, people shot by the thousands. Every day I told myself I wouldn't listen to more news. But the next evening at six if I was near the radio I'd turn it on again. I couldn't help myself. I had to hear the news.

"Annie, you better turn that stuff off," Mama said. "It'll just make you sad."

"But what if we was to get into the war?" I said. "You know Velmer and Troy and Muir might all have to go."

"We're not in the war," Mama said. "Velmer and Troy and Muir are safe."

It come to me I should be comforting Mama, not the other way around.

Mama was as worried as me, but she never said nothing. She just tried to help others. I felt guilty for making it worse for her. But I didn't stop listening to the news.

And then in August we got a terrible shock. It was on a Friday, the day Sharon come for a weekend visit. It was a little card, the size of a business card, and it come in the mail. It had print on the back and the name Troy Richards was filled in with ink.

"This is to inform you that Troy Richards has joined the United States Army Air Corps at Fort Jackson, South Carolina." I was so surprised I thought it must be a joke. When I showed it to Mama she turned away and went and set in her chair by the door to the dining room.

"It must be a mistake," I said. "Or somebody is playing a trick on us."

Sharon took the card from me and looked at it. "This is no mistake," she said. "This is an official card. There is no postage stamp on the front. He has done this without telling me." She was so mad she slammed the card against her hip.

"Didn't he mention this to you?" I said.

"All he said was he was thinking about it," Sharon said. "I begged him not to and he said he would think about it."

"Why would he go now?" I said.

"He said that with war coming anyway it was better to get ahead of the game, to get a better deal. And it would be much safer to be in the Air Corps than in the infantry."

"At least he told you he was thinking about it," I said.

"I begged him not to."

When Papa and Muir and Velmer got home that night they said Troy had joined the Air Corps at the office in Fayetteville and rode with other recruits to Fort Jackson. The Air Corps had promised that he could go to mechanics school, and if he did well he'd be trained to work on airplane motors. It was the promise of work on airplanes that made him decide to go. Troy said that after the war, or if there was no war, he could work for an airline as a mechanic.

"I told him airplanes was dangerous things," Velmer said. "Stay away from airplanes. But he said that was true only if you flew in them. A fighter plane or a bomber might be dangerous but not to them that worked on the ground."

That weekend it seemed like the world had been twisted out of shape to some crazy angle. With Troy gone into the service it was like some terrible change had come over everything. The country was not at war, but everybody believed the war was coming.

"Where is Old Pat?" I said to Papa.

"They're keeping her at the kennel until she has her pups," Papa said. "After that I'll bring her home."

It was no fun to have Sharon at the house that weekend. I felt bad and I know Mama felt bad, but Sharon was more mad than anything else. She acted like Troy had joined the Air Corps just to spite her, like he'd slapped her face. Nothing I said seemed to cheer her up the least bit. We walked out to the milk gap to get the cow and I said Troy must have done what he thought was the right thing for his country.

"I told him that if he was going to join up we should get married first," Sharon said.

"Maybe he didn't think that would be fair," I said. "To marry you and then go away."

"It seemed fair to me. It was what I wanted."

I told her that Troy would write a letter soon explaining his plans. Now he was too busy to write.

"A soldier's wife gets special benefits," Sharon said. "But you have to be married to be eligible for them."

❧

AFTER TROY FINISHED basic training at Fort Jackson he was home for a few days. Sharon come down to stay with us and I don't think she ever left Troy's side. She was determined they'd get married either on this leave or when he had his next furlough. I don't know what all she said to him, but I'm sure she kept telling him one way or another that she wanted to get married now. Once I heard her say to him, "What if you was to meet some other girl way off from here?"

"Now you know that won't happen," Troy said.

Everywhere they went Troy asked me to go along. It was like he wanted me there to help him or protect him. It surprised me a little that he resisted getting married the way he did. Most boys going away in the army want to marry the girl they love. And Troy showed every sign of loving Sharon. He'd wrote letters to her from the Air Corps and he went to get her in town in Papa's Model A truck. He liked to spend time with her and Lord knows she was crazy about him, as most girls was. And Sharon's claim that she would get benefits if she was an army wife was all too true. And though nobody mentioned it, she would get insurance and maybe a pension in case of his death.

But something held Troy back. Nice and easygoing as he was, he could be firm when he wanted to be. I thought maybe he didn't want to start on a marriage and then have to leave. No telling where he might be sent or what might happen to him if a war come. He liked to finish the things that he started. He may have thought it was unfair to Sharon, as much as she wanted it, to marry her and then leave for who knows how long, maybe forever.

They was a good-looking couple together, her dark skinned and petite, him tall and broad shouldered with fair skin and wavy red hair. The army had made him more muscular, harder, more mature looking. He must have been the handsomest soldier in his unit.

But I wondered if he was really as attracted to Sharon as he seemed. Troy was the kind of person that had liked to spend hour after hour working at paintings, doing things like exploring the river in the canoe. He was curious about everything and liked to meet different kinds of people. He may have held back from marrying Sharon because he wasn't sure it was what he wanted. Deep down he may have sensed that she just wasn't right. That's what I decided later, when I seen how she acted. As much as she clung to him he may have seen that she was kind of spoiled.

Sharon certainly sulked after he was gone. She wouldn't hardly speak to me and Mama after Troy left on the bus to go all the way to Biloxi, Mississippi. I know she was terribly disappointed. I could understand that. She had her heart set on being an army wife and now she was left behind with nothing but a promise for a later time. I was glad when she was gone. We didn't see her again for many weeks.

What Troy was doing in Biloxi was studying mechanics. He was learning about airplane engines and all about airplanes, how to fix them and keep them running, how to load ammunition and bombs in them. From time to time we got a letter from him wrote with a pencil on tablet paper. He said he was having a good time learning about those big airplanes, bomber planes, and that much of the time it was raining there on the Gulf of Mexico. I think he loved what he was doing for he loved mechanical things.

I'll never forget the first Sunday in December of that year. It was the weekend Papa and Velmer and Muir brought Old Pat back from Fort Bragg. She'd had her pups and they'd been weaned. The army would raise them to train for guard dogs. Old Pat was so happy to be home and to see me she jumped right up on me, putting a paw on either shoulder. She like to knocked me down.

"Don't do that," I said, and give her a hug and pushed her away. I'd forgot how big she was. Maybe she'd growed a little bit while the army was keeping her. It was like having a member of the family back at home. I run my hand through her fur. We missed Troy, but it helped to have his dog back at the house.

After we got home from church that Sunday Mama and me put on our aprons and fixed dinner. We had fried chicken and rice as usual, and green beans and canned peaches. And Mama had made one of her special coconut cakes. When Papa and Velmer and Muir was home Mama liked to put on the best meal that she could.

Just as we set it all on the table Papa said he was going to turn on the radio to get the news. He'd got in the habit of checking the war news the same as me. There was always bad news from Europe and Russia and North Africa. I reckon he was getting more and more worried because Troy was in the Air Corps.

"We're about to eat," Mama said. "Let's not ruin dinner listening to bad news." So Papa didn't turn on the radio then, and we set down and he said the blessing. It felt good to have Muir and Papa and Velmer with us.

"How much longer are you going to work at Fort Bragg?" I said to Papa when we was eating the cake. Mama had made a fresh pot of coffee to go with the cake.

"As long as they keep building barracks," Papa said. "There's no work around here."

"A thousand recruits a week arrive at Fort Bragg," Muir said. "They have to have some place to put them."

"What are they going to do with all them soldiers?" Mama said.

"They're getting ready for war," Papa said.

"Who is getting ready?" I said.

"The army is getting ready. The president is getting ready," Muir said.

"The president don't want war," I said. "That's what he told us."

Papa took his coffee into the living room and turned on the radio. I was clearing dishes from the table when I heard him call out, "Listen to this!" I stepped to the door to the living room and heard an announcer all excited and talking about ships burning.

"The whole fleet is either sunk or burning," he said. "Hundreds, maybe thousands of sailors have been killed. There has also been an attack on Schofield Barracks and the air base at Hickam Field. We're still unsure of the extent of the damage. The Japanese are still attacking even as I speak."

"What is happening?" I said.

"The Japanese are attacking us," Papa said.

"Where?"

"At Pearl Harbor. That's in Hawaii."

Muir come from the bedroom and listened. It sounded like the whole island and the whole navy had been destroyed. "They will pay for this," Muir said.

We listened to the report and Papa slammed his fist on the arm of his chair. I seen Mama standing by the stove, but she hadn't said nothing. I knowed she was thinking about Troy.

"Troy is safe," I said. "He's in Mississippi. That's a long way from Hawaii."

But it was like she didn't even hear me. She knowed then, as we all did, that the war was here and whoever was in the service would be in it.

I stepped out on the porch to catch my breath and to get some fresh air. It was a cold gray day, and the mountains all around was dark. Old Pat set on the steps looking at a car stopped down the road halfway to the milk gap. I thought at first it must be having trouble and that was why it was stopped. I thought it was one of the Huggins boys from down at the cotton mill. I seen him bent over toward the dashboard and realized he was listening to the radio. He was so astonished by the news he'd stopped the car just to listen to what the announcer was saying. The day was so dark the taillights of the car looked especially bright.

Muir had come out on the porch and stood behind me. "All over the country people must have stopped what they are doing to listen to this news," he said. I shivered and he put his arms around me before we went back inside.

"Maybe it's not true," I said to Papa when I got back to the living room. "Maybe it's just a trick, like that story on the radio that Martians had landed in New Jersey."

"It's on all the stations," Papa said.

There was nothing to do but help Mama with the dishes. I heated water on the stove and piled dirty dishes in the pan. I tried not to think of all those burning ships and burning buildings they described on the radio. I wasn't sure where Hawaii was exactly, except it was out in the ocean, but the descriptions on the radio was as real as if it was happening right here.

"Who is that?" Mama said, looking out the kitchen window. I opened the door and seen Sharon getting out of her daddy's car. She run up the steps and grabbed me in her arms. "Oh, Annie, it's just so awful," she said.

"It is," I said. Old Pat come up to Sharon and whimpered. It was clear she remembered her.

"All I can think about is that Troy will go to war," Sharon said.

"Troy is far away in Mississippi," I said. But I knowed nothing I said would make her feel better.

"It's not fair," Sharon said. "It's just not fair."

Sharon reached out to pet Old Pat on the head, and that's when I seen the ring on her finger. It had a little diamond that flashed.

"You have an engagement ring," I said.

"Troy sent it from Biloxi," she said, and held up her hand so I could see it better.

"It's beautiful," I said.

"Oh, Annie, I'm so scared," Sharon said.

"Come in where it's warm," I said.

3·

WHEN TROY FINISHED the course at Biloxi he got to come home for Christmas for just a week. After that he'd go on to Sarasota, Florida, to study B-17 motors. The B-17 was called the Flying Fortress, but in his letters he referred to it as "the Fort." I thought that sounded funny, calling an airplane a fort, like it was a big wall of logs or stone.

By the time Troy got home there was Christmas decorations up everywhere as usual. Old Pat went with us to find a tree on the hill above the pasture and flushed a covey of quail out of the edge of the pine thicket. People had put lights in their houses, and stores in town had decorated windows with snowmen and Santa Claus. There was Christmas carols on the radio and people at the church was preparing the annual Christmas pageant.

But after Pearl Harbor everything was different. I don't think we felt much like celebrating Christmas. Boys was being drafted and them that wasn't drafted had plans to join. Velmer tried to enlist, but was told his heart was too weak. I reckon the typhoid fever had damaged his heart. Wherever you went people talked about the Japs and the Germans. There was rumors about German spies and Japanese spies and a story in the paper said a man with a cousin in Germany had tried to pour poison into the Greenville reservoir.

I think Sharon expected Troy to marry her before he went on to Sarasota. After all, he'd sent her a ring. Maybe he had planned to while he was still at Biloxi. If that was so, something changed his mind once he got home and seen Sharon. I don't know what it was that changed him, but she sulked and sometimes cried all through the holiday. I never seen a girl so disappointed. One time I heard them talking and Troy said, "It just wouldn't be fair to you, to marry and then leave you for who knows how long."

"You mean it wouldn't be fair to you, to be tied down in case you met somebody better?" Sharon said.

"You know that's not what I mean," Troy said.

Again Troy made sure I was with them everywhere they went. Muir was still working at Holly Ridge and wouldn't be home until the day before Christmas. We drove to Asheville to look for presents and see all the Christmas lights in the square. Troy bought Sharon a fine necklace with amber jewels like drops of honey. We walked down in the pasture to break limbs of holly off the big tree there.

"What we need is some mistletoe," Troy said. He looked at Sharon and laughed. "Some kissing mistletoe." He was trying his best to cheer her up and have a normal Christmas. He got Papa's shotgun and we climbed up on the ridge of Meetinghouse Mountain. Muir couldn't go with us because he was fixing a window in the Powell house that had been broke in a storm. There was some old oak trees at the far end, away from the ruins of Muir's rock church, that was just full of mistletoe. Troy said he wanted to shoot down enough to put a sprig over every door.

It was refreshing to get up on the ridge above the valley. With the trees bare you could see all the way up the river valley to Chimney Top and Pinnacle. "My feet hurt," Sharon said.

"I can carry you down," Troy said. "But you'll have to hold the mistletoe."

When we got to the far end of the ridge we come to an old field that was full of briars and weeds. The oaks with the mistletoe stood right at the edge of the field. Troy got out in the field so he could see better and raised the gun. But before he pulled the trigger we heard this droning sound and then something like a cough way off to the south. Troy lowered the gun and looked through the trees. He backed farther out into the field where he could see better.

"That airplane's in trouble," he called.

"How do you know?" I said.

"Listen."

The sky had been full of airplanes in recent weeks. I reckon they come from the Air Corps base south of Greenville. They had stars on their wings like war planes.

"He's not going to make it," Troy said. Sharon and me run out into the field to see what he was looking at. Far to the south we seen an airplane, with things dropping out of it. It looked like the airplane was blowing bubbles from its belly. "They're parachutes," Troy said. "They're bailing out."

"What's going to happen?" I said.

"It's going to crash," Troy said. Sharon screamed and Old Pat whined and yelped. I froze where I stood in the briars.

"Is there something you can do?" Sharon said.

The airplane coughed and then was quiet. Two more parachutes opened below it. The airplane rocked a little like it was hit by wind, but come on straight toward us. It got bigger and bigger and I could see the numbers painted on it.

"Is it a bomber?" I said.

"No, a transport, the kind that carries paratroopers," Troy said.

It was awful to watch the plane come on toward the mountain and know there was nothing we could do. It was like a nightmare where you're paralyzed and can't even speak. The plane rocked and dipped a little, but it glided right in our direction. The motors was quiet. "He must have dumped the fuel," Troy said.

I wanted to run but didn't know which way to run. The plane would tip to the right and then to the left. A breeze could tip it either way. I backed away toward the left since it seemed to be leaning toward the right.

"Lord help us," Sharon said. Old Pat yelped and run to the edge of the woods and then back to Troy. As the plane got bigger you could see the wheels folded up under it, and the open door on the left side. The windows in front reflected the sun and you couldn't see nothing behind them.

"Is it a Japanese plane?" Sharon said.

"It's an army plane," Troy said.

As the airplane got closer you could hear a kind of whistle in the air. I guess that was the sound of the wind on the wings. As it got bigger and bigger I started to run one way and then I run the other. And then I dropped to the ground as it went right over us. I could smell gasoline as the shadow passed just overhead. And then I heard a bang and thud and screech. When I raised my head I seen the plane turn sideways as it skidded across the briars and brush of the old field. There was a terrible grinding and rattling and swish like metal rubbed with steel wool, and then a squeal and bang as the plane slammed into a tree at the far end of the field.

Troy and Sharon and me stood up and Old Pat yelped. We looked at the airplane and waited for it to explode, the way crashed planes was supposed to do. But there wasn't even any smoke from the motors. We waited a long time and then started walking across the field, picking our way through blackberry briars and brush while Old Pat run on ahead.

"Let's be careful," Troy said. "There could still be a spark to set off an explosion." When we got pretty close we stopped to see if there was any sign of fire.

"They must have all jumped out," Troy said.

Just then Old Pat started yelping and whining. She was near the front of the plane, and then she run around to the side.

"What is it, Old Pat?" Troy called. She yelped and whined and stopped at the door in the side where the men had jumped out.

"What do you see?" Troy called. He moved closer and Sharon and me stayed behind him.

"I'm afraid to look," Sharon said.

Old Pat kept whining and Troy stepped to the door and looked inside. There was a strong smell of oil and gasoline but still no sign of a fire. Old Pat jumped through the side door and Troy followed her. "Oh my God," I heard Troy say.

"What is it?" I called. There was no answer, but then I seen Troy backing into the door pulling a body. The man was covered in blood. He wore a leather jacket with patches on the shoulders. His face was all bloody and mashed up. At the doorway old Pat grabbed the leather jacket in her teeth and helped Troy pull the body out onto the ground. Troy drug the man through the briars until he was well away from the airplane.

"He must have stayed with the plane and tried to land it," Troy said. "But all his men got out." He laid the pilot in the weeds between two clumps of briars. Blood was everywhere, covering his face and neck and seeping out from under the leather jacket.

"He'll bleed to death if we can't stop the wound," Troy said. He got his hands bloody trying to unzip the leather jacket. When he opened the jacket we seen the man's chest was covered with blood. More blood was coming through the shirt.

"I think his lungs have been punctured," Troy said. He was trying to think of something he could do. He looked around at the field and at me and Sharon.

"You could run to the store and call the ambulance," he said. I stood up and wondered how you call an ambulance to come way up on the mountain where there was no road.

"No, call the government, call the army," Troy said. He looked down at the pilot and told me not to go. He would go hisself since he could run faster. Sharon and me could stay with the man. And then he looked at the pilot and said it was no use, he was already dead. The bleeding had stopped and the blood was starting to dry. Just then we seen men in uniforms coming out of the woods.

"You get away from there!" one called. "Tampering with a crash is a federal offense." We backed away from the man on the ground as the company of soldiers advanced across the field.

THE CRASH OF the airplane on the mountain seemed so awful I wondered if I'd imagined it. Seeing it happen and trying to help the pilot and then being ordered away by the soldiers like we was criminals left me confused and more worried about Troy working on airplanes. We read in the paper the next day it was a training plane from the air base down below Greenville. When it got in trouble the pilot radioed for help, and all the men on board jumped out except him. It just happened that an army unit on a training patrol was nearby and got to the crash in less than half an hour. That was who had ordered us away. I had bad dreams about the awful cough of the engines we heard, and the blood on the pilot's chest, and the sound of the airplane crashing into the trees. It seemed the war had been brought right to the ridge behind our house, and there was no safe place anywhere.

MAMA GOT LETTERS from Troy in Sarasota and Sharon got letters from him also. He talked about working all day on the big B-17 motors, memorizing all the parts so he could take one apart and put it all back together in the dark. He talked about going to the beach and swimming in the ocean, and he asked about Old Pat. He said he was going to be posted overseas, but before that he was going to be sent to the factory in Massachusetts where they made the engines he was working on. And before he went to Massachusetts he'd come home on a furlough for a week. He'd be home for the Fourth of July. He didn't mention anything about marrying Sharon before he went overseas.

When Troy come home me and Papa met him at the bus station in town. Papa and Muir had come home from Holly Ridge for the holiday. Troy looked leaner than before, like he'd been working awful hard. And he looked older too. He told us that when he went overseas he'd be sent to England with the Eighth Air Force. He said the Air Corps was now called the Army Air Force.

"What will you do in England?" I said.

"Work on airplanes," he said, and laughed.

We'd read in the paper about bombing planes lost in Europe. But, like Troy said, he'd not be flying in them, only working on them. Sharon was already at the house when we got there. Her daddy had brought her and left her for the weekend. She'd brought her overnight bag. The engagement ring flashed on her finger. When Troy hugged her I seen there was tears on her cheeks.

Old Pat come running from up in the orchard and Troy noticed at once the right front paw was a little crooked. "What happened to her foot?" he said.

"She got caught in a fox trap over on the Squirrel Hill," I said. "But it's all healed up long ago." Velmer had seen a red fox on the hill and set a trap in the trail to catch it. When Old Pat stepped in it it broke some of the bones in her right front paw, but they'd healed up pretty quick.

Now we usually didn't do much to celebrate the Fourth of July, maybe because we was too busy working in the fields then. They celebrated in town with speeches and band music and fireworks, a parade down Main Street, and flags and banners all over the place. But out in the country there was never much notice, unless you heard somebody fire off a shotgun. But this year it was different, maybe because we was at war. All up and down the valley people had hung flags from their porches and second-story windows and even from their barns. You never seen such an outpouring of patriotic feeling. And there was supposed to be a parade at the cotton mill, with speeches and a picnic.

For some reason firecrackers was always something that local boys had shot off at Christmas. From midnight on Christmas Eve until late Christmas Day, the river valley would shake and boom and crackle with all kinds of firecrackers. Shotguns would be fired on Christmas morning and sometimes somebody would even light a stick of dynamite.

Just after the war had started before last Christmas, Velmer had bought up all the firecrackers he could find. He said that because of the war, gunpowder wouldn't be available until the war was over. All the gunpowder would go to the armed services. So he'd bought boxes of cherry bombs and six-inch firecrackers and big silver firecrackers called TNTs, and saved them in the attic where they would stay dry.

"Because Troy is home, we'll shoot them all on the Fourth," Velmer said.

"You better save some for Christmas," Muir said. "You won't be able to get any more."

"We'll celebrate the Fourth while Troy's at home," Velmer said. Velmer had his barber license and would be cutting hair at the army base in Columbia, South Carolina.

Velmer said the time to start fireworks was just at dark. Then you could see the flash of the explosion best. He'd wait until after supper and then light all the big firecrackers in the field across the road.

Troy said we'd go for a canoe ride after dinner, so me and Sharon and Muir helped him carry the canoe down to the river. It was a hot day and we took our bathing suits to go swimming. Old Pat was excited to see us get our suits. She run along beside us on the road, kicking up little puffs of dust with her paws. By the time we reached the sandbar and put the canoe down we was all covered with sweat.

"Let's go swimming and cool off," Muir said.

Old Pat jumped into the water ahead of us and splashed Troy, and he splashed her back. And then he splashed water on Sharon and me. Muir joined in and soon we was splashing water on each other. The air was filled with spray that made rainbows in the sunlight. We got to laughing with our hair soaked and our faces wet.

"Oh my God," Sharon screamed.

"What is it?" Troy said.

"It's gone," she said, and held up her left hand. "My ring is gone."

"That can't be," I said.

"How would you know?" Sharon said. "I've lost weight this summer and the ring was a little loose."

"It's got to be here somewhere," Muir said. We stood still to let the water clear so we could see the bottom. Old Pat come paddling over but Troy pointed to the bank and told her to go set. We looked down into the water but couldn't see nothing but sand. Troy got down in the water and searched the bottom, and then come up for air. Muir done the same, and they done it again and again, but couldn't find any sign of the ring.

"Maybe if we just felt along the bottom with our feet we could find it," I said.

Sharon cried and wiped her eyes with the back of her hand. "I don't think you planned to marry me anyway," she said.

"You know that's not true," Troy said, and took her in his arms. Me and Muir looked at each other and then looked away. I searched on the bottom a little more and then went back to the sandbar where Old Pat set.

THAT EVENING AFTER supper and after the dishes was washed and dried, we set on the porch talking until it was near dark. Sharon didn't say much. I guess it broke her heart to lose the ring and to know that Troy wasn't going to marry her before he went overseas. I felt bad for her but knowed there was nothing I could do to cheer her up. I'd married the man I wanted to and couldn't share her misery. She'd be left alone when Troy went to England.

Velmer got out his boxes of firecrackers and two boxes of kitchen matches, and him and Troy and Muir carried them out into the yard. Because Old Pat was sensitive about loud noises, as most dogs are, Troy told me to hold her on the porch by the collar. She was nervous, maybe smelling gunpowder. I gripped her collar and patted her head.

Velmer lit the first cherry bomb and throwed it into the field across the road. We watched the sparks of the fuse and then the flash, and the boom echoed off the trees on the Squirrel Hill. Old Pat jumped and whimpered. "It's OK," I said to her. "It's OK."

Every time a firecracker flashed and boomed Old Pat jumped. Dogs hear better than people and I reckon the blasts excited and scared her. I hoped she'd get used to the noise and calm down, and I talked soothing to her.

"Now this is a six-incher," Troy called. We seen the flare of a match and the sparks of fuse arcing through the air. Old Pat made a leap and jumped right out of my hand. She was bigger and stronger than me.

"Oh no," I hollered as she bounded away. "Stop her!"

I guess she'd seen the big firecracker in the dark and thought it was a stick Troy had throwed for her to retrieve. It may have been an automatic thing: if a stick was throwed, she was supposed to go after it.

Muir made a grab at her but she run around him. There was just enough light to see her dash across the road and seize the big firecracker in her teeth. She'd started back across the road when there was this big flash. Sharon screamed and the boom echoed off the mountain. "Oh no," I cried.

I run toward the road, but Troy yelled, "Bring a flashlight." Papa went into the house and brought a flashlight out.

"Let's get her out of the road," Troy shouted. Troy and Muir carried Old Pat up the steps and into the yard and laid her in the grass.

"She's still breathing," Troy said. When he shined the light on Old Pat's head I seen blood and hair and turned away.

"You don't want to look," Troy said. "Her tongue and jaw has been blowed away, and her mouth is burned."

"Is there nothing we can do?" I said.

"We must put her out of her suffering," Troy said. "You all go back on the porch."

Mama and me led Sharon back on the porch and Papa come out of the house carrying his .22 rifle. I figured Troy couldn't bear to kill his dog and would let Papa or Muir or Velmer do it. But I heard him say, "Give me the rifle." Troy ever did have a nerve of steel in an emergency.

"Let's go in the house," I said to Sharon and Mama. We'd just reached the living room when we heard the shot. Sharon winced and started crying again.

Troy didn't come inside for a while. I reckon he got a shovel and him and Muir dug a hole at the edge of the garden and buried Old Pat while Papa held the flashlight. Troy was all sweaty when he finally did come in. He washed his hands and face in the kitchen and come back to the living room.

Sharon must have been reaching into the pocket of her dress for a handkerchief when she gasped and cried, "Oh my God." We all turned to her as she held up the engagement ring.

"I forgot I put it in my pocket when I changed into my bathing suit," she said.

Seventeen

In the months after we got the telegram Mama wouldn't talk about Troy at all. I thought it was a good thing at first. While everybody else was asking about how he died and saying what a fine man he was and how handsome and talented, Mama just stayed quiet and kept her thoughts to herself. I could understand why she just wanted to go on with her work and not rub salt in the sore of her grief by reminding herself of her loss. Sharon, when she come to the house, would talk about nothing else, and Mama just let her talk.

I got mad at Aunt Lou who come with Garland one Sunday after dinner and asked Mama when she was going to have a funeral for Troy. Her and Mama had always been outspoken to each other.

"We can't have a funeral until the body is returned," I said.

"Who says?" Lou answered. "He's dead and the boy deserves a funeral."

"The army will send his body back after the war," Papa said. "The letter they sent says he's buried in a cemetery in Cambridge."

"Who knows when the war will be over, and who knows whether they *will* ship the casket back?" Lou said.

"We'll just have to wait," I said.

Mama had gone back into the kitchen where she was sorting silverware into the drawer under the counter.

"After the explosion I wonder if they found anything to put in that casket," Lou said.

"We don't need to talk about that," I said to her.

"I mean, how could they tell one body from another after such a crash," Lou said.

"Will you stop it!" I said, my breath short with anger.

Lou looked at me like I'd slapped her with a dirty dishrag. "I'm just trying to help," she said.

But as the weeks and months went by I seen it was not necessarily a good thing that Mama wouldn't talk at all about Troy. She'd sealed up her thoughts and her grief inside her and she wouldn't let any of us touch it. What she felt and what she thought was pushed down far from the light of day. Whenever I brought up Troy she just turned away and went on with her work. Before that I'd always thought of her work as soothing and healing for her, but it seemed to me she used work the way a drunk used liquor or a drug addict took morphine. Work was a way of avoiding herself and her connection to what had happened.

"You ought to rest some," I said to her. It was spring and she'd started working in the garden, planting the first peas and lettuce, dropping taters.

"There'll be plenty of time to rest," Mama said.

"When will you take the time?" I said.

She used to sweep the yard and scour away any chicken piles and sprinkle branch sand on the dirt once a week. Now she done it at least twice a week. She took her bucket all the way to Kimble Branch and carried back the sand. When she finished with the yard it was bright as a sheet of fresh paper. It was so perfect you hated to see chickens come back and mess it up.

The first change in Mama I noticed was that she started looking older. She'd always been so strong and her hair had stayed light brown. But after

Troy died there was streaks of gray, and by the next year her hair was almost all gray. In just a few months she looked like an old woman. She'd always stood so straight and had strong shoulders from all the work she'd done. And now her back was bent and her shoulders slumped, like she was carrying a great burden.

And then I noticed she'd act different. She would suddenly snap at you. She had always been kind and polite, but sometimes she'd turn sarcastic. If I made a suggestion, she'd blurt, "Are you telling me what to do?" And sometimes she'd forget things too. She'd always been the kind of person who never forgot nothing. She could remember what frock she wore to the first day of school on Mount Olivet. She could remember what Ma Richards had said to her on Gap Creek. But one Saturday the next summer I looked in the egg basket in the dining room and seen it was nearly full.

"Why have you not took the eggs to the store?" I said.

"I did," Mama said.

"You ain't."

"I reckon I know what I've done," Mama said.

When I showed her the basket full of eggs she got flustered. She'd forgot to take the eggs and butter to the store that week. That had never happened before. The money she got from the eggs and butter was her money. All her life she'd depended on that money, and she'd forgot it.

From time to time I'd find a pot boiling on the stove that she'd forgot. That can happen to anybody of course, but it was not the kind of thing that had happened to her very often. She'd always been able to do several things at once, as a woman has to, a woman that has took care of a house and raised younguns and worked on a farm and canned things for winter all at once. The beans that got burned and the water that boiled away didn't bother me at first. That could happen to any of us, especially if we was worried and tired.

But one day I come into the kitchen and Mama was standing in front of the stove watching water boil in a saucepan. Fire was blazing in the stove and the kitchen windows had steamed up. The bag of grits was open on the counter and I seen she must have been fixing to make grits for supper.

"The water's boiling," I said.

Mama looked like I'd woke her up. "I hate grits," she said. She kept standing there, and it come to me she'd forgot what she was doing.

"Here," I said, and picked up the bag of grits.

"I'll do that," Mama said, and took the bag from me.

Mama had always liked to be in charge of her kitchen, but she appreciated help too, especially when I helped her fix dinner or wash the dishes or mop the floor at the end of the day. But now she acted sometimes like she feared I was trying to take over the kitchen. If I started to mix batter for corn bread, she'd say, "I'll do that" or "Will you dump these peelings in the backyard?" It was a side of her I'd never seen before. She acted like she was afraid I'd try to run her house while Papa and Velmer and Muir was away.

One time I seen she was out of sugar, and when I got off from work at the cotton mill I stopped at the store and bought a five-pound bag of sugar. But when I reached home and put the bag on the counter Mama said, "Where did that come from?"

"You're out of sugar," I said.

"That's not the kind of sugar I use," Mama said.

"It's exactly the kind of sugar you use," I said. "See, it's Diamond Brand."

"I never used that in my life," Mama said.

"It's what you always used."

"Are you telling me I don't know what I use?" Mama snapped.

"I know what you use," I said, but seen I shouldn't have argued with her. It just made her mad.

"Are you out of your mind?" Mama said. "Have you completely lost your mind?" I didn't say nothing more, for it wouldn't have done no good.

Mama had always been the most patient and kind person I'd ever knowed. She almost never lost her temper, and she helped everybody that she could. She give meals to hoboes and beggars and cooked dinner for the preacher. She made clothes for her children and worked like a man in the fields and done everything she could to make us healthy and comfortable. And some of the time she was still like her old self, calm and attentive. But her temper got short more quick and more often. She'd lash out all of a sudden at the least little thing. A loud noise would bother her. And sometimes if she was looking right at you she couldn't hear what you said. She was by herself most days while I was at work. I started to worry about her, and I worried about what I could do for her.

One Sunday when Papa was home I told him I was a little concerned about Mama, that she was acting strange.

"She's getting old, like all of us," he said.

Papa had always refused to admit that Mama got sick. He'd get mad if she was sick. I reckon it was because he depended on her so. He couldn't stand to think that she was sick. He was irritated by the idea that she was not well, and he refused to admit there was anything wrong with her.

And Mama was the kind of person that tried to ignore her own sickness. All her life she'd just brushed aside whatever fever or headache or cold she had. She waited on other people that was sick. She'd nursed Papa when he had pneumonia and took care of Mr. Pendergast and Ma Richards when they was dying. She helped all us younguns when we had measles and mumps, whooping cough and scarlet fever, chicken pox and pleurisy. If she got sick she said nothing and went on with her work. And most of the time she just throwed the sickness off. Ignoring it was the best medicine. That was how strong she was.

But this time was different. She insisted on working, but I'd never seen her so weak. If she set down it took her a big effort to push herself up. And it was like she had to remember how to get up. One evening she went out to gather eggs in the henhouse while I was peeling taters for supper, and when she didn't come in for a long time I waited and finally figured I'd better go see about her. When I got beyond the hawthorn bush I found her standing in front of the chicken house looking toward the big walnut tree. She was holding the eggs she'd collected in her apron and looking like she'd lost something.

"You better come in," I said. "It's getting cold out here."

"I'm trying to remember where the guinea nest is," Mama said.

"You don't have no guineas," I said. "You haven't had guinea hens for years."

"I have to find the nest," Mama said. "I don't want the eggs to rot."

I seen it was better not to argue with her. She'd not had guineas for ten years, since a mink got into the henhouse and killed all her guinea hens.

"You go in and get warm," I said. "I'll look for the guinea eggs later."

Because Mama had always worked hard she slept well at night. She was never one to stay up all night reading the way her mama had done. But one night that next winter I woke around two o'clock in the morning and thought I smelled smoke. I got up and put on a housecoat and when I opened the bedroom door I seen a light in the living room. I wondered if Papa or Muir had come home in the night and started a fire. Or I thought maybe something had caught fire. I hurried to the living room and there set Mama in her rocking chair wrapped in a blanket. Wind pushed against the side of the house and rattled the windows, and a little smoke escaped from the fireplace. The wind must have been from the southeast, for that was the direction that made the fireplace smoke.

"It's smoky in here," I said.

"Can't help it," Mama said. "It's a windy night."

"It is," I said, and stood with my back to the fire to warm my butt.

All wrapped up in the blanket Mama looked like some figure out of the Bible. I'd never seen her setting up in the middle of the night before, unless somebody was sick and she was nursing them.

"Sometimes I just want to scream," Mama said. "The headache's busting behind my forehead and the blood is thundering behind my ears."

"Did you take some aspirin?"

"And I can't sleep. Nobody could sleep with such a headache."

"I'll get you some aspirin," I said. I went to the kitchen to take two aspirin from the bottle on the shelf and I got a glass of water. When I brought them to Mama she waved me away.

"Aspirins won't do no good," she said.

"What you need is some coffee," I said. When I had a headache a cup of coffee was the thing that made it go away fastest.

"Coffee won't help," Mama said.

I made her take the two aspirins and then I went to the kitchen to start a fire in the stove. It took me several minutes to get the water boiling for coffee. I hoped that by the time the coffee was made Mama would be asleep, but she wasn't. She set by the fire looking at the flames like the fire was a moving picture. I know a fire can look like whatever you imagine it to be, a road winding way back into the mountains, a storm at sea, a crowd of people waving.

"The church at Gap Creek was built with bootlegger money," Mama said, like she could see the church in the flames.

"That's what I've heard," I said.

"I reckon bad money can go for a good purpose," Mama said.

I thought maybe she was feeling better because she was remembering the old days on Gap Creek when she was first married. But the next thing she said was, "I won't never see that place again."

"Of course you will," I said.

Mama drunk some of the fresh coffee and I drunk a cup, and I set up with her until it was almost daylight. But the headache didn't go away.

The aspirin had no effect, and neither did the coffee. I got her to go back to bed finally and then I fixed breakfast and went to work.

Mama didn't go to church the next Sunday. Papa and Muir went to church, but I stayed at the house with Mama. And I fixed dinner while they was away. Mama tried to help and I let her do what she could. But she found it hard to keep her mind on whatever she started. She begun to scrape some carrots, but I found her standing with the scraper in her hand and looking out the kitchen window.

To my surprise Papa brought the preacher back to the house for dinner. It was like Papa didn't think Mama was sick. He acted like if he just went on as usual she wouldn't be sick. Mama had fixed dinner a hundred times for different preachers, but now she couldn't even fix dinner for herself. But I'd killed and fried a chicken and made rice and biscuits, gravy and peas, and opened a can of sliced peaches the same as Mama would have. But I hadn't made a coconut cake. I didn't have time for that.

I got the table ready while the men talked in the living room by the fire, and I hoped everything would go like normal. When we all set down at the table the preacher said grace, but I noticed Mama didn't even bow her head. That sent an icy splinter through my bones. When we started eating the preacher looked at Mama and said, "Mrs. Richards, I hope you're feeling better."

"I don't feel no better," Mama said. She said it like she resented being asked how she felt. It was completely unlike Mama to answer the preacher in that tone of voice.

"Would you like a biscuit?" I said, and passed the plate to Preacher Rice.

Muir seen that Mama wasn't at herself, and he tried to steer the conversation in another direction. "I like the new electric lights in the church," he said.

"It makes a big difference," the preacher said. "Now I can actually read my text at the night service."

"Lantern light is mellow," I said.

"It's a lot easier to read scripture by an electric light," the preacher said.

"Someday we ought to replace the woodstove in the church with a furnace," Papa said.

"When the war's over and the soldiers come home we can add onto the church," the preacher said. "Maybe we can put in new windows and build a Sunday school building. When this war is over we'll start a lot of things."

I wished the preacher hadn't mentioned the war and the boys coming home. It broke my heart to think Troy wouldn't be returning except in a casket. I hated for anybody to remind Mama of the war and of Troy.

"Maybe the Depression will come back after the war," Papa said.

"The economy is booming," the preacher said. "There may be a slowdown, but there'll never be a Depression again. I don't think the Lord will let it happen."

Mama didn't say nothing else throughout the meal, and she didn't hardly eat nothing either. Whatever was wrong with her it had killed her appetite. For dessert we had peaches and vanilla wafers, but she didn't eat none.

After everybody got up from the table I helped Mama to the living room, and then went back to the kitchen to wash the dishes. When I heard the preacher speak to Mama again a shadow of sick dread passed through me.

"Mrs. Richards, I'll keep you in my prayers," the preacher said. "The Lord will look after his own."

"The Lord didn't look after Troy," Mama said.

"It's hard for us mortals to understand the ways of the Lord," the preacher said.

"I prayed every day for Troy and it didn't do no good," Mama said.

There was quiet in the living room and I felt ice sink through my legs into my feet.

"Julie's not feeling good," Papa said.

I dried my hands and hurried into the living room. "Mama needs to rest," I said. I helped her up and led her to the bedroom. As soon as we was out of the room the preacher started talking about the war again.

When I took Mama to the doctor in April of 1945 he couldn't find what was giving her the headaches. He said it must be a migraine. It was a migraine that made her confused, made her act strange. Dr. Fauntleroy scratched his head and said if the headaches didn't go away he'd send her to the hospital in Asheville for x-rays. He give her some pain pills and said he expected the headaches would clear up. By then it was late spring of 1945.

Sharon come down one weekend to visit. I wished she hadn't come because she reminded Mama of Troy. When she arrived I whispered to her that Mama had been sick and it was important not to upset her.

"I didn't plan to upset her," Sharon said.

"I know you didn't."

Sharon had brought Mama a box of candy, one of the big samplers that had been hard to get since the war started. "It's a sign that the war is almost over, that you can get chocolate again," Sharon said.

"I pray that the war will be over soon," I said.

"The other boys will be coming home," Sharon said, and I seen a tear in her eye.

When Sharon give the candy to Mama, Mama nodded and set the box on the table beside her chair. It surprised me that she didn't thank Sharon. I knowed she'd lost her appetite for almost everything, but Mama had always been the most polite person I'd ever seen.

"How are you feeling, Mrs. Richards?" Sharon said. Mama looked at her without answering. "I hope you're feeling better." Mama still didn't speak and Sharon went on and told her she'd quit working at the dime store and now worked as a sales clerk at Efird's department store. She said she enjoyed selling clothes, now that the store could get clothes again.

"What are you doing here?" Mama said.

Sharon looked at me and then turned back to Mama. "I'm Sharon," she said. "Sharon Peace that was engaged . . ." Sharon stopped and turned to me. I thought she was going to cry, and I thought I was going to cry too. It had been several months since she'd come for a visit. But even so I was stunned that Mama would say that to her.

Since we didn't have a telephone I had to walk down to the store on the highway the next week to call Dr. Fauntleroy and tell him Mama was no better and seemed a little worse. I had to wait a long time before he come to the phone. When I told him how Mama had acted to Sharon he said it was time to take her to Asheville for an x-ray. And when they'd done the x-ray it would be time to bring her back to see him.

"Is she continent?" he said.

"What?"

"Does she wet herself?"

"Only sometimes," I said.

As soon as the doctor hung up I tried to think how I'd get Mama to Asheville. We could catch the bus at the store, but how was I going to get her to the store? She couldn't hardly walk without falling. I put another dime in the slot and called Effie in Flat Rock. When she finally answered the phone I told her her and Alvin would have to drive Mama from the house to catch the bus.

"We won't drive her to the store," Effie said.

"Why not?" I said. "Somebody has to."

"Now that we can get gas we'll drive her to Asheville. Mama's in no shape to get on and off a bus anyway."

If Effie had been there, I would have hugged her and kissed her. She must have heard in my voice how scared I was. She must have been scared herself. For all our lives Mama had never been really sick before.

At the hospital in Asheville they put Mama in their machine and took pictures of her head from every side. She'd never had an x-ray before. To calm her down I told her it was just like having your picture made. Except this was a picture of the inside of your head.

"Maybe there ain't nothing in there," she said. It was good to see her try to be funny.

After they made the x-ray she talked to the doctor in a white coat who asked her to stand on one foot and then the other. He asked her to look at the point of a pencil and he moved it back and forth from left to right. Then he asked her what day of the week and month it was. When Mama said it was a silly question and she wouldn't answer it he wrote something down on his clipboard.

When we got Mama home that day she had wet herself. I took a towel and dried the backseat of Alvin's car the best I could. After that I put a towel in the chair for her to set on. And I found myself washing almost every day, the way you do when you have a baby and lots of diapers and sheets to clean. Three days later I walked down to the store and called Dr. Fauntleroy. I could tell from the way he said hello that he didn't have good news.

"Annie, as you know, your mother is very sick," he said.

"She has never been sick before."

"That may be," he said. "But she's sick now. I'm afraid she has a brain tumor."

"Is it cancer?" I said.

"The x-ray can't tell if it's malignant or not."

My mouth felt dry as sandpaper. My tongue stuck to my lower lip. "How big is it?" I said.

"Almost the size of a large egg. I don't know how fast it's growing. She may have had it for some time."

"What should we do? What can we do?"

"That's for you and your family to decide. Surgery is the usual option. It could be removed, hoping, if it's cancer, the malignancy hasn't spread. If it has spread, there's not a lot that can be done. Talk it over with your father and the rest of your family and let me know what you decide."

As I walked home I kept repeating in my mind what Dr. Fauntleroy had said. I was hardly aware of the cars passing me until Carl Whitmire stopped in his pickup truck and offered me a ride to the church. I hope I thanked him when he let me out, but I don't remember. All I could think of as I walked to the house was of that dark tumor the size of a big egg that showed up on the x-ray.

At the house Mama was laying on the floor in front of the fireplace. I reckon she'd got up to walk to the bedroom where the pee pot was and had fell. It took all the strength I had to get her back into the chair. And then I had to get her up again to change her clothes. I knowed then I could never leave her alone again.

When Papa and Velmer and Muir come home that Friday I told them what the doctor had said about the size of the tumor and about the operation that needed to be done.

"I don't think that doctor knows what he's talking about," Papa said. "What if he's wrong and they saw open her head for nothing?"

"Something bad is wrong with her," I said. "Anybody can see that."

"Did he tell you how likely it was she would be cured?" Muir said.

"He didn't say."

"What is the risk of doing nothing?" Velmer said. "Sometimes a tumor will go away."

"I don't think this is going away," I said.

"Julie may be just run down," Papa said. "What she needs is time to build up her strength. Now that the weather is warmer she'll get better."

I know that Papa loved Mama, but for some reason he couldn't stand to think of her being sick. She'd always took care of him and the rest of us. He refused to consider just how sick she was. I seen he was going to keep pretending it was just something temporary, like a bad cold. It surprised me how stubborn he was about it.

When Effie come that Sunday she said she agreed with me: if there was any chance of helping Mama by operating on her brain and taking out the tumor, then it had to be done.

"What if it left her without any sense?" Papa said.

"It's the only chance she has to live," I said.

"Where would they do the operation?" Muir said.

"Dr. Fauntleroy said the best place to take her is to the Baptist Hospital in Winston-Salem."

"That's a long way off," Velmer said.

"It's what has to be done," I said. I seen that Muir and Velmer had come over to my side. That was four of us against Papa and he had to give in. I think he also seen it would have to be done.

"How will she go there?" Effie said.

"She'll have to be took there in an ambulance," I said. "She's too sick to ride that far in a car."

That night instead of sleeping Mama kept talking about the old days on Gap Creek. She remembered the awful flood on Christmas when both her and Papa had almost drowned. "There's water coming in under the door," she said, and pointed to the door to the front room. It took me a minute to see that she thought she was still back there in Mr. Pendergast's house.

"There's no water," I said. "Look, the floor is dry."

"If it gets to the hearth, it'll put out the fire," she said.

"You're at home," I said. "There's no flood."

"Hank, where are you?" she called. I bent down and looked into her face, and then she seemed to remember where she was.

"You was just dreaming," I said.

"Hank left me in the middle of that flood," she said. "I thought he must have drowneded."

I put my hand on hers and asked if she wanted a cup of coffee. She shook her head.

Eighteen

It took a while for Dr. Fauntleroy to arrange the operation in Winston-Salem and to schedule an ambulance to take Mama to the hospital there. By then the war with Germany was over. President Roosevelt had died back in April, but I was so concerned about Mama I hadn't hardly noticed. The day the ambulance come for Mama it rained so hard the road looked like a river. Water stood in pools in the yard. Rain fell out of the sky in sheets. Everything seemed to be washing away.

The ambulance was a kind of gray-green, the color of snot. It backed up to the back porch and one of the attendants stepped out in the mud where we throwed dishwater and scraps for the chickens. He tried to wipe his shoes on the steps. The driver got out too and they opened the back door of the ambulance as rain and runoff from the roof soaked them and they pulled out a stretcher. I led them into the living room where Mama set in her chair.

"Sorry to drip on everything," one of the men said.

"That's OK," I told him.

When Mama seen the men in white coats with the stretcher she give a kind of cry and turned away.

"They're going to take you to the hospital," I said. "At the hospital they're going to make you well." I'd not told her she was going all the way to Winston-Salem. There was no use to tell her that in her condition.

"No," Mama said. "I want to stay home."

"Don't you want to cure your headache?"

Mama didn't say no more. She looked away from me toward the fire.

"I'll be coming with you," I said. "And I'll stay with you."

With the help of Velmer and Muir we finally got Mama onto the stretcher. She looked tiny once she was laying there under the white sheet. She'd fell off more than I'd realized. She'd always been strong and worked so hard, it was hard to believe it was her. Her hair spread out on the pillow. I got my coat and overnight case and followed them out the back door. I held an umbrella over Mama as they slid the stretcher into the ambulance, and then I climbed in and set on a kind of jump seat beside her.

After they closed the door and started driving out of the yard I seen Mama trying to look out the window. She turned to look at the house and yard and the arborvitae tree as we drove away. I think maybe she knowed it was the last time she'd ever see the place. She looked until we went around the bend and the house and barn was out of sight. And then she closed her eyes.

Papa and Velmer and Effie and Alvin followed us in Alvin's car—Muir had volunteered to stay at the house and take care of the cow and horse and chickens. It was raining so hard you couldn't hardly see them through the back window. I held Mama's hand and hoped she'd sleep on the trip. I'd give her one of the pain pills Dr. Fauntleroy had prescribed. The ambulance bounced on the rough muddy road, and Mama opened her eyes and then closed them again.

The trip to Winston-Salem was one of the strangest things I'd ever done. We was going all that way at such an expense and we didn't even know if it would do any good. I'd never gone that far from home in my life, and neither had Mama. I don't reckon Mama had ever traveled farther than Asheville. I kept my eyes on Mama but she seemed to be asleep, or half asleep. It was a shame she was taking her first trip and didn't even know it, or was too sick to enjoy it.

That drive is all a blur to me now, of driving through towns and getting splashed with the spray from big trucks, of winding around and around the curves on the highway down out of the mountains. My ears popped and I thought I was going to throw up as we turned and lurched. I swallowed and set real still to make my stomach settle. I expected all the rocking and turning to wake Mama up, but it didn't.

When we got down into the foothills it was still raining, but I was sweating. It felt like there was a heater on in the ambulance. The windows got fogged up and I wiped the one closest to me to look out. I wondered if I'd took a fever. It was steamy hot. And then I seen the heat was coming from the outside. As we got down out of the mountains into the flat country it got hotter and hotter. I wiped my forehead with the back of my hand.

We passed through little towns and big towns. We passed towns with water tanks and grain elevators. We passed a pile of sawdust that was burning, and we run alongside a railroad track and passed a train. There was so many soldiers on the train you could see them standing up and looking out the windows. We crossed a long bridge over a river that was all pimpled with falling rain.

When we finally did get to Winston-Salem it took us forever to wind around the streets to get to the hospital. The place had a special smell that filled every inch of air. It was a scent I knowed but couldn't name. And then I recognized it was tobacco. There was long brick buildings that was warehouses for tobacco.

When we finally got Mama into a room in the hospital it was after dark. She'd gone to sleep in the ambulance and had not waked up when they wheeled her into the elevator and up to the fourth floor. I waited with her in the room for the doctor, and Papa and the others waited in the hall outside. When the doctor come in I told him Mama was asleep. He looked at her and lifted one of her eyelids. "She's in a coma," he said.

The word *coma* shot through me like a long, cold knife. A coma meant she wouldn't wake up.

The doctor looked at the papers Dr. Fauntleroy had sent, and the x-rays from Asheville. He frowned and shook his head. "You have waited too long," he said.

"Can't you operate?" I said.

"Wouldn't do any good; she's already in a coma."

"We have drove all the way from Henderson County," I said.

"I'm sorry," the doctor said.

I asked him if he would talk to Papa. I'd never felt so hopeless. We walked out in the hall where Papa and Velmer was standing, and Effie and Alvin set on a bench nearby. The doctor looked at the charts on the clipboard and then spoke in a very low voice, "Mr. Richards, I'm afraid it is too late to operate; she is already in a coma."

"She was awake when we left the house," Papa said.

"Her condition is advancing rapidly," the doctor said.

"We was told you could operate and take out the brain tumor," Effie said. She begun to cry. She lifted her glasses and wiped her eyes with a handkerchief.

"We have brought her all the way down here," Velmer said.

"The tumor has grown too far," the doctor said. "I wish I could be more hopeful, but that is the truth."

We all stood there like we couldn't think of nothing else to say. I guess we was all wore out from the long day of travel and worry. I'd never felt so helpless in my life. The light in the hospital was gray, like dishwater, and it seemed the smell of tobacco had seeped into the air. It was a sickening smell. It was so hot the back of my dress was wet. There was cigarette smoke coming from one of the rooms. I felt I couldn't breathe. I felt like I was going to sink right down on the floor. Papa and Velmer both acted like they was stunned. And then a shock of anger surged through me.

"So you're not going to help us?" I said to the doctor. "After we brought her all this way."

"Mrs. Powell, I wish there was something I could do," the doctor said. He was so calm it made me madder. He wasn't even going to try to do nothing for Mama. I'd heard that doctors try to stay away from a patient that's dying. It looks bad if they are treating a person that dies. Something about the way he looked at the clipboard and spoke in such a low voice made me madder still.

"The least you could do is try to help her," I said.

"If I knew anything that would help her, I would do it," the doctor said. He looked at his watch.

A nurse come up and said he had a call at the front desk. "You'll have to excuse me," the doctor said.

"You just want to wash your hands of her," I said, and looked him in the eye.

He started to walk away, and then he turned back to me. "The only place they can operate at this stage is in Charlotte," he said. "There is a brain surgeon there named Rogers. That's the only thing I can recommend."

"How do we make an appointment?" I said.

"I'll have my office call ahead and make an appointment," the doctor said. "Dr. Rogers will be waiting for you." Then he hurried away.

"He's just trying to get rid of us," Velmer said.

"Can we go all the way to Charlotte tonight?" Alvin said.

"How far is it to Charlotte?" Effie said.

Suddenly I knowed we had to get Mama out of that hospital and out of that town stinking of tobacco. I wouldn't let her die in that place where

they would not even try to help her. I would never forgive myself I we
didn't take her to Charlotte.

"Charlotte is our only choice," I said. "We have to take her."

The ambulance we'd come in had gone back to Henderson County.
We had the woman at the front desk call another ambulance to make the
trip to Charlotte.

THE RIDE TO Charlotte in the dark I don't hardly remember at
all. Mama never woke up as we passed through towns and strange lighted
places. It was just getting daylight when we finally reached the hospital in
Charlotte. Dr. Rogers was there waiting for us and he seemed completely
different from the doctor in Winston-Salem. He shook hands with each
of us and had us set down on a settee in the lounge.

"Any surgery at this time is a very long shot," he said. "But I'll do what
I can to save Mrs. Richards." He looked me in the eye when he said that.

"What are her chances?" I said.

"Not good; she's already in a coma." He said the first thing to do was
relieve the pressure on Mama's brain, if there was pressure. He'd do that
by cutting a hole in her skull and letting the built-up fluid out. Then he'd
open up the skull to see if the tumor had spread. Dr. Rogers talked to us
like he'd knowed us all his life and like he really cared what happened to
Mama.

"I can make no promises," he said.

"I understand," I said.

A nurse give Papa a form to sign saying he granted permission to operate. I seen them roll Mama into the operating room at the end of the hall,
but we couldn't go down there. We had to stay in the waiting room where
there was a few couches and magazines on a coffee table. The blinds was
down but you could tell it was getting daylight outside.

Velmer and Alvin said they was going to get some coffee and maybe something to eat. Effie and Papa and me stayed there in the waiting room. Papa had said almost nothing since we left home. It was so unlike him to have nothing to say. I'd been too worried to pay much attention to him. In all my life I'd never seen him so quiet. It was like he was in shock and didn't know what to say. He'd always depended on Mama to look after things. Without her I don't reckon he knowed what to do or think.

There was a clock on the wall that said seven o'clock in the morning. But I tried not to look at it. There was no telling how long the operation might take. I felt sticky in my clothes and remembered I hadn't took off my clothes since yesterday morning. I went to the restroom and washed my face and hands. When I come back Papa was still setting where he was but Effie had gone out to look for Alvin and Velmer. Only a few minutes had passed.

I was thinking what a strange place this was for Mama to be in, so far from home, when I heard somebody holler way down the hall, "Out of the way! Out of the way! We're coming through." I jumped up to see what was happening and seen this nurse hurrying down the hall waving everybody out of the way and two men pushing a gurney behind her.

"Out of the way!" she hollered at me, and I stepped back. As they went by I seen a body on the gurney with the head all bloody and mashed in on one side. A man in overalls and a woman in a print dress that buttoned all the way down the front tried to keep up with the gurney. Another nurse told them to stay there in the waiting room. They watched the men push the gurney all the way down the hall and disappear into the operating room.

The woman turned away from me and sobbed. The man, who looked like he hadn't shaved in a week, just stood there looking at the floor. I noticed his shoes was laced with binders twine. The woman got a handkerchief out of her pocketbook and wiped her eyes, and blowed her nose but kept crying. I tried to think what I could do to help her. I stood up and spoke to the man in a low voice. "Is that your son?"

"Grandson," the man said.

"I sure am sorry," I said.

The man said his grandson had drove his car over a bank and hit a tree. He'd been throwed out and his head had hit another tree. Because the car had gone down the bank, nobody had seen him there till daylight.

"It's all my fault," the man said. Tobacco juice seeped out of the corners of his mouth.

"How is it your fault?" I said.

"Cause I let him take the car. He ain't but fifteen and don't even have a license."

"No, it's my fault," the woman said without turning around. "I give him a dollar to buy gas so he could drive to Gastonia."

I tried to think of something comforting. "This is the best place for brain surgery," I said. "Everybody says so."

"It's all my fault," the man said again. He put his hand in the pocket of his overalls where something heavy weighted the cloth down. "These doctors don't pull him through, they'll answer to me," he said.

Just then a doctor and a nurse come down the hall from the operating room. It wasn't Dr. Rogers but another doctor. They come straight to the man in the overalls and the doctor said in a low voice, "Mr. Lindsey, I'm afraid your grandson was already dead when he arrived here. He must have died in the ambulance."

The man in the overalls looked around like he didn't know what to do. And then he reached into his pocket and pulled out a silver-colored pistol. "You will fix him up," he said to the doctor.

"He was dead when he arrived," the doctor said. "There was nothing we could do." I was surprised how calm the doctor was. He didn't seem at all afraid of the man with the pistol.

"Give me that thing," the woman said, and reached out for the gun. The man backed away.

"Cletus, do you always have to act the fool?" the woman said. "Give me that gun this minute." He handed over the pistol and put his hands over his eyes and turned away.

"I'm awful sorry," the doctor said to the woman. The woman led the man in overalls down the hall toward the elevator.

I'd been so busy watching them that I was surprised to see Dr. Rogers standing beside me. He still had on his white cap, and his mask was pulled down under his chin. He nodded to Papa and asked us to come with him. He took us to a room adjoining the operating room. Mama laid on a gurney with her head all wrapped up in bandages.

"The tumor has grown since the x-rays were made," Dr. Rogers said. "She must have been in some pain. I wonder that she has lived this long."

"Did you take out the tumor?" I said.

"I did not," he said. "It has spread too far."

"Then there is no hope?"

"She will die within hours." He said Mama's brain was so damaged it could not send out messages to keep her body alive, or something like that. I wasn't really listening no more. I went over and looked at Mama. She'd never waked up since we left the house the day before. I wondered if we should take her home. But even if we did she wouldn't know the difference.

They rolled Mama into a room farther away from the operating room. Papa come in to look at her, and then Velmer and Effie and Alvin come in. They all went back to the waiting room and I stayed with Mama. I looked at Mama's hands all calloused and rough from hard work. I felt guilty for bringing her all the way to Winston-Salem and then Charlotte where they couldn't help her at all. She ought to have been left at home where she belonged. Mama had spent her life working on Mount Olivet, on Gap Creek and on Green River. She'd done a man's work of chopping wood, plowing fields, killing hogs, as well as a woman's work of washing and cooking and cleaning, sewing and raising kids. She looked so tiny there under the covers on the gurney it was hard to believe the tons she'd lifted and carried, the back-breaking work she'd done every day of her life.

I was mad at myself because I hadn't done enough to help her. If I'd took her to the doctor earlier they might have found the tumor and cured her. If I'd paid more attention I might have helped her. She'd worried herself to death after Troy was killed. She'd not let out her grief. And that grief had poisoned her. I should've done something to relieve her mind and I hadn't.

Mama laid there and I couldn't even tell if she was breathing. And then she moved her head a little sideways. There was a kind of twitch and a shudder or tremble run through her body. Her foot moved and then she was still. I stood there waiting for her to move or breathe again, but she didn't. I waited some more and looked to see if her chest rose, but it didn't.

Instead of going out to tell anybody I just stood there to be with Mama. It was my last chance to be with her. I kept thinking of all the things I'd done wrong, and all the ways I should've helped her and hadn't. And then a nurse come in and took her pulse and said Mama was dead. There was no use to stay with her after that. I went out to the waiting room and told Papa and Velmer and Effie and Alvin. Papa just shook his head and looked down at his feet. I knowed he was confused, because for more than forty-five years he'd depended on Mama to keep things going. Even when he'd fussed at her he'd relied on her to tell him what things meant.

THE DAY AFTER we got home people brought all kinds of things to eat to the house. It was the custom of the community. They brought platters of fried chicken and casseroles of all kinds. They brought apple pies and peach cobblers. Chocolate cakes and coconut cakes. They brought lemonade and jugs of iced tea. Some brought boxes of dough-nuts. When Sharon come down she brought a cherry pie. It was hot hazy weather, the kind we usually had in August. I knowed a lot of food would go to waste cause only a little would fit in the icebox. I invited everybody that come by to eat something, and I tried to give away as much as I could.

Now the surprise to me was that I never did cry when Mama died. I didn't cry at the hospital when I seen her die or on the ride back home to the mountains. Effie cried and Papa cried, and I expected to cry, but I never did. I'd worked so hard taking care of Mama, and worrying about Mama, I was too tired to cry. I wanted to cry but I couldn't. And somehow I seen what had happened was too sad for tears. Tears was for ordinary grief and hurt feelings and surprise. To know that Mama had grieved herself to death over Troy's death, and that she was gone forever, left me too numb for words. There wasn't nothing to be done or said. It's the *reality* of death that touches you too deep for weeping. There was nothing that could be said.

Sharon would run to me and cry and get my shoulder wet, and I'd pat her back. I know that she was awful sorry that Mama had gone because Mama had always been good to her. But then Mama was good to everybody. She'd go without new clothes for herself so her children could have decent clothes. She would get up in the middle of the night to fix grits for somebody that had been sick and was suddenly hungry.

Even Muir cried, for he was devoted to Mama. When I got home from Charlotte and told him Mama was dead he bawled like a baby, and there wasn't nothing I could say that would comfort him.

I guess people thought it was strange that I never cried. And I thought it was odd myself. I didn't want people to think I didn't care. But at the same time I knowed I was too close to Mama and her passing. Her death was too big for me to see yet. It would be a while before I understood what had happened.

Though Ginny had died only five years before, it had been a long time since there'd been a funeral in the Richards family. I think the last had been the funeral of Ma Richards who died when I was just a little girl. I was afraid of her and stayed away from her. If Ma Richards seen me in the room she'd ask me to bring a coal from the fireplace to light her pipe. If she caught hold of me she'd turn me over her knee to see if my underwear was clean. I wasn't sad at all when she died.

I went with Papa and Effie to the funeral home to pick out a casket. You could buy a casket at the store down at the highway, but Papa decided to use some of the insurance money from Troy's death to have an undertaker funeral. I agreed that it was the right thing to do. There was a whole big room of caskets at the funeral parlor and we picked a blue metal one that cost $299.95. Blue was Mama's favorite color.

We asked Lorrie and her sisters to sing at the funeral. They'd sung at lots of funerals and they harmonized perfectly together. I asked Muir if he wanted to preach at the funeral, but he said no, it was Preacher Rice's job since he was pastor of the church and Mama was a member. He didn't want to take the pastor's place. I reckon he was still remembering all the trouble with Preacher Liner about Moody's funeral too.

I know it's said that people enjoy funerals. They enjoy getting together with family and neighbors and remembering the one who has gone on. They enjoy the dignity and sadness, the respect and solemnness of the occasion. Most of all a funeral takes you out of the boredom and confusion of ordinary life and makes you think of everlasting things. But I never did like funerals. I had a horror of the way preachers talked at funerals, referring to mansions in heaven and them that might be left behind at the Second Coming. When Moody died Muir had preached the best funeral I ever seen, but he didn't think it was his place to preach at Mama's.

Before we got in the undertaker's limousine to drive to the funeral I took two aspirins to cool me off. Sharon rode in the car with Papa and Muir and me. Effie and Velmer followed in Alvin's car. Hot as it was I shivered. And I shivered again when we got in the church and they played the sad organ music. The smell of flowers around the casket at the front of the church made the heat seem stickier. Maybe it was dust in the air that made me want to sneeze.

Lorrie and her sisters sung and they sung real pretty. They sung "How Beautiful Heaven Must Be," one of Mama's favorite songs. But I couldn't hardly listen. I kept thinking about the way Mama couldn't enjoy nothing after Troy was killed. Sharon sobbed on the bench beside me, and Effie cried. But I felt like I wasn't hardly there.

Preacher Rice prayed and said amen. And then he started to read from the Bible. It was the passage that was always read at funerals. "In my house are many mansions. If it were not so I would have told you . . ."

Just then we heard a car blow its horn. It must have been going up the river road, for we heard the horn again and again as it faded away. It seemed strange that anybody would honk their horn while a funeral was going on. They could see all the cars and trucks parked at the church, not to mention the hearse and limousine. Did someone just want to be mean and irreverent? Was it someone like Edward that was mad at Papa or the family?

Preacher Rice kept speaking and then there was the sound of another horn. Somebody was banging their horn again and again as they got closer, and then they stopped. I reckon they seen all the cars and the hearse parked at the church. It seemed crazy that two cars would pass on the road honking their horns.

Preacher Rice kept talking about what a fine Christian woman Mama was and how she now had her reward in heaven. He talked about how she'd served the Lord all her life, how she set an example for us all, how she had true compassion and love for her fellow man. It was all true, but it was like I couldn't listen. I was somewhere else in my mind. I was streaming sweat and yet I was cold. My feet was icy. I wasn't sure where I was.

Then as Preacher Rice was closing with a prayer we heard this terrible boom, like a big gun had gone off. And then boom boom boom boom, and the booms echoed off the mountains. The preacher finished praying, but I could tell he was shook by the blasts. It sounded like war had broke out and that we was being attacked. His voice trembled as he spoke. And then Lorrie and her sisters sung again.

It was the thought that a war had broke out that made me realize what all the horns, what all the noise, was about. War had not broke out: the war had ended. Japan must have surrendered. It was August 15, 1945, and the war must be over. There was no other explanation for the shots and blaring horns. The world would always remember this day because it was the end of the war. I would always remember it because it was the day of Mama's funeral.

We'd been so worried about Mama we'd paid little attention to the news in the last few weeks. I'd seen in the paper the headlines about the big bombs exploding in Japan, and people had talked about a new Atomic Age and how the whole world might be blowed up. But I'd hardly noticed the talk. All I could think about was Mama and wondering what we could do for her.

When the funeral was finally over and we walked out of the church into the hazy heat, a whole string of cars come up the road with their lights on, horns beeping and blaring. There was even a Model A making its *oogah-oogah* sound. Some of the cars when they seen us stopped honking, but others just kept blowing their horns. I reckon people was beside theirselves with the news.

When we got into the limousine Sharon said, "How dare those people make such a fuss? They're just a bunch of hoojers."

"It's the end of the war," I said.

"That's what it must be," Muir said. He took my hand.

"How do you know?" Sharon said.

"What else could it be?" I said.

As we drove up the road to the cemetery we met cars blasting their horns one after another. One had a big sign on the side that said, THE WAR IS OVER. OUR BOYS ARE COMING HOME. Most stopped blowing their horns when they seen us. But some didn't.

"They should be ashamed," Sharon said. "They have no consideration."

"They're so thrilled they're not thinking," Muir said.

"They're making all this racket, knowing Troy won't be coming home. He'll never come home," Sharon said.

"They're not thinking about that," Muir said.

"They ought to have some decency," Sharon said.

For once I agreed with Sharon. I knowed Troy's death was the furthest thing from these people's minds. They didn't intend to hurt us. But even so, it was thoughtless. I resented their mindless enthusiasm and serenading. I was angry in spite of myself.

After we drove around the hill and to the top of the cemetery knoll and got out of the limousine and walked to the tent and set down, we heard the cotton-mill whistle blow again and again. Guns went off and there was a boom like a stick of dynamite had been lit. Truck horns on the highway and car horns all up and down the valley echoed off the ridges. Church bells rung at Mountain Valley and Cedar Springs and Mount Olivet. There was such a racket you couldn't hardly hear the preacher's prayer beside the grave. I kept thinking how the dirt piled there beside the grave was almost the same color of red as Troy's hair.

Nineteen

After the war was over and the world was at peace, everybody expected things to be better if not perfect. After the long Depression and the years of war it just seemed things had to get better. The boys was coming home and there was now electricity all up and down the valley and even on Mount Olivet and Mountain Valley. The paper said there was a new age beginning, the Atomic Age. There would be big rockets, and people might go to the moon. To hear the newspaper tell it, there was to be a new day of peace and prosperity.

Except what really happened was that when the war ended a lot of people got laid off from their jobs. All the work for the war effort was over, and with the soldiers coming back there wasn't near enough jobs to go around. Most soldiers had been too young to look for work before they went into the service, but now they needed jobs. There was no more work for Papa and Muir at Fort Bragg, and Velmer had quit his job as a barber at Fort Jackson before he was laid off. Papa still had the little checks from Troy's insurance coming every month, but that was all. Both Muir and Velmer went back to farming in the summer of 1946, because that was all they could find to do.

And just when we thought the world was at peace you started hearing talk about the Russians. People said the Russians had gobbled up half of Europe and wouldn't let go. They made everybody there become a communist and killed them that wouldn't. The newspaper was full of stories about communists taking over everywhere, in places I never heard of, like Bulgaria and Albania. The newspaper warned that there was communists in this country, infiltrating government and almost every organization. You never could know what was legitimate and what was a communist front. People said there was Russian spies everywhere, in the government, in the army, even in schools all over the country. Spies was stealing the government secrets and giving them to the Russians. Papa said the Russians was worse than the Germans.

One day this letter from the government come to Papa. It said if he filled out the enclosed form and sent it back, Troy's body would be brought from England and buried wherever he chose in the United States. One big ship would carry all the coffins dug up from the cemeteries over there and bring them home at no cost to the families. It occurred to me when I read the letter that bringing the casket here and having a funeral and burying Troy beside Mama might just make us all sadder. But it was what we'd promised Mama we'd do. And it was what Papa wanted too. So I helped him fill out the form and we mailed it in.

Now you never know how things will turn out. What you predict will almost never happen. I guess the world likes to surprise you. Like I said, after the war was over almost nobody could find work. I stayed on at the cotton mill and Muir preached at a church when he was invited. And when he had some free time he started working on the church on the mountain again. Weeds had growed up around the place, and the road up the mountain had washed out in several places. He took a shovel up there and smoothed out the road, and he cut the weeds with his mowing blade. One pane at a time he replaced windows that had been broke by storms or kids throwing rocks. Papa helped him put new shingles on the roof.

I guess people thought it was strange that Muir, now that he was older, returned to his dream of finishing the church on the mountain. With Ginny gone nobody supported him except Papa. I thought it was strange myself, but I didn't say nothing. Because he didn't have a job and didn't have a regular church to preach in, he needed something to keep him going. I could see that, and I reckon Papa could too.

Suddenly in the spring of 1947 Preacher Rice had a heart attack. He didn't die, but he was too weak to preach anymore. Muir was asked to fill in for a week or two, and I can't tell you how pleased he was to be invited by his own neighbors. There was grumbling, of course, as there always is. People said he'd left the church and tried to build a rival church on top of the mountain. He hadn't meant for it to be a rival church, but that's what people said. And some people remembered how Muir's mama and grandpa had gone to the Pentecostal revivals way back yonder before he was born, and they still held that against him.

I was happy for Muir, for even if it was just for one or two or three weeks he'd get to offer sermons here to his own people. He'd been traveling around to speak and this would be a kind of homecoming for him. This was the place where he was embarrassed when he first tried to preach. I knowed it made him nervous to think of speaking there again. It made me nervous too.

Muir got out his best herringbone gray suit and polished his black shoes. He had a tie of dark ruby red. He put oil on his black hair so it shined. All dressed up he looked like a lawyer or a banker.

I expected the worst, because so many bad things had happened to him on Green River. It was a place where things just seemed to go wrong. Nothing that had to do with the church ever seemed to work out. I was so nervous that morning as I set in the choir where Mama had always set I was wet under my arms. I was almost afraid to look around, for I knowed people was just waiting for Muir to make a fool of hisself. Christian people can be the meanest people there is, and nobody can gossip and quarrel like members of a Baptist church.

Imagine how surprised I was when Muir stood up behind the pulpit and acted so calm. He acted like he'd done this every Sunday all his life. I hadn't heard him preach in a long time, for mostly he'd preached at some distance from home. He was older now, and his work away from home during the war had matured him, and maybe marriage had matured him too. I liked to think that. He was my husband, and these days I seen him every day, but even so, I was surprised at how natural he acted. And it was partly acting, for I was certain he was nervous, though he didn't show it. Even his voice was soothing.

"We have gone through the trials of a great war," Muir said. "And we've lost many loved ones. But for those of us who've survived, who are here now, the Lord has given us a new chance."

Muir seemed so strong and quiet and sure of hisself the air in the church was soothing. There had been so much hardness, such bitterness in that church, but Muir's voice seemed to ease the tension. It was a voice of con-ciliation and openness. I was not surprised when he opened the Bible and read from Ecclesiastes 3: "To everything there is a season, and a time to every purpose under the heaven; a time to be born, and a time to die, a time to plant, and a time to pluck up that which is planted."

Muir talked like a sermon was natural as rain falling on an April morn-ing or the leaves turning yellow in the fall. Even though he was my hus-band he didn't seem hardly like the nervous and excited man I'd knowed and lived with. He talked like the right words just come to him without effort. He was speaking his thoughts. It was not the way he talked at home. It was a different voice and a different manner. As I watched him I thought how he was like an actor, a good actor, playing the *role* of a preacher.

Through practice, years of thought and study and practice, he'd learned the role. That was thrilling to me, for I'd always loved acting. I seen that we are always learning our roles, rehearsing our roles, and playing a part. It was strangely comforting to think that as I watched Muir be a preacher in front of the whole community, in the church where he'd embarrassed hisself many years before.

In spite of some people complaining, mostly women that hadn't liked Ginny, the deacons invited Muir to preach again another Sunday and then another. They give him fifteen dollars every time he preached. It was the most money we'd made in a long time. During the weekdays Muir worked in the fields, and on Saturdays he worked on the church on the top of the mountain, and on Sunday he preached at the church at the bottom of the mountain.

One Monday night just after supper a car drove up to the house. Curtis Stepp that was chairman of the board of deacons and three other deacons got out. "Is Muir here?" Curtis asked. Muir was out at the barn. I told them to go set by the fire and I'd get him. It passed through my mind that they'd come to tell Muir he couldn't preach no more at the church. I knowed Curtis had never liked Ginny and had voted to throw her out of the church when she attended the Pentecostal services many years ago.

Muir was drawing water for the horse, and he was as surprised as me when I told him the deacons had come to the house. As soon as we got back to the house I told the deacons to set down and I'd make some fresh coffee.

"This won't take long," Curtis said. Then he turned to Muir. "Would you be interested in being the pastor of the church?" he said.

"If people want me to be pastor that will be fine," Muir said. "If people don't want me to be pastor that will be fine too. But as far as I know Preacher Rice is still the pastor." Muir didn't sound as sure of hisself at home as he did in the pulpit. He'd not learned to play the role of preacher out of the pulpit yet.

"Preacher Rice has resigned. His health will not permit him to pastor a church anymore," Doug Williams said.

"I'll serve the community as best I can," Muir said.

"Then we invite you to be our next pastor," Curtis said.

"Won't the whole congregation have to vote?" Muir said.

"They will follow our recommendation," Curtis said.

"Then I will humbly accept," Muir said.

I couldn't hardly believe what I was hearing. Muir becoming the pastor was the last thing I expected. Given all the troubles with the church building on the mountain and his quarrels with Preacher Liner a few years ago, it didn't seem possible. It was strange that in a few short years things could change around so much. I knowed that Papa as a deacon would have supported Muir, but I also knowed that Papa would have had to excuse hisself when they voted on his son-in-law. When the deacons left I wasn't sure whether I wanted to laugh or cry. But there was a smile of deep satisfaction on Muir's face.

I'D HEARD THAT Sharon had got married and I'd seen her once up town with her husband. Sharon had not told me she was getting married. She just quit coming to the house or sending cards at Christmas and Easter the way she had done. She had every right to get married. It'd been five years since Troy had died, which was more than a decent amount of time. The war was over. And besides that, she'd never even been married to Troy. She was not exactly a war widow, much as she'd acted like one.

She had no reason to feel ashamed or embarrassed about marrying someone else. Except she obviously did feel ashamed, the way she broke off from us and never did tell us. I thought about it a lot and decided the reason she felt bad was maybe because she'd overacted a little when

Troy died. Troy's death was so sad it just made Mama set in the corner and brood and say almost nothing for days. But Sharon had acted like it was the end of the world for her. She'd acted like there was no meaning in anything for her now that Troy was gone. She acted like she could never be reconciled or happy again, and nobody could take Troy's place. And yet here she was married to somebody else. What must have embarrassed her was the way she herself had done.

I got a ride to town with Velmer in the ugly army surplus truck he'd bought for almost nothing. He always parked in the lot behind the feed store where you still sometimes seen a horse and wagon or a mule and wagon parked in the years right after the war. The lot was only a block from the old A&P store on South Main right across the street from the courthouse. But to get to the store from the parking lot you had to cross the side street at a place called Greasy Corner where all these old hoojers in overalls hung out talking and spitting tobacco juice and laughing at dirty stories. When a woman walked by, these unwashed and unshaved geezers from skid row and back in the hills, some of them red eyed from liquor, would watch her like she didn't have a stitch of clothes on. It always scared me a little to walk by there.

I'd got out of earshot of them old lechers and almost to the A&P store when I seen this neat-looking man in a tan jacket and brown hat. He was not a tall man, but he walked like somebody proud and determined. The woman beside him wearing a light blue dress and a dark blue jacket looked familiar, and I recognized with a start it was Sharon.

When I spoke to her she turned around and when she seen me she blushed so that even though her skin was dark you could see the flush. "How have you been?" I said.

"This, this is Albert," she said.

"How do you do?" I said.

"This is Annie Richards, no I mean Powell." The man tipped his hat to me, and then it must have occurred to him who I was, for he backed away, pulling at Sharon's hand. But when he seen she was going to stay and talk to me he hurried on up the street, like he was afraid I had some catching disease or he was very late for an appointment. Sharon watched him go and then turned back to me.

"It's good to see you," I said. "We heard you was married."

Sharon stepped closer to me and said, "Albert don't like for me to mention Troy."

"I'm sorry," I said, not sure exactly what I meant. I looked her in the eyes, trying to be as friendly as I could.

"He gets mad if anybody mentions Troy," Sharon said. "He throwed away the boxes of arrowheads you give me. He took the boxes and flung them in the creek."

I shook my head because I didn't want to say nothing critical about her husband.

"Albert said he could compete with a living man," Sharon said. "But he couldn't compete with a dead man."

I took her hand and squeezed it. I could see she'd lost weight. It was pretty clear her marriage had not been a happy one. I tried to think what to say to her.

"We're bringing Troy's body home," I said. "Papa signed the papers. When the casket comes we'll have a funeral."

"Where will the funeral be?"

"At the Green River Church where he was a member. Muir will preach the funeral. He's the new pastor there. Can you believe it?"

"I'll try to come, if you can let me know."

"There will be an announcement in the paper."

It made me sad just to watch her as she walked on up the street to catch up with Albert. I tried to think of what I could do to help her but couldn't think of a single thing.

W HEN T ROY ' S COFFIN arrived finally at the funeral home in town Papa got a letter asking when he wanted to schedule the service and saying there'd be no cost for the funeral. It was the undertaker's gift to the family of a soldier who'd been lost. I drove to town with Papa and we set the funeral for the following Sunday. The funeral parlor director suggested that we have a visitation hour just for family at the funeral parlor the day before the service.

"It often helps families at this sad time to spend an hour with the loved one the day before the funeral," he said. That seemed thoughtful of him and we agreed.

So on Saturday evening we all met at the funeral home, Papa and Velmer, me and Muir, Effie and Alvin, Lou and Garland, and they brought Carolyn, Mama's younger sister that had never got married. Her other unmarried sister, Rosie, had the flu and couldn't come.

It was an awful feeling, going into the fine room with carpets and lamps and this gray casket with a flag spread over it. It was hard to think Troy, who we hadn't seen in six years, was laying in that box, and it has hard not to think he was there. Papa had never looked so old as he did when he walked up and put a hand on that casket. He trembled a little and I nudged Muir to stand close to him in case he started to fall.

"Hank, are you going to open it?" Carolyn said.

I turned to look at her. I couldn't hardly believe my ears. When Carolyn was young she was a terrible flirt. She had busted up couples that was about to get married and would then drop the boy and move on to another that was engaged. Mama said she done it just to prove she could. Now that she was old she mostly liked to gossip and to stick her nose in other people's business.

"Why would he open the casket?" I said, giving Carolyn a hard look. Mama had once hinted that Carolyn had tried to break her and Papa up after they was first married and living on Gap Creek.

"Because it's his only chance to see Troy one last time," Carolyn said. "Didn't they give Hank the key to the casket?"

It was true the undertaker had give Papa the key to the coffin. I shuddered to think what might be in that box. That airplane had exploded and burned up. There might not be anything but a few burned bones or a skull, or a few rags of clothes. Can you imagine the horror of looking at the burned-up remains of somebody you loved? After five years who knew what the condition of such remains would be? It might be a nightmare for Papa to see. And then again there might not be anything at all in the coffin, for the bombs had blowed everything to pieces. It could be the worst thing of all for Papa to look in that casket and see nothing at all.

"The coffin will not be opened," I said.

Papa didn't say nothing, and nobody else said nothing.

"You could let him speak for hisself," Carolyn said.

"It ain't your place to say what he does," I said, and looked at her as hard as I could. Carolyn was not used to people standing up to her. She was spoiled. Her sisters had always let her have her way, because she was the youngest.

"Carolyn is just trying to help," Lou said.

"Let her help somebody else," I snapped.

Carolyn turned and walked out of the funeral parlor, and I was happy to see her go. She waited in Garland's truck until we come out after dark, and she didn't speak to me when I walked by the truck.

Now that Muir was pastor of the church, we could have the funeral in the old church at the foot of the mountain or at the new unfinished church at the top of the mountain. Muir had been hoping to hold the service in the new church, but it rained the night before and the road up the mountain was muddy and mushy. So the funeral was held in the old church down by the road, which the hearse could reach easy.

I'd never been to a military funeral before. The honor guard with their rifles and fine uniforms lined up on the steps outside the church before we went in. The undertaker had us wait until everybody else was in the church before we entered. It had stopped raining and clouds was parting so you could see some blue. Just then a checker-painted taxicab pulled into the parking lot and a woman dressed in black got out. I seen it was Sharon and she was by herself.

The undertaker was about to tell us to start walking into the church, but I said, "Wait." Sharon come right up to us and I moved around to let her stand beside Papa. It seemed the polite thing to do. She tried to smile, but she couldn't quite manage it she was so out of breath.

"I had to come," she whispered as we started to march in.

I don't remember much about that service. I know we sung "Battle Hymn." And I know that Muir talked about what a fine man, a brave man, an athlete, an artist, Troy was. But I don't recall the words he actually said. All I could think about was Mama and how she would've felt if she'd been there.

But I remember the graveside service very well, every second of it. The limousine we rode in behind the hearse wound up the little road to the top of the cemetery hill. It always seemed a lonely place to me, with crows in the trees and the mountain looming above. The cliff they call Buzzard Rock looked down. Water on the rock made it gleam in the sun like it had eyes. There was always wind in the broomsedge on the hill.

Troy's grave was right beside Mama's and it made the back of my mouth tight and sore just to look at the two graves side by side. The tent was up over the fresh grave, and after we set down, the soldiers assembled in a line on the other side of the grave. The creases on their pants was so sharp you'd think the uniforms was made of metal. Their shoes shined like hot tar.

When the leader called out an order they all jerked to attention and looked straight ahead. When another order was give they raised their rifles straight up and down in front of their faces. Next they put the rifles to their shoulders and worked the bolts to put a cartridge in. Then the order to fire was give and they all pulled the trigger at once. The boom of the guns echoed off the mountain and made the crows call out their warnings like they was being shot at. The crows had no way of knowing the soldiers was using blanks.

And then the soldiers worked the rifles to put in another shot and fired again. I winced with the roar of the blasts. And then they done it again. On command they lowered the rifle butts to the ground and stood at attention.

I thought the ceremony must be over, but two of the soldiers handed their guns to others and walked to the casket over the grave. One got on either side and they begun to fold the flag. It was a big flag and they folded it this way and that way, again and again, until it was smaller than a pillow, and then they folded it once more so it was three cornered and brought it to Papa.

As Papa held the flag on his lap I thought it was a fine and impressive kind of ceremony. But it was mostly sad that such a ceremony had to take place. Tens of thousands of such ceremonies was being conducted all over the country and all over the world. People had to be crazy, the world had to be crazy, to fight such wars. Smart people would never do such a thing to each other. They would find a better way to settle arguments rather than just killing each other. And for what? So they could have fine ceremonies and make speeches on a hillside at the end of the war?

I was thinking such grim thoughts when I noticed a black roadster pull behind the last car on the driveway around the cemetery. I didn't think nothing of it at first. People sometimes come to the graveside service even if they missed the funeral. Papa set on one side of me and Sharon on the other. Sharon give a kind of gasp when she seen the roadster. The man that got out of the roadster was her husband, Albert. He took something out of the trunk of the car and started walking toward us.

"Oh no," Sharon groaned.

It was just then that Muir stood up at the side of the grave and started reading from the hundred and third Psalm. "As for man his days are as grass . . ."

Muir paused, and then said, "Let us bow our heads."

The crows on the mountainside was making a terrible racket and wind blowed in under the tent making the flowers around the coffin tremble. As Albert got closer I seen that he had something in his hand. Light flashed on it and I thought at first it might be a pair of glasses or a fountain pen. And then I seen it was a pistol. It looked like an army pistol, the kind you could buy for a few dollars at a surplus store.

As Muir begun to pray, "Lord, we are here to honor our fallen brother, who we know is now at home with you," Albert called out Sharon's name. Everybody's eyes turned toward him. Albert wore the same tan jacket and brown hat he had the time I'd seen him up town. I hadn't noticed then it was an army jacket, but in the bright sun you could see where the patches had been tore off the sleeves and shoulders.

Muir paused for an instant and then continued the prayer. Surely nobody would want to interrupt the prayer at the end of a funeral.

"Sharon, you come here," Albert said in a shaking voice. He didn't point the pistol at nobody. He held it pointed at the ground. I'd not knowed he'd been a soldier in the war hisself. It occurred to me he might be shell shocked, as so many boys who'd been in battle was. I could see he was shaking as he stood there in the wind with the crows screaming in the trees beyond.

Muir cut the prayer short and said "Amen," then turned to Albert. He'd never seen Albert, but must have guessed who he was, and he held out his hand. Holding out your hand is a gesture that you want to be friends; it says there is nothing here to fear. But instead of shaking hands, Albert backed away, still holding the gun pointed down.

The soldiers with their rifles just stood there. I reckon a man with a pistol who was probably shell shocked was the last thing they'd expected at a funeral. There was nothing in their rifles but blanks.

"You get out of my way; this ain't your business, preacher," Albert said, so short of breath he could hardly talk.

"This is a funeral," Muir said, "for a fallen soldier."

Albert looked all around the crowd, and then he looked hard at Sharon before turning back to Muir. "You think the only brave soldiers are them that died?" he said. "Them that returns is just as brave as them that died."

"Nobody is arguing with that," Muir said.

The sergeant of the honor guard stepped out of the line and faced Albert. "Soldier," he snapped, "take that pistol back to your car and leave here. That is an order."

"I don't take orders no more," Albert said.

"Don't disgrace the uniform," the sergeant said.

Albert turned toward Sharon and said, "You're coming with me." There was both threat and begging in his voice.

The sergeant stepped closer to Muir and they both stood between Albert and Sharon. I was afraid Albert would raise the pistol and shoot, or the sergeant would try to hit him with the rifle. It was an awful thing to happen, at the end of Troy's funeral.

"Wait," Sharon said. "I'll come."

I almost blurted out that Sharon shouldn't go with him; he was too dangerous. But I didn't. I guess I thought that any way we could get Albert away from there would be good. If it was the thought of Troy that upset him so, then she should stay far away from Troy's family.

It looked like Sharon was going to take Albert's arm, but she didn't. Instead she walked on toward the black roadster and he followed her. She walked like somebody that has been give a long sentence. I hated to think what it would be like when she got home, away from all the curious eyes of the congregation. As I watched her get in that car and the car drive away, I thought how the war wasn't really over. For us in Troy's family, for those that had loved him, and for former soldiers like Albert, the war was far from over. In fact it would never be over for any of us.

Nobody said anything after Sharon and Albert was gone. Nobody knowed what to say. Usually after a funeral people come up to the family and say what a beautiful service it was, how fitting for the honor and memory of the loved one who has been lost. But after what had happened it was hard for anybody to think of what to say.

Lorrie come and up hugged me with tears in her eyes. "Oh, Annie," she said. "I know you'll always miss Troy."

"We all will," I said.

I held the tightly folded flag while Papa shook hands with each of the pallbearers and thanked them for taking part. Then he thanked each member of the honor guard. Lou and Garland had brought Rosie to the funeral and I talked to them a little. Carolyn had not come. It was like her to stay mad after an argument. Mama said she'd always been that way.

As people started drifting back to their cars I told Effie and Alvin to be sure to come back to the house for supper. People had brought heaps of fried chicken and tater salad, and somebody had to eat it. I took Muir's arm and we walked back to the limousine. Muir had never give up on me over the years. No matter what else had changed Muir was still there.

Twenty

I won't say having a baby ain't hard, for everybody knows it is. The pains and then the waiting and then the pains getting worse are harder than anything you ever imagined. The pain shrieks through you and out of you as you push and strain and scream to high heaven or deep hell, all melted in sweat and hair sticking to your forehead. You think you can't stand it no more, that you're going to die and wish you could die. But you don't. And finally it's over and you're wore out and have a glistening baby that has to be wiped off and held close.

But the hardest thing for me, because it lasted so much longer, was the summer leading up to the birth of Angela, my first child. Because I kept getting infections, bladder infections, kidney infections, uterine infections, Dr. Fauntleroy said it might be necessary to take the baby, to save my life. He said he was afraid there'd be a miscarriage anyway, so it would be safer to end the pregnancy. But I'd waited too long to have a child to do that. If the Lord wanted me to have a baby, he would let me have the baby anyway, no matter what the doctor said. I remembered Mama's stories of having her first baby when she was alone in that old house on Gap Creek. I knowed it could not be as bad as that because I had a doctor and could go to the hospital in town.

"Then you must stay in bed until the baby comes," Dr. Fauntleroy said.

"But that'll be all summer."

"That's why I think we should take the baby now," the doctor said.

But I told him I'd stay in bed, if that's what it would take. I wouldn't leave the house all summer.

"And you must restrict your diet," he said.

"What do you mean?"

"Only eat the things you can hold on your stomach," he said. He recommended toast and milk, ginger ale and soda crackers. Light things like that.

"I'll get poor as a whippoorwill," I told Muir.

But the doctor was right about the diet. If I eat anything raw or the least bit greasy, I'd throw it up. Nothing that was spicy would stay down. I found I could eat grits or cream of wheat three times a day. And what I preferred most was sourwood honey, honey on toast, honey on biscuits. And banana pudding because it was so cool.

I'll say this about Muir: he took care of things and the house while I laid in bed all that hot summer. He washed dishes and brought me tea and done the washing. When he was off at work I was by myself except when Papa was around, or sometimes Effie or Lorrie come to visit.

Sometimes Muir brought me a magazine, but I didn't feel much like reading. I didn't even want the light on. I kept the curtains pulled and laid still to keep my stomach settled. If I moved around, I'd throw up. I could feel the baby growing inside me. Everything I eat, I eat for the baby. It was so hot you didn't want to move anyway. Even with the window open and the breeze pushing the curtain the heat built up in the afternoon and made me feel so weak I couldn't hardly move. I was weak from not eating much anyway. I laid there and tried not to think about Mama and Troy and Old Pat.

AFTER ANGELA WAS born I was still weak. Because I'd eat so little that summer, she was poor, with legs like pipe stems and toes little as beads of dew. Dr. Fauntleroy said I might not want to nurse her but give her formula, but I wouldn't hear of that. She was my baby and it was my place to feed her out of my own breasts. And once I started nursing her I was glad I had for it was about the nicest thing I'd done. If there is something more satisfying than nursing your own baby, I don't know what it is. As I held Angela to my nipple it seemed there couldn't be nothing more important in the world.

Whatever men think is important may be important to them, but nothing to me could be more important than taking care of Angela. If men had babies, maybe there wouldn't be such awful things happening all the time I thought. If men had babies, they'd know what was more important than wars and always fighting about things.

Every time I picked up Angela I felt that sweetness inside me where she'd been. Her skin was soft as a petal, and when I give her a bath she glowed all over. I liked to watch her upper lip as she took the nipple. I thought I'd bust when she smiled the first time. And then a few weeks later she laughed when I took her hands and went patty-cake, patty-cake, the baker's man. I wished Mama was there to see her. It hurt to think she'd never see her granddaughter.

It's hard to explain how having a baby and taking care of a baby changes the way you look at things. It sounds a little silly when you try to put it in words. But the truth is having your own baby makes you feel connected to everything else. With a baby you ain't alone in the same way as before. You're taking part in the future and with the people that come before you. All you have to do is take care of this little living thing to have a part in all creation. You feel foolish telling that to somebody, but that's the way you feel.

Even when Angela had the terrible colic I still had the satisfaction of taking care of her. Her belly hurt and she would cry. I'd feed her and then she would get the bellyache again. I set up with her and rocked her and walked around with her. Muir got up and rocked her and toted her around while I got some sleep. Dr. Fauntleroy prescribed some paregoric, and that helped a little. It seemed like I must be doing something wrong, and that the colic would never end. And then it did.

The reason you feel so important as a mother is because you are important. Nobody else in the world will care as much and love as much this little thing that cries and don't know where it is and needs its butt cleaned up from time to time. Nobody can ever love it like you do. All its life depends on what you do for it now. The most important thing is just to let it know that it's loved. Having a baby of my own made me understand Mama better.

Having a daughter is special to a mother. I know having a son must be exciting and wonderful too. You want to raise a son to be a man you admire. Having a son gives you a special chance to have some effect on the world. But the same could be said for having a daughter. For you feel a closeness to the little girl, a likeness. You feel she understands you. You watch a little girl learn to flirt with people, with her daddy, even with strangers. You recognize yourself in the way she smiles and gestures for affection.

One day when Angela was crying with the colic and I couldn't get her to stop, I decided to take her outdoors to see if that would help. It was a cool day in late spring. It didn't seem like I'd hardly been outside for the past year. I put on a jacket and wrapped Angela in a blanket and tied a pink knitted cap on her head. The light was so bright I blinked when I stepped into the backyard.

When you've been inside for a long time it surprises you how close and intimate things outdoor are. The wall of the smokehouse, the dirt of the path, the cedars by the gate, was so familiar, like friends you ain't seen in a long time. I walked out to the springhouse, then up to the gate and out into the pasture where I could look across the valley. The sway of walking did calm Angela, and I held her close and swung from side to side to rock her.

After she was asleep I stopped and looked across the pasture to Meetinghouse Mountain. What I seen give me a shock, for a sharp thin blade rose high above the tops of the trees on the mountaintop, pointing right at the center of the sky, like a rocket or an unknown space machine from science fiction. And then I laughed at myself, for it was a steeple and I could see the rock tower it stood on. While I'd been laying in bed before Angela was born, and then all fall and winter while I stayed inside taking care of her, Muir had been building the steeple of his church. He'd mentioned it from time to time, but I'd been too busy to pay much attention.

The several-tiered tower rose over the trees, and the spire shot up far above the trees. It was the most beautiful thing, that steeple pointing straight to heaven. It made the mountain and the valley and the whole community seem to reach up to that point of hope, far above the sinkholes and mud and confusion of the everyday things. All these years that was what Muir had seen in his mind, the "idea" of the building, the spire, the inspiration. And nobody, except maybe Papa, had understood it. The stone church, the steeple, would be there for years and years, long after Muir and me and even Angela was dead, and Muir had built it with his sweat, his own rocks and wood, his own dimes and quarters, his own vision, with some help from Papa. As I looked I wondered how he'd made the steeple so high and sharp. It looked impossible to get up on something that steep. What kind of scaffold had he used, I'd have to ask him.

By the time Angela was a year old she delighted everybody with her laugh, with the way she clapped her hands when she was excited, with the way she seemed to notice everything. Her blond curls and fair skin made her shine out in the sun. Women on the street would stop to tell me what a beautiful baby I had. When she cried at church while Muir was preaching

I had to carry her outside. But some other woman would usually come out to help me hold her.

One summer day when Angela was almost a year old, I decided I'd done enough work. I'd been breaking and canning beans for a week. The kitchen was hot and the house was clammy from the steam from the canner. Bean strings was scattered on the floor. I finally loaded the last rack of jars in the canner, then swept the floor. Angela was asleep in her crib, but I knowed she'd wake up soon and want some dinner.

I washed my face and arms at the pan on the back porch to cool off and thought of the rocks by the shoals on the river. A cool breeze always come up the valley there. Instead of fixing dinner in the hot kitchen I thought it would be good to take a picnic down to the shoals and relax by the rushing water. The sound of the river always soothed me and cooled me off. The summer before I'd just laid in bed in the awful heat and waited for Angela to come. Now she was a bright happy child and it would be nice to have a picnic at an unexpected time on a work day.

While Angela was still asleep I made some tomato sandwiches with bacon left over from breakfast and boiled three eggs. I made a jar of lemonade too and packed it in the egg basket with a tablecloth, glasses, salt and pepper shakers, and napkins. The stove was starting to cool and I just left the cans of beans in the canner. When Angela woke up I changed her and then started toward the river with her in the crook of my right arm and the basket in my left hand.

It was the brightest summer day I can ever remember; there'd been a rain and the air was washed clean. I knowed Muir was working in the bottom field by the river, stretching wire for the pole beans. He'd put in more crops this year because he needed extra money to pay for benches for the church on the mountaintop. When we come down the pasture hill by the old molasses furnace to where he was working he said, "Where are you going?"

"To a picnic," I said.

"Where?"

"By the shoals." I told him I had his dinner and lemonade in the basket. He was took by surprise but then wiped his hands on his overalls and took the basket from me. We followed the path under the birch trees along the river bank down to the Bee Gum Hole and then the shoals. It was cool in the shade along the river. Spotlights of sun fell through the trees onto the trail.

When we come out to the open place where the big rocks was I told Muir to spread the blanket on the flattest rock. I put Angela on her blanket there. The river was clear except for froth around the rocks. Two lavender butterflies circled each other above the water in a kind of dance over the chute where Troy had made his great leap. The roar of the shoals made the rest of the world seem faraway.

"Everybody will think it's funny to have a picnic on a workday," Muir said.

"We have to eat lunch somewhere," I said. "Might as well be by the river."

Angela started to cry with the sun in her eyes and I moved her to my side so she set in my shadow. The warm sunlight near the splashing water made me feel so easy I thought I could set there forever.

ACKNOWLEDGMENTS

First I want to acknowledge my mother, Fannie F. Morgan (1912–2010) whose gifted storytelling inspires much of my fiction, including *Gap Creek* and this sequel.

I am extremely grateful to my agent, Liz Darhansoff, whose enthusiastic support contributed so much to the completion of this book. Also I want to thank my longtime editor, Shannon Ravenel, for once again guiding me through the complex process of editing and finishing this story. Her excitement about good writing is contagious and sustaining. I am indebted to Jude Grant for her unique and priceless skills as copy editor. Also I want to thank Peter Workman, Elisabeth Scharlatt, Chuck Adams, and the staff at Algonquin Books of Chapel Hill for making this publication possible, especially Anne Winslow for her superb designs, and Brunson Hoole, managing editor, for his exemplary coordination of all our efforts.